Praise for Wo[...]
Jeanne Cavelos
and *Babylon 5: The Shadow Within*

"A book that's a real book, rather than just a TV tie-in knock-off. . . . Absorbing and affecting . . . Excellent."
—Andy Lane, author of *The Babylon File*

"From the explosive opening . . . to the chilling ending, *The Shadow Within* fires on all cylinders. . . . Ms. Cavelos does a wonderful job of deepening the layers of the *Babylon 5* universe. . . . A highly enjoyable reading experience with a powerful and chilling ending. Best of the B5 media novels."
—*The Zocalo*

"One of the best TV tie-in novels ever written."
—*Dreamwatch* magazine

"Most satisfying. . . . [I] devoured this flashback book (which takes place before the first episode) cover to cover. The plot involves realistic political intrigue, a sparkling interstellar mystery, and a sense of doom so thick you can smell it on the pages. Still, the sharply defined characters display so much wit, intelligence, and warmth that you root for them to change history anyway. . . . This is no by-the-numbers knock-off. . . . Perhaps the best TV tie-in novel ever."
—Captain Comics, *The Sunday Telegraph*

Published by Ballantine Books:

CREATING BABYLON 5 by David Bassom

Babylon 5 Season-by-Season Guides by Jane Killick
SIGNS AND PORTENTS
THE COMING OF THE SHADOWS
POINT OF NO RETURN
NO SURRENDER, NO RETREAT
THE WHEEL OF FIRE

BABYLON 5 SECURITY MANUAL

BABYLON 5: IN THE BEGINNING by Peter David
BABYLON 5: THIRDSPACE by Peter David
BABYLON 5: A CALL TO ARMS by Robert Sheckley

The Psi Corps Trilogy by J. Gregory Keyes
BABYLON 5: DARK GENESIS
BABYLON 5: DEADLY RELATIONS
BABYLON 5: FINAL RECKONING

Legions of Fire by Peter David
BABYLON 5: THE LONG NIGHT OF CENTAURI PRIME
BABYLON 5: ARMIES OF LIGHT AND DARK
BABYLON 5: OUT OF THE DARKNESS

The Passing of the Techno-Mages by Jeanne Cavelos
BABYLON 5: CASTING SHADOWS
BABYLON 5: SUMMONING LIGHT
BABYLON 5: INVOKING DARKNESS*

*forthcoming

Book II of
The Passing of the Techno-Mages

Summoning Light

By Jeanne Cavelos

Based on
an outline by
J. Michael Straczynski

A Del Rey® Book
THE BALLANTINE PUBLISHING GROUP • NEW YORK

A Del Rey® Book
Published by The Ballantine Publishing Group
TM & copyright © 2001 by Warner Bros.

www.randomhouse.com/delrey/

Library of Congress Catalog Card Number: 2001116594

ISBN 0-345-42722-X

Manufactured in the United States of America

First Ballantine Books Edition: July 2001

10   9   8   7   6   5   4   3   2   1

To Jamie Ferris,
friends forever

acknowledgments

Thanks again to J. Michael Straczynski for allowing me to add a small piece to the Babylon 5 universe. Thanks also to all the wonderful actors on *Babylon 5* and *Crusade* who brought their characters to inspiring life.

Thanks to my group of *Babylon 5* experts, for keeping me accurate and alerting me to some intriguing possibilities: K. Stoddard Hayes, K. Waldo Ricke, Merryl Gross, Don Kinney, John Donigan, Patricia Jackson, Alec Ecyler, Penny Rothkopf, William (Pete) Pettit, Marty Gingras, Allen Wilkins, and Bill Hartman.

For generously sharing their scientific expertise, thanks to Tom Thatcher, Dr. Charles Lurio, Elizabeth Bartosz, Dr. Stephanie Ross, Dr. Michael Blumlein, Dr. Korey Moeller, Dr. Stuart Penn, Dr. Dennis C. Hwang, Bruce Goatly, Megan Gentry, Dr. David Loffredo, Dr. Gary Day, Dr. Reed Riddle, Beth Dibble, Dr. Gail Dolbear, Dr. John Schilling, Britta Serog, and Dr. Paul Viscuso.

Thanks to those who provided extremely useful information on a variety of bizarre topics: Julia Duncan, Thomas Seay, JoAnn Forgit, Matt Winn, Deirdre Saoirse, Marty Hiller, Elaine Isaak, Susan Winston, and Tony Gangi.

Thanks to all the people, including many of those listed above, who read pieces of this book in manuscript form and gave very helpful feedback: Keith Demanche, Barnaby

Rapoport, Martha Adams, Michael Flint, Keith Maxwell, and Margo Cavelos.

Thanks to Sue Gagnon and the rest of the staff at Saint Anselm College's Geisel Library.

Thanks to my husband for telling me about Confederate General John Bankhead Magruder, an amateur actor whose big act was deceiving Union General George McClellan, and about U.S. General George S. Patton, whose phantom army in Britain decoyed the Germans. An additional, passionate thanks to him for keeping me stocked with Russell Stover chocolate, Diet Coke, and chocolate chip ice cream throughout the writing of this book.

Thanks to my agent, Lori Perkins, and my editor, Steve Saffel.

And thanks to Igmoe, my iguana, for redeeming himself after his poor behavior during the writing of Book 1 by being quite a good boy this time around.

WHAT ARE YOU?

The greatest obstacle to discovery is not ignorance—it is the illusion of knowledge.

—Daniel J. Boorstin

January 2259

— chapter 1 —

The ship sang of the beauty of order, the harmony of the spheres. The peace of its silent passage through space, the symmetry of its form, the unity of its functioning wove through its melody. But within the song, Kosh was disturbed.

The maelstrom was spreading.

Only a short time ago, the forces of chaos had been limited to their ancient home of Z'ha'dum. While that planet remained their stronghold, they had now spread to over a dozen worlds in the surrounding systems.

Kosh altered his ship's song, slowing its speed, drawing it carefully closer to the fourth planet orbiting the star called Thenothk. Near the end of the last war with the ancient enemy, Kosh had visited this place. It had been a sphere of red in the darkness of space, a frigid, barren desert, unable to sustain life. He had left a buoy nonetheless, and over time, it had perceived changes.

Soon after the buoy had begun its observations, a great ship had arrived, an engine of transformation sent by the ancient enemy. It was but one of many sent into the systems surrounding their home, designed to create habitable environments for them and their allies. Finally they had realized their vulnerability in remaining concentrated on a single planet.

Over the years, the great engine released many smaller ones, in wave upon wave upon wave, each designed to perform a

3

specific function. Some took up residence above, some burrowed below, some spread over the land. The planet warmed. Ice frozen for eons melted. Floods raced across the lowlands. The atmosphere thickened, and storms raged through it. Lifeforms were seeded and flourished, performing necessary chemical reactions. When their purpose was accomplished, they were replaced with others, one species after the next, until the work of transformation was complete. Gradually the storms lessened, conditions stabilized. From chaos, order came. As was inevitable.

Then other ships began to arrive, and a settlement was built. While the ancient enemy preferred to live underground, they built the majority of this settlement above, erecting structures that would feel comfortable and familiar to many of the younger races. It was to be a place where they could meet and interact with allies, where the maelstrom could present itself with a false face and draw others into its grasp.

The small settlement quickly grew, spreading its tentacles in chaotic form, until now over twelve million of various species lived there. Several other settlements appeared as well, where more secret work took place.

Now the planet was busy with activity, and Kosh took care to make sure his ship was not observed. He directed it to extrude several new buoys, which would take up positions around Thenothk 4 and provide more complete information about the activity occurring within the thick haze of the atmosphere. As the war cascaded from hidden attacks to outright aggression, the Vorlons would need to know their ancient enemies' actions.

A new harmonic entered the ship's song, alerting him to the presence of several other probes. They were small, nearly as small as Kosh's buoys, and they orbited a bit closer to the planet than the Vorlon buoys would. He recognized them immediately. He had come across the probes of the fabulists numerous times. They too observed many things in many places. Apparently, they too found the activity here of interest.

To Kosh, the probes held no negative significance. But some among the Vorlons, he knew, would say the probes revealed a further connection between the fabulists and the forces of chaos, an interest that could perhaps lead to alliance.

Kosh feared that talk of destroying the fabulists would gain strength. Their position was precarious. They carried great power; they could be the pivot on which the war turned. The Vorlons would not allow that pivot to turn against them.

At the fabulists' recent assemblage, their leaders had decreed that they would go into hiding, that they would leave the coming war for others to fight. Although the plans of the fabulists were always difficult to decipher, Kosh believed this was their true intent. Yet others believed the plan a deception.

Kosh had watched as the fabulists left the assemblage and journeyed back to their homes. A few at a time, they destroyed those homes and set out for the place where they would gather in preparation for their migration. They gathered slowly to disguise their mass activity. Yet soon they must leave, or more among the Vorlons would doubt their intentions.

A dissonance entered the ship's song, and Kosh saw through one of his buoys that a jagged black silhouette was rising up out of the thick greyish atmosphere. If any would detect him, it would be this monstrosity created by the maelstrom. He would observe it through the currents of the buoy without revealing himself. Kosh directed his ship to withdraw to a safer distance. It obeyed eagerly. Obedience was its greatest joy.

The great black vessel screamed up out of the gravity well. It was an abomination, a failed technology that required at its center a living, intelligent being, enslaved to the needs of the ship and the directives of its masters.

Once beyond the atmosphere, the abomination stopped, waiting.

Kosh wondered if it carried any passengers within, but he could not look inside or he would be noticed. Instead, he too waited.

Shortly, another ship approached, a sleek dark triangle. It belonged to one of the fabulists. Kosh's concern increased. He located the hidden sign on the side of the ship. This ship belonged to the fabulists' former leader, Kell. Kell had left the fabulists after his students had joined with the forces of chaos. Since then, he had been searching for those students. Kosh had observed one of them arriving at Thenothk, not long ago. Perhaps Kell had discovered his student's location. Perhaps that student was even now within the enemy vessel.

Or perhaps Kell had decided to join with the enemy himself. Kosh had believed him an honorable leader, yet the fabulists were in a difficult position, caught between order and chaos. The ancient enemy could have made great promises; the dream of the maelstrom could infect any not Vorlon.

The underside of the black monstrosity stretched open like a hungry maw. Kell's ship entered the beast, and the darkness swallowed it.

Over the years, Kosh had observed Kell only from a distance, yet now he felt both loss and disappointment. Whatever Kell's intentions, the fabulist would not leave the vessel alive, unless he swore himself to chaos. He could have accomplished much more in the great war. Instead, with his actions, he might well condemn the rest of his kind.

Many among the Vorlons would believe this another fabulist defection, and would argue with new fervor that they must all be killed, before it was too late. Kosh knew he must take at least some action to placate the other Vorlons.

If indeed more fabulists did consider joining with the enemy, let him frighten them a little. He would destroy their probes. They would believe the forces of chaos had discovered their spying, and had been angered. That, perhaps, would help keep them away, keep them on the path to their migration.

It would also please the Vorlons. They liked to think of themselves as the ones who stood on high and watched, controlled. They did not like to think of others standing beside them, watching as well.

So he would destroy their probes. And then he, alone, would watch. If Kell emerged from the abomination, then Kosh would take the news back to the Vorlons. And it would very likely trigger the destruction of the fabulists.

He hoped it would not come to that.

The others would say Kosh spent too much time among the younger races. They would say he allowed sentimentality to weaken discipline. They would say he had forgotten his place.

But the destruction of the fabulists, he believed, would be a great tragedy.

With a cry of joy, Anna shot up into the sky. The gases of the atmosphere, layers of moisture, pollutants, and dust pressed against her, fighting her forward motion. She disliked spending time on the planet, the atmosphere constricting her, gravity holding her down. She strove upward. The atmosphere thinned, the pressure lessened, her weight grew light, and the cold sent exhilarating tingles across her skin. Then she was free, cutting through the invigorating vacuum of space.

She wanted to dance in the vast darkness, to celebrate her freedom. But her four passengers directed her to stop, and wait. Waiting could be done as easily in motion as in stillness, yet they cared nothing for her joys. She would have preferred not to carry these intruders, but the Eye had told her they were critical to the war, and by carrying them and aiding them, she was helping to attain victory.

The greatest joy is the ecstasy of victory.

She stopped where they directed. These creatures made her uneasy. She could feel them moving around inside the dark chambers of her body, running their hands over her curves, eyeing the shifting black brilliance of her skin. She had extended chairs from the walls and floor of her largest chamber for their comfort, and when they sat, their heat and oily excretions soaked into her.

Three, the Eye had told her, were techno-mages, with machinery incorporated into their bodies. From listening to them speak, she had learned their names: Elizar, Razeel, and Tilar. Anna found their bodies vastly inferior to her own. They generated some low-level energies, but they were irritants, no more.

Yet the fourth passenger was more, a torturous, repugnant presence. Her name was Bunny. The Eye had long ago taught her what a telepath was, and told her telepaths were enemies. Yet today the Eye had told her that this telepath was an ally, one who would fight with them.

When Bunny had first approached, Anna had immediately sensed the threat, a vague pressure that pushed at her mind, intrusive, confusing, quickly generating a dull, pulsing pain. She had not wanted Bunny inside her. All her instincts screamed against it. As Bunny stepped into her orifice, Anna sealed the telepath within, unwilling to expose herself to this enemy. But the Eye told her she must admit Bunny; this telepath meant no harm; Bunny's thoughts simply carried a power that Anna could feel. To a lesser extent, Bunny would feel the pressure of Anna's thoughts surrounding her. Anna was glad of that.

She had at last admitted Bunny, but she did not trust the telepath. Bunny was challenging her in some way she didn't quite understand. Concentrating, carrying out her tasks had become more difficult in Bunny's presence. At the first sign of aggression, Anna was prepared to expel Bunny out the nearest orifice. In the meantime, she bent her mind toward the telepath, hoping at least to make Bunny as uncomfortable as she was.

As she waited above the planet, Anna realized it wasn't only Bunny's presence that disturbed her, but her duties for this day, as the Eye had explained them. She longed to swoop down upon an enemy, to shriek out her war cry, to rush with the rapture of fire. For that she had been well trained. But for what she must do today, she had not been trained.

She resented having to take direction from Elizar, rather than from the Eye. More than that, she feared performing poorly, failing the machine that was so perfect and was a part of her. But if it was perfect, and it was a part of her, then she would not fail. She could not fail.

The intruders were speaking. Anna would have preferred to ignore them, to concentrate on the tasks at hand. But she had to keep close watch on Bunny, and she must try to understand this unfamiliar situation, so that she would perform well. Anna absorbed their words, their images, through her skin.

Though he was young, Elizar was the leader of the group. He had an angular face and pale skin. His scalp was bare, but on his chin dark hair grew in an intricate pattern. He wore a long coat of maroon velvet, with a gold and maroon vest underneath. At first Anna had thought the clothes lent him stature, but she realized the aura of authority came from Elizar himself. He calculated his movements as carefully as Anna plotted a course. What intrigued Anna most, though, was Elizar's platinum staff, which he held braced against the floor. From it she sensed signs of life.

Elizar and Bunny stood to one side in Anna's largest chamber, speaking privately. "If you're successful," Elizar said, "you will prove your value to me today. You will not share the fate of the others."

Bunny was tall for a woman, as tall as Elizar. A thinness to her face made her look a few years older than him, and somehow gave Anna the sense that Bunny was hungry—for something. She had long, curly blond hair and wore a tight-fitting pink dress. She shrugged. "I don't know why you won't let me go at him first. You don't need torture or tricks. I'll get what you need."

"I respect your abilities, Bunny. But if he does not give us the information willingly, I fear we will not get it. Mages are trained in mental discipline and focus. Kell is the most adept of us all. He may have defenses we do not suspect."

"No one can stand up to me, except another P12 telepath. There're about a dozen of those on Earth. I went through Tilar fast enough for you, didn't I? Had him reliving his potty training. The poor thing is still scared of me." Bunny glanced toward Tilar, who sat across the chamber, watching them.

"Tilar is a failed mage," Elizar said.

"I could do the same to you, sweet cheeks, anytime, any-where." There was a lightness to her tone that made Anna un-certain whether she meant the threat or not.

Elizar ran the head of his staff down the side of her face. "But it would be the last thing you would ever do, sweet Bunny."

She twirled her long blond hair. "That's what makes our arrangement so perfect. Live and let live. Except for our enemies."

"If I am forced to call upon you, that means all else has failed. He'll fight you. You may have to destroy his mind to find the truth."

"I hope so. There's a real rush in ripping through some-one's brain, through all those tired ideas and pathetic worries. It feels like—taking a bunch of poor old gerbils out of their rusty exercise wheels. And then blowing them up."

"So long as you first find what we need," Elizar said.

"I'll find it." The lightness had drained out of Bunny's voice. "Don't start getting all repressive on me. I'm not big on obedi-ence. I wouldn't follow my parents' rules, so they turned me in.

I wouldn't follow Psi Corps' rules, so they locked me up. I wouldn't follow the rules of the goddamn blips, so they volunteered me for the sleeper tube express. Why should I listen to a bunch of hypocrites and users?"

Elizar lowered his voice. "But wouldn't you want to make new rules of your own, eliminate the hypocrisy?"

She laughed with a toss of her head. "My rules would be the most hypocritical of all. I'm all for chaos. That's why I agreed to help you." Her ice blue eyes narrowed. "I thought you felt the same."

"I told you," Elizar said. "We believe in the same things. We were both taken from our homes and forced into a mold we did not fit. We both found hypocrisy, secrets, and oppression. And we both rebelled."

Outside, a ship approached. Anna recognized it as the techno-mage ship they had been sent to meet. It was like the one who had first brought Elizar here. Like his staff, it carried some trace of life. Anna was interested in these techno-mage ships. They were not soulless, like the other ships she had encountered. Yet they were not like her sisters, either. In a way, they seemed similar to the Vorlon ships about which she'd been warned. Their life seemed an extension of the being riding within, a being who might come and go independently. These ships weren't truly alive, as she was. They were a sad echo of life. They had no will of their own; they had no freedom. They were forced to follow orders. A techno-mage and his ship were not one; she and the machine were one, working together toward common goals: chaos and destruction.

Anna informed her passengers of the ship's arrival. She had learned little from their conversation.

"You're about to meet the biggest hypocrite of all," Elizar said.

Bunny's lips parted, the tip of her tongue pushing through. "The fun begins." She turned to Razeel and Tilar, extending her hands. "Come on! You guys don't laugh enough. We're going to kill the king of the techno-mages today! Can I get a smile out of you, at least?"

Tilar stood. "This is too easy. I'll laugh when it's done, if there's something to laugh about. You underestimate Kell."

Bunny shrugged. "I think you all overestimate yourselves. You may have some fancy machinery wired into you, but artificial power can never stand up to the real thing." She waved her hands down the length of her body. "A machine, after all, can always be"—she snapped her fingers—"turned off."

That comment, Anna felt certain, had been directed at her. Perhaps Bunny needed to be reminded of her own weaknesses. A telepath, after all, could always be killed.

The small mage named Razeel said nothing, but stood with the others.

Elizar directed Anna to open herself to the techno-mage ship. She didn't want to accept the inferior ship within her. It was not worthy of her, and it could do much damage to her unprotected interior.

Yet admitting the ship was part of her duty. She must do it. At least she would hold the ship for only a short time.

Before proceeding, she scanned it carefully. Its weapons were inactive, and she found no explosive devices, though such things could be hidden. Reluctantly, she opened herself to the stranger. With crude, clumsy maneuvers, he entered her.

In her large chamber, Tilar removed the strange hat he wore, and Anna realized now that it was some living adjunct, like Elizar's staff. He put the lumpy greyish organ into a liquid-filled canister, then fluffed the short crest of hair that crowned his head in the Centauri fashion. He wore a brilliant white shirt, an ornately decorated vest. He had something of Elizar's authority in his posture, but somehow seemed anxious instead.

"His ship could destroy us all once he's inside," Tilar said. "I don't know why they didn't allow him to land."

"They did not allow him to land," Elizar said, "for that very reason. They would rather he destroy us than an entire city."

"I'm just saying it would be much simpler to do this on the planet."

Elizar's jaw tightened. "And by 'do this,' I assume you mean interrogate and murder Kell."

Tilar stopped his fluffing. "You say that as if it's a bad thing. You're not having second thoughts, are you?" There was something menacing in Tilar's voice.

"Don't be a fool. Kell lied to us. He misled us. You have no idea my depth of hatred for the man. You wouldn't understand, because you never loved the mages, only yourself. What I find offensive is your imprecise speech. Did Regana teach you nothing?"

"So you have no feelings for him at all?"

"Just because I hate him, doesn't mean I want to be the one to 'do this.' "

"I can do it."

"No, you can't. He does not trust you."

Tilar said nothing more, though his gaze lingered on Elizar.

After Anna had closed and repressurized herself, the techno-mage newcomer left his ship, and what little life Anna sensed within it vanished. The mage himself looked weak and aged. He walked slowly, with the aid of an ivory staff, his shoulders hunched. He wore a black robe with a short white fur cape over it. His skin was lined and dark. Like a negative image of Elizar, white hair on his chin grew in an elaborate pattern. This must be Kell, one of the Circle of five that ruled the techno-mages. He seemed no one to be afraid of, despite what her passengers had said.

They met him.

"So," Elizar said. "You have found me."

"And now I will die."

"Yes," Elizar said. "In time." His manner had changed,

though Anna couldn't say exactly how. He seemed somehow younger, his tone bitter. "You should have stayed away. I don't know what you hoped to accomplish."

"To face my failure with my own eyes." Kell's voice was rich, resonant.

"A mirror would be more suited to that task."

"You are my mirror," Kell said.

Anna's attention was drawn to the small mage, Razeel. Short, thin hair drifted around her head. Her lips moved, though no words emerged. A darkness gathered in the air before her, casting her pale skin into shadow. Anna wasn't sure what was happening. She examined the area; energy was building. The darkness took on an undulating cylindrical shape. Then, at its top, the darkness seemed to unfold, revealing an even darker mouth. It shot at Kell. The black mouth swallowed his head and slid down his body, the cylinder encasing him. After a moment, it grew transparent, vanished. Anna couldn't tell if the darkness had moved inside of him or simply dispersed.

Kell moaned, and his knees buckled. Elizar and Tilar caught him. Tilar took his staff, and they dragged him into the small chamber that had been previously prepared. They thrust him into Anna's chair.

Kell's weight pressed against her, the heat of his body spreading into her. Anna extended long black fingers around him, embracing him tightly so he could not escape. From those fingers she extended wire-thin tendrils, pierced his clothing to make direct contact with his skin. She sent the tendrils over his body to the areas where she'd been told nerve endings gathered close to the surface: the inside of the ears, the nape of the neck, the spine, nipples, abdomen, genitals, the inside of the legs, the soles of the feet. His heart pounded against her.

Razeel remained in the doorway.

"You know you can't be in here," Elizar said to her. "Do you want your voice to go silent?"

Razeel gave a single nod and left, and Anna sealed the

opening. Elizar leaned his staff against the wall, sat cross-legged on the floor, and rested his head in his hands. "Activate the device, Anna."

As Anna did, she also opened herself again to the vacuum of space, as they had planned. Kell's ship could not be within her when he was killed, for it might be programmed to destroy itself. Eagerly, Anna expelled the inferior ship from her body. It fell toward the planet. She waited until it was a safe distance, then wheeled and shrieked out her war cry. Red ecstasy flooded her. Her beam impaled the hated ship, utterly destroying it.

She closed herself, feeling better. She and the machine were tireless, invulnerable. They could do anything. She would accomplish the duties the Eye had assigned her.

Within the small chamber, Elizar stood. Kell's head hung to the side, and his eyes moved aimlessly. He was disoriented.

"It doesn't take much to get the better of one of you," Bunny said.

"He never intended to fight." Elizar turned to Kell. "Did you." His words sounded like a challenge.

Kell lifted his head, squinted his eyes. "I will tell you nothing."

"We're reduced to crude, makeshift methods here," Elizar said, "but I think you'll find them extremely effective. Anna, begin."

As Elizar had previously directed, she started by sending through her tendrils only a moderate shock.

Though Kell said nothing, his muscles spasmed violently. His fingers dug into her skin; his heart hammered against her.

She gave him a few moments. She had to monitor him carefully so that he did not become unconscious or die before they wished it. When his heart had stabilized, she sent the next shock, slightly greater than the first.

Kell's body bucked. Through clenched teeth, a low sound escaped him. His blood pressure dropped, and his heart raced. She waited carefully until they had returned to normal limits.

This activity did not come naturally to her. She had been taught to attack and never break off until the enemy was utterly destroyed. These timid torturings, as they were called, seemed frustratingly ineffective. She sent the next shock, at yet greater intensity.

Kell's clenched teeth parted, and he released a cry. His chest bowed outward, pushing against her. Then it fell back, and his body convulsed violently, his breath coming in short, quick puffs.

Anna waited for him to stabilize. His sweat drenched her skin.

"I will tell you nothing," Kell said, his voice breathy, weak. "Where is the point to this, Elizar? Where is the good?"

"I find it very good," Elizar said.

"Beg for mercy," Tilar said. "That will make it even better."

Anna increased the intensity and sent the next shock.

Kell's leg jerked against her as his body was racked with wave after wave of spasm. His muscles writhed, unable to coordinate themselves enough for him to scream, or even to breathe. His heart fluttered within her hand, and Anna's heart jumped as well. She didn't want to fail. He must not die until they directed.

After a few moments, Kell's heartbeat returned, though it was erratic. His breath came in rapid gasps.

Elizar must have noticed, for he raised a hand. "Stop."

She discontinued the shocks.

Elizar approached Kell and stood over him. "You see that we're serious. We can go on like this for days. Tell us what the mages are planning. What action has the Circle decided?"

"I will—tell you nothing," Kell said.

"You will tell us everything. You have no choice." Elizar moved away. "I realize I haven't properly introduced you to everyone. You remember Tilar, of course. And earlier you saw your embarrassingly strange, constantly neglected student, Razeel. But I haven't introduced you to our latest addition." Elizar's hand extended with a flourish. "This is Bunny. Bunny is a telepath. I've promised her that if you don't tell us everything we want to know, she can tear your mind to shreds to get the information. She's looking forward to it. She's a bit unstable."

Bunny put her hands on her hips.

"So you see, it's foolish to suffer," Elizar continued. "Either way, we will find what we want. Isn't it for the good to tell us now and die quickly?"

"I think you were right before," Kell whispered. "The good—is for me to be tortured. And to die having revealed nothing."

Elizar's dark blue gaze fixed on Kell. "Leave us," he said.

"Hey, it's my turn," Bunny said.

Elizar turned on her and Tilar, and his voice rang with authority. "Leave us. Now."

"This wasn't part of the plan," Tilar said.

Yet it was. Bunny and Tilar were incorrect; the plan had been torture, then Elizar questioning Kell alone, and then, if necessary, telepathic interrogation. Bunny and Tilar knew this. They were lying, she realized.

Anna opened the door briefly so that the others could leave. Then Elizar and Kell were alone.

"Anna," Elizar said, "release him."

Anna withdrew her tendrils, her fingers, leaving only the conventional shape of a chair. Kell wiped the sweat from his eyes with a shaky hand. His dark gaze followed Elizar.

"If you came with the intention of killing me," Elizar said, "I am sorry to disappoint. I will not be killed."

"That was not my intent," Kell said softly. His heartbeat was becoming more regular, his breath slowing.

"Then why did you come?"

"I had to see whether it was true. Whether you had truly betrayed the mages."

"I killed Isabelle. Was that not proof enough?"

"For one who loves you? No." Kell straightened. "I knew the difficulty of your position. I put you in it."

"What do you . . ." Elizar rested a hand against the wall, bowed his head. For a long moment he was silent. Then, haltingly, he continued. "You incited me to break into your place of power. You allowed me to access your files. You wanted me to discover your secrets."

"I acted alone. The others knew nothing."

Elizar shook his head. "You sent me as your unknowing agent to gather information from the Shadows. And all the time I thought you had betrayed us, by hiding all you knew. How could you keep such secrets? The Shadows . . ." Elizar's voice had a strange quality to it. Anna couldn't tell whether he was upset or angry.

"It is the legacy of Wierden. I allowed you the knowledge when I thought you were ready. Secrecy was necessary. I believed you were the only one—who could save us. I still do."

Elizar turned his head away from Kell, and the hand resting against the wall tightened into a fist. "Then why have you come here? Why do you force me to kill you?"

Kell ran his index finger over the white hair on his chin. "Because if I'm wrong, and you have betrayed us, I want to die. And if I'm right, and you are trying to save us, then I give my life as evidence beyond doubt for the Shadows that you have joined them. So they will give you the information you need to save us. To allow us to fight the Shadows and defeat them."

Elizar faced Kell again. "I haven't betrayed the mages. I'm trying to save them. But I don't want to save them by killing you. Not now that I know the truth. How could you come here and lay your death upon me? And how will the mages survive without you?"

"I have already resigned the Circle. They must survive without me." Though Kell was the one tortured, he seemed calm, while Elizar grew more agitated.

"Resigned?"

"My secrecy led to the deaths of Burell and Isabelle. I made a desperate gambit, and they paid the price. Does any chance remain of success? If not, there is a third alternative. Together, perhaps we can escape this ship of darkness, or die trying, so we cannot be used for ill."

Elizar's hand curled closed, and his thumb circled nervously about his fingertips. "I believe there is a chance for success. They have trusted me more since—Isabelle's death. But I don't yet know all I need."

"What have you learned?"

"I've learned the workings of their ships, and some of their devices. I know a few of their secret alliances. But I need more time." He crouched before Kell. "Tell me of the mages' plans."

"Of their plans I know nothing. I resigned upon Galen's return and have not seen them since."

"You must be watching them. You watch all."

"No longer," Kell said.

"You know them. You know what they will decide before they decide it. You have said as much in the past."

"No one can be sure of another's actions."

Elizar jerked to his feet, pacing in a small circle. "Still you keep secrets from me! Do you think I'm so foolish? You seek to learn what I know while giving nothing in return. You have no faith in me."

He stopped, and they stared at each other in silence, until at last Kell spoke. His voice had regained its resonance. "You attempt to manipulate me like an outsider. Sending the others from the room so we can speak 'privately.' I reveal that I have manipulated you, and you pretend no ill will, hoping to gain my confidence."

"You taught me well. How should I trust you, after all the secrets you've kept and the lies you've told?"

In a precise motion, Kell extended two fingers toward Elizar. "And how should I trust you? You killed one of us."

"You have the gall to say that to me! What incredible ego!" Elizar brought his hand down sharply. "You set me on my path. And you sent Galen and Isabelle into that path. Because of your manipulations, I have her blood on my hands! I had no choice. It was the only way to maintain the pretense. If only Isabelle had pretended to join them, as I did. I convinced them to spare Galen."

Kell took a tired breath. "Your loyalty is not pretended when you kill for them. There comes a point when the pretense and the reality become indistinguishable. When you killed Isabelle, you passed that point."

"But my way is the only way to save us. We must learn the Shadows' secrets. You said so yourself."

"Perhaps, if that is the price, we are not worth saving."

"We are not worth one life?" Elizar spread his arms. "This is your own plan. I am your pawn. And now you reject it? You reject me?"

"I love you. But I fear that my plan has failed. I fear that you have become a pawn of the Shadows. I fear that they will never tell you enough. I fear that, even if they did, you would use that knowledge for your own good, and the good of the Shadows, rather than that of the mages. It is what you are doing right now. And I fear that, even if you took your knowledge back to the mages, they would never accept it, or you."

Elizar nodded to himself. "Of course they will. When they need my knowledge, they will take me back."

"You can never again be one of their number. You can never have a place in the Circle."

"When they are forced to fight the Shadows, they will be grateful for my help."

Kell's lined face tightened. "You fool yourself, perhaps, better than you fool me."

"When they are dying, they will have no choice. They will take me as their leader."

For a few moments, Kell's intense, dark eyes studied Elizar. Then at last he spoke. "They needn't fight."

"Of course they . . ." Elizar looked sharply at Kell, wiping a hand over his mouth. "Will they hide, then? Will they bury their heads in the sand and pray for mercy? I should have known it." He crouched again before Kell. "Where will they hide, then? Where are they now? Preparing? Tell me all."

Kell's expression seemed pained. "I tell you nothing, except that your quest has become pointless. They will leave, and you will never find them. They will never accept you or your knowledge. There is no point to your remaining with the Shadows, unless you wish truly to join them. I put too great a burden on you. The task was impossible, though I did not want to believe it. If your intentions are true, then let us attempt escape from this ship, and if we die, we die for the good."

"If they refuse to accept me and what I might learn, then the mages will die."

"Then they will die. But they will never accept you. Unless perhaps you return to them now, as my savior. Come with me now, Elizar. We can take my ship."

Elizar gave a ragged laugh. "Can you still believe I would ally with you? Your ship is destroyed. And I would not save you no matter how much good it might do me. You and the Circle have lied and lied and lied. It is you who have led us into this dire situation. Your resignation simply saves me the trouble of overthrowing you."

"There is still the other alternative."

"Kill myself? Destroy the line of Wierden? And the hope of the mages? I think not." Elizar stood. "The mages have a great capacity to do what is convenient, as you well know.

They've practiced that skill over hundreds of years. They will accept me, when they need the knowledge I have." He bent over Kell, put his arm over Kell's shoulders. "Tell me where they will hide. I will share the information with no one. I will use it only to go to them, once I know all that can be known."

"I don't know their plans."

Elizar straightened. "You know. And damn you to hell for making me torture it out of you."

"You will be unsuccessful."

Elizar stood silently, his face downcast. Then he strode to the door. "Anna, open."

She did, and he called out.

"Bunny! Your time has come."

Bunny and Tilar returned to the room. Anna sealed the door behind them.

"He let slip that the mages are going to retreat to a hiding place," Elizar said. "He must be getting old."

Tilar frowned. "They're going to hide? While the rest of the galaxy is at war? I don't believe it. How does that satisfy good?"

"It satisfies fear and self-interest, which have apparently always been stronger than good."

Tilar studied Kell. "They're planning to fight us. They have to be. They sent him to plant false information. That's why he came."

"You're wrong," Elizar said, "but I don't have the patience to explain all the reasons why. In any case, sweet Bunny will find out everything soon enough." He turned to her. "We need to know where the mages will hide and when, and where they will gather for this exodus."

Bunny flipped her hair back over her shoulders. "You could say please."

"Please will you rip into this old hypocrite's mind and pull out the information we need."

She winked. "Happy to."

Bunny crossed her arms and stared at Kell, and in her thin, tense face, Anna saw insatiable hunger. Suddenly Anna felt the pressure of Bunny's thoughts increase. They pushed at Anna's skin, at her mind. For a moment every thought, every sensation was lost in a blinding blaze of whiteness. Then the pressure lessened, sensation returned, and as the dull, pulsing discomfort of the telepath's presence faded away, she realized Bunny's power had found a focus.

Kell's body went stiff. His head jerked to one side, his cheek pressing into her skin. From a face rigid with pain he forced out a series of words, so softly that she had to strain to hear them. "Seven. Eleven. Thirteen. Seventeen. Nineteen. Twenty-three." As the numbers increased, his heart beat faster and faster.

"He's—" Bunny's eyes narrowed.

"What is it?" Tilar said.

Elizar's fists were clenched, his face as still and inexpressive as marble.

Kell's body temperature was increasing, and with trembling lips he pushed the words out, his short, hot breaths grazing her skin. "Twenty-nine. Thirty-one. Thirty-seven." Kell's heart raced with a beat it could not possibly sustain.

"Stop it!" Bunny yelled.

"Forty-one. Forty-three." With a cry Kell launched himself out of the chair at Bunny. He slammed into her, and they twisted and fell to the floor.

Through her skin, Anna felt his heart stumble.

"Forty . . . seven," he breathed against her.

The erratic beat cascaded into chaos, then, with one final, tired contraction, his heart stopped.

The normal pressure of Bunny's thoughts returned. The telepath pushed at Kell. "Get him off me! Get him off me!"

Tilar kicked Kell in the head.

"He's dead, you idiot," Bunny said.

Tilar gave Kell one more kick. Then he and Elizar pulled the body off of Bunny. Kell sprawled across the floor, still.

Bunny sat up, rubbing her forehead. "The son of a bitch gave himself a heart attack. Maybe he thought he could take me with him." She held up her hand, waiting for someone to assist her. Elizar did.

Some low-level ultraviolet radiation was coming from a spot on Bunny's forehead. Anna wondered if it was a result of her exertion.

"What did you find?" Elizar asked.

"He was trying to block me by reciting the prime numbers. It caused a minor delay, but I got through quickly enough," she said, straightening her tight dress. She was swaying slightly. "They are going to hide. He doesn't know where. They have some method of creating a hiding place almost anywhere they want, so it can't be detected. He thought it would be somewhere out of the way."

"Somewhere out of the way?" Tilar said, nudging Kell's head with his foot. "That helps a lot."

"I didn't have much time."

Elizar's eyes were fixed on Kell. "Anything else?" he asked.

"Mmmm, well"—Bunny twirled her hair—"I found out where they're gathering now. At least, where he thinks they're gathering. Someplace called Selic 4."

"You got that?" Tilar said.

"Got it."

Tilar snorted. "He couldn't keep his secrets better than anyone else."

Bunny tossed her head. "You could give *me* some credit."

Anna considered the possibility that Bunny might be at fault for Kell's death, but her passengers seemed satisfied with the telepath's actions.

Tilar's foot nudged again at Kell. "The leader of the Circle. He wasn't so great. He was easy enough to kill."

Elizar looked to Tilar. "He killed himself."

"Now we can send the message the Shadows directed," Tilar said. "Right, Elizar?"

"Straighten his limbs," Elizar said, "and I will begin."

Anna had little interest in the technical work that followed. Kell's skin was sliced open; blood flowed out over her. It was time for her systems check, and she was simply glad that she had completed her unfamiliar duties successfully. She had obeyed both the Eye and Elizar, and she had delivered the required torturings without killing. She had furthered their path to victory. The greatest joy was the ecstasy of victory.

Soon she would return these passengers to the planet below. She would be glad to have them gone from her body. The Eye had told her she would have to stay nearby and carry them again when there was need; they were critical to victory. Anna hoped the need never again arose. She would prefer to go on to other duties, to use the machine as it was meant to be used.

The machine was so beautiful, so elegant. Perfect grace, perfect control, form and function integrated into the circuitry of the unbroken loop, the closed universe. All systems of the machine passed through her. She was its heart; she was its brain; she was the machine. She kept the neurons firing in harmony. She synchronized the cleansing and circulation in sublime synergy. She beat out a flawless march with the complex, multileveled systems. The skin of the machine was her skin; its bones and blood, her bones and blood. She and the machine were one: a great engine of chaos and destruction.

— *chapter 2* —

Galen had unpacked only a few weeks ago. Now he was packing again, this time for good. He and Elric would leave Soom. They would flee with the mages.

Packing was a strange thing. It involved imagining oneself in a different place, doing different things, projecting which items might be necessary or useful under those circumstances. But Galen couldn't imagine himself anywhere, doing anything. His mind could not form the picture.

He remembered the last time he'd packed, for the trip to Zafran 8, weighing the value of each item against the space it would take. Yet now, it was impossible to distinguish one item from another. Nothing seemed necessary, nothing potentially useful. He could leave it all behind, or he could bring it all with him. It made no difference.

He stood at the side of his bed, which was covered with boxes of various sizes, filled to various levels. He did not know how long he had been standing there. He decided it did not matter.

Elric had gone to town to say good-bye. He had asked Galen to go with him, but Galen had wanted to stay behind. Stay behind and pack. They would leave before dark. And so here he stood.

The four rough wooden shelves above his worktable were half-empty, items taken or left behind at random, the remaining items disorganized. The disarray would normally have bothered him, yet now it did not. His thoughts simply drifted away.

A cool breeze blew in through the window, and Galen shivered. He was always cold now. Outside, the mak, the plain of moss-covered rock on which he lived, was shrouded in thick mist. It was as if he lived within a formless limbo where neither light nor darkness could find definition. They could only mix in shades of grey.

On the floor below the window he saw a square shape. He went to it. He bent, picked it up. He opened the cover, flipped through the pages, the recognition delayed a few seconds. *Mirm, the Extremely Mottled Swug.* It was Fa's book. She had not come to his house in a long time. He had frightened her away. The book must have lain there since . . . before.

If he had found it earlier, he could have given it to Elric to return. Now. Here it was. He squeezed it tightly, forcing the memories to remain within. It was her favorite book. If he left it behind, it would be destroyed with the house. He must return it.

He had not treated her well. He had never treated her well. She had given him friendship and kindness. He had given her arrogance and impatience. And lately, not even that. He owed her something. He owed her, at least, a good-bye. The picture formed in his head: a smiling, black-robed figure wrapping Fa in a warm embrace, speaking words of love and reassurance, exchanging sleights of hand one more time.

But the figure in the black robe was not he. What he owed her he could not give. He could not find the words, could not perform the actions. He looked down at the book clenched in his hands. He would return it to her through a messenger.

He left his home of stacked stones behind and passed into the mist. He felt like a ghost, lacking in substance or reality. The wind drove him along.

He knew Fa's house, though as he approached the back of it, he realized he had never been inside. She had always come to him; he had never gone to her. He was still a stranger in this place, among these people, after eleven years of living here. He had never opened himself to them, or to Fa, and now there was nothing of him left to open. He was transparent, empty.

He heard her voice coming from one of the windows. He imagined his mind as a blank screen, carefully visualized an equation written upon it. The spell gave him access to the probe in the ring he'd given her, his father's ring. The image appeared in his mind's eye.

She was staring right at him, right at the stone in the ring. Below the curly white wisps of hair that covered her face, her skin was the deep pink it became when she was excited. Her eyes were wide, bright, engaged in play. Her head turned back and forth as she studied the ring.

Seeing her in his mind's eye was like peering through a telescope at some impossibly distant past. It was a past to which he could not return.

"Make me great flowers of light in the sky," she said in the language of the Soom. The probe's image turned away from her, swooping over the stone walls of her room in dizzying circles as she waved her arms and twirled, imagining the flowers falling around her. Of course the ring would do no magic for her.

"Pretty, pretty flowers." She again held the ring up to her face. "Blow all the flowers to Gale. Tell him not to be sad anymore. Tell him to be happy. Tell him not to go away."

Galen turned, nearly starting for home. He did not want to think. He did not want to feel. Yet he had taken the easy path and ignored her for too long. He must say good-bye.

"Turn me into a great lady carried in a chair," Fa said.

He needed a messenger. He had once, for practice, created an illusion of Mirm, trying to combine the feel of the book's hand-tinted engravings with realistic swuglike movements. He had never been happy with the illusion, but it would have to do.

On the screen in his mind's eye, he visualized a second equation, one to create the image of Mirm. His tech eagerly echoed the spell, and the massive swug stood before him, chest high, skin brightly mottled with shades of pink, purple, and blue, a friendly tilt to his head, just as in the book. Galen added another equation, creating a small flying platform on top of Mirm's snout. He laid the book upon it, so it appeared as if Mirm carried the book balanced there. Galen conjured an equation of motion, and Mirm approached Fa's window. The swug's ample fatty deposits jiggled as he trotted on thin legs.

Holding the spells in his mind, Galen withdrew behind a short wall of stacked stones that marked the boundary of the property. He created a new equation of motion, sending Mirm scrabbling up through Fa's window, then knelt among the grasses, out of sight. He closed his eyes, focusing on the image from the probe.

The image had been waving all over the room as Fa played. Suddenly it froze in place. "Mirm! Is it really you?"

Galen had created a voice for Mirm, which quavered like the deep bleats that swugs usually made. He conjured the voice, composed the words Mirm would say as if he were writing a message. The illusion spoke. "Hello, Fa," Mirm said. "I brought your book." With a flick of his nose Mirm flipped the book toward Fa. She caught it.

"I left it at Gale's house," she said, running her hands over the book, amazed. "I didn't think I should go there." She looked up eagerly. "Is he with you?" She ran to the window, looked out.

Galen bent forward, bracing his hands against the cold ground.

"Gale isn't here," Mirm said. "He sent me. To say good-bye."

"Honored El said that they must leave." She turned back to Mirm. "Can't Gale stay?"

"No," Mirm said. "He must go with all the others like him."

Fa crouched beside the window, her head bent. "He's my best friend."

"He asked me to tell you he is sorry he has not been more friendly."

"He is sad. I understand. I wish he wasn't so sad, though."

Galen's fingers tightened, digging into the dirt. "He worries that you will be sad," Mirm said.

"I wish we could be sad together."

Galen needed to end this. "Gale said that wherever he is, he will look up at the stars in the sky and think of you."

"I want to create lights in the sky, just like him. If I do, can I go where he goes?"

"You cannot create lights. Not from the ring. You can use it only to call Gale by saying his name three times. But you must not call him unless you are in dire need. The ring will watch over you. He will watch over you."

She stared at the ring—at him—and began to cry. He was a coward.

"But I don't want the ring," she said. "I want Gale. I don't want him to leave."

This was only making her more upset. As usual, he had no skills for dealing with others. Galen moved Mirm toward the window.

Fa lunged at the swug, extending her arms to embrace him. They passed through the illusion, and she fell to the floor. She lay there sobbing, her skin a bright pink, the hair below her eyes matted with tears. "Mirm!"

Mirm hesitated at the window.

Fa pushed herself up on her hands. "Tell Gale I love him."

Galen's heart pounded. "Good-bye," Mirm said.

He conjured equation of motion. Mirm scrambled out the window, ran away between the stone houses into the mist.

Fa stared into the ring. "Gale," she whispered. "Gale." She stopped herself before saying his name a third time. She would not abuse the gift he had given her. "Don't be sad anymore. Do you remember our picnic with Is? Remember how she laughed? She would want you to be happy."

She rubbed a finger over the ring. "I will look up at the stars and think of you. I will hope that, wherever you are, you are laughing."

Galen broke the connection with the probe, dissolved the illusion.

He willed his heart to slow, his mind to go blank. He would not think. He would not feel. He would regain the transparency of a ghost.

He had done what he needed to do; he had said good-bye to the past. Now he could fade away.

He pushed himself to his feet and walked stiffly back toward home.

In his place of power, Elric sat in darkness. He dreaded what he had to do. He had given himself to Soom, sunk his bones deep into this planet. He was a part of it, and it was a part of him. He could not imagine splitting them asunder.

Soom lived and breathed. The planet's core generated the heat that gave it life. Driven by this heart, magma pumped to the surface, carrying the energy that moved continents, raised mountains, and built volcanoes. From the volcanoes magma and steam escaped, enriching the atmosphere and driving rains that spread precious water upon the surface. Sustained by this living planet, life flourished in many forms.

On the far side of Soom, the coarse-haired wild tak stood on a rocky mountainside, sleeping in the predawn darkness. The tiny krit, eyes closed, clung to thick stalks of grass as they blew in the breeze. Across the continent, shadows in the desert city of Drel shortened as the sun climbed toward its zenith. Sand blew across the vast open plain.

Closer to home, the sea shril began their migration south with the warm currents. Above the waterline, the coastal city of Tain was busy with traders leaving the marketplace and heading for their evening meal. The Rook of Tain, corrupt leader of that city, stared once again into the great chest of gems that had arrived a few weeks ago from his new friends on the rim.

In the town of Lok, a few discussed Elric's departure with regret, though for most, the event was only a curiosity, nothing more. Farmer Jae and Farmer Nee shared their afternoon drink, as had become their custom. After their last fight, Elric had directed them to have three mugs of brew together each day for three days. The punishment had been more successful than he had ever hoped. Drinking together each day had broken down the barriers between them, and they had found in each other, if not a kindred spirit, at least someone to listen. Though they still often quarreled, they had become friends, of a sort.

Unnoticed, Farmer Nee's Jab marched into Farmer Jae's barn, where the prizewinning swug, Des, lay. Elric's probe, stuck between Jab's eyes, shifted back and forth as her low body drove forward with powerful legs. Des raised his head at Jab's approach, but did not rouse his vast bulk. He returned his attention to something else, to a chunk of brownish food that had fallen into the grasses of his bed. Jab approached the chunk of food. Tiny wormlike creatures struggled over the damp surface. They were perhaps one-quarter inch long, with barely visible arms and legs. Jab sniffed at her offspring. Des watched them with great interest and, if Elric was not mistaken, some pride. After all, they had incubated beneath his skin.

Out on the mak, the brilliant lime-green moss thrived, covering the rocky plain like a carpet. Within the mist stood Elric's circle of seven great moss-covered standing stones, and below it, a chamber carved out of rock, his place of power.

He lingered there, caught between necessity and dread. He had to act. Yet the planet and its inhabitants needed him. He did not want to desert them. And as much as they needed him, he needed them. They endowed his life and his conjuries with meaning and direction. They gave him a center, a place that nourished his spirit and called him to a purpose greater than his own interests. They enriched him.

Before Galen had come, Soom and its inhabitants had been his primary companions. Even now, they reminded him of what was truly important, of the struggles for life that went on every day, in every place; of the temptations to do ill, great and small; and of the need to do good where one was able.

Over thirty years ago, within this chamber of stone, he had connected a large portion of his chrysalis to a variety of devices he had built, creating a place that amplified and channeled his power, that made Soom as much a part of him as his heart. He did not want to cut out that heart. And yet he must.

He must support the decision of the Circle, though he had voted against it. He must leave with the rest of the techno-mages and go into hiding. Any mage tech that was left behind would simply become an attraction for opportunists who would use it for ill; entities like the EarthForce New Technologies Division were aggressively seeking more sophisticated technologies to exploit. Nothing could be left for them to study.

And an even greater danger existed. If he left his place intact, it could become a target for either the Shadows or the Vorlons, who might well attack the homes of the mages, anticipating their eventual return.

He could leave no trace of himself upon the planet, no trace that would allow him to remain a part of it, no trace that would protect the inhabitants as he had always done. No trace that would endanger them. He must abandon his home, amputate the best part of himself.

In the past, each time he had left Soom, he had been diminished, weakened. Limited to his own body he had felt partially blind, partially paralyzed. The sensation had been unpleasant enough that in recent years he had left home only when required by his duties. Yet even in those instances, his place of power had remained connected to him, though the connection had grown tenuous with distance.

Now there would be no connection. There would be nothing with which to connect. That great piece of his chrysalis, which over the years had grown, intertwining itself with the various devices, driving threads deep into the planet itself, would be destroyed. The devices he had built, his house, the hall would also be destroyed. A part of him would be destroyed.

All that would remain were the faster-than-light relay in orbit and the probes he had planted. The mages had such relays around many planets, not just their homes, and they would keep their network active for as long as they could, to gather information about the galaxy they refused to face, and the war they refused to fight. So they might know when it was safe to come out again.

Through these, he could still observe Soom, but it would be with the attenuated, lifeless objectivity with which he could observe any world.

Elric thought of the many mages who had formed places of power, perhaps three-quarters of their number. Up until a few weeks ago, no mage had destroyed his place within recorded memory. Now the destruction was nearly complete. He would be one of the last of their order to take this irrevocable step. Of the long-term effects, they knew nothing. Of the short-term effects, accounts remained scattered and vague. Elric sensed they were too private to be discussed. Their severity would differ, certainly. The longer such a connection existed, the stronger it became, and the more discomfort a mage felt in leaving. Ing-Radi, the oldest of them, would likely suffer the most, and emerge severely debilitated. Of the four members of the Circle, only Herazade had never formed such an attachment. She found the idea of putting down roots old-fashioned. And perhaps she was right. Roots certainly made it inconvenient to flee.

As a group, the mages would be much weakened. Yet they had decided to cripple themselves rather than stay and face further risk. They feared that more of them would be killed, as Burell and Isabelle had been. They feared that more might turn to the Shadows. They feared what they might be forced to do.

The mages had lowered their expectations of themselves. Rather than seeking to do good, they hoped simply to survive. It frustrated and infuriated him when he allowed himself to dwell on it. But he knew that, above all, they must remain united. Without obedience to the Circle, the mages would fracture and fall to chaos. And so he must abide by their decision.

Through a probe on one of the standing stones, Elric saw that Galen had arrived at the circle above. "I've finished packing," Galen said, knowing Elric would hear. "Everything is on the ships."

Galen's brilliant blue eyes were blank, his face inexpressive. At the convocation, Elric had given him over to the Circle, to accomplish their task, and he had returned deeply hurt. He was still in shock from Isabelle's death. Elric had given him time, an extra month, making sure they were among the last mages to leave for the gathering place, hoping Galen would return to himself. Yet the delay had made little difference. For the most part, Galen's mind remained in his own private hiding place while his body moved absently, an empty vessel.

Galen was much as he had been after his parents' deaths.

Elric had learned then that Galen's major defense against
trauma was withdrawal, and that forcing him to confront
that trauma simply made him withdraw further. Some things,
he simply refused to face. Over time, Elric had been able to
help him slowly return to normality, as he became more secure in his new life and home. Yet Elric feared that after today,
he would lack the energy to help Galen. And that their life
would lack the stability that might allow Galen to feel safe
again. Galen did not cope well with change.

Elric thought that perhaps he too was not quite himself,
since the return of the Shadows, the resignation of Kell, the
betrayal of Elizar and Razeel, and the decision of the Circle.
For he could not believe he was about to do what he would do.

Yet he had no choice. He could delay no longer. Elric laid a
hand on the rough rock of the chamber. Soom was his heart;
Soom was his soul. And now he must tear them apart.

Elric conjured a flying platform and ascended the rocky
chimney that led to the surface, emerging from the hidden
opening in one of the standing stones. He approached Galen,
who stood just outside the circle, in the mist. "You have removed everything from the house?"

"Yes."

"You are prepared to leave?"

"Yes."

He would get nothing more from Galen. "Very well. Step
back." The massive standing stones were over twenty feet tall,
shrouded in moss. Each marked with one of the seven runes
of the Code, together they embodied his commitment to the
principles of the techno-mages.

Galen moved a few feet away, obviously reluctant to leave
him. Elric had to stay close to the circle, for as with most mage
powers, the ability to conjure magical fire was limited in
distance.

Elric knew he should dissociate from his place before destroying it, but he could not. He had not dissociated from it in

many years, and somehow it seemed wrong to break contact now, to force it to die alone. He accessed a probe in that dark stone chamber beneath the ground and began the conjury.

To cast a spell, he simply visualized what he desired. Yet this time, the visualization was no desire, but a nightmare: his place of power filled with magical fire. The tech echoed his command, and brilliant lime-green flames blazed light through the stone chamber, whirling in a vortex of fierce, searing heat. The flames played over the smooth surfaces of the devices he had built, their heat penetrating inward. Clenching his teeth, Elric increased the fire's intensity, hoping to complete the process as quickly as possible.

The heat melted through the top layers of metal and burned inward. The information he had stored there—information about the planet, its history—faded from his mind. One by one, connections to various instruments across the planet failed, those tools that had always been at his command now falling suddenly out of reach.

The dazzling green sizzled deeper, contacting the outstretched threads of the chrysalis.

Elric gasped through clenched teeth. Fire boiled into his hands, searing down middle and index fingers and thumbs, following the lines of the tech. He raised his shaking hands, determined not to scream for Galen's sake. Green flames blazed down his fingers, joined in the palms, sizzled across his wrists and up his arms. He was burning from the inside out.

"Dissociate!" Galen was at his side. "Dissociate!"

Wildfire seethed up his arms.

Within the chamber of rock, the vortex of flames spread down the length of the chrysalis' threads toward its main body.

He had to finish it. Before he lost the power.

Elric found untouched threads of the chrysalis, urged the conjured flames outward along them. Across the mak, the house and training hall erupted in torrents of green.

Fire seared up his arms to his shoulders, burned along lines of tech to his spine.

Though he could no longer access them, he sensed the destruction of one after another of the devices he had planted across Soom, pieces of himself being consumed with burning green.

Within the stone chamber, the heat built higher and higher. The metal surfaces boiled now, and inside, the green tongues of flame reached the main body of the chrysalis itself, the translucent golden piece of himself with which he had trained so long ago.

The fire seized Elric, surging up his spine and into his brain. Soom's lands, its oceans, its volcanoes and magma, its heart—all became unreachable beyond the brilliant burning incandescence. Great flames spouted from the mak, engulfing each of his standing stones in a towering column of fire. Then the heat became unbearable, consuming every thought in a blast of searing greenness.

A crystalline pain pierced directly through his skull into his brain, transfixing him. The next thing he knew, he was lying on the mak, the fire at last running out of him. The circle of flames roared high above. Below, the golden body of his chrysalis had vanished within a furious vortex of green. It had burned to death, he knew. He knew, for within him, something had died, something had shriveled to ash, leaving a throbbing, echoing emptiness.

The green fire faded from his body, and the columns of flame surrounding the standing stones dwindled, revealing their charred remains, like the fossilized bones of some long-extinct creature.

The rocky plain began to shake, and the tall stones slowly gained motion, swaying slightly back and forth. Galen fell to his knees beside Elric, shielding Elric with his body. One of the charred stones swayed past the point of return and toppled inward through the mist, this sign of his commitment to the

Code falling silently, unremarkably. As it hit the mak, it disintegrated, throwing up a thick cloud of ash.

The shaking increased, and with a sudden gust that felt almost like an exhalation, the plain on which the circle stood collapsed like a bowl. The standing stones fell inward one by one.

Galen bent lower over him as great clouds of ash filled the air. But Galen could not shelter him from what had already happened within.

When most of the dust had cleared, Galen straightened, allowing Elric again to see. The standing stones were gone, the ash of their remains filling the depression that had formed. The house was gone. The hall.

Within him, where once a planet had been, there was now a great emptiness. He was diminished.

Elric pressed a hand against the mak and pushed himself into a sitting position. Strangely, neither his skin nor his clothing was burned. The damage had been internal, not external. His body felt strange to him, as if he were missing limbs. Now he knew how Burell had felt when sections of her tech had become inert, and she'd been separated from a part of herself.

"The ground here is unstable," Galen said. "We should move away. Can you stand?"

Fear had brought Galen's face to life. Galen feared that Elric would die and leave him, as his parents had. Elric wanted to reassure Galen. He would be all right.

Preparing to stand, he braced one foot against the ground. It required a surprising amount of effort. He pushed his hands against the ash-covered moss, attempting to rise.

Galen grabbed him beneath his arms and pulled him up, helped him move farther from the broken circle of stones.

"I'll be fine," Elric said, and he was appalled at the weakness of his own voice. He took a breath, gathering his strength, and asserted voice control. "I just need a moment."

He had always been fit, and aging into his late fifties had done little to lessen his physical condition. Yet in a moment he had become an old man. Simply standing was an effort, from which his muscles quivered, and something deep within his head throbbed, a cavity of darkness that felt as if it had swallowed his very soul. Elric feared it was a mortal wound that would, eventually, kill him.

Galen's face revealed how bad he looked. "We should wait a few days before leaving."

Elric forced himself to straighten. "No. We have been directed to leave today. I am simply tired. I will have my ship follow yours. You can guide us to the gathering place. You are able, are you not?" Elric knew that questioning Galen's ability would distract him.

"I can do it. But I wish we could ride together."

"We may need both ships." Shaking off Galen's support, Elric began to walk toward the two black, triangular-shaped vessels. The soft mak gave beneath his feet, yet it was no longer a part of him. "I will rest, and you will have the first true test of mastery of your ship."

Thankfully, Galen did not question him further, for it took all of his energy to reach the ships. There, he paused, gathering himself before attempting to climb up the ramp. "Make sure we are not followed or observed. If anything unusual occurs, rouse me."

Galen nodded, wide eyes anxious.

Elric looked across the mist-shrouded mak that had been his home for so many years. The brisk breeze caressed his face, carrying the sharp smell of the sea. He could see no remnants of their house, or the hall. "It is as if we had never come here."

"No," Galen said. "Things are much better because of the years you've spent here."

Elric nodded a single time, gratified by Galen's comment.

Perhaps the need created by Elric's weakness would bring Galen back to himself.

Elric took a final breath of the sea air and forced himself up the ramp. Galen at last turned to his own ship, so Elric could slow without being observed. He took one more look back at the mak. Life was fragile, fleeting. He hoped that no ill would come to this place.

He had done what duty required. And as he was abandoning Soom, so the mages would abandon the galaxy. So they had abandoned their vow to do good. Elric could not imagine how they might regain their commitment to the Code, how they might survive the coming conflict as the order he had loved. Perhaps the rest of the Circle knew better than he did. For Elric could not see the path to their survival.

But he was tired. Perhaps, after he rested, he would see new possibilities. He must not give in to despair. He must stay strong for the mages.

He continued up the ramp, and he did not look back again.

—— chapter 3 ——

The ship responded eagerly to Galen's direction, echoing his commands and carrying them out. Behind, Elric's ship followed.

Galen sat in darkness, his heart pounding, and tried to think of nothing, to be nothing. Let the time slide by, and let him slide through it, like the ships gliding through the endless currents of hyperspace.

Yet his mind would be still no longer. The blank emptiness that had been shielding him these past weeks had finally slipped away. Since the convocation, he realized, he'd been insulated in that place deep inside, where he hid from himself. Now worry had drawn him out, and he couldn't go back, couldn't drift away and dissolve into mist like a ghost. He pushed the worry down, focused on his surroundings, on the workings of his ship.

A piece of his chrysalis had been incorporated into it, just as with his staff. Two of the Kinetic Grimlis, the group of mages that made the ships for all of them, had stayed behind after the end of the convocation to help him integrate the chrysalis, and to train him in the ship's operation. He had listened with little interest to their rapid instruction regarding engines, weapons, maintenance. What good was a ship, if the mages were all to withdraw to a hiding place for the indefinite future? He might as well travel with Elric, as he always had in the past.

Elric had convinced him to take a few training flights, but Galen had felt little desire to explore the capabilities of the ship, or the nature of his connection with it. More than that, he had found the connection uncomfortable. Associating with the ship, as with his staff, triggered a startling surge of nervous anticipation, as if he'd been injected with adrenaline. The energy from the chrysalis interacted with the restless undercurrent of the implants in a phenomenon mages called parallelism. Thoughts and feelings echoed back and forth between ship and implants, repeating themselves again and again, trapped in a rapid, swelling reverberation that could easily become overwhelming. It was a state he preferred to avoid.

This time, as he associated with the ship, it had been his concern for Elric that had echoed between him and the chrysalis—thoughts of Elric weakening, of Elric dying, quickly escalating into panic. He had done a mind-focusing exercise to calm himself, and gradually the panic had lessened. He had maintained control of himself, and the tech. Yet still his fear persisted, holding him pinned to the present and the pounding of his heart.

Elric had been the one certainty in his life, the wall of strength beside him. Out there on the mak, he had thought Elric was burning to death. He'd thought Elric would die. And though Elric had survived, the fire had left its mark. He had aged before Galen's eyes, the frown lines between his eyebrows deepening, his chest curving inward, his body growing weak. Elric's standing stones had crumbled to dust, just as Elizar had foretold. Perhaps Elric himself had not yet crumbled, but the process had begun.

How rapid his deterioration might be, how many years might be cut from his life, they would learn only with time. But after Kell's resignation, the mages could not afford to lose Elric. And Galen could not stand to lose him.

In his mind's eye, Galen checked again on Elric's ship,

seeing through his ship's sensors. They gave him the full view of the area surrounding his ship, as if its walls were transparent. A steady distance behind and to starboard, the sleek black triangle of Elric's ship cut through the billowing red turmoil of hyperspace. Its side radiated the three frequencies high in the ultraviolet in which mages hid signs. Correctly combined, the three signals revealed the rune Elric had chosen to represent himself. The rune came from the language of the Taratimude, the ancient, extinct species who had, a thousand years ago, created the tech and made themselves into the first techno-mages. Elric's rune signified integrity.

The familiar symbol offered no reassurance, though. Elric's strength was broken. Their home was destroyed. So much had been lost. Nothing was the same as it had been. Nothing ever would be.

His anxiety was echoed by the ship, echoed again by his tech. His pounding heart quickened.

Again he forced his mind away, focusing instead on the steady stream of data communicated to him by his ship. It fed him information about hyperspace currents, surrounding conditions, thrust output, fuel consumption. It calculated and updated his position. As the ship did all these things, it felt as if he were doing them, as if a part of his mind were engaged in these tasks, just as a part of him might be engaged in walking while the rest of his mind concentrated on other things.

To direct the ship, he selected from a menu of options in his mind's eye. The result was a ship that, while not alive in and of itself, was an extension of him, like an extra limb. The intimate connection allowed him to control the ship more quickly and with greater instinct than any traditional pilot.

Galen had long daydreamed about having his own ship, going on grand quests to restore the glory of the techno-mages, quests he had planned with Elizar. Now he had his ship. But he no longer dreamed of quests. He no longer believed the glory of the techno-mages could be restored. Not when they had decided to turn their backs on the universe.

But they certainly had fast, sophisticated ships in which to flee.

Galen realized that his ship had reached the end of its hyperspace course and was preparing to form a jump point for the drop into normal space. Elric's ship would follow.

He formed the jump point, an immense vortex of orange with a tiny heart of blackness at its very center. With a great rush of speed he was sucked into it. For an instant the ship's readings went blank, and he lost all sense of direction or movement.

Then the calm blackness of normal space appeared around him. He looked anxiously toward the jump point behind him, now a swirling blue. From the eye of the vortex Elric's ship emerged.

They were on the outskirts of the Selic system. Here all the mages were gathering in preparation for their flight to the hiding place. The system and those surrounding it were unoccupied, unfriendly to life and of little commercial interest. The gathering place was on the fourth planet, where two hundred years ago a religious cult had built a retreat. Poor organization and corruption had left many of the loyal believers without food, and those who hadn't been able to flee on the few available ships had died after a brief descent into cannibalism.

Elric had commented that he hoped their use of the facility would be more successful.

Blaylock had discovered the unused facility some years ago, and had proposed it to the Circle as the perfect place for the mages to cloister themselves from outsiders and focus on realizing their destiny: forming a perfect union with the tech. Although the Circle had rejected his proposal then, they had realized Selic 4 was the perfect place for them to gather now in secrecy. The facility had required numerous repairs and upgrades to sustain them for even this short time, but under the direction of Blaylock, the work had quickly been completed.

As Galen's ship moved past the massive fifth planet, he visualized the equation to create a message. He didn't want to disturb Elric's rest, but Elric would not appreciate Galen landing their ships while he remained asleep. And Galen would feel much better knowing Elric's condition. He composed the message. *We are nearing Selic 4. Shall I continue to control both ships?* He sent it to Elric.

While he waited anxiously for an answer, he noticed an object approaching the fourth planet at right angles to their course. It was another mage ship. It displayed the rune for knowledge, Kell's sign.

Memory flashed through him. He had last seen that symbol as Kell had flown away from Soom, leaving the mages after revealing all he had done. The shape burned into Galen's mind, reaching down into buried layers. Alone with Elric for the past month, Galen had been able to forget much, to turn his back on the memories surrounding the last convocation, as he had turned his back on those of his parents years ago. But Kell had been the mover behind those recent events. He carried with him those memories, and as Galen looked at his ship, they closed around him with increasing pressure, threatening to bleed through.

Galen had thought he would never have to face Kell again. Kell's knowledge could no doubt be useful to the mages, and for any help Kell might offer them, Galen would be grateful. But while part of his mind carried on these superficial, charitable thoughts, in another, deeper place, anger was seeping out from where he had buried it, anger at all Kell had done: the deceptions, the reckless manipulations. And when Kell's plans had failed, he had simply walked away. Galen's anger was echoed by the ship, echoed again by his tech, the echoes overlapping and quickening, reflecting back and forth, building like the tolling of a bell in a bell tower to over-whelming intensity.

Kell had known of the Shadows' return. Kell had kept secret the Shadows. Kell had encouraged Elizar to go to the Shadows. He had helped to create a killer. Kell had sent them needlessly into danger. Kell had sent them to know what was already known. There had been no need. They could have stayed. Then everything would not have changed. Everything would not have been lost. But because of Kell, she was dead. Dead.

She.

Isabelle.

He had spent a month hiding from that name, and now it rang inside him. The tech's agitating energy welled up in a rush of heat, energy driving through him, urging him toward action.

Isabelle. Isabelle.

He could not see her face, only the small clear tube of ash that had lain on his palm. In conjured fire her body had been reduced to dust. Dust to dust.

The rage swelled, reverberating through him. He had been holding it inside all this time, holding it so tightly he hadn't even known it was there. He had kept it in so long; could he not be allowed, finally, to act?

His body was trembling, fists clenched, heart racing. Fire burned along the meridians of his tech, the same fire that had consumed Isabelle, that had crippled Elric. But in his case the fire was a source of strength, a source of hate and destruction. Morden had told him, and Morden had been right. Galen was just like the Shadows. All he wanted was destruction.

He would take that hate and strike back against the pain, strike back at his enemy. Kell's ship was well within range of his weapons. He brought them to bear.

He need only select *fire* from the menu of options. And Kell would be killed.

Then her face came to him, slack in death, as it had looked after Elizar's spike had wound its way into her brain. Her head was tilted to one side. A partially healed cut ran down the right side of her forehead into her thin, upslanted brow. Her lips were slightly parted, her grey eyes blank and cold. Her skin carried an odd shininess, a sense of artifice. This was not her. This was an empty vessel. The light of her essence had gone.

And he had failed to save her.

The full weight of his grief at that moment fell upon him, and more than anything he wanted to lash out, to find some release from the pain. Yet he knew. She had died because he had upheld his vows. He had sworn to be worthy of the Circle's trust. He had sworn to follow the Code. And he had done so, even when it had cost her life.

Now would he break that Code? Would he reveal that she had died for nothing?

No. No.

He took refuge in a mind-focusing exercise, blocking out the images of the ship's sensors, closing down his thoughts, burying the memories, narrowing his attention to a blank screen in his mind. First he visualized just the letter A in glowing blue on the left side of the screen, fixing on it with ferocious intensity. The image echoed back to him. Then he visualized B appearing beside A, and he held the image of them both in his mind. Then it was $A\ B\ C$, all in his mind at once, each individual letter clear while the whole also remained clear. Retaining clarity required concentration, and became more difficult as the exercise progressed.

He added letter after letter in a neat row, keeping the images of them all in his mind at once. The orderly progression echoed back to him. Bit by bit, the energy calmed, decreased. Gradually his heart slowed; his trembling stopped. The heat dissipated from his body. The anger remained, and the constant undercurrent, yet he would not act on them.

He had almost slipped, as he had when he'd attacked Elizar at the convocation. He had determined then never to let it happen again, and he had maintained control through much more difficult circumstances than this. Yet over the last weeks, in his desire to lose himself, to fade into transparency, he had relaxed his tight control. And today he had nearly attacked another mage.

Galen realized he had a message from Elric. He opened it quickly, worry echoing through him.

I have tried to contact Kell. There is no response. No life signs in the ship beyond those of the chrysalis.

He had been so blinded by anger, he had nearly attacked an empty ship.

Galen used his sensors, confirmed Elric's findings. Then where was Kell?

They had received reports of some mages being attacked, and of others who seemed to have disappeared, not arriving at the gathering place at their scheduled times. Whether they had encountered Shadows or Vorlons, decided to stay behind in defiance of the Circle, or died with the destruction of their places of power, no one knew. There was no time to investigate.

If Kell had been killed, his ship should not have been able to function without him. If Kell still lived, elsewhere, he could have associated with his ship and sent it on this course. Although he would remain connected to it, the connection would become tenuous as the ship moved away from him, so eventually he would be unable to alter its orders. A risky situation.

But why would Kell send his ship to the gathering place without coming himself?

Galen could think of only two reasons. First, Kell might be injured and unable to reach his ship, sending it instead to bring help. Second, Kell might have no intention of coming. He might have decided to betray them and send a weapon in his place. Galen couldn't believe that of Kell. No matter what else he had done, Kell had meant the mages no harm. Nevertheless, Galen scanned the ship for explosives, found nothing.

The ship was drawing close to the planet, as were they.

Another message arrived from Elric. *The ship is preparing to land. The Circle has agreed to allow it to do so. We are to follow and observe it for signs of danger. You may release my ship now.*

Galen resisted the temptation to ask Elric how he was. He was ashamed that he had nearly failed Elric again, with another loss of control, especially after Elric had made so great a sacrifice.

I will follow, Galen wrote. He released Elric's ship, and Elric took the lead, his movements clean, assured.

Kell's ship revealed no unusual activity, so Galen examined the planet, trying to retain his focus, his fragile calm. Selic 4 was a world of ice and stone, whites and browns. It had a thin atmosphere, unbreathable by Humans. As Galen descended toward the surface, details of the towering mountains and vast ice fields seemed unnaturally vivid.

On a massive sheet of ice between two great mountain ranges sat the religious retreat, a plain grey rectangular structure. Galen knew it must be surrounded by mage ships, but they were not visible. Maskelyne was in charge of camouflaging their presence here. She must be generating an illusion to hide the ships, while allowing the facility to remain visible, so that nothing would appear changed. She had volunteered to make Selic 4 her place of power, even though they would stay only temporarily and she would soon enough have to destroy it. Establishing Selic 4 as her place would enhance her ability to create large-scale illusions.

As Galen came close he could pick out the boundaries of the illusion, which ran in a semicircle around the facility, covering several square miles. The crudeness of the illusion was apparent, the artificial simulation of ice too shiny, angular, and uniform. It was impossible to create such a vast illusion and retain realistic quality. Yet from a distance, the illusion would be convincing to both observers and instruments.

Kell's ship set down about a mile from the facility. Elric landed a short distance away, and Galen directed his ship down beside Elric's.

To leave the ship, Elric would probably conjure a containment shield around his body that would hold within it enough of the heat and oxygen from his ship so that he could walk a short distance outside. Assuming he was not too weakened.

But Galen had never been skilled with shields of any kind. He would need a breather and something warm to wear.

He had only a lightweight coat, long and black. The temperature seldom fell to freezing on the mak. He dug the coat out of his valise, slipped the breather over his face, and hurried into the air lock. As he descended the ramp, he had to shade his eyes. The sun was too bright, the landscape too clear. No comforting mist enfolded the land; no buildings obscured the landscape. He could see miles across the barren ice sheet to the ragged mountains.

As soon as he was clear of the ship, he visualized the equation to dissociate. Twin echoes from the tech and the chrysalis confirmed the conjury, then his connection to the ship broke; the second echo faded into silence.

Yet the undercurrent of energy from the implants remained with him, and it felt stronger than ever. It was restless and endless, quick to respond. And there was no dissociating from it. He was determined to remain in control, no matter what happened.

He jammed his cold hands into his pockets and tramped across the crunchy ice pack. Elric stood already before the empty ship. The ramp was lowered.

"This is not Kell's ship," Elric said. "It has been disguised." His voice had regained its strength, and he manipulated it with his old skill, extending certain sounds, pausing at specific places, and modulating his intonation to almost hypnotic effect. In the bright sun, though, Elric's face looked worn. Perhaps it was the blue tinge of the shield covering his body that gave his skin a pale cast. With his scoured scalp and high-collared black robe, he still appeared stern and severe, yet now Galen sensed a weariness in the thin line of his lips, an effort in the frown lines between his brows.

"Whose is it, then?"

"We will know soon enough."

They walked up the ramp, Galen matching Elric's slow steps. As they reached the air lock, the outer door opened for them.

"Only one of us need go," Elric said.

"But which one?" Galen replied. He knew Elric would prefer him to wait away from the ship, and danger. As one of the Circle, Elric could order him to remain behind. But Elric had not given him an order since Galen had ceased being his student and had been initiated as a mage. Galen didn't think he would do so now. And Galen didn't want Elric to enter alone.

Galen stepped into the air lock, and Elric entered with him. The door closed behind them.

They waited while the air lock pressurized. Then the inner door opened. Inside, all was dark. Galen removed his breather. The recycled air carried a faint stale smell.

Elric conjured a globe of light. Around the ship, other lights suddenly flashed on, one after the other. They all pointed in the same direction. Sitting in the spotlight was something that Galen, at first, could not identify. Then he recognized the white goatee scoured into the shape of the rune for knowledge. From there his gaze rose to Kell's face, which had fallen back, white teeth gleaming in a mouth fixed in a rigid grimace.

The sleeves of Kell's robe had been ripped open, and beneath, a single clean incision had been made down each of Kell's arms, the skin spread back like the petals of an alien flower, revealing a great mystery of darkness speckled with brilliant flecks of white. His hands were two great blossoms, the skin of palms, of thumbs, index and middle fingers peeled back, muscle elegantly split, delicate canyons of bone exposed.

Kell had been flayed.

In the early days of their history, rogue mages had been flayed for refusing to obey the Code. Removing all of the tech from a mage, unless it was done soon after initiation, was always fatal. The body and the tech quickly became intertwined. Although flaying remained the punishment for serious violations of the Code, it hadn't been administered for hundreds of years.

Elric approached Kell. Galen wanted to tell him not to move, not to speak, that perhaps the vision in the light was an illusion. If they did not move, if they did not touch it, perhaps they could come to believe it was not real.

Kell had not deserved this.

Elric laid one hand on the back of the chair and turned Kell away from them. Galen thought at first that Elric wanted to shield them from the image. But then Elric brought his hands to either side of Kell's head, lifted it. A shudder ran down Elric's body.

Galen could not see. He found himself moving forward.

The spotlights shone into the back of Kell's skull. A neat circle of bone had been cut away, revealing the emptiness within. Most of his brain had been removed. Elric's hands moved to Kell's shoulders. Galen wanted him to stop. He could not see any more.

Elric pushed the shoulders forward, away from the chair. The back of Kell's robe had been cut away. Three parallel furrows transected him from shoulder to shoulder. From neck to tailbone, his spine was one wide, ragged wound, the skin peeled back to reveal the white bone of vertebrae. Down each side of the spinal cord, deep channels had been carved, and periodic clumps of tissue, muscle, and nerves scooped cleanly away where they'd become inextricably intertwined with high concentrations of tech. Tiny holes revealed channels cut deeper within. The work was so extensive, only a few traces remained of the stippled black discoloration along Kell's spine and shoulder blades.

There were easier ways to kill him. And the removed tech could be of no use. It had fused with Kell's system. It had adapted to his body, his mind. It could be commanded by no one else.

Elric pulled Kell's shoulders back, gently rested him against the chair. For a moment Kell's dark eyes pointed up at Galen, and Galen remembered how that gaze used to make him feel, as if Kell saw right into him. But those eyes saw nothing now. They were as empty as hers had been.

Kell's head shifted, his empty gaze falling away. Elric straightened his head against the back of the chair, turned the chair to its original orientation, as if that could somehow erase what they had seen.

Only a mage could do such detailed work. Tilar was only in chrysalis stage; he wouldn't have powerful enough sensors to detect all the fine threads of the tech. Razeel, Galen thought, wouldn't have the skill to cut it away so precisely. But there was one who had proven himself expert in his knowledge of the body and its vulnerabilities, who had shown the skill to use that knowledge effectively.

Galen's anger had been misdirected. Kell had erred, but he had not been the one to betray the techno-mages. He had not been the one to join the Shadows. He had not been the one to kill her. The grief and fury he had felt at the sight of Kell's ship returned full force, and a sudden surge of energy drove through him, burning to act, to strike back.

"The ship belongs to Elizar," Elric said.

Behind them a door slid open and Galen spun, ready to attack. With fierce focus he forced his mind to be still, to be blank. He would not conjure on instinct.

Two dark figures emerged from the air lock.

Galen stepped out of the spotlights, saw that it was Blaylock and his former student, Gowen. Galen struggled to slow his breathing, to regain control.

"The blessing of Wierden upon—" Gowen's greeting broke off in a gasp.

"He has been flayed," Elric said.

Blaylock addressed Gowen. "Turn away. Come no closer." Gowen obeyed.

Blaylock's pale face, scoured of all hair, seemed to float in the shadows. "They know where we are," he said.

One after another, the ship's lights went out, leaving only the light globe Elric had conjured. Then in the near darkness, brilliant red fire spread down Kell's arms. The fire curled into runes, formed a message.

We will reclaim the techno-mages.

The tech echoed Galen's outrage. Elizar still had dreams of overthrowing the Circle, of leading the mages with Razeel and Tilar at his side. He believed it was his right as an heir of the line of Wierden. Yet Galen had thought Elizar's hopes would have died when he'd become a murderer. How could he think they would ever accept him now, after all he had done? And how could he have the arrogance to treat the mages as if they were his to command, his to "reclaim"?

Elric glanced at him, but Galen could read no reaction on his stern face.

The fiery runes faded, leaving them in the light of Elric's single globe.

"The Circle should meet at once," Elric said.

"We must remove Kell to the facility," Blaylock said. "This ship must be destroyed."

Elric nodded and conjured a platform beneath Kell that

lifted him from the chair, then straightened so that he lay flat. With a wave of his hand Elric created the illusion of a sheet shrouding Kell's body, and in Galen's mind the image rose unbidden: Elric walking from the fire of the explosion, the bodies of Galen's parents floating behind him, supine, shrouded in sheets.

Energy churned inside Galen, searching for outlet. "I will destroy the ship," he said.

Elric hesitated, studying him. Galen tried to make his face impassive. He didn't think he fooled Elric, but Elric didn't seem to have the energy to argue. Instead Elric nodded and moved with Kell toward the air lock.

"Use your ship to destroy this one," Blaylock said. "Remove yourself to a distance. Take no unnecessary risk."

"Yes," Galen said.

Soon the others were gone, and he was left with darkness and the smell of blood and decay. He visualized his mind as a blank screen on which to impose equations. First he conjured several light globes, illuminating the area. Next he accessed his sensors, studied the walls of the ship, confirming what he thought. Then he went to the panel in the wall behind the chair. He slid it open, as the Grimlis had taught him. Sometimes maintenance or repair was necessary.

There, within the recess, like a thick silvery worm, clung a section of Elizar's chrysalis. Ripples on its skin revealed the tension of its muscles as it held to the interface pane. Processors ringed it, the nexus for them all. Silver filaments spread from its plump body in a web, intertwining themselves with the ship's systems, with the ship itself. Galen touched the warm translucent surface. A subtle light glowed from within.

It carried Elizar's DNA, and during Elizar's training as an apprentice, it had grown into an echo of him, mirroring his brain structure, his patterns of thought. It had become a part of him, an extension of him.

Galen had last seen Elizar a month ago, through a probe, in

the Thenothk system on the rim of known space, thousands of light-years away. If Elizar was still there, or at any distance from the ship, he would have only the most tenuous connection to it.

Yet even a tenuous connection could carry sensation. The sensation of a single hair being pulled from the scalp, the sensation of a needle-thin sliver slipping under the skin. The sensation of the devil walking over his grave.

Galen's heart pounded, the pounding echoed back to him by the tech. He had agreed to leave Elizar behind, to run with the mages to their hiding place.

But here was one piece he did not have to leave behind.

Galen removed his hand from the soft silver surface, took a step back, then another. The hatred welled up in him, no longer willing to be buried or contained. Energy bloomed through him. Fire raced along the lines of the tech. Heat spilled out from his skin. He visualized the equation.

A fireball appeared in the air before him, coruscating with light. He formed an equation of motion, hurled the fireball at the chrysalis. Fire splashed across the silver form and the interface pane. The chrysalis made a slight, squirming movement.

He formed a second fireball in the air. Shot it at the chrysalis. A third ball. Slammed it into the fiery recess.

The wormlike form was black, engulfed in flame. It moved no more.

Smoke billowed out of the wall, and with the sizzle and pop of melting machinery, the smell of charred meat carried on the air. He recognized the smell from when he'd burned Elizar's arm. It was the smell of his old friend's flesh.

If only he had killed Elizar then. If only he had burned Elizar to a handful of ash.

Galen's hands had tightened into quivering fists. He realized with surprise that he was crying, wiped impatiently at his eyes with the back of his fist. Smoke was filling the interior. He knew he should leave. Yet the fire that raced through him would consume him if he did not release it. These small conjuries had only increased its pressure.

He thought of letting it all come out, of making the ship into an inferno, destroying it from the inside out, with him still inside.

But that would kill Elric.

He had to leave. He had to leave before he lost all control. He stumbled to the air lock.

He would get into his ship. He would retreat to a safe distance. He would fire at Elizar's ship, destroying it. And he would bury these thoughts of destruction once again. He would not feel. He would not remember.

But he would remain vigilant. He could not allow himself to retreat completely to that place deep inside, to fade into transparency, to haunt the living like a ghost. It was too dangerous. For in the blaze of fire, he had revealed himself. He was no insubstantial ghost, but a monster, one who would kill in a moment if he did not hold tightly to the tech.

So he would maintain his focus. He would stay in control. He would go with the techno-mages to their hiding place. And he would hide.

─── *chapter 4* ───

Galen entered the squat, rectangular structure through an air lock marked with the rune signifying solidarity. He had brought his valise and staff from the ship, leaving the rest of his possessions behind. As he waited for the air lock to pressurize, he dreaded facing the others, feeling the self-consciousness that inevitably arose when he was with anyone other than Elric. People, particularly mages, always gave him the uncomfortable sensation that they saw in him things he did not wish to reveal, things that, in some cases, he did not even know existed. And with all that had happened, he feared what they would now see in him, and what they would say. Whatever they said, he would keep the memories, and the emotions they carried, buried. He could not face them again.

He composed his face. The inner door opened, and he slipped the breather off, stepped into a vast hangar filled with crates and supplies.

Fed stood beside the air lock, a crooked smile on his face.

"Federico," Galen said, feeling awkward. "Good to see you." His tone sounded more distant than he intended.

"Nice work on Elizar's ship," Fed said. "I think you got it the first time."

"I felt thoroughness was warranted," Galen replied.

"Oh, absolutely. You don't want to leave the job half done." Though many mages scoured their scalps regularly in honor of the Code, as did Galen, it appeared that Fed had not undergone scouring since their initiation in November. His bushy beard and short, wiry hair were quickly regaining their old wild-man look. That Fed forwent the scouring of the scalp was not surprising; his former teacher, Herazade, did the same.

Fed exuded the sharp smell of cologne, and he'd discarded the plain black robe he'd worn as an apprentice in favor of a short yellow jacket and pants covered with elaborate embroidery. For some reason, he looked like a pirate. Galen could imagine Elizar saying something very clever and cutting about Fed's appearance. But Elizar was across the galaxy, torturing and killing people.

"I'm supposed to brief you on our luxurious accommodations," Fed said.

Galen found he had received a message from Fed with several files attached—maps, schedules, plans.

"They have some rules. Everyone is required to help with the preparations, and work assignments are being coordinated by Herazade. Don't complain about your assignment, or you'll be—assigned to something less pleasant." Galen got the impression Fed was speaking from experience. "You're staying in Room 244, with me. We're roommates. Your lifetime dream, I'm sure. My stuff's a little messy right now. Just ignore it; I'll clean it up later.

"All the rooms are claustrophobia traps, so don't get your hopes up. If we keep to schedule, we should be out of here in two weeks. Any disputes should be brought immediately to a member of the Circle. I have to say that, because there have already been so many fights, things are getting pretty crazy. It's air-lock fever; it's the tension." Fed shrugged. "It's us."

"Where is Elric?"

Fed jerked a thumb toward the far end of the hangar. "If you go out that door, you'll find him in Room 288, down the hall to the right. The Circle has gathered there." He added, hesitantly, "I think they're examining Kell's body."

Galen started down through the tall rows of supplies, his staff and breather in his right hand, valise in his left.

Fed followed. "Is it true that Elizar and Razeel killed Kell?" His voice had grown softer.

"Yes," Galen said.

"You saw Kell?"

"Yes."

Fed bowed his head, uncharacteristically thoughtful. "Kell helped me once. With some trouble I was having. It was nothing major. It was pretty stupid, actually. But he took the time to talk to me." Fed was silent for a few seconds. Galen didn't think he'd ever seen Fed quiet, except when someone else was speaking. "When I saw Elric come out of that ship with a body, I felt—outrage, I guess is what it was. How could they do that?"

Galen kept his voice neutral. "The same way they killed before."

"Elizar always seemed to take that mage arrogance thing a little too seriously. And Razeel, she was just plain creepy."

Galen wondered how Fed would categorize him.

"How could they have overpowered Kell? And how could they have found out where we are? Kell resigned the Circle before those decisions were even made," Fed said.

"I don't know."

"A traitor?"

Galen did not answer. They didn't have enough information.

"We're going to have to move, aren't we? If they know we're gathering here, they could follow us to the hiding place."

"I expect so." They had reached the far side of the hangar, and Galen stopped, hoping that perhaps Fed would return to his post.

Fed glanced into the plain beige hall and seemed to force the crooked smile back onto his face. "I'm lobbying for some-place warmer and more comfortable for our next gathering place. A nice resort with a beach. A bunch of pale-skinned techno-mages in black robes would fit right in."

Down the hall to the right, a large group of mages blocked the passage. Carvin stood out in her colorful Centauri silks, her head buried in her hands as she sobbed. Alwyn stood beside his former student, an arm over her shoulders, his jaw tight with anger. After Elric, they were the two mages he felt closest to. But Galen did not want to join them in their mourning.

"Word travels pretty fast around here." Fed shrugged.

Galen had no doubt Fed had been the one to start the news spreading. He had always been a conduit of gossip. Secrecy seemed to be a part of the Code with which he was unacquainted. "Which way is our room?"

Fed nodded down the hall in the same direction as the crowd. "No way around them." Fed tilted his head. "Have you noticed, Galen? I can never get more than a sentence out of you."

"I haven't much to say."

"But I've never known someone more full of things to say." Fed's eyes were narrowed in humor, though they remained fixed on him, revealing a more serious intent. Perhaps Fed wanted more gossip to spread. Or perhaps Fed simply wanted to be his friend, to encourage him to unburden himself. Fed had always behaved as if they were good friends, though Galen felt they barely knew each other. He certainly didn't understand Fed. He didn't know how someone could become a mage with minimal discipline, no sense of mage history, and little respect for the Code. In any case, Galen had no desire to speak, about anything, to anyone.

"If I feel the urge to talk, I'll make sure to let you know."

He left Fed behind and walked toward the mages gathered in the passage. Perhaps fifty or a hundred of them blocked the way, crowding outside the closed door to Room 288, where the Circle now studied Kell's remains.

Galen composed a message to Elric. *I have destroyed Elizar's ship. Do you have need of me?*

Gowen stood in the center of a large group who seemed to be bombarding him with questions. They would want to know what he'd seen aboard Elizar's ship. Gowen's round cheeks were drawn up in dismay, his hands clenched together in white-knuckle prayer. He caught sight of Galen, fixed on him as if seeing a specter. Circe and Maskelyne, standing beside Gowen, stopped their questioning, and they too looked toward Galen. They would know that he had been with Elric, that he had seen Kell's body.

Elric's response arrived. *No. I am occupied with the Circle. You did well in getting us here. You should rest.*

A few feet away, Alwyn followed the gaze of the others to Galen. His tight jaw relinquished a smile. Alwyn looked the same as he had last month, at the convocation. He wore his favorite loud, multicolored robe, a long black cape over it. His receding silvery hair, the bags beneath his eyes, his generous girth—all suggested a softness that Alwyn often displayed, yet one that could vanish instantly when his anger was aroused. Galen didn't see any new weakness in Alwyn, though he too must have destroyed his place of power.

Carvin seemed to sense that something had changed. She raised her face, wet with tears. "Galen!" she cried. She ran to him, seizing him with a rustle of her Centauri silks, and enveloped him in her sobs.

Galen's body went rigid. As always, close contact made him uncomfortable. He did not like to be touched. And he did not want to be the dumping ground for her pain. Let her keep it to herself. He did not want to feel it. He refused to feel it.

Her whisper ran down the side of his face. "It is one death after another."

The words ripped the memory from him, the image of Carvin's face wet with tears, watching as magical fire consumed

Isabelle's lifeless body. She had cried for Isabelle, cried when Galen could not.

Alwyn came to stand beside her, and he rubbed her back in a circular motion. Carvin had never withheld her emotions. During Alwyn's visits to Soom, Galen and Carvin had often studied together. To Galen, she had always seemed strangely fearless—passionate, outgoing, open. She did not hide from life, but lived it. It was an existence foreign to him.

At last she released him, and he let out a breath, trying to relax his muscles.

Carvin wiped at her eyes. Her spell language was the language of her body. When she performed an elaborate conjury, she directed her power with strong, graceful movements. Galen remembered the perfect illusion she had created in the training hall on Soom with Alwyn's boots, the intricate patterns traced by her body. Now her shoulders were curled inward, her back hunched.

Alwyn embraced him. "It's good to see you well."

"And you," Galen said, wondering how he would ever get through the entire group of mages. But he could not pass without talking to Alwyn and Carvin. He set his valise down, rested the end of his staff against the floor.

"Was it Elizar?" Carvin asked.

Galen's throat was tight. He nodded.

"We have to stop him," she said.

Anger stirred inside Galen. Didn't she understand how hard it had been to put to rest? "That is up to the Circle," he said.

"You don't know all that's happened," Alwyn said. "Djadjamonkh and Regana are missing. They should have arrived here last week. And as Carvin and I traveled here from Regula 4, we were attacked by an unmarked ship of great power. We barely escaped from it. The Shadows are determined to stop us."

Galen didn't need Alwyn to tell him of the Shadows. It was

their hand behind all that had happened, their hand that had brought so much pain. They sought to consume the galaxy in chaos. But he would not be consumed.

Circe inserted herself into their conversation. "Djadja-monkh and Regana may have fallen ill after destroying their places of power. Or perhaps they joined with the Shadows." Her voice now sounded almost like an outsider's, weak, lacking resonance. And beneath the shadow of her tall, pointed hat, her face showed signs of change as well. The lines on either side of her mouth had deepened, along with the tiny lines above her lip. She, like so many of them, had destroyed her place.

"They would not have joined the Shadows," Alwyn said. "And if ill, they would have contacted us. Do you believe Kell, too, fell ill?"

"You speak as if you've made up your mind what we must do."

Alwyn gave her a hard stare. "I know what's right, without waiting for the Circle to issue a proclamation."

Circe frowned. "We must all follow the Circle. We are sworn to solidarity. Besides, they may well have information we do not."

"Of that I've no doubt. They may know who killed every Earth president from Santiago back to Kennedy. They may know the number of angels that can dance on the head of a pin. They may even know the meaning of the universe. But it doesn't change what I know."

"And what is that?"

"That we must fight the Shadows," Alwyn said.

Galen looked anxiously down the hall toward his room. He didn't want to be drawn into this debate.

"We haven't the numbers or the technology to win," Circe said.

Alwyn dismissed her comment with an impatient wave of his hand. "I didn't say we must fight them to win. But we must fight them. If our Code is anything more than a convenient balm to our conscience, we must make a stand. Besides, the Shadows won't relent. They'll find us in our hiding place, cowering like cowards, and they'll destroy us. Better to go down fighting. And we may even surprise you; we may be able to do them more damage than you suspect."

Circe pursed her lips. "If that's how you feel, Alwyn, then why have you come here? Why aren't you out killing Shadows?"

"Because I still foolishly hope that the Circle may see the light and change their minds."

"That they 'may see the light.' You're a great man for talk, Alwyn. Superior in wisdom, superior in morals. Yet what of action? Your superiority truly shines in carousing and probe-spitting contests. Look at Galen. He of all of us has faced the Shadows, and fought them. And he leaves for the hiding place with Elric. He knows that if we fight, more of us will die."

Alwyn looked at Galen. "Each must decide for himself."

"That way lies chaos." Circe turned to Carvin. "And you, do you share your teacher's rash judgment?"

"He has told me the decision is my own, and I will not make it lightly."

"The decision," Circe said, "is the Circle's. They have made the only choice they could, the one best for us."

Alwyn shook his head. "Aren't you tired of always defending them, of always seeking to impress them, hoping that someday you will be one of them?"

Circe glanced behind her, as if afraid others might overhear. "You go too far, Alwyn. You always have." She turned and pushed her way into the crowd, her pointed hat marking her retreat.

"And she never goes far enough, unfortunately," Alwyn said. He turned to Galen. "Elric is my last chance of swaying the Circle. I've talked to the rest of them, but they don't give my opinion any weight. If Elric would argue to stay, perhaps he could convince one other, and the vote of the Circle would be tied. With the arrival of Elizar's ship, they must reevaluate their plan. Might Elric be swayed?"

Galen unbuttoned his coat. The undercurrent of energy from the tech had risen again to the level of discomfort, generating an agitating unrest.

At the last meeting of the Circle, Elric had voted to stay and fight, but the other three members of the Circle had voted to hide, and so Elric had bowed to the will of the majority. He had told Galen that the mages must remain united, above all. *We must support the Circle with all our energies, or it will not hold. And if it does not, the mages will fall to chaos, and the Shadows will have triumphed.* Elric had not wanted to leave Soom, to destroy his place of power. Yet he had done it. He had weakened himself, for the sake of solidarity.

"I think it may be too late," Galen said, "for any of them to change their decision now."

"I'll do my damnedest to convince him, in any case," Alwyn said. "But what of you, Galen? Is what Circe said true?"

Galen looked again down the crowded hall, wishing for the refuge of his room. Alwyn was forcing him to reconsider his decision, to relive the events that had brought him to it. He could not think of them, could not allow those memories to resurface. He had chosen to obey the Circle and the Code before. Just as Elric could not change, he could not change, could not admit that his earlier obedience had been unnecessary. How could he live, if he admitted that? "I have sworn myself to the Circle and the Code, and I will do what they direct."

"And if the Circle dictates one thing, and the Code another?"

"Then I will follow the Circle, for the first word of the Code is solidarity, and we must remain united." He said the words, but they brought him no peace. The possibility of staying and fighting, though he tried not to think of it, lingered in his mind, unsettling him, promising him the satisfaction he desired. The tech echoed his restlessness.

He knew he must go with the others, but it was no longer enough simply to know. He had to hear it confirmed, had to hear again the reasons.

Alwyn planned to make his argument to Elric. Elric would explain why the mages must leave.

Galen reached down with his right hand, which held his staff and breather, and picked up the valise. Meanwhile, with his left, he reached into his robe pocket, where he had a packet of probes, and dipped his index finger into the dust-sized grains.

"But—" Carvin said.

As Galen straightened, he saw on her face what she was about to say, and he didn't want to hear it. He spoke over her.

"What about Elizar?" she said.

"I must find my room," Galen said. "It was a long journey, and I must rest."

"Yes, of course," Alwyn said, putting an arm across Galen's shoulders.

Galen brushed his index finger against Alwyn's cape, depositing several probes there.

"Get some rest," Alwyn said.

Galen put his head down and worked his way through the crowd. Others called to him—Muirne, Beel, Elektra, Tzakizak. They had shown him only minor interest in the past, but now they sought to find out what he'd seen on Elizar's ship. But it was more than that, Galen thought, as he nodded and moved on. They had left him alone after his return to the convocation, its final night a shock to them all. But they would leave him alone no longer. Somehow, now, they felt the need to speak to him, to extract from him the details of his ordeal, to include him in their deliberations. Though he tried not to meet their faces, some flashed past him, with smiles of forced cheer, or grim expressions of sympathy. Hands touched his back, his arms. He thought he heard the word, whispered, "Condolences." He pushed ahead, as if he did not hear, did not feel. He could not stop again.

He should not have put the probes on Alwyn. It was improper for one mage to secretly use his powers on another. And Alwyn would eventually discover the probes. But hopefully not until after Alwyn and Elric spoke.

The decision that he had made a month ago, and that the Circle had made, now seemed in doubt. Elizar and the Shadows knew where they gathered. Mages were missing or killed. Would it even be possible to hide when the Shadows pursued them so closely?

Galen broke free of the crowd and continued down the passage. In everything the mages said there were echoes of what Galen tried to bury. He had thought leaving Soom would help him drift further away from himself, just as leaving his home many years ago to live with Elric had helped him to forget. Yet things were only more difficult here. As Circe had said, he was the only one of them who had faced the Shadows and lived. When the mages looked at him, they thought of that, and of those who had faced the Shadows and died.

He was trapped here with those memories. And even once the mages reached the hiding place, it would be no different. The memories were everywhere. The pain was everywhere. There was no hiding from it. How could he continue to face it, day after day?

And how could he face, day after day, the fact that Elizar was out there, living his life?

Perhaps, if he heard Elric's response to Alwyn's argument, if he heard again the reasons they must go, it would put his thoughts to rest and calm the racing energy inside him.

He hoped that it would, for he could not remain this way.

*   *   *

"Must we speak now?" Elric said.

"It cannot wait," Alwyn replied.

The images from the probes Galen had planted on Alwyn weren't very revealing. The microscopic devices were caught in a fold of Alwyn's cape, and showed mainly a shifting curtain of black as Alwyn moved, with only occasional glimpses of the surroundings. At least Galen could hear their voices. He listened anxiously, relieved that Elric had finally emerged from the examination of Kell's remains, hoping at last for the confirmation he needed. The tech echoed his anxiety.

Apparently Elric followed Alwyn into a room where they could speak privately, for Alwyn continued. "We barely had a chance to talk after the Circle made its decision at the convocation. I know we disagree about—almost everything. But I respect you, and I believe I know you. And I believe you must agree that the right thing for us to do is stay and fight the Shadows."

"I will save you the effort of convincing me, though I know you would enjoy the debate. I voted to stay and fight. The others disagreed."

"There's hope for you yet." Alwyn sounded surprised. "Must be my influence. All the better, then. You must convince just one of them to change votes. Then the Circle will be deadlocked, and they'll be forced to consider other alternatives."

"I cannot. But even if I could, I would not."

"We have a responsibility. You to Soom, and I to Regula 4 and its people. I know you don't want to leave your place undefended."

"Yet I have done so, for duty."

"Duty. Do you have a duty to be a fool, if the Circle orders foolishness?" The black folds of Alwyn's cape billowed. "I'm sorry. I'm sorry. I know you've not made this decision lightly. But we have a responsibility that extends beyond our places of power, all of us to all the rest out there. We have power they do not. If we fail to use it for good, then what justification can we possibly claim for having it?"

"I made this argument to the Circle before. It did not sway them."

"How can they be such colossal hypocrites?" Alwyn's voice rose, and Galen could imagine his jaw growing tight, as it did when he became impassioned. "We have access to the tech, and to the power it carries. We keep it to ourselves, claiming we don't want it abused. We say that with it we'll seek knowledge, create beauty and magic, and do good. Then along come the Shadows, determined to drive all of known space into a war that will kill billions, and all we think about is saving our own skins. It goes against everything we claim to be. It proves that we have no right to the tech at all. It—it's rank cowardice, that's what it is. How can those jackasses justify themselves?"

Galen's breath quickened. Alwyn was right. Surely there must be some way that they could convince the Circle. They must fight the Shadows. They must fight Elizar.

Elric's tone remained even. "Blaylock believes fighting would go against our holy destiny. Ing-Radi believes we should fight only if we have a chance of winning. Herazade does not know how to cope with a universe in which we are not the strongest, except by hiding."

"I accept Blaylock as a lost cause. But couldn't Ing-Radi or Herazade be turned?"

"I tried and failed."

"Why not try again?"

That was exactly what Galen found himself asking.

"Because we have begun down this road," Elric said, "and as much as I wish we had not, we no longer have the choice to turn back. We are too weakened to form an effective fighting force. And with the murder of Kell, the attack on you and Carvin, and the other mages missing, it is clear we are besieged. Thus far they have attacked only a few of us, to frighten and intimidate the rest. But now we have gathered ourselves in one place, a place the Shadows have discovered, a place that is undefended. They can destroy us easily, at any moment. We must be very clever if any of us are to survive. The only reason they have not yet destroyed us is because they still hope for our alliance."

"We could use that against them."

"Pretend to join them, as Kell sent Elizar to do? We dare not. And the truth is, some among us may already have joined the Shadows, and may only be pretending loyalty to us. That may be how Elizar learned our location."

"Then what good will it be to hide, if the Shadows will know our hiding place?"

"No one will know, save the Circle. And no one will be allowed to send communications outside the hiding place, save the Circle."

"The hiding place will be our prison, then."

"That is not—" Elric's voice broke off oddly in the middle of his sentence, as if he had lost his breath. "That is not what I said."

"I can't believe you're going to go along with this," Alwyn said. "You're going to leave all the beings in known space without defense against the Shadows."

"We are not the only defense."

"But we're the ones best equipped to defend. What purpose do we have, if not this?"

Galen didn't understand what Alwyn meant. Certainly the mages were powerful. But weren't the Vorlons even more powerful?

"I too thought it might be our destiny to fight the Shadows, perhaps even to defeat them. Yet the Circle finds it otherwise. And as powerful as we are, we have many vulnerabilities when it comes to the Shadows. They can see through our illusions. They can penetrate our shields. It's likely they can do even more. We don't know if Kell surrendered willingly to Elizar, or if he was overpowered."

"Kell was the most powerful of us. How could he be overpowered?"

"That is the . . ."

"Elric. What is it? Sit down." The folds of Alwyn's cape shifted as he moved. Galen struggled to catch a glimpse of Elric. He saw the flash of a chair, nothing more. "You aren't well," Alwyn said.

"You have not destroyed your place of power." Elric's words sounded as if they were forced through clenched teeth.

Galen grabbed the edge of the cot where he sat, staring anxiously at the tiny room strewn with Fed's possessions. Fear held him still. Elric was in pain. His condition was worsening. And they had no idea how serious it would become.

"Is that what this is?" Alwyn said. After a few moments, he continued, his tone subdued. "No. I won't abandon it. I had hoped the mages would change their minds and stay. But if I must, I'll stay alone. You could stay with me."

"I have made my decision." Elric's voice sounded stronger, the only remaining hint of pain a slight brittleness in his words. "I am no longer what I was. Over half of us are now so afflicted, including the oldest and most powerful."

If Elizar had not betrayed them, perhaps the Circle would not have decided to flee. Elric would not have had to destroy his place of power.

"Even weakened, we can still put up a fight. If we're to die, why not die fighting?"

"That would be my preference," Elric said. "But my personal wishes are irrelevant. It is my responsibility to hold the mages together, and that means following the will of the Circle."

"You could lead a group of us against the Shadows. Let the others flee."

"I will not break from the Circle. Without the authority of

the Circle and the Code, we would fracture not into two factions, but into many. We would quickly descend into chaos, and the Shadows would have won. We must remain united."

Elric was right, of course. Solidarity, above all. It was the same answer he himself had given to Alwyn earlier. Yet Elric's assertion brought him no peace. Elric had paid too great a price. And Galen raced with the restless urge for revenge.

"How much are you willing to sacrifice to that end?"

"I have already given nearly everything I have."

"What about Galen?" Alwyn said. "He's trying like hell to remain loyal to you and your exalted Circle, and it's killing him."

Galen rocked back and forth, uncomfortable with the mention of his name.

"He has spoken to you?" Elric said.

"Of course not. He's barely speaking at all. I was shocked to see that he's in no better shape than he was a month ago. The poor boy's been sleepwalking through life like some kind of zombie since Isabelle was killed. Another bright idea of the Circle—sending two inexperienced initiates into danger."

"To answer your question, no, I will not give up Galen. I have given him over to the Circle once, and I will not do so again. He is the one thing I am not willing to sacrifice. He is another reason I must go to the hiding place."

"But he needs to fight. He needs justice for Isabelle."

Galen closed his eyes, though it did not matter. His fingers dug into the mattress.

"No. He is in shock. I believe he has had thoughts of suicide, as well as thoughts of mass destruction. He needs stability, not war. That is his path to recovery."

"Stability, in a confined place filled with mages? It sounds more like a powder keg."

"There is no further need for discussion. You have asked

and I have answered. The Circle has made its decision. As for Galen, keep him out of your plans. He is mine."

Galen heard footsteps. Elric, he supposed, walking to the door.

Alwyn turned, and Elric's image flashed momentarily into view. He stood a few feet away, a severe figure in his high-collared black robe.

"Don't you think the time for secrecy is over?" Alwyn's question sounded more like a challenge. A long silence followed. Finally Alwyn continued. "The mages deserve to know the full situation. And I believe if the Circle told them, they would want to stay and fight."

"Kell allowed Elizar to learn the secrets of Wierden."

"Everyone is not Elizar."

Galen stiffened. What was this?

The Circle retained more secrets, he realized, and somehow Alwyn knew at least one of them. His heart pounded. What was it? A secret of power? Elizar had spoken of such secrets, and he had learned some of them when he had invaded Kell's place. Did the mages have more powers of which they were unaware, and did Alwyn believe those powers could be used to fight the Shadows?

If the Circle did hold such secrets, then it should reveal them before the mages went into hiding. It should have revealed them before it had forced so many to destroy their places of power. It should have revealed them before ... everything had gone wrong.

Secrecy was the way of the mages, necessary to manipulate others, to create illusions and deceptions, to perform acts that seemed magical. But their secrets should be kept from outsiders, not one another. Kell's secrets had already caused irreparable damage. What reason could the Circle possibly have for keeping secrets now?

He must find the truth. The secrets had to be uncovered.

That was just what Elizar had told him, a lifetime ago.

"The Circle will never agree to tell the mages," Elric said. "We have discussed it many times."

"I could tell them."

"You know the penalty."

"The Circle would do to me what Elizar did to Kell. You could tell them."

"The penalty is no different for me," Elric said.

"How can you keep this from them? Don't you think they have a right to know? And how could you have kept Galen in the dark all these years? How could you have seen him through initiation and all that's followed, and never said a single word to the boy?"

Agitating energy surged through Galen. What had Elric kept from him?

For a long moment the room was silent. Then Elric answered. "We do what we must. Perhaps once we are in the hiding place, the Circle will feel differently."

"Hiding from this war solves nothing. What if the Shadows are victorious? What then? Or worse, what if the Vorlons are victorious?"

"I can see no path by which the mages will survive this war. Not in any form that we would recognize. If that has not been clear to you, then I offer it as an additional bit of despair. Our time is ending."

Galen couldn't believe Elric had said that. He knew Elric had disagreed with the decision of the Circle, yet Elric had behaved as if retreating to a hiding place, while perhaps not the best solution, was a viable one. Galen had never seen his hopelessness.

Could it be that the situation truly was hopeless?

"I can't believe that," Alwyn said. "You're tired."

"I am more tired than I hope you ever know," Elric said. Then he added, "I will tell the Circle nothing of your plans."

The nearby sound of laughter distracted Galen, drawing

him back to his small room. He sat on his cot, bent forward, rocking back and forth, his hands clenched around the edge of the mattress. His valise and staff lay on the floor beside him. Fed's bizarre, colorful wardrobe and half-assembled inventions surrounded him as if Fed's suitcase had exploded. The air reeked of cologne. The laughing came from outside the door. He heard Fed's voice.

"I didn't realize what a great idea this hiding away was. Once we get there, we're going to have plenty of time, and not much to do with it. Except have fun."

Some muffled sounds followed.

In Galen's mind's eye, Alwyn's cape billowed in a regular rhythm. He seemed to be walking down the hall. His conversation with Elric was over. Galen broke the connection.

"You're very good at that," a woman said, just outside the door. "Did I ever tell you that I had a hiding place of my own? I'd like to show it to you sometime."

"I'm free now," Fed said, and more muffled sounds followed. Galen realized they were kissing, their bodies rubbing against the door. "Want to take a spin on my flying platform of love?"

Galen stood.

Fed could go to the hiding place. Fed could be happy there. But how could Galen stand it?

He pulled open the door, and the two stumbled in, nearly falling on top of him. Fed's companion was Optima, one of the younger members of the Kinetic Grimlis. She pulled down her glowing purple shirt.

"Sorry," Galen said. He started out the door.

They both laughed. "Take your time," Fed said, "wherever you're going."

Galen closed the door behind him. He didn't know how long he could stand to be cooped up here, inside, with so many others. The utilitarian facility packed one tiny room beside the next, with only thin metal walls separating them. There was no privacy, no space.

Giggling sounded from the other side of the door. "I think we shocked him," Optima said.

Galen started down the narrow beige hall. Listening to Alwyn and Elric's conversation had not helped. He felt more unsettled than before, thoughts racing, energy churning, memories bleeding through. He crossed his arms over his chest, holding tightly to control. What was he going to do? Defy the Circle, defy Elric, abandon him in his time of need? Go to the home of the Shadows, find Elizar, and kill him?

That was what he wanted to do, but to do it, he would have to forswear the Circle and the Code. He would be no different from Elizar.

He had to see Elric. He had to know the secret of which Alwyn had spoken, the secret that might convince the mages to stay and fight.

Just as Galen reached the main passage, Herazade and Blaylock rushed by. Gowen followed a few feet behind.

"Gowen," Galen called.

Gowen continued down the hall. "I can't talk."

"What is it?"

"Another meeting of the Circle."

Galen went after him, fell into step beside him. "Will they change plans because of Kell?"

"That is what they must decide."

Galen had to talk to Elric before the meeting, before the Circle made any decision. He glanced back and found others following, anxious to learn whether their plans would be altered. He didn't see Elric. But if he followed Herazade and Blaylock, they would lead him to the rest of the Circle.

He tightened his arms across his chest, desperate to hold everything inside. Searching for something to quiet his mind, he fixed on Gowen.

Since the initiation, Gowen had apparently been scouring the hair not only from his scalp, cheeks, and chin, but from his entire body, as most of Blaylock's followers did, in imitation of their leader. Without eyebrows, Gowen's round face looked even rounder. Usually his expression conveyed a sense of serenity and sincerity, making Galen think of a monk. Yet now Gowen's cheeks were drawn up in dismay, his thick lips turned slightly upward. He turned to Galen.

"I only saw Kell for a moment," he said, "when we first entered. But I can't get the image out of my mind. How could Elizar do such a thing?"

Why did they keep asking him this? Elizar had done it to Kell the same way Galen would do it to Elizar, given the chance. Cut pathways down the arms as the victim screamed, pull back skin, carve through muscle, tendon, and blood vessels down to bone, and for maximum satisfaction, rip the tech out with bare, bloody hands.

Gowen awaited an answer.

"Some people delight in hurting others," Galen said.

"I can't understand that. And Elizar always seemed so devoted to the mages. I never knew him to be cruel—except perhaps with an insult. Now he seems as determined to destroy us as the Shadows are. Did Alwyn tell you that he and Carvin were attacked?"

"Yes."

"A number of others are missing. The Shadows seem to be targeting us."

Galen's mind suddenly jumped to what he had overheard. *We are the ones best equipped to defend,* Alwyn had said to Elric. And Elizar, in the last moment before the universe had changed forever, had told him that Isabelle must die because she knew the secret of listening to the Shadows. The Shadows were attacking them because the mages formed a threat. The mages did have some potential to fight the Shadows. So why wouldn't they?

Following Blaylock and Herazade, they turned down another passage, this one wider and higher. Two great metal doors on the right side of the passage swung open as they approached, and Blaylock and Herazade entered. Galen and

Gowen stopped outside, and as the doors closed, Galen caught a glimpse of a plain dais at the far end of the large, empty room. Elric was not inside.

"That's where they had their religious services," Gowen said.

Galen looked back down the passage for Elric. The area was filling with mages.

"I never got a chance to talk to you after you returned to the convocation," Gowen said.

Galen searched desperately for Elric, for a way out of the conversation.

"I'm sorry for your loss," Gowen said.

What did Gowen know of it? How did he know Galen had suffered a loss? Galen had been sent on a task with another mage. The other mage had died. How did Gowen know what he felt about that death? He had said nothing, to anyone. He had told no one that he loved her, not even her. Did they all speak of him as Alwyn had? Did they note his silence? Did they call him a zombie? Didn't they have enough to concern themselves with?

"I'm sure you did all you could," Gowen said.

But he had not. That was the whole point, wasn't it? He had not used his spell of destruction to stop Elizar. And when she lay—dying—he had not accepted Morden's offer to save her.

I wonder, Morden had said, *whether you'll be able to live with that decision.*

Galen saw Elric coming down the far end of the passage. "Excuse me," he said.

Again he tightened his arms across his chest, cold, though he still wore his coat. Inside, the memories were rising up, one by one, from where he had buried them. They slipped silently into his system, circulating through him like a fever. He could not face them again, not without losing all control.

He could not go on this way. He could not spend years in hiding like this. He could not hold it inside forever.

He had to find a way to end it.

— chapter 5 —

After his conversation with Alwyn, Elric was barely able to find his way into an empty room before he was overwhelmed. He pressed his forehead against the cold metal of the wall, his hands to either side, and ran through one mind-focusing exercise after another, searching for some way to manage the pain.

Its source was the cavity of darkness in his skull, a place that had been connected to the chrysalis, and Soom, a place that had shriveled to ash. That emptiness pushed outward, like a tumor of desolation, pressing at the backs of his eyes, at his forehead. It throbbed, a phantom pain, the pain of what had been lost. It threatened to consume him.

During the journey to Selic 4, the discomfort had faded as he'd rested, never leaving him entirely, but allowing him to sleep for a short time. It had begun to gain intensity while he and the others of the Circle examined Kell's remains. And as he'd spoken to Alwyn, it had built into a startling, incredible pain.

At last, in its own time, it faded.

Elric did not know whether such attacks would continue, or whether they would grow more or less severe. But he was determined that no one would know of them. The mages had to have faith that their Circle was strong and capable if they were to follow. Those within the Circle needed to respect his power and authority if he was to have any influence. And Galen struggled enough without this additional burden.

When the pain finally passed, he was exhausted. His body was covered in sweat, and his legs quivered with the effort of standing.

It would be morning now, where he once lived. The sun would be shining through the mist, turning it brilliant white. The smell of the sea would be on the air. The townspeople of Lok would be stirring. Before, it would all have been a part of him, it would have been him. But the lava of Soom no longer flowed through him, its waters no longer soothed him, its life no longer enriched him. Now there was nothing but emptiness.

But his was not the only loss. As he had walked the halls of this place, he had felt sick at heart to see so many of his order now weakened. The mages had elected him to the Circle, had entrusted him with their care and guidance, and they were dying before his eyes. He had failed them. And Kell, their longtime leader, was gone.

Elric discovered that he had received a message some minutes ago; the Circle was meeting immediately. He wiped his face on his sleeve and took a moment to focus inward, to moderate his body temperature, heartbeat, respiration. Then he moved quickly toward the room the message indicated as their meeting place. He would betray no sign of weakness.

As he neared the meeting room, Galen approached him. Elric could see in a moment that he was agitated. His arms were crossed over his chest, his breathing was rapid, and color had risen in his cheeks.

"I must speak with you," Galen said.

Elric slowed but did not stop. "I am required for a meeting of the Circle. We will talk when my duties are completed."

Galen stopped in front of him, blocking his way. "No. I must speak with you now. I think Alwyn is right. We must stay and fight the Shadows. Will you argue his position before the Circle?"

Galen must have spoken with Alwyn, and Alwyn had upset him with talk of fighting in this war. Elric cursed his impetuous friend. Galen had made his decision, at great cost. He should not be forced to revisit it. "I have already made that argument and lost," Elric said.

"But now that the Shadows know where we are—"

"We may alter the particulars of our plan. But the plan has already been put in motion, and we cannot change course now."

"But—"

"I don't have time to debate this with you." Elric was growing hot.

"What harm is there if some of us stay behind to fight?"

"If we don't stand together," Elric said, "we will fall."

"If we don't fight, then what do we stand for?"

"You agreed to go with us. You pledged to follow the dictates of the Circle. Does your word mean nothing?" Elric broke into a sweat. He would not suffer an attack in front of Galen.

Galen fixed him with his brilliant blue eyes. "You're keeping something from us. The Circle has more secrets."

Elric realized that Galen had contrived to listen to his conversation with Alwyn. Galen had violated the trust between mages. It was not like him. He was closer to losing control than Elric had realized.

Elric quickly tried to recall what he and Alwyn had said. "It is part of the Circle's duty to be the guardians of knowledge. Some we share, and some we safeguard, as we see fit."

"How then does Alwyn know?"

"You spied on us, and now you demand an explanation."

"Alwyn believes the mages might stay and fight if they knew this truth."

"Alwyn believes what Alwyn believes. The Circle has chosen the path they feel best."

"Even you voted to stay and fight."

"Yet I follow the will of the Circle."

"The Shadows attack us because they fear us. We have the power to fight them."

"And they have the power to fight us. Already five of us are dead, and more missing."

Galen shook with a quick, violent shiver, and he bit out his words. "This is not some test by which you will train me. I am no longer your student. Tell me the secret."

"But it is a test." Elric paused, stressing his reply. "It is the most important test of all, and one that will continue for the rest of your life. It is the test of what you are. A techno-mage or a traitor. One who kills, or one who does good. One in control, or one consumed by chaos. One who brings darkness, or one who brings light."

Galen's voice rose. "How can I bring light, when you keep us in darkness! You're keeping something important from us. Some secret of power that would help us fight the Shadows. If the mages knew, they would want to stay and fight. But you won't tell them. You're lying to us! Manipulating us! Haven't you learned anything from Kell? Secrets are killers!"

Galen broke off, panting, looking as shocked as Elric was to find himself yelling. Those gathered outside the meeting room, including Ing-Radi, were staring at them.

Elric had thought Galen could handle the move to their new home, with his support. Yet Galen was crumbling. If only they had not been the ones to find Kell's body. If only he had been free to help Galen settle in, rather than occupied with his duties to the Circle. Yet Galen had seen Kell, had faced Alwyn and the rest of the mages alone, and he had been pulled from his own private hiding place before he was ready to deal with reality, his emotions still raw.

And even now, Elric had no time for him.

"You are out of control," Elric said.

"I know," Galen said, his face bare. His shivering had grown more violent. "I can't stop it."

Although Elric's face and chest were hot, his back was cool. Elric realized the heat was coming from Galen, radiating from him like a furnace.

Elric searched for the words that would help him reassert control. "Then think of the last time you lost control, and how much you regretted it. Think of how much you owe the mages, and how grateful you were that you were given a second chance. Think of your tribute to Wierden, the care you put into it, the passion you felt for all she believed. Remember your commitment to obey the Code, and to prove yourself worthy to the Circle."

Galen averted his gaze, and his mouth tightened in a way Elric recognized. He was performing a mind-focusing exercise.

"We do what we do for the good of all," Elric said. "Our situation is grave. There is no simple answer, despite what you may think. It is our burden to find the best path. And it is your burden to follow. Think on that, while I am within. And know that if there is any opportunity for us to do good, I will fight for us to do it."

Galen glanced up at him, and the look on his face made his words unnecessary. "I am sorry."

Elric wiped his forehead. The heat was decreasing. "Violate the trust of the mages no further."

"I will not."

Elric only hoped that Galen could maintain control until the Circle's meeting was over. And that he would have the strength, then, to help Galen. "We will talk when I come out. I promise it."

Galen nodded, looking downward.

With a final, anxious glance at Galen, Elric continued toward the meeting room. Once again, his duties to the Circle kept them apart.

The others in the passage seemed to remember that it was rude to stare and moved about, looking anywhere but at Galen or Elric. Ing-Radi followed him inside, and the large doors swung closed behind them.

Galen walked stiffly down the passage away from the others, shivering, arms still wrapped across his chest. Energy raced through him, searching for outlet. He added letter after letter to his mind-focusing visualization of the alphabet, and as the neat row grew, it became more and more difficult to hold them all in his mind at once. Yet even the demanding exercise could not calm him. He had energy he must release.

He turned down a narrow side passage, found himself alone. A small maintenance room provided privacy. The energy could not be allowed to do harm. He wanted no one to detect it, no one to question him. Yet if he could just release some small piece, he hoped he would be able to wait through the Circle's meeting until Elric returned.

Releasing his energy in the attack on Elizar's chrysalis had brought him no relief, but Galen could think of nothing else to try. If he did not expend some of the energy burning through him, he feared it would slip out of his control. And if some conjury slipped out, no one could alter or dissolve it but him. He felt feverish, racked with chills.

He was ashamed of his conduct. The anger he'd tried to bury after attacking Elizar's chrysalis had welled up out of him again—a great anger at everything that had happened, an anger much deeper and more intense than he'd known. And with it he had struck out at the one person who had tried to help him. He had yelled in public at Elric—Elric, to whom he owed everything. He must not do so again. He must bring himself back under control.

What had happened was his fault, more than anyone else's. His choices, his failures. If there was anyone he should be angry at, it was himself. If there was anyone the energy should strike at, it was himself.

He would bring the energy down upon himself. Perhaps it would shock him back into stillness.

He regularly scoured his scalp, cheeks, and chin of hair, in a limited way re-creating the experience of his initiation. The pain was intense but brief; he had grown used to it. To release a greater amount of energy, generate a higher level of pain, he would scour his entire body. He would leave his head untouched, so there would be no sudden loss of eyebrows to draw attention to what he'd done.

He made the plan in a moment, visualized the blank screen in his mind's eye, imposed the equation upon it. The tech eagerly echoed the spell.

A ball of brilliant blue light appeared above him, shot downward. Fire rushed over his body like living lava, searing him, consuming the hair from his body. His skin screamed with pain. He gasped.

Again.

The blue fire fell upon him with ragged claws. They raked down his skin, scouring the outer layer away. Galen stumbled, doubled over.

His hands quivered, red, raw. The touch of his robe against his skin awakened pain in countless nerve endings. He had forgotten how much it had hurt.

The tech raced, eager to bring the fire down upon him again. Galen forced the screen in his mind's eye blank. It already hurt like hell, and now he realized that, sharing a room with Fed, it would be hard to hide the damage he had inflicted upon himself. Much of his epidermis was gone, burned away. Soon would follow inflammation, and some weeping of the skin. He realized the irony. He had wanted to become a mage to heal.

He slowed his ragged breathing, trying to calm himself. This had to be one of the stupider things he'd done.

Yet it had helped. As he straightened, he found he was no longer shivering. And the pressure to act had lessened somewhat. The agitating energy of the implants had faded, overshadowed now by pain.

He had released some of the anger, and he had hurt only himself. It hurt so much, he could think of little else. If he could not fade like a ghost from the present, he could at least distract himself from it.

Trying to move normally, he went out into the passageway, walked back toward the Circle's meeting room. He would wait for Elric, and he would apologize for his conduct.

The tops of his boots dug into his burning skin. His robe scraped like sandpaper against his shoulders. Even so, he found his mind returning to the harsh words he had spoken. When he'd yelled at Elric, he realized, he'd sounded just like Elizar, talking of secrets of power and deceptions by the Circle. The similarity frightened him.

And yet, nearly everything Elizar had told him had proven true. Kell had known of the Shadows' return. He had sent two inexperienced mages to investigate rumors of that return, hoping they would find nothing. If those accusations were true, then were the others Elizar had made true as well?

I tell you that the Circle has led us astray. They have lied to us, again and again. They have so constricted our powers that we are now only a shadow of what we once were.

Galen took a place against the wall, away from the others. He could not allow himself to be drawn into those thoughts. He pressed his back against the cool metal wall, his robe scraping against his raw skin. He must remain calm.

He focused on the two large doors opposite him. Eventually they would open, and Elric would emerge, and Elric would help him. Perhaps there was a task he could be assigned that would take him out of the facility, that would allow him to work alone. Perhaps he could be allowed to stay on his ship. All the mages were being housed within the facility, for security, but Elric might get special permission for him. It was common knowledge that mages did not get along well with one another. Surely they could make some accommodation to separate him from the rest.

Then, perhaps, he could force the anger away, still the restless energy, bury the memories one last time.

About a hundred mages waited in the wide passage. Though a few glanced his way, none approached him, for which he was thankful. Word of his argument with Elric had no doubt spread. Now that the sleepwalker had awoken, perhaps they would leave him alone and allow him to return to sleep.

Yet no sooner had he thought this than Alwyn came toward him. Why couldn't they just leave him alone?

Galen began an inventory of his pain, beginning at his shoulders and working his way down, intensifying the burning, prickling discomfort with his focus. Everything Elric had said to him was true. Galen had sworn himself to the Circle, to earning their faith in him, and he must not lose his way. The Circle and the Code had brought the early technomages to peace, had allowed them to focus on knowing all that could be known, and on using that knowledge to create magic, beauty, and good. He must put the Circle and the Code first, even if it was more difficult than he had ever imagined. It was no more than Elric demanded of himself.

Alwyn stopped beside Galen, appraised him with obvious concern. "I heard about your fight with Elric. I didn't mean to be the cause of trouble between you. Elric is a good man. Very nearly as stubborn as I am. But he's trying to do what is best for the mages. My concerns are a little more selfish. I want to do the best thing for me. And for me, the best thing is to stay and fight. I've made my decision. I was a fool to think the Circle would change." He shook his head with a glance upward. "I ought to know better after all these years. Wishful thinking, I suppose. I'll offer any help that is wanted or needed to bring the mages safely to their hiding place, but I will not enter."

Alwyn was going to defy the Circle. Galen hadn't thought he would go through with it. And if Alwyn refused to go, perhaps others would as well. A group might remain to fight the Shadows.

Galen followed a line of pain down his spine. It wasn't enough. He should have brought the fire down upon himself a third time. He squeezed his hand into a tight fist, his nails digging into the raw skin of his palm. No distraction could ever make him forget. He had made his decision. Now he must live with it.

Several followers of Blaylock were standing nearby, including Gowen. They had overheard Alwyn, and they gathered around him.

"You can't defy the Circle," Gowen said in disbelief. "We are all sworn to them. Wierden established it: 'Our five wisest will form the Circle, which will guide and rule the techno-mages.' "

Alwyn dismissed the comment with a wave of his hand. "Many times in our history the Circle has been defied, even overthrown. It's not my fault no one has had the guts to stand up to them in recent memory. It's about time someone shook things up."

But now was not the time, Galen thought. They needed to be focused, orderly, disciplined. Not shaken up. Calm. He forced his fist, finger by finger, to open, relax.

Gowen's round cheeks drew up in displeasure. "The Circle has been our salvation. They have held us together for a thousand years. They maintain our holy traditions and mysteries. They are the core of our order, the best of us. They stand between us and chaos."

Alwyn's jaw was tight. "More accurately, they cower between us and chaos."

Several mages, including Gowen, grunted disapproval, as Blaylock was known to do. Gowen's bare eyebrow ridges contracted. Galen had never seen him this angry before. But then, no one had ever declared his intention to defy the Circle before. Gowen and the other mages crowded more closely around Alwyn, looking ready for a fight.

Carvin came to stand beside Alwyn. Galen pushed his back against the wall, adrenaline preparing him to meet any threat.

Gowen's voice was hard. "We carry a special blessing, bequeathed to us by the Taratimude in trust. The tech taps into the basic powers of the universe. It offers us connections: to devices, to one another, to planets, and ultimately to the universe. We cannot let it be corrupted."

"It is technology," Alwyn snapped, revealing he too was ready for a fight. "There's nothing inherently good about it."

"Our goal must be to attain a complete, spiritual union with the tech, and to gain the insight that enlightenment will provide. We are not meant to be soldiers."

Alwyn gave Gowen a hard stare. "You mean the mages don't *want* to be soldiers. But then who does?"

As the two glared at each other, Carvin broke the silence. "But the Shadows are targeting us. How effective can we be at fighting them if they're attacking us?"

She was asking the question backward, as Galen had been until earlier today. The true question was this: Why were the Shadows attacking the mages unless the mages *could* be effective at fighting them?

And if that was so, then why didn't they stay and fight? He realized he had returned to where he'd begun. He could not disobey the Circle; he could not obey. He was trapped, his thoughts caught in a loop, like the ouroboros, the snake that took its own tail in its mouth, consuming itself just as quickly as it regenerated. He would not go through it again. Yet he had no choice.

The doors to the meeting room swung open, and a rune of blue fire appeared in the doorway, the rune for solidarity.

Galen found he had a message. It was from Blaylock to them all, calling them to gather. The Circle had news.

"This is their last chance to get it right," Alwyn said.

Galen started across the hall, trying to make his mind a blank. Elric had told him the Circle would not change its course. There was no sense hoping for it. He had searched for an end to this and found none. Wherever he went, whatever he did, his failure, his loss, would haunt him.

He had thought he could not live with it. But he had no choice. He would live with it, and he would retain control. If he had to scour every last cell of skin from his body.

—— chapter 6 ——

Nearly five hundred mages were now packed into the same room where the Circle had met. Galen waited with them. Gowen had said it was a place designed for religious services. A plain dais ran across the front of the room, and narrow metal benches had been pushed aside to clear the rest of the space. Windows along one wall revealed the ragged mountains, their stone and ice tinted orange in the late-day sun. Other than that, the room was bare. Galen wondered if the last surviving members of the religious cult had prayed here as they'd starved to death. He could almost hear them, their voices whispering, pleading to be released quickly.

Galen stood at the front, since he'd been one of the first to enter. Carvin and Alwyn stood to his left, Gowen and other followers of Blaylock to his right. Farther down he saw Circe's pointed hat sticking out of the crowd.

The presence of so many in the confined space was oppressive. Bodies brushed against his. The cacophony of their voices was too loud. He imagined himself back on Soom, standing alone on a flat rock at the cliff's edge, looking down into layer upon layer of mist, listening to the susurration of the sea: *The sound of death,* Razeel had called it. He imagined stepping quietly off the cliff, falling peacefully through the soft, enveloping mist.

He could not sustain the image, though. His mind would not be still.

He'd been unable to apologize to Elric, who stood on the dais conferring with the other members of the Circle. Soon they would announce their plans, and whatever those plans were, Galen would comply. Then he would speak with Elric at last, apologize for his loss of control. And perhaps Elric would find some way to help him.

To quiet his mind, Galen studied the members of the Circle. He had admired and respected them as the wisest, the most skilled of their order. And though he had learned that they were fallible, he admired them still. Yet now they appeared diminished: aging, failing.

Only Herazade, who had never formed a place of power, seemed unchanged. Her long hair was a thick, glossy black, her movements strong, authoritative. When he had been called before the Circle, she had worn a formal black robe, her hair up. But now she wore a deep blue sari, and her hair was down. Apparently she had not had time to change for the meeting. Or perhaps, without Kell, she no longer felt the need.

Ing-Radi looked the weakest of them. She was the oldest, almost two hundred years, and now, with the destruction of her place, she finally showed it. Her orange skin had faded, revealing blue veins beneath the surface that ran in a pattern of starbursts over her bare head. Her four arms had always seemed active before, offering healing touches, adding graceful emphasis to her words. Now they hung at her sides. Something in her stance gave the impression the balance of her tall body was precarious, as if at any moment she could topple.

Blaylock too showed signs of change. He had been one of the first to Selic 4, which meant that he must have destroyed his place nearly a month ago. His black robe hung on him as if he were little more than bone. His pale face, scoured of all hair, was gaunt, and his skin had an almost waxy sheen. The black skullcap he wore formed a dramatic contrast against his high, pallid forehead.

Turning his attention to Elric, Galen saw a difference greater than the deepened frown lines between his brows. Elric's posture had changed. He had always stood erect, and he still did, yet now Galen sensed effort. His shoulders seemed forced back, held where they no longer naturally settled. His actions were stiff, hesitant, as if he was afraid movement might betray his condition. He would want to appear strong, Galen knew, for all of them.

He had suffered some kind of attack when he was with Alwyn. Galen berated himself again for arguing with Elric. Elric had cared for him for the last eleven years. Elric had brought order to his life, had taught him nearly everything he knew. Elric had been the unyielding wall of strength beside him in times of need. Galen had often thought that Elric was all he had. Now he realized that he was all Elric had. He should not be thinking of ways in which Elric could help him; he should be thinking of ways in which he could help Elric. Elric needed him, and Galen must be his wall of strength.

Many others were also weakened. They had crippled themselves before they had even tried fighting. Now it was too late. The only chance for him to fight was to break with the Circle, to break with Elric, to break Elric. He could not do that.

But if he stayed, could he stop himself from breaking?

Elric glanced toward him, and Galen realized he had a message. He opened it. *We will speak after the meeting. I regret that we must be sent on different tasks. Duty requires— much. But I will not leave until I am sure you are all right.*

Elric was leaving, and he was not taking Galen with him. Elric feared Galen was unstable. Every word of his message showed it. And he was right. Galen didn't know how he could continue here without Elric.

The four members of the Circle faced the mages, and there was silence. Blaylock spoke, his voice harsh and certain. "We come together as techno-mages in service of a common

Code: solidarity, secrecy, mystery, magic, science, knowledge, and good. In the quest to preserve our integrity we have gathered here, in preparation for our migration to a place of hiding. But new information requires that we alter our plans.

"The Shadows have said that we must join with them or die. It seems they have grown impatient for our decision. Our probes and relays in the Omega sector of the rim have been destroyed, including those we placed recently at Tau Omega, or Thenothk, in response to information gathered by Galen. We are blind now to the activities of the Shadows.

"The last of us were scheduled to arrive here this morning. Eight have not. We have confirmed that Djadjamonkh and Regana are killed. Six others are missing: Walkyra, Dedi, Athanasius, Barlinda, Ling Lau, and Alipio. Our attempts to reach them have failed."

The mages listened in silence. It felt odd to have Blaylock speak for the Circle. Blaylock lacked the warmth Kell had projected. His dour expression and cold delivery conveyed power, yet no emotion for those missing.

"Kell's body arrived a few hours ago aboard Elizar's ship. He had been flayed, we believe by Elizar. From this we may assume that the Shadows know our position. How they learned it, we do not know. Kell was not privy to our plans, though he may well have deduced them. Or perhaps the Shadows' information came from a different source.

"In any event, we must leave this place immediately. We have decided upon a new site at which we can prepare for our exodus. The majority of you will proceed there at once, where you will finish the arrangements. As part of our heightened security measures, you will not be told where this new gathering place is. In addition, from this point forward, no communications will be sent off-planet by any but the Circle. We cannot allow our gathering place again to be discovered by the Shadows.

"Three groups will not proceed to this new gathering place.

They will split off to perform critical tasks. Herazade will lead the first group directly to the hiding place, to prepare it and secure its safety. Elric and Ing-Radi will lead the second group in an attempt to misdirect, to convince the Shadows that we are actually gathering in another location. The third group will acquire intelligence about the Shadows' activities, since we have lost access to our probes on the rim. We must know all that can be known about their plans for us. To minimize the danger of discovery, only two will be sent, to get as close as they can to the Shadows' ancient home, to learn what they know of us, and to discover their strategy. Circe will accompany me on this task."

Something stirred inside Galen, and he found himself stepping forward. "I must go with you."

Elric turned on him, the three frown lines of grave disappointment between his brows. "Silence! It has been decided."

Energy surged through him. This was the escape he had sought from the endless loop of his racing thoughts, the escape he had believed did not exist. They had to let him go.

He forced himself to speak in a measured voice. "I mean no disrespect to the Circle. But I am the only one who has faced the Shadows and lived. My knowledge could help in the success of this task."

"We have had our debate and determined our course," Elric said.

Galen could think of only one way to convince them. From his lips, he forced her name. "Isabelle discovered a technique to listen to the Shadows. I hold her knowledge. I may be able to re-create it."

Blaylock's gaze was sharp, appraising. "This is a mission of stealth and intelligence-gathering, not vengeance."

"I seek only to serve in the way I can be most useful."

"We will confer," Ing-Radi said.

As the Circle turned inward, a shield came down over them

to secure their privacy. Someone grabbed his robe from behind, fingers scraping his raw back.

Fed whispered in his ear. "Are you crazy? Going to the
rim? It's a suicide mission."

Galen studied the Circle anxiously. They must allow him to
go. It was a way to act against the Shadows, without defying
the Circle or breaking the Code. It was a way to escape the
others and the memories they carried. And perhaps, finally,
he would find an end to this.

Circe moved to the front, and under the brim of her hat she
watched Galen.

"Tell them you changed your mind," Fed whispered, the
scent of his cologne wrapping around Galen. "Temporary in-
sanity. Let the old folks go. They're not going to last long
anyway."

The Circle ended its deliberations and turned back to face
them, the shield dissolving. Elric did not look at him.

Blaylock spoke. "Galen, you will go in place of Circe. As
for the rest, Herazade is sending your instructions. We must
all be gone from this place in four hours."

Circe was glaring at him. Galen felt a great sense of relief.
The restless energy of the tech declined. At last, he realized,
he could breathe.

"In seventeen days, we will converge on the new gathering
place and leave immediately for the hiding place. To minimize the chance of discovery, we will move in one single
group, and only the Circle will hold the key to entering our
new home. Any who do not arrive in time will be assumed
lost and left behind.

"Before we give ourselves over to these preparations,
though, we face a grievous task. Kell must be sent to the other
side. Ing-Radi?"

Ing-Radi laid her four hands, palms up, on top of each
other, and bowed her head. "It was long, long ago that I first
became a mage. We had great ideals, yet few followed them.

They were for the lips only, not for the heart. Many years later, Kell was initiated as the latest of the line of Wierden. What he said with the lips, he felt with the heart. He made us see that we need not squabble and maneuver for power, but instead we could do good. He made us see that we must not only speak the words of Wierden, but believe them. His vision and wisdom drew us to him. And so a new age of relative peace and cooperation was born. His leadership brought us together. His example inspired us. I hope that we may live on in his example. These trying times shall be the test of how well we have learned what he taught us: to put the needs of our order above our own.

"My first experience with Kell's leadership came at the convocation at which he was initiated." As Ing-Radi spoke of the accomplishments of Kell, Carvin, beside him, began to cry. Galen cast his eyes downward, trying to block out the sound.

In four hours he would be headed with Blaylock for the rim, for the home of the Shadows, for the last place where he had seen Elizar. The chance that he would encounter Elizar was minuscule, but Galen couldn't stop the image from forming in his mind, of Elizar turning and seeing him, of Elizar's angular, arrogant face filling with fear.

And then the next image. Galen's hands covered in blood, clutching the broken threads of Elizar's tech.

Ing-Radi had finished her eulogy, and the mages were filing out. They would go outside the facility to watch as Kell's body was consumed in magical fire.

Elric separated from the rest of the Circle and took Galen aside. His lined face was stern. "You must withdraw your request. The task is too dangerous. It was meant for one of the Circle, but there are not enough of us to do what we must. You lack the necessary experience."

"Where would you have me go?"

"Ahead to the hiding place. You can set up things there to

your liking. You can create a new home for us. I will join you shortly."

Galen could not give up his opportunity, force himself back into the endless loop. He had chosen the right course. "I cannot."

Elric studied him. "It may be difficult, but you can."

"I must go with Blaylock."

"It would be wiser if you did not."

Galen shook his head. "I must. I'm sorry. I mean no disrespect." He met Elric's gaze. "I apologize for my earlier outburst. I was angry at myself, yet I struck at you. I deeply regret what I said. It was undeserved and untrue. I know you do what is best for all of us." The words seemed inadequate. Galen wished he could say something more, but he could think only to end his apology as the Soom did. "It is a mark against my own name."

At the reminder of home, the tension in Elric's face lessened, the frown lines between his brows dwindling from three to two. "I erase the mark." Elric had spoken in the language of the Soom, and he continued in it. "These are difficult times. Alwyn should not have spoken to you as he did."

Hearing the simple, orderly language comforted Galen. He spoke in it as well. "It's not only Alwyn. It's all of them. It's what they remember when they look at me."

"That will pass, in time."

"I don't have time."

"You have your whole life, which may be short or may be long. I prefer to think it long, long enough that one day you might be elected to the Circle and lead the mages more wisely than I."

"You told Alwyn you didn't believe the mages would survive this war."

"Perhaps I am wrong. And if I am, the mages will need you to help guide them."

"And you."

Elric said nothing. His lips formed a thin, straight line. Elric had promised never to lie to him, and Elric had kept that promise. He might not return from this task. That was what he was telling Galen.

Once again Galen had been thinking only of himself. For the first time he thought of Elric's task. Elric must draw the attention of the Shadows, make his group their target to spare the rest. He was not well. He should not go. Galen couldn't imagine what he would do, if he returned from his task and Elric did not. He could not lose Elric too. He could not.

"If you truly want to stop me," Galen said, "then withdraw to the hiding place with me. I will not go on my task, if you do not go on yours. You are weakened; while with Alwyn you were overcome by pain. You should not be sent into danger." He didn't know how he would honor the promise, but if it would keep Elric safe, he would.

"I am capable," Elric said.

"The mages cannot afford to lose you."

"The mages will lose much that they cannot afford to lose before this war is over. Nevertheless, I do hope to return from this task unharmed."

"Can Circe not be sent in your place?" Galen asked.

"Members of the Circle must be seen, for the deception to be convincing."

"Let them see an illusion of you."

"I must create the deception, with the help of Ing-Radi and the resources at hand. The task must be successful if any of us are to survive." Elric paused, and he looked tired. "But you need not go with Blaylock. Your time is to come. Let Circe go with him."

"Blaylock and Circe are both weakened. Is it not better to send someone who remains strong?"

"Wisdom is often more important than power, as Elizar never learned." Elric raised a cautioning hand. "You admitted only minutes ago that you were out of control. You must not accompany Blaylock in that condition. You may endanger his life as well as the information we need. You may endanger yourself."

"I will maintain control. I swear it."

"You cannot make such a promise. You know that. You are not fit to go."

That might be true, but Galen refused to admit it. "Going to the rim can be no more difficult than remaining here."

"You will torment yourself with the temptation to act against the Shadows. It is a test greater than I would put you through."

"And yet the Circle has voted to send me. As you obey the Circle, so shall I."

Elric looked toward the windows, where the mountains had fallen into the long shadows of the setting sun. "I have often thought we are too much alike."

Galen was shocked into silence. He didn't have the skill of Elric, or the control, or the direction. "If I am like you in even the smallest part, that is the greatest praise you have ever given me."

Elric turned to Galen, his movement stiff. "Someday, perhaps, you will not think of me so kindly. I hope, if that day comes, you will try to understand why I have done what I have done."

"I understand," Galen said. Elric was in an odd mood. He was probably tired, and the death of Kell had upset him.

"If you have need," Elric said, "contact me at once. I will send assistance."

Galen nodded.

"And beware of Blaylock. If you stray from the task, he will not hesitate to stop you." Elric seemed to rouse himself. "We should join the others." He laid a hand on Galen's shoulder. "Come."

The room had emptied, and they left it, catching up with the last of the mages in the passage. They were going outside through a nearby air lock. Elric and Galen joined the others, and as the air lock closed them inside, Elric conjured a containment shield around them both, holding within it heat and a breathable atmosphere.

Outside, they moved quietly across the vast field of ice, their shadows long before them. The shield echoed the sounds of their own breathing, the movement of their robes. Galen's raw skin prickled in the confining warmth. The voices of the other mages were faint, distorted.

At the base of the great mountains, upon a stone boulder, lay Kell's body. There was no sign of the wounds he had sustained. An illusion made him appear intact. Galen remembered him as he had been on Elizar's ship, his arms split open, skull hollowed out.

It was the end of an age for the mages, the end of the line of Wierden. Perhaps the beginning of the end for them all, if Elric's fears came to pass.

The mages encircled Kell's body, their skin tinged blue by their shields. Many looked older, weaker. Some, who lacked the skill of shields, wore breathers. A few joined two within a shield, particularly those with young apprentices who hadn't yet reached chrysalis stage. Galen wondered if those young ones had a future.

Galen looked to Elric. His face was impassive, composed. He would remain strong. He always did.

Wisps of blue fire caressed Kell's body, running up the length of it in gentle waves. They gathered about his head, intensified into a brilliant corona. Then the fire swirled, building rapidly to surround him, obscuring him. The flames grew brighter, hotter. And with a sudden gust they whirled up into a great pillar of fire, rising to rival the mountains. The mages were dwarfed by it.

Kell had erred, erred horribly. But without him, the mages were diminished.

The churning of the flame stirred memories of fires past,

losses of which he did not wish to be reminded. He lowered
his head. Kell had believed he could control everything. In
that, he was no different from the rest of the mages. They all
desired control. They wanted to direct events, to manipulate
perceptions, to impose their designs upon the universe. They
did not realize that, in reality, all was chaos.

But even in their failure, they had done much good. They
had plumbed the secrets of the universe, created transcendent
beauty, healed wounds, inspired with magic, brought living
spirit to their homes. As for himself, Galen no longer knew if
he could do good rather than kill; if he could remain in control rather than falling to chaos; if he could bring light rather
than darkness. But he would do his best to help the others survive this coming war, to prevent the end that Elric feared.

With a sharp movement Elric jerked his hand up to cover
his face. His fingers quivered, pressing hard against his skin.
His eyes were closed, his chest rising and falling with deep
breaths. For a terrible moment he seemed like a stranger,
weak and vulnerable.

Galen averted his eyes. He stood tall, trying to be Elric's
wall of strength, trying to be strong enough for both of them.
In four hours they would say good-bye to each other, perhaps
for good. Galen memorized the sensation of Elric standing
beside him—the height of his body, the shape of it, the heat of
it. Perhaps they would never stand together again. As so much
had been lost, Elric, too, could be lost.

That thought terrified him.

"I am not Elric," Blaylock said. "I will not tolerate disobedience. I will order and you will obey. Do you understand?"

"Yes," Galen said. They stood in the large hangar where
Galen had first entered the facility. The rows of crates and
supplies were now nearly gone, the hangar nearly empty.
Gowen hovered a few feet away, listening as Blaylock laid
down the rules for Galen.

"I allow you to accompany me because you have handled yourself well under difficult circumstances, and because of your experience with the Shadows. But I am well aware that you disobeyed my orders in the destruction of Elizar's ship." Blaylock's eyes narrowed. "Do not defy me again. This is your only warning."

Blaylock had ordered Galen to destroy the ship from a safe distance. Somehow he knew that Galen had attacked Elizar's chrysalis while still on board. He must have planted a probe when he'd been on the ship. Galen bowed his head, embarrassed that his rage had been uncovered.

"Yes," Galen said. "I'm sorry."

Blaylock grunted. Maskelyne and two of the Kinetic Grimlis entered the hangar, and Blaylock moved away to consult with them.

"He likes you," Gowen said.

"I have that to be grateful for," Galen said.

Most of the mages were now in their ships, awaiting the signal to depart. Gowen was assigned to go with Elric and Ing-Radi's group, yet he continued to linger, seemingly unable to leave Blaylock.

The last few hours had been filled with activity as the mages mobilized to leave Selic 4. Blaylock had taken charge of Galen, separating him from Elric and directing him to help with the dispersal of supplies. Galen had worked to get the right combination of materials to each group, attempting to keep the process orderly as everyone rushed to meet their departure time. The frantic activity had been interrupted only once, as Blaylock's followers, over sixty in number, had marched into the hangar, bidding farewell to their spiritual leader in a grim, impassioned ceremony of repentance and self-denial. Galen was shocked to see some of them crying as they left Blaylock behind.

Carvin ran into the hangar, looked about, her gaze stopping on Galen. She rushed over to him with a rustle of her

Centauri silks, Alwyn following in a more measured gait. Galen found that the prospect of speaking with Alwyn no longer upset him. He had discovered the solution he needed. He was at peace with it. And he would like to say farewell.

"I had to say good-bye," Carvin said, turning belatedly to include Gowen in her statement. "Alwyn and I are going to help Elric create the deception. Elric asked specifically for me, can you believe it?"

"You excel at illusions and misdirection," Galen said. "I'm sure you will be a great asset."

Carvin smiled at the compliment, though her eyes had grown serious. "Afterward, I won't be going to the hiding place. I've decided to stay with Alwyn and do what I can to fight the Shadows."

She hesitated, her lips sucked inward. "I know you don't like this, but I'm going to do it anyway." She threw her arms around him. "I'm going to miss you, Galen. Please be careful." She squeezed his raw skin.

"I will miss you," he said, realizing it was true.

She released him, moved on to Gowen, giving him an energetic hug. "Oh—we're going in the same group, aren't we."

"Yes," Gowen said, looking frustrated.

Alwyn stood before Galen. "You're a more tolerant man than I, accompanying Blaylock. I'd be ready to wring his neck before we got halfway to the rim."

"Please watch over Elric," Galen said. "He is not well."

"The stubborn bastard. I'll make sure he behaves himself." Alwyn shook his head. "Apparently he and the rest of the Circle are going to look the other way, ignore our defiance. It surprised me, to tell you the truth. I expected more of a fight. Kind of looking forward to it. Officially, of course, once we fail to show up at the gathering place, they'll sentence us to flaying, as they have Elizar and Razeel. But it will be a hard sentence to impose with all of them cloistered away in the hiding place." Alwyn laughed to himself. He embraced Galen. "If you come to your senses, you know how to contact me."

"I won't change my mind."

Alwyn hesitated, his mouth falling open. "You're making a mistake. Your father . . . he never walked away from a fight."

It had been a long time since Alwyn had invoked his father. Once, years ago, Galen had overheard Elric telling Alwyn never to mention his parents again. For the most part, Alwyn had obeyed. The few times Alwyn had persisted, Galen had refused to respond.

"I do what I must," Galen said.

"That sounds like Elric."

"Be well," Galen said. As passionate and unreasonable as Alwyn could be, he had been a good friend.

Alwyn gave a sour smile, realizing he was being dismissed. "Come, Gowen. You're going with Elric's group, aren't you?"

Gowen nodded. "I'll follow in a moment."

As Alwyn and Carvin crossed the hangar, Gowen turned to Galen. "I'll watch over Elric as well. Please see Blaylock safely back to us. He claims he is unchanged since the destruction of his place of power, but he has aged. And he barely eats." Gowen glanced nervously toward Blaylock. "In his quest to become one with the tech, he has encouraged his systems to intertwine with it more intimately than most of ours do. I fear the destruction of his place will lead to the failure of his body. He will not make any concessions. He treats himself harshly."

Blaylock's voice rang across the hangar. "Gowen, if you have need to discuss me, do me the courtesy of speaking in my presence."

"Yes, Blaylock," Gowen called.

"His hearing seems unimpaired," Galen said.

Gowen started across the hangar toward Blaylock, looking anxiously back at Galen. Galen gave a single nod. He doubted that either he or Blaylock would return from their task, but he would do his best to keep Blaylock well.

Gowen smiled, nodding back.

As Gowen bowed before his teacher for a final good-bye, Galen saw that Elric had joined Blaylock and the others. After a few moments, Elric took his leave from them, coming toward Galen. His movements again seemed stiff, brittle. He looked tired. Galen met him.

"You will depart?" Galen asked.

"Yes," Elric said.

They stood in silence. Galen didn't know what to say. There was so much he had never said. It was too late now. There was no time.

"Do not make me see you to the other side," Elric said.

Galen nodded. He didn't want to let Elric go. He wanted to run with Elric to the hiding place, to keep Elric safe there.

"Galen!" Blaylock's voice carried across the hangar. "Come."

He had failed to say the words to her, and they had haunted him ever since. Yet still he could not say them to Elric. She was wrong. She had said he could transcend himself, but he could not. He was who he was.

"Be careful," he said, beginning to move toward Blaylock. The words sounded empty, weak.

"I am glad to have been your teacher."

Galen nodded quickly, his throat thick. As he continued toward Blaylock, he found that he had a message from Elric. *You have made me proud.*

He thought to send something to Elric in return, but he could not form the words. He didn't know why. But he could not. Elric knew, didn't he? Didn't he know how Galen felt?

"Gather your things," Blaylock said. "We go at once."

Galen turned back; the air-lock door slid down, blocking the last of Elric's black robe from sight.

He was gone.

Galen took a deep breath. He and Blaylock were left in the empty hangar with Maskelyne. She had volunteered to stay behind and maintain as long as possible the illusion that the mages remained on Selic 4. She had made the planet her place of power so that she could more skillfully disguise their presence. Now she would disguise their absence. She did not know the location of the new gathering place, so when the Shadows came for her, they would not get the information from her.

Galen did not know her well, but she was a master of disguise and illusion. She constantly shrouded herself in full-body illusions, so that Galen wasn't sure what she truly looked like. She appeared now as a scarred warrior suited in glittering silver armor.

Blaylock bowed his head. "You do us a great service."

"I will be satisfied if I can take some of them with me."

"Then I wish you great satisfaction."

"And I, you."

Galen bowed. "Thank you."

"The blessing of Wierden upon you," Blaylock said to her.

Blaylock strode toward the air lock, and Galen retrieved his possessions and followed. As they stepped into the confined space, Galen slid his breather over his face.

For a few moments they were closed inside together, then the outer door opened onto the dark landscape. Faint moonlight reflected off the ice. As they stepped out, Galen heard the whisper of mage ships in the blackness overhead. He accessed his sensors, scanned the infrared for a hint of them. The ships were well shielded; only the slightest traces of their exhausts appeared as faint red fans against the night sky. A formation of fifty or so shot overhead. Elric and Ing-Radi would be leading them. Where they were going, Galen did not know. All was secrecy now.

Another group of ghostly red fans headed off to the south, this one smaller, perhaps thirty ships. Led by Herazade, they would go ahead to secure the hiding place. The red faded, vanished.

Finally, as he and Blaylock rounded the corner of the facility, he saw the main body of mage ships rising up from the ice field like a great flock of birds. With only a whisper they disappeared into the sky.

Blaylock climbed into his ship. *Follow me,* his message read. *Remain close.*

Galen headed toward his own ship. The mages had been driven from their homes, and now were driven from this place. They were pursued, in decline. Elric believed they would not survive.

The cold wind burned into his skin. On the vast landscape he was alone, the mountains towering dark above him. The universe was a cold, empty place, empty with loss, empty of all the things that had once been there, and were no more. For a moment Galen thought it did not matter if he went to the rim, or if he returned within, or if he walked across the icy plain until his oxygen ran out. With the debate between fighting and fleeing, he had forgotten that simple truth. There was no justice in the universe, no order, no God. Killing Elizar would not bring Isabelle back. When she had died, the universe had not cared; the universe had continued. And now, what would happen to Elric? Would he die, and would the universe continue along its maddening course of chaos and death?

He didn't want Elric to be gone, as others had gone, leaving only a painful hole in memory. Whether Galen came back from the rim or not, Elric had to be all right. He had to. Galen stared up at the countless stars.

Please don't die, he thought. *Please don't.*

February 2259

— *chapter 7* —

Elric stood at the window as the transport approached Babylon 5. Bathed in light, the station was five miles of spinning metal, containing one quarter of a million beings. As a construction, the space station was primitive. As an idea, however, Babylon 5 aspired to the highest goal: good. It had been designed to promote communication and understanding between various species, to prevent unnecessary conflict.

Unfortunately, not all conflict was unnecessary.

While most on Babylon 5 remained unaware that the first skirmishes of a great war had already taken place, the influence of that coming war spread all around them. Here the early stages were fought quietly, in microcosm. Intelligence was gathered, alliances formed, alliances broken. Plots and counterplots were launched, some successful, some not. The mages' deception would be among them.

Yet this could be no ordinary deception.

The mages were more powerful and advanced than any but the Vorlons and the Shadows. Over their history, the mages had performed successful deceptions on members of nearly every intelligent species—save the Vorlons and the Shadows. Techno-mages were adept at manipulating perceptions, at influencing thoughts, at using the desires of others for their own ends.

Yet Elric could not manipulate the perceptions of the Shadows, when they could penetrate his illusions. He could influence their thoughts only crudely, with the limited knowledge he had of them. He hoped, at least, he knew their desires, for in those lay his only chance of success. And he must succeed, for the survival of the mages depended on it.

Elric looked to Muirne and Beel, who stood beside him. They were both only in their forties, yet they too had been weakened by the loss of their places of power. Their weakness was less severe, since they had been connected to their places for a shorter time, yet he could see new signs of aging in them. The roots of Muirne's blond hair were going prematurely grey, and Beel's eyes seemed to have withdrawn into shadowed hollows.

They stood before the large window at the front of the passenger compartment, drawing attention to themselves without seeming to do so. All three wore black robes, and to make himself even more conspicuous, Elric had chosen the robe Isabelle had given him, curving silver and copper cords adorning the front in a bold pattern. In the crook of his arm he cradled his staff. It was short, in the ancient fashion, only three feet long and of a dull, unadorned silver. He wanted to make sure they were recognized by as many as might have memory of them. Once the transport docked, the news that mages had arrived must spread quickly through the station. Elric anticipated their strategy would be successful, for the other passengers shot them nervous glances and kept their distance.

"We have only fifteen minutes until our arrival," Muirne said.

Elric gave a grim nod, shifting his attention to the images in his mind's eye, which he knew the others watched as well. Through Babylon 5's security cameras, he saw Alwyn and Carvin loitering in one of the station's less reputable bazaars, among the crowds and noise. They were disguised with full-body illusions as Drazi, covered with thick grey scales, wearing coarse tunics and pants, and purple scarves about their necks. Although Elric and his two companions would be the first mages to officially arrive on the station, nothing was as it seemed. Alwyn and Carvin had arrived a day earlier, in disguise.

Through another camera, Elric monitored an empty corridor on the station. To the left stood a door that remained stubbornly closed, a door that must open before Elric arrived. It marked the room where the Drazi Rabelna Dorna stayed.

The plan had been for Alwyn and Carvin to encounter Rabelna the previous night and leak information to her. She was a thief and spy who operated out of the station, and in recent months, she had made several trips to the Thenothk system. After each trip, her bank account grew significantly. She was the perfect vehicle through which to convey a certain piece of news to the Shadows.

Alwyn and Carvin were to contrive for her to overhear them speaking. Since, to all appearances, techno-mages had not even arrived on the station, no deception would be suspected.

Yet last night, as Alwyn and Carvin had entered a bar where Rabelna gathered information, a fight had broken out between members of two Drazi factions: one wearing purple scarves and the other wearing green.

The Drazi had arrived at the end of their five-year cycle, and as custom required, they had split themselves into two groups by drawing scarves of either purple or green from a great barrel. For the next year they would fight, and when the fighting ended, the winning side would take over for the next cycle. Their custom was mindless, pointless, the seeds planted long ago by the Shadows. In a small way, it reflected the very conflict that would soon envelop them all.

Alwyn and Carvin, wearing purple, had been drawn into the fight, and had barely escaped being rounded up by security personnel. Rabelna had retreated to her quarters, and had not emerged since. The information had not been delivered.

Elric had not yet stepped foot on Babylon 5, and already his plan had gone awry.

If Rabelna did not receive the information until after mages had "arrived" on the station, she might suspect it. Even if she did not, her clients on the rim surely would. The information must not be tainted by the shadow of suspicion.

Elric watched the empty corridor, the closed door. She went to the bazaar every day at the same time. Yet today, she had failed to emerge. And he had no idea what she was doing within.

One of their greatest weaknesses in operating out of Babylon 5 was a lack of information. Their knowledge of the station and those who lived on it wasn't as extensive as it might be, for no mage had taken the station as a place of power. The fates of the previous Babylon stations had deterred interest, and this fifth station had not existed long enough to prove itself worthy of a mage's lifelong commitment.

The mage most closely associated with the station was Muirne. She had visited a number of times, though never revealing her identity. She had tapped into security, communications, and other systems soon after the station went on-line, but had never bothered to plant probes of her own. The primitive cameras used by station security provided superficial background information, though little more. They were limited to public areas and offered only rudimentary visual and audio functions.

Yet the Circle had chosen Babylon 5 as the false gathering place in the belief that the Shadows would not make a direct attack in such a public setting. While the Shadows' powers were great, they would not want to reveal their abilities here. However, a more subtle attack was certain, and indeed necessary if Elric's plan was to succeed.

Whether the Shadows themselves were on Babylon 5, Elric did not know. On Zafran 8, Galen had learned that techno-mage sensors sometimes showed the Shadows as anomalous bodies of static. The mages must search for these. He only hoped they would find none. For if Shadows moved freely on the station, his deception would almost surely fail.

Their main chance of success lay in the Shadows' inclination to work quietly, through puppets. That best served Elric's purposes.

The Shadows had another trait that could work to the mages' advantage. They were arrogant. Sending Kell's body to Selic 4, revealing that they knew where the mages were gathering but still need not strike, demonstrated that arrogance. They believed they could exterminate the mages at any point. Elric hoped their confidence unjustified.

Yet it would not be, if they had made allies of any of the fifty mages within his group. Before leaving Selic, Elric had warned the fifty that they might be required to give their lives. None had objected. He believed he had chosen wisely. Yet how could Elric be sure that one among them would not have second thoughts, would not resent the fact that he might be asked to die so that the rest could live? One word from any of them to an agent of the Shadows, and the deception would fail.

For a moment, the hopelessness of the task overwhelmed him. They were a small group, weakened, on the run. They could not trust one another. The Shadows had powers of which they knew nothing. How could they possibly succeed?

These feelings, Elric knew, were unlike him. The unrelenting throbbing in his head was taking its toll; his energy was not what it once had been. The plan could work if he did not fail it. Once again, he reviewed all that had been done over the last two days.

Their ships had been safely hidden away and awaited their return. He and Ing-Radi had split the group into smaller teams. They would take different transports to Babylon 5, leading the Shadows to conclude the mage ships had been destroyed as part of their attempt to disguise their movements.

Each team would subtly draw attention to its arrival. They must create the appearance that mages were gathering on Babylon 5 from different places, and that, rather than fifty of them, there were five hundred. Once all fifty had arrived over the next few days, the arrivals would appear to continue for several more days, through a combination of falsified ships' records and illusions.

Elric would serve as spokesman for the group, coordinating the deception that must fool the Shadows. Ing-Radi, who was less adept at deception, would work mainly behind the scenes. If they were successful, they would rejoin the others within fifteen days and retreat with them to the hiding place. Only through a flawless plan and perfect coordination could they prevail. The Shadows must be convinced that they had killed all the mages, or there would likely be no escape for any of them.

It had been some years since Elric had orchestrated so elaborate a deception. Of course, he had never outwitted such a sophisticated enemy, nor had the stakes ever been so high. Yet the principles remained the same. The best deception was elegant and seemingly effortless, like a simple sleight of hand, a shell game. All the elements must be set up in advance, everything prepared, perfectly practiced and timed. Once the plan was set in motion, it must allow only a single, inevitable conclusion.

To the targets of the deception, events must seem to be under their control, when all along they were being directed, ideas planted in their minds, actions anticipated and used. Elric had quickly determined who on Babylon 5 might serve the mages' purposes, and had examined their records, their activities, gathered information to shed light on the secret darkness of their hearts. Some mages operated on instinct, or learned to read body language or voice inflection. For Elric, history was everything. Know a man's past, and you would know his future. The past was prologue.

History suggested that Rabelna Dorna would go to the bazaar. And yet, she had not emerged. They had only ten minutes before their ship would arrive.

Then, in the empty corridor, the door slid open. Rabelna appeared. Muirne gave Elric a tense smile. Time was short.

Elric switched from camera to camera, following Rabelna's course. She wore no scarf of purple or green. She did not dress like a Drazi at all, but like a Human, in a brown plaid jacket and skirt. The clothes bulged with the thick grey scales beneath them. Elric knew she spoke English nearly fluently, quite an accomplishment considering the difficulty Drazi had with other languages. The clothes and the language skills revealed both insecurity and determination. Most of her contacts on Babylon 5 were Human, and she obviously desired to fit in among them and to impress them. For other Drazi, she seemed to have little patience or affection.

She made her way toward the bazaar. The marketplace was one of the less reputable on the station, crowded with small, dimly lit stalls that offered exotic and often illegal items.

Well aware of Rabelna's progress, Alwyn and Carvin positioned themselves at a stall where she often stopped. The Human proprietor traded in stolen wares.

Rabelna wound her way through the bazaar, stopping periodically. At last she approached the stall where the mages waited.

Alwyn had planted probes there, and Elric now accessed those, using the common key they had all agreed upon. Elric selected a probe stuck on a display case. Rabelna stood over it, waiting for the proprietor to finish with another customer. Alwyn and Carvin stood to one side, their backs to her. They spoke in well-rehearsed Drazi.

"Captain Vayda fired us because he was afraid we'd win," Alwyn said.

"It's not our fault we two drew purple and the rest of the

crew drew green," Carvin said. "We had to fight. That's no reason to fire us."

"It's Green oppression," Alwyn said.

Rabelna's expression soured with the talk of the Purple/Green conflict.

"I'm going to file a complaint with the shipping commission. Those techno-mages are paying a bonus. We should have gotten a share."

At the mention of techno-mages, Rabelna glanced subtly in their direction. Suddenly she was interested. She reached into her pocket, activated a small recorder.

Alwyn took Carvin's arm, lowering his voice. "I have a better idea." Rabelna inched closer. "The *Zekhite* will arrive here in ten days to take the techno-mages away. When the ship comes, we can lead the Purples of Babylon 5 in an attack. Teach Captain Vayda and those Greens a lesson."

"That's brilliant!" Carvin said. "Let's find the Purple leader."

They began to walk away, and Rabelna deactivated the recorder, the grey scales of her face twisting with a sly smile. She looked curiously after Alwyn and Carvin.

To follow their progress, Elric accessed one of the security cameras in the bazaar, continuing to maintain his connection with the probe on the stall. The two images appeared side by side in his mind's eye.

Alwyn and Carvin didn't get far. They ran into a trio of Purple Drazi, who were staring down a group of Green Drazi across the marketplace. The Purples, encouraged by the increase in their numbers, slapped Alwyn on the back and headed toward the Greens, eager for a fight.

Never one to undertake an illusion with anything less than one hundred percent commitment, Alwyn took the lead. He walked up to one of the Greens and rammed his shoulder into the Drazi as he shoved past. Apparently he didn't take the weight of the Drazi into account, for the force of the impact spun Alwyn around, and in that moment of vulnerability, the Green hauled off and punched him.

Alwyn fell stumbling back, and Carvin jumped to his defense, pummeling the Green with a few quick blows. A brawl broke out.

Rabelna turned to the stall's proprietor with a condescending shake of her head. "I'll be moving up my trip," she said in perfect English. "I need to leave immediately. Do you have anything for me?"

Elric relaxed a bit. She'd embraced the deception completely. Their first step had been successful. News that the techno-mages had hired a Drazi freighter, the *Zekhite*, would reach their enemies when she did. Records would show it could carry over five hundred, promoting the illusion that all five hundred mages were leaving together from Babylon 5.

That was one of three means of transportation Elric had arranged for their departure. In the shell game of his deception, the shells were the three ships, the mages the pea hidden within one of them. The second ship was an Earth transport, the *Tidewell*. It too was scheduled to arrive in ten days and could carry five hundred passengers. The mages had purchased it under the name of a false holding company Alwyn had long ago established. The transaction had been carefully disguised so that their enemies, when they searched the records with sufficient effort, could discover the true owners. Elric expected they would apply that sufficient effort within a day of his arrival on Babylon 5.

Once they discovered that the mages had purchased the *Tidewell*, the Shadows would destroy it, hoping to delay the mages and throw their plans into disarray. At the same time, the Shadows would continue their investigations. They would assume that the mages had some second method for leaving the station; their order's use of deceptions and misdirection was well established.

But of the mages' arrangement with the *Zekhite*, no records existed, so it could not be discovered—except through this "chance" leak. When Rabelna brought news of it to the Shadows, they would believe the *Tidewell* had been the mages' misdirection, and the true plan was to leave on the *Zekhite*. In their arrogance, they would believe they had discovered the whole of the mages' strategy.

What they would not know was that there were not five hundred mages on Babylon 5 but only fifty. And of those, only half would board the ship that was to be the target of the Shadows—an unavoidable sacrifice necessary to maintain the illusion. For the other half, Elric hoped, there was the third shell in this game, a third method of transportation: twenty-five tickets bought under a variety of names on a small luxury liner, the *Crystal Cabin*.

In the bazaar, security arrived to break up the fight. Alwyn was being pounded by two Greens; Carvin climbed up onto a nearby display counter, ran down its length, and launched herself at them. Elric had told Alwyn and Carvin to bond with the station's Purple Drazi, though he hadn't envisioned the bonding taking this form. He knew that Alwyn, at least, was enjoying himself, and he thought Carvin was as well. He just hoped they would be able to slip away before they were detained.

Elric broke the contact, leaving them to their own devices. The transport was entering the station's vast docking complex. Elric nodded to Muirne and Beel, directing them to retrieve their few belongings.

As they did, he accessed the cameras in the busy customs area where he and the others would disembark. He was gratified to see, amidst all the activity, three Centauri. He had timed his arrival perfectly.

One of the Centauri was critical to his deception.

When reviewing Muirne's records, Elric had been pleased to learn that Morden, the "dead" archaeologist, frequently visited Babylon 5 and was currently on the station. Even if

Elric could not deceive the Shadows, he could deceive their Human servant. Morden would be the mechanism through which his deception worked.

To reach Morden, he would have to operate through a pawn. That pawn would be the Centauri ambassador, Londo Mollari. Londo was a man of great appetites, and a man of great appetites could be easily manipulated. Apparently Elric was not the first to think so.

Londo appeared to have some preexisting relationship with Morden. What exactly their relationship was, Elric had not been certain until just an hour ago. While Morden had spoken with many on Babylon 5, just as he had spoken with many at the mages' convocation, including Elric, that did not always mean the subjects of his interest became his allies. Yet Morden had gone to Londo's quarters several times, and they seemed also to visit the station's gardens at the same time, where they could meet within the vast hedge maze without being observed by security.

More than that, Morden kept Londo under observation. Elric had discovered that Morden had several agents working for him. These agents would meet with Morden, and later appear in the casino when Londo was there, or follow him through the Zocalo. Elric had even seen one of these agents gambling with Londo, winning a great deal of money from the ambassador. Elric wondered how many of Londo's extensive gambling debts were Morden's doing. Limiting Londo's resources would help keep him under control.

Initially Elric had imagined that, when faced with the question Morden seemed to favor—*What do you want?*— Londo would ask for money to repay those never-ending debts, or for women, or for some advantage over his nemesis, the Narn ambassador, G'Kar. He had not yet grasped the depths of Londo's evil.

The Narn base in Quadrant 37 had been destroyed by the Shadows at the end of last year, ten thousand Narns killed.

Elric had assumed the Shadows had undertaken the attack to secure an alliance with the Centauri, sworn enemies of the Narn. But Elric had not believed Londo the one to request the attack—it seemed too bloodthirsty for the petty, dissolute, discarded diplomat Muirne had described.

Yet he had learned differently.

Since their arrival the day before, Alwyn and Carvin had planted probes on as many of the station's residents as possible, and in particular—following Elric's instructions—on Vir Cotto, Londo's attaché. Elric dared not plant a probe on Londo, for fear Morden or the Shadows might detect it and realize the ambassador had been targeted.

But the probe on Vir had proven extremely valuable. Only an hour before, Vir had been present at a meeting between Londo and Refa, a lord among the Centauri.

Elric had anticipated the meeting. In his earlier examination of station records, he had noted that Refa's personal transport was scheduled to both arrive and depart on this day. Further investigation had revealed a connection between Refa's visit and the arrival of the Centauri freighter *Ondavi*, which carried grain for sale. Refa tried to hide the fact that he and his family owned the ship and the grain, since participating in such commerce was deemed unworthy for a Centauri born of high ancestry. But the wealth of Refa's family had greatly declined over the years, debts had accumulated, and entering into commerce was a desperate attempt to maintain the lifestyle in which he believed he must live. Through his visit, Refa clearly hoped to expedite some sales without revealing his own stake in the matter.

Elric had assumed Refa's brief stay would include a meeting with the Centauri ambassador, though he had thought that for Refa, one of the most powerful men outside the royal family, the visit would be pro forma, Londo barely worthy of his attention.

But at that meeting, Refa had revealed that Londo had

been behind the attack on Quadrant 37 and the death of ten thousand Narns. How Londo had accomplished it, and with what hidden forces, Refa did not know, and Refa very much wanted to know. But Londo would not tell him.

The answer was obvious enough. Londo had sold his soul to the Shadows so that the Narns would be crushed, and the Centauri would regain dominance within the galaxy. Londo could not stomach the fact that the Narns, once slaves of the Centauri, had not only gained their freedom but built themselves into a power greater than their former masters.

The Centauri, in contrast, were in decline. They had not the will nor the resources to fight the growing Narn threat. Instead of accepting the loss of a few Centauri colonies, or motivating his own people to fight, Londo took the easy way, the way that would add most to his own personal glory. He was much more ruthless and power hungry than Muirne had painted him.

Perhaps, she had argued, Londo hadn't fully understood what he had done. Yet thousands had died. He must understand. And now he formed an agreement with Refa to replace the aged emperor, upon his death, with their own puppet. His ambitions were growing by the moment. He had no thought for consequences, no thought for the price that must be paid for his actions, nor who would pay it. His recklessness infuriated Elric.

If not for Londo and those like him, the Shadows would be forced into the light, forced to fight their own war. If not for those like Londo, the Shadows would have been seen long ago for what they were, bearers of chaos and death, and they would have been defeated. If not for those like Londo, the mages would not be compelled to give up everything and flee. Londo allied himself with the Shadows for the most fleeting, petty rewards. The mages refused to ally themselves with the Shadows, even though that refusal would likely lead to their complete destruction.

In the meantime, however, Londo would serve his purposes perfectly, would be his puppet as well as the Shadows', though it provided little comfort. Elric only wished his plan included Londo's death.

With the discipline of long practice, he suppressed his anger. The transport had docked, and the passengers began to leave. The throbbing in his head was growing stronger—the phantom pain of the chrysalis, and the planet, that had once been part of him. It would soon grow acute. He must rest again, already. But there was no time.

Near the rear of the passenger compartment, Muirne pulled her small bag out from beneath her seat. As she stood, she swayed slightly, and Beel steadied her.

When selecting those who would accompany him and Ing-Radi, Elric had tried to choose not only those he felt he could trust, but those who were older, weaker. Perhaps Kell could have devised a stratagem by which they might deceive the Shadows without losing any life. Elric had failed to conceive such a plan. He believed some, at least, would have to be sacrificed, so that the rest could be saved. He pressed his hand briefly to the decorative pattern that adorned the front of his robe. He had worn the robe not only to draw attention, but also to serve as his own private tribute to Isabelle. She had sacrificed herself so that Galen could live. Many of them would now have to follow her example. Yet, he hoped, not all.

To ensure that they accomplished their task, he had been obliged to take a handful of those who remained young and strong. He had determined to do everything in his power to spare them.

Above all, though, their deception must be successful, so that the main body of the mages could escape unmolested to the hiding place. Yet even with success, the mages would no longer be what they had once been. They were abandoning their commitment to the Code. They were fighting not for good, but for themselves. They were fleeing, leaving the rest of the beings in the galaxy to death and chaos. Elric could not imagine how they could recite the words of the Code after that. Eventually, their time would pass. Once the last of them died, their history, their Code, their deeds, their discoveries would die with them.

They kept their secrets, perhaps, too well.

Muirne and Beel approached, and he straightened, wanting to reveal no sign of weakness. They proceeded together toward the hatch with swift, authoritative steps, and most moved out of their way.

As they emerged into the busy customs area and waited to be cleared by security, Refa passed by him. The Centauri lord was boarding his personal transport. Everything was falling into place for the next step in Elric's plan: they must plant an idea. That was all.

Beyond the security checkpoint stood Londo and his at-taché, Vir. They had just finished saying good-bye to Refa. Londo looked like a peacock in his pretentious pseudo-military garb, with its gaudy gold braiding, epaulettes, and buttonholes, and an ostentatious golden starburst brooch that echoed the mages' ancient influence. Londo's hairline was re-ceding, a great tragedy for a Centauri male, whose status was reflected by his hair. To compensate, his hair was erected in a great fan around his head, higher than Lord Refa's or even the emperor's. Though Londo did not realize it, the hair served as his own personal black halo.

Beside him stood Vir, subservient, his clothes more under-stated, his crest of hair trimmed shorter. He was a nervous, overweight man who had not yet been tested and so did not yet know who he truly was.

Elric presented his identicard, flicked a probe onto the se-curity guard, and pretended not to notice as Londo and Vir noticed him. Londo's expression revealed that his presence had elicited the desired reaction. Vir said something, and Londo responded. Elric accessed the probe on Vir, which had

been planted on his cheek, and received an unflattering pro-
file of Londo.

"—seen one in years," Londo said. His voice carried the
thick accent of the northern provinces. "They almost never
travel. They don't like to leave their places of power. To see
even one of them is a rare thing. To see more than one at a
time is considered a very bad omen."

Londo knew of the mages, as Elric had expected and
hoped. Londo's superstitious image of them, coupled with his
ambition, would be very useful.

Security allowed Elric to pass through. The throbbing in
his head was being echoed by his tech, filling his body with
the pain of absence. As he waited for Muirne and Beel, he
thought of Galen. Galen's was another unaccustomed absence. Before Galen's initiation, they had never been separated, not since Galen had come to live with him. On Soom,
he nearly always knew where Galen was, what Galen was
doing. Now he had only fears. Galen's task was extremely
dangerous, and he had not only the Shadows to fight, but
himself.

Elric wished that they could be together. Yet he did not believe they ever would be again. He'd told Galen he hoped to
return from this task unharmed, and that was true. But while
he might hope it, he did not expect it. His life was required,
along with the lives of the others. That knowledge had made
his parting from Galen awkward; he hadn't wanted Galen to
sense his despair.

Galen, though, must survive. Elric had made it clear to
Blaylock that returning without Galen would be unwise. But
in truth, he knew that if Galen decided to engineer his own
destruction, Blaylock could not stop it. And if the Shadows
discovered their activities, neither would escape.

Of course, that was true for all of them.

Muirne and Beel were passed by security, and they continued single file through the customs area as Elric had di-

rected, echoing an image from a famous Centauri painting of three techno-mages arriving to bless the first emperor of the Centauri Republic. They passed by Londo and Vir while completely ignoring them.

"Three," Londo said. "This is definitely not good."

That much, at least, was true.

—— chapter 8 ——

Galen followed Blaylock to a table in the ship's lounge. They sat beside the wall, where they could have a good view of the rest of the room.

Galen had barely seen Blaylock for the last eleven days, and they had exchanged few words. They'd traveled as close to the Omega sector on the rim as they dared in their mage ships. Then they'd stopped in an obscure port, ships disguised, and hidden their vessels, switching to public transports. They had taken three different ships under different identities to help mask their origins. The ships, up until this one, had been crowded and poorly constructed, offering unhealthy accommodations and no privacy.

This last ship, though, which would bring them to Tau Omega—the system G'Leel had called Thenothk—was a luxury cruiser. Though Blaylock had not shared his reasoning in selecting the ship, Galen thought he wanted to observe some of the more powerful immigrants to the rim.

Based on the little data the probes on the rim had been able to collect before they'd been destroyed, Thenothk seemed the system with the most activity, members of many different races converging there. On the fourth planet a great city had arisen, millions drawn to this beacon of darkness for their own secret reasons. Whether this planet was also Z'ha'dum, the legendary home of the Shadows, they did not know. But Galen and Blaylock could fit in.

They posed as owner and employee of a company that produced high-tech FTL relays. This gave them an excuse to bring one such relay as a "sample," which would allow them to send a message to Elric or the others if they had critical information they were unable to deliver in person. Considering that the Shadows might be able to intercept their communications, it was to be used under only the direst of circumstances.

In one of the few communications between their ships, Blaylock had directed Galen to allow his hair to grow, had even explained how he could slightly accelerate its growth. Blaylock did not want them to use illusions to disguise themselves once they came close to the rim, since the Shadows might penetrate those illusions. Galen had managed only about one-quarter inch of growth on his scalp, but it was enough that he did not stand out. He wore a plain black sweater and pants, with his black coat always over them. His feeling of cold had intensified since leaving Selic, as if he were suffering from a constant fever.

Blaylock had discarded his black skullcap, leaving his head looking oddly naked. His skull had a striking, sculpted shape, all the more so because Blaylock was so gaunt. His eyebrows had grown in a heavy black, yet he kept his scalp bare. Galen supposed that at his age, baldness would not draw attention. Blaylock wore a dark blue business suit with a dark blue shirt. Although the suit was slightly large for him, he wore the clothes well, as if he had been wearing them for years. He had even added two small gold lapel pins and a heavy gold ring to complete the effect. And he had changed something in his manner, so that he carried himself, somehow, not like a mage, but like a businessman. Galen couldn't figure out what it was.

They took the menu-pads from the holder beside the window and ordered lunch. Discarding his menu in the middle of the table, Blaylock turned his sharp gaze on the other passengers in the lounge. Galen took Blaylock's menu and his own and returned them to the holder. The holder had been turned slightly askew. Galen straightened it.

Blaylock did not seem interested in talking. Reluctantly, Galen pulled the dirty tan scarf from his coat pocket and laid it carefully across his lap, his fingers grazing its complex, textured surface.

Over the last eleven days, he had forced himself to study the files she had sent him as she lay dying. He had not wanted the files, the records of her spells and her research. He had not wanted to look at them. But he had led the Circle to believe he could translate her spell for listening to the Shadows, and that spell was probably the only way to discover their secret plans, to learn whether they believed Elric's deception, and what action they planned to take against him. Yet Galen didn't know if he could translate her conjury; their spell languages were very different. His was the language of equations, hers the language of weaving. Her strong fingers had intertwined, moving in subtle, complex patterns. He could still feel the movement of her hands beneath his.

She had created an odd shorthand to record her spells, the movements that each finger must make, in sequence. The files were filled with bizarre symbols in strange configurations. Galen had gained only the most basic understanding of them. He had managed to translate several of her simpler spells, spells in which she used only one hand, made only a few simple movements. But the more complicated spells using both hands he found impossible to equate to his own language. The spell to listen to the Shadow communications was one of her most complex.

She had recorded some of her spells by another method, in tapestries that had hung on the walls of the apartment she'd shared with Burell. That method of recording would be simpler and more natural, Galen thought, since her spells were so like weaving. If he had some of those tapestries, it would give him another way of understanding her work. All that was left, though, was the scarf. Her gift to him. He knew she had encoded a message for him within it, but he had not yet been able to decipher it. In truth, he did not know if he wanted to decipher it. Yet he felt the scarf held his only hope for translating her more complex spells.

He preferred to study it in private, but now time was short. They would arrive at Thenothk in less than an hour, and he had not yet accomplished what he must.

He ran his fingertips over the irregularly spaced bumps, as if reading braille. Grains of dirt imbedded in the weave scratched his raw skin. The dirt, of course, had come from the mines where he had taken her, where she—

He turned his thoughts away. He must not lose control here, in front of Blaylock.

Handling the scarf, as studying her files, unsettled him. Her spells reflected the way she thought. They were pieces of her. Pieces she had given him as she'd struggled for her last breaths. He did not want to go back to that time, to that place. He did not want to remember.

When he studied her spells on his ship, alone, and the memories became too much for him, he had found two solutions. If he stopped himself soon enough, he could simply move on to another task. The task that most helped to order and focus his thoughts was organizing his own spells, grouping them into progressions as he had begun to do so long ago. Already he had defined two other progressions, spells that built on one another, becoming more and more complex, their equations containing more and more terms. And following those progressions backward, he had discovered a one-term equation lying at the base of each, just as he had discovered the one-term spell of destruction. He did not know what these new one-term spells would do, and he knew that he must never conjure them, but arranging his spells in these neat columns helped to calm him. It allowed him, he supposed, to briefly fool himself into thinking there was an order to things, as neat and reassuring as the arrangement of objects on his shelves at home had been.

If he didn't stop himself from working on her spells soon enough, he found that he could not focus on his progressions or on anything else, until he had brought the fire down upon himself several times. He'd last done it four days ago. In a fury of grief, he had called down the fire five times. His skin was still red, raw. Even the organelles could not heal such injuries instantly.

After scouring himself, the cold would leave him for a time, and he would regain control. Then, as he worked with her spells, the memories, the feelings, the cold, would return.

As he sat there with Blaylock, he could feel the energy building inside him. It would be time, soon, to bring the fire down again.

"The Centauri in the red jacket," Blaylock said. "Why is he here?"

Apparently Blaylock had decided to test him. It was a welcome distraction. He and Blaylock had spent the last few hours separately circulating through the ship, planting probes, picking up what they could, accessing databases to gain further information on the passengers. Galen had seen the Centauri earlier and overheard a fair amount from him.

"He's been told about jobs that pay ten times what he was getting on Centauri Prime."

"And that Narn. What does he eat for breakfast?"

Galen had not seen the Narn before. But he wore a pleated white collar, a symbol of the Narns' former slavery adopted by members of an extreme political group that advocated the complete extermination of the Centauri. "As a member of the Kha'dai, he eats a morning meal of acotu as a reminder of the deprivations they suffered as slaves."

"How long has that couple been married?" Blaylock indicated them with a subtle turn of his hand.

Galen had accessed data on the man earlier, when they had

passed in the corridor. His name was Trent Barkley. Galen wondered what relevance his marriage could have to their task. "Twelve years," he said.

Blaylock's hand tapped against the table. "You look but you do not see. Look. And see."

Galen studied the couple. Trent Barkley was the head of a large datasystem corporation. He wore an expensive suit, his wife a tight-fitting black dress. She fiddled with the hair above her ear, and Galen noticed a delicate diamond bracelet on her wrist. When she lowered her hand, she adjusted the bracelet.

They sat close in a corner booth, her foot, shoe discarded, rubbing against his ankle. Two Bloody Marys sat on the table before them. As he spoke to her, his lips paused in a half smile. They were obviously in love. Was that what Blaylock wanted him to see? He didn't care to see it.

Perhaps the information he had accessed on the date of marriage had been incorrect or incomplete. He could check her records and see if they showed the same.

"Don't search the databases. I asked you to look."

Galen would not watch them further. "I did. I have given you my answer."

Blaylock studied him. "I have often tried to convince the Circle that we should cloister ourselves from the outside world, its petty distractions, and pleasures, so that we can concentrate on the inner life and fulfill our destiny. But if one is raised in a shelter, one must take great care in leaving that shelter."

"Elric has not sheltered me. He has taught me all I need to know."

"Have you known any couple," Blaylock said, "that has been together for twelve years?"

His parents had been together for twelve years. But Galen would not say their names. "Among the Soom I know, some have been mated for that time."

Blaylock's eyes narrowed. "I know little of the Soom, but do those couples behave like this?"

"The Soom enjoy arguing. When they're not, they lick each other on the cheek as a sign of affection."

"Human couples argue as well."

Galen looked down at the scarf in his lap.

"This couple has not been married for twelve years. They are not married at all. Look at the woman. Look! How old is she?"

Her face had only the slightest hint of wrinkles. The skin on the back of her hands was tight. Galen realized his error. It was foolish. "Perhaps twenty-five," he said.

"Twenty-five and married for twelve years. Do you see the bracelet?"

"Diamond."

"Yes. And from the attention she gives it, it is new. You see her hand, the way it touches her ear, her hair?"

"Yes."

"Human females flirt by showing the inside of their wrists. It is an unconscious instinct. She is with a man she wants to control, not one whom she already controls. Her foot is also working to that end. Now look at his eyes. Where are they pointed?"

"He is looking at her mouth."

"A sign of sexual attraction. And you see him smooth his collar? A preening gesture. Not something a man does with a partner of twelve years."

Galen took a deep breath, feeling he had done a disservice to Elric in performing so poorly.

"If you are to be effective out in the universe, you cannot close yourself off from it. You must know what is going on around you. You must know how people work. You must study them. Tell me of the Drazi."

Galen turned toward the table against the opposite wall.

"Simply look, and tell me what you see."

"She dresses like a Human." The Drazi wore a brown jacket and skirt with a subtle plaid, something a business-woman on Earth might wear. It had obviously been tailored for her anatomy, though still it bulged from her thick grey scales. Her shoes were of the Drazi style, since Human shoes would not fit her wide feet, and would probably look strange if adapted to do so.

"Why does she dress like a Human?"

"Perhaps she spends more time with Humans than with Drazi."

"And?"

"She wants to impress someone. To be taken seriously. To fool herself into thinking she is better than others of her kind." Her briefcase was open on the table, and within it Galen caught the sparkle of a pile of data crystals. On the table, she had several neat stacks of materials laid out before her. Two of the stacks appeared to be credit chits; two others were comp-pads. Perhaps she was a thief.

The waiter came and refilled her cup—she was drinking coffee. His hand touched one of the stacks, knocking the comp-pads just slightly out of alignment. When he left, she brought her grey, scaled hands to either side of the stack and straightened it. "She is neat," Galen said.

"Such compulsive ordering is a sign of insecurity. She fears she will lose what she has. One straightens the comp-pads, or puts away the menus, because one finds one's life out of control."

Galen's head jerked toward Blaylock, and he found Blay-lock's attention not on the Drazi, but on him. This was not a test of his abilities at all. Blaylock was dissecting him just like these outsiders. He folded his hands tightly in his lap and looked back to the Drazi.

A Human came to the table, and she stood, shook his hand. As they spoke, she glanced several times at the table, as if checking its contents.

"Does she want him to join her?"

"No," Galen said. "She doesn't want him near her things."

"Is she honest with him?"

"Do you intend me to use my—"

"No. Look."

Galen had studied the ways in which heart rate, respiration, and other physiological signs might reveal lies. But without his sensors, he could detect little. He knew that eye movement and gestures were tied to lying, but they varied greatly with the individual and required a much better knowledge of the person. Galen didn't know what he was supposed to see. "She looks into his eyes. Her hand is in her pocket."

"The hand in the pocket, in almost every species with hands and pockets, is a tell. When the palm is shown, one is usually speaking the truth. When the palm is hidden, the truth is hidden as well. She is hiding something. And she is anxious about it."

She shook hands again with the man, and he left. She sat back at the table, straightening her piles.

Galen turned to Blaylock. "Do we really care about any of these people? Or are you simply evaluating me?"

"They may all be useful, to varying degrees. Her presence, in particular, concerns me."

"Why?"

The waiter came with their food, and Galen found he had a message from Blaylock. In it were the records of the Drazi's travel. Her name was Rabelna Dorna. Most recently she had been on Babylon 5. Galen saw no particular relevance in that. She had left only nine days ago, though, on a transport that could never have gotten her this far, this fast. Rabelna had disembarked from the transport a few systems away from Babylon 5. Then records showed her on a planet near the rim, boarding this ship, only two days later. To take her from one transport to the other, she must have found another ride, a much faster one.

In his mind's eye, Galen scanned back through the record to see where she had been before Babylon 5. Rabelna seemed to spend much of her time on the station, though in mid-January she'd made a trip to Curesse, the system beside Alwyn's home of Regula. Two of the planets in the Curesse system had been engaged in a vicious war for the past six months. As Galen wondered whether her visit might be connected to that, he realized that Alwyn and Carvin had left Regula for Selic in mid-January. And when they'd begun their journey, they had been attacked by an unmarked ship of great power. Could Rabelna have been involved in that?

Blaylock had before him a small plate with three boiled potatoes. His head was bowed, and Galen realized he must be directing the tech to deactivate the taste center in his brain, as he was known to do. With such bland food, Galen wondered what difference it would make.

Galen had ordered a wrap, and it had come on a large platter with all sorts of stylish vegetation, so that, compared to Blaylock, he seemed to have a feast. He remembered what Gowen had said.

"I seem to have a lot," he said. "I'm glad to share."

"No, thank you," Blaylock said.

"Do you think she was involved in the attack on Alwyn?"

"Yes." Blaylock was dissecting one of the potatoes with his fork.

"She works with the—" Galen thought it wiser if he did not say their name here. "With them."

"Yes."

"Why has she come to Tau Omega?"

Blaylock chewed with efficient, automatic movements. "Why has she come to Tau Omega from Babylon 5?" He had switched to the language of the Soom.

Galen shook his head, startled that Blaylock would know it. He must have learned the language so they could converse privately. Blaylock had warned that they must not send messages to each other once they arrived at Thenothk. If they spoke in the language of the Soom, though, the chances that the language would be understood were virtually nonexistent. "She seems to be a thief," Galen said, continuing in that language.

"What has she stolen?" Blaylock's pronunciation was harsh, but accurate.

Galen looked toward the stacks of credit chits, comp-pads. Surely the Shadows weren't interested in stolen merchandise. He turned to Blaylock. "Information."

Blaylock's eyes narrowed. "What information?"

Information that would concern Blaylock. "Information about our order."

Blaylock gave a single nod. "I believe so, yes."

"How do you know that?" As Galen asked the question, the answer came to him. "Elric and the others. They're on Babylon 5."

Blaylock set down his fork, apparently finished. He had eaten only one of the potatoes. "Eat your food."

If Rabelna brought word that the mages were gathering on Babylon 5, that would mean the deception was proving successful. Yet it would also mean the Shadows would take action against those gathered there. Galen picked up his wrap. "Can't we send a warning to Elric?"

"No. It is quite possible, in any case, that Elric himself has sent her, as his unwitting agent."

Galen nodded as he chewed.

"You asked if I evaluate you. Of course I do. If we are to work together effectively, I must know you. Elric felt you should not come with me." Blaylock paused. "Your hands are red."

Galen put down his wrap self-consciously. "It is dry on the ships, and cold. Not what I'm used to."

"One should beware what one becomes accustomed to.

The body can withstand much, but one should act out of discipline, not a lack of it."

Galen felt his face flush with shame. His hands clenched the scarf in his lap.

"That scarf was made by Isabelle, was it not?"

Galen nodded. There was no escape from her name, or her memory.

"You seek to understand the pattern embedded there."

"Yes."

"You believe it may help you translate her spell for listening to the Shadows."

"Yes."

"She had great skill, for one so young," Blaylock said.

Galen was shocked to hear him speak well of her. "But she studied the tech, which you condemn. She sought to understand its workings. You denounced Burell for such research."

"As I would have denounced Isabelle, had she continued. What we have been given, Galen, is a mystery beyond our understanding, a true blessing. It taps into the basic force and fabric of the universe, into God, as some call it. Our place is to use that blessing in the best way possible, to be the best agents of the universe that we can. Is it an angel's place to dissect the genes that gave him wings? I think an angel who does so misses the point of his existence. His place is to generate awe and belief in God, to do good as he can, to try to understand and follow God's will. I believe we must try to learn as much of the universe as we possibly can, to understand and follow its will."

"In understanding the universe, can we not understand ourselves?"

"Throughout our history, many have tried to unlock the secrets of the tech, and all have failed. I believe our understanding of it, and of our relationship with it, will be the very last to come to us. I didn't want to see Burell and Isabelle waste their lives in that vain pursuit."

Anger quickened Galen's breath. He tried to keep his voice even. "It was not vain. They had learned much. And if that was what they desired to study, why should they be condemned for it? Why should they be denied access to the tech?"

"To dissect a thing is not to understand a thing. I can dissect a frog and record all of its parts. I may even deduce the absorption of nutrients through its digestive system, the passage of oxygen through its blood vessels. I may electrically stimulate a neuron in the frog's brain and make its leg jump. Yet what understanding do I have of the frog itself?"

"Science is part of our Code. How can you deny it?"

"In order to investigate things scientifically, we break them into parts. Yet some things cannot be understood in their parts but only in their totality." Blaylock paused, allowing the words their importance. "And to what end is this scientific investigation? We investigate things scientifically in order to learn how to control them. But control of the tech should not come from some artificial electrical stimulation. It is a cheap method, unworthy of us. Control should come from the perfect, transcendent joining of a mage and his tech. We control it so imperfectly now, struggling with spell languages, with discipline, with focus. Only through perfect discipline, through perfect control, though a perfect connection, can we truly understand it. A mage who forms a complete union with his tech will undergo an enlightenment in which he learns the will of the tech, and the universe. As one, they may carry out that will."

Galen knew that the universe had no consciousness, no will. And if it did, if it had willed all that had happened to happen, then the universe was vicious and cold. Rather than seeking to join with it, Galen would do everything in his power to fight it, to destroy it. He bit out the words. "And why would one want to carry out the will of the universe?"

Blaylock's gaze lingered on him. "We devote our lives to

learning and understanding. What greater wisdom can we gain than this? If we can learn the will of the universe, we can bring greater understanding to all. We can break the cycle of war and chaos that has recurred so many times."

"What if war and chaos *are* the will of the universe?"

"Then the universe would not have embodied itself in matter subject to constant, physical laws."

"Then science can help us understand."

"Certainly."

"Then why was Burell reprimanded and ostracized for her work? Why was she forced to cripple herself in the pursuit of knowledge?"

Blaylock paused before answering, his expression unreadable. "I did not know that, though I suspected it." His gaunt face tightened. "You are not privy to all that Burell has done. Know that she committed unforgivable atrocities in her pursuit of answers. The tech is alive, though in a form we do not understand. To dissect it is no less a crime than flaying a mage."

Galen wondered how Blaylock could be so certain the tech was alive, if he had never studied it. Of course, the Circle must know something of it, in order to replicate it. "Scientific study can be done without dissection. Why is that, too, discouraged?"

Over the speakers, a voice announced in Interlac that they were arriving at the Thenothk system. Galen's heart jumped, his excitement echoed by the tech, and he suddenly realized that he had no interest in continuing the conversation. Let Blaylock believe they were connected to some great universal order—it no longer mattered. Though Galen hadn't known it, for the past eleven days, beneath the traveling and the studies, beneath the unrest and the scouring, he had been thinking of only one thing: of arriving at this place, of finding Elizar, and of killing him.

Blaylock stood. "Let us make ready."

Galen hesitated. "You haven't finished your lunch."

Blaylock gave him a dour look. "If I had wanted Gowen with me, I would have brought him."

— *chapter 9* —

In his mind's eye, Elric watched as Vir stumbled through yet another dark passage in the section of Babylon 5 known as Down Below, searching for the techno-mages as his master had commanded. The Centauri attaché tripped over a pile of rags and discovered a sleeping figure beneath. Fed—for that was who it was—stumbled to his feet, his wild dark hair sticking out in all directions as he let out a mad howl. He chased Vir through several preplanned twists and turns before allowing Vir to "escape" him.

Vir stood with his back against the wall, gasping, his eyes wide with terror. He didn't yet know that today was his lucky day. Today was the day when he would at last find the mages. Because today was the day when it served them to be found.

Once they had arrived on the station, it had taken only hours for Londo to conceive the plan of seeking the mages' blessing. Obsessed as he was with power, he considered the arrival of the techno-mages only in how it might further his ambitions. He had told Vir of the important role techno-mages had played in Centauri history. Centauri history, however, was only distantly related to the truth.

One thousand years ago, a minor noble in the Centauri Empire had led his people in the extermination of the Xon, a sentient species who shared their home planet of Centauri Prime. To celebrate this great realization of their destiny, the

145

butcher declared the beginning of a new era, that of the Centauri "Republic"—which was nothing but the Centauri Empire under another name—and appointed himself the first emperor of that republic.

This outrage was coupled with one of the lowest moments in techno-mage history, when Frazur and two other mages gave their blessing to the butcher's assumption of power. Their arrival on Centauri Prime was immortalized in a famous painting, a painting whose image Elric and the others had evoked with their arrival.

The three ancient mages had sought power for themselves, the power behind the throne. As Frazur said, "Magic enables clever men to dominate others." In short order they fell to fighting amongst themselves, until they destroyed each other in spectacular fashion. Some memory of this seemed to lie behind Londo's comment that seeing more than one mage at a time was a "very bad omen."

The debacle had occurred in the early days of the mages, before Wierden's Code was widely accepted. But this was the action for which the Centauri most remembered the techno-mages, this "blessing" that somehow justified all that their species had done, and all they might do.

Londo sought a similar blessing for his own atrocities and for the ascension to power he envisioned. It was clear now that Londo's ambitions stretched even to imagining himself emperor.

Though in many ways Vir was a fool, he had wisely feared seeking out the mages to request an audience. Yet every day he searched the station for them. Vir himself had no discernable desire for power, but he served his master loyally. Loyalty to a butcher was, of course, no virtue.

It had taken Vir a few days to discover that they were staying in Down Below, and since then he had each day descended to those lawless levels of the station with great trepidation, questioning any he dared about the rumored territory the mages had taken for their own. He had learned that it was large, large enough to house hundreds of them. Its location had been described to him several times, yet he had never been able to find it. Vir had tried to pay someone to show him the way, yet no one dared approach, even for a fee. Ing-Radi and the others had done an excellent job of instilling fear in the inhabitants of Down Below. If there was one thing at which mages excelled, it was that.

Fed followed Vir, remaining out of sight, manipulating his course. They had covered Down Below with probes, so they could observe his progress easily. Through illusions, passageways appeared or disappeared, obstructions blocked one path while lights revealed another to be safe.

Movement drew Elric's attention back to the silent grey room in which he sat, a dozen other mages with him, each observing different areas of the station.

Ing-Radi stood over him. The globes of magical light that floated above, illuminating the room, revealed that her orange skin had grown even more pale, the blue veins becoming more prominent, cutting across her face in an elaborate pattern. The slit of her mouth was dry and white. She leaned slightly to one side, as if her balance was off, and her four arms hung limply at her sides. Each day she grew worse. Elric knew she continued only through sheer force of will.

"I have intercepted a communication on Gold Channel you should see," she said. Her voice, at least, retained its rich, calming tone. With a slight motion of her hand, two frozen images appeared in the air between them. On Elric's left, a woman sat behind a desk in a richly appointed office. Behind her on the wall hung the seal of EarthGov. Across the front of her desk lay two matching metal sculptures, abstract twisted patterns. She appeared in her mid-thirties, with a self-assured expression. She wore a tan cashmere jacket with a black shirt beneath, the lines clean, forceful. Her wavy dark hair was pinned up, a single strand curling down each side of her face.

"That is Senator Norman," Ing-Radi said. "She is a member of the Senate Intelligence Committee, as well as a member of the Babylon 5 Oversight Committee. A powerful person."

On the right was John Sheridan, captain of Babylon 5. Elric had first become aware of him during the Earth-Minbari War, and since then had followed his career. The captain was an energetic, charismatic leader—a good man, moral and loyal, though also a fierce and canny military strategist. He was a practical man who had not yet given up his dreams, a rare combination. Though he had risen far in his career and fought already in one war, he was just entering early middle age. In charge of this place devoted to good, he would be a major force in the great war, either fulfilling the promise of Babylon 5 or undermining it completely. He stood in his office, hands clasped behind his back, fit, young, ready, he believed, to face any challenge. He had no idea what would soon confront him.

Ing-Radi set the images into motion.

"Captain Sheridan," the senator said, her mouth sliding into a smile that somehow seemed condescending. "It's a pleasure to finally speak with you. Congratulations on your new post."

"Thank you."

"I'm afraid I have to keep this brief, though it is a matter of grave importance. It has come to our attention that a large group of techno-mages has gathered on Babylon 5."

John Sheridan nodded. "We're aware of the situation." His voice, though untrained, carried a compelling resonance. He had learned how to give orders and command respect.

"Do you know their plans?"

"Security tells me they may be leaving within a day or two, though we haven't yet confirmed that. They've acted peacefully." He hesitated. "May I ask what your interest is?"

She tilted her head, the vague smile remaining on her face. "The techno-mages aren't simple magicians, Captain. They're extremely powerful, and as such, their movements raise planetary security issues. Particularly such mass movements. We need you to look into the matter. Learn their plans. If they fail to cooperate, you'll have to detain them."

John frowned. "On what grounds would I detain them? They've done nothing."

Her tone remained mild, her expression friendly. "I hear they're staying in the sector you call Down Below, which is officially off-limits. You could hold them for that, at the least."

John gave a quick shake of his head. "But that will only create unnecessary hostility."

The smile faded from her face. "You may believe they're harmless, Captain, but they're not. Their plans are of great concern to us, and you're the only one in a position to discover them. I hope I don't need to remind you of your duties."

"No," John said. "You don't."

"Good." Her smile returned. "We will expect your report shortly."

Ing-Radi dissolved the images. "The Shadow influence is everywhere."

"How could we have been blind for so long?" Elric said. The assassination of the Earth President Santiago had revealed the strength of the Shadows' influence there. Elric should have realized that the Shadows would try to use that influence to compel the EarthForce personnel who ran Babylon 5 to detain them. If the mages would not be detained, then they would have to fight. The station and those on it would be endangered, and the mages could be drawn into the great war.

John had been posted to Babylon 5 only since the beginning of the year. How he would react, if given orders that conflicted with the purpose of Babylon 5, remained unclear. He would have to make a choice between loyalty and morality.

Elric considered creating a deceit that would trick John

Sheridan into helping them. The mages not only required that John allow them to leave, their best chance of leaving safely would be with the active help of John and his security staff. But for some reason, Elric did not want to deceive the captain. He wanted to believe that John, given the chance, would act for good. Perhaps he simply hoped to convince himself that those billions of beings that the mages were leaving behind would have a good leader to follow, and a chance to survive. The Shadows planted the seeds of division and conflict; countless numbers would die unless the races could be brought together, united against the true enemy.

He would not deceive John. Instead, he would test John with the truth.

Carvin ran up to them, breathless. Her hands twisted anxiously together. "The *Tidewell* has exploded."

Elric nodded. He should have been relieved that the Shadows had acted as he'd anticipated. But instead he found himself filled with dread. As Ing-Radi questioned Carvin about the details, he told himself there was no reason for his reaction. Yet the explosion somehow seemed a harbinger of greater destruction to come, of an intelligence that could not possibly be manipulated, a power that could not possibly be survived.

It was the emptiness inside him, pushing him again toward despair. He reminded himself that the explosion was part of his plan. He'd been only an hour off in his expectations, believing the Shadows would strike a bit sooner. The *Tidewell* had just been leaving its last stop before Babylon 5, where it was scheduled to arrive tomorrow. The Shadows sought to delay the mages, to limit their options, to frighten them. Soon would follow one last attempt to gain their alliance. When that failed, their enemies' focus would turn from delay to destruction.

Within a few hours, the Shadows would learn of the mages' other ship, the *Zekhite*. The Shadows would pretend they knew nothing of it, hoping to trick the mages into boarding so they could then destroy it. They would believe themselves in command of the situation, the mages desperate after the destruction of the *Tidewell*. They would not know that they had done exactly what Elric wanted.

Unless they had somehow discovered the mages' true plan.

The possibility of a traitor remained one of the greatest dangers they faced. In secrecy, Elric had assigned Gowen to observe the activities of the other mages. Elric had no doubt of Gowen's loyalty; Blaylock had indoctrinated him thoroughly. The choice of Gowen carried another advantage: It kept Gowen occupied, when he had seemed determined to hover over Elric. Elric suspected Galen had asked Gowen to watch over him. Now Gowen's full attention was taken watching his fellow mages. It violated their basic etiquette, yet Elric needed to know if any would betray them. Gowen had as yet seen no sign of it.

Elric stood, suddenly tired, and dissolved his chair. Carvin's face carried a mixture of expectation and nervousness. In her Centauri silks she appeared a beautiful young woman, nothing more. She was perfect for their purposes. She had grown into an exceptional young mage, skilled and inventive. Alwyn had taught her well. After leaking the information to Rabelna Dorna and joining in the Drazi brawl, she had spent a night in the brig with Alwyn and several angry Purple Drazi, yet never revealed a hint of her true identity.

Elric turned his attention to the casino, accessing those cameras. There, in safety and luxury, Londo gambled and drank, as was his habit. "Wait thirty minutes," Elric said to Carvin. "Then go."

Carvin sucked her lips in nervously, nodded.

"All is according to plan," he said. "They will believe we have sent you in a desperate attempt to secure another transport, another misdirection. You are prepared?"

With a quick flick of her hand she produced an ace of diamonds between index and middle fingers. On her index finger she wore the signet ring engraved with the rune for solidarity.

Elric smiled. "You will do well."

Carvin's grin lit up her face. With a flourish of her hand the card vanished. She hurried off.

In his mind's eye he visualized a blank message screen. *Begin*. He imagined the message being broken into bits of information, traveling through the air to Fed, reassembling itself.

Fed would steer Vir toward them now. The extra hour the Shadows had taken meant that Vir had made a few extra trips around Down Below, but he would arrive only a bit worse for the wear.

Elric looked up at Ing-Radi. "I will take care of John Sheridan. I had planned to meet him, in any case."

"If I may. You must first take care of yourself. Else our task will not succeed."

She reached toward him, and he stepped back. It was her nature to heal where she saw hurt, as she had always done. Yet now she had no organelles to spare. She needed all her healing powers for herself.

He straightened, trying to hide his fatigue. "I am well enough. In two more days, we will have eternity to rest."

"It is not yet your time. That element of your plan is flawed. You must save yourself for the mages. And for Galen. He still needs you."

Elric pushed thoughts of Galen from his mind. What Galen needed, or what he himself needed, could play no role in their plan. "What the mages most need is for us to succeed. No matter the cost. I am sorry. I must go."

"We will discuss this again."

Elric left the observation room through the heavy circular metal hatch and made his way through the shadowy, irregularly shaped spaces that comprised the large section of Down

Below they had claimed for themselves. These levels had not been built for habitation, but to contain the machines and structure necessary to support the rest, in an arrangement that allowed maintenance personnel access when necessary. The recycled air, confining dimensions, and unrelenting lifelessness were oppressive.

He entered the corridor that marked one boundary of their territory. Like much of Down Below, it exhibited a peculiar structure, stretching two stories high, with a catwalk running above. The overhead lights had been dimmed and repeatedly faded on and off, creating a forbidding atmosphere. To warn off intruders, the mages had marked the walls with glowing runes and arcane diagrams. The rune for solidarity occupied a prominent place.

Elric reached an intersection. Vir would come from the left. Elric withdrew to the right and created the illusion of a solid wall to hide his presence. Here he would wait.

Over the next two days, Elric knew, his deception would either succeed or fail, and their fate would be sealed. Events must be controlled precisely, each falling into place at exactly the right time. His energy and concentration must not flag. Elric worried that he would not be equal to the demanding schedule. Yet the best deceptions happened quickly, before the targets had time to think. And all was ready.

False arrivals had continued for days, and the fifty of their group were constantly appearing in many different guises in various locations throughout the station, so that their numbers seemed much greater, and so that mages who were not here, including the other members of the Circle, appeared to be among them. Their numbers had been increased in the station database as well.

Extensive food and supplies had been ordered, as if to sustain them over a long period. It had been made clear to all the vendors that the supplies must be available by the day after tomorrow, when they were leaving.

Three of the younger mages—Emond, Chiatto, and Ak-Shana—were generating an elaborate web of false communications, from mages who were not here to other mages who were not here, discussing their fictitious activities. All on the chance that the Shadows could detect their communications.

Of course that was the great unknown: the Shadows. Their powers and their thoughts. The mages had searched the station for anomalous bodies of static and found none. Shadows, if they were here, had to be few. But it would take only one to see through their illusions. Elric hoped that the Shadows, if here, remained hidden, depending on Morden to serve as their eyes and ears.

Elric had studied Morden as much as time had allowed. Though the Shadows' servant remained an enigma, Elric believed he knew enough to manipulate the man. As Elric had expected, Morden had avoided the mages since their arrival. Instead he used others, whether they knew they were being used or not. Morden used the senator and John to try to detain the mages, Londo and Vir to gather intelligence on their numbers and purpose. And in just the same way, Elric would use Londo and Vir to carry what information he desired to Morden.

But soon, Elric knew, Morden would confront him. And Morden would present the Shadows' final offer.

In his mind's eye, Elric saw Vir drawing close. Several mages in disguise ran past Vir, as if fleeing.

"What is it?" Vir cried out in panic.

"Techno-mages!" Beel yelled, pushing past him.

Vir pressed himself back against the wall, murmuring to himself. "Attaché to an ambassador. How dangerous can that be? They never told me that the ambassador was a madman. 'Go to the techno-mages, Vir. Arrange it, Vir.' Obviously they don't want to be bothered. Obviously they won't be happy to be bothered. And who will they take that out on, I wonder."

He took several heavy breaths, straightened, continued onward.

From Elric's position, the illusory wall he'd conjured appeared no more than a dark screen. Through it, he watched Vir approaching the intersection. It was time now to convince Vir that the mages wanted nothing to do with Londo, when the opposite was actually the case.

Vir peered around the corner into the corridor that separated them, took in the glowing runes on the walls. He withdrew his head, then, after a moment, extended it again. "Hello?"

Vir took a few steps into the empty hallway. He spoke loudly into the silence. "I am Vir Cotto, diplomatic attaché to Ambassador Londo Mollari of the Centauri Republic. I am told by the people running that way that this is where I can find the techno-mages. I am here on behalf of Ambassador Mollari, and I need to speak to someone who is in charge."

Fed was positioned at the next cross-hallway down. A low growl came from there, and it began growing steadily in volume. Elric accessed the probe on Vir's cheek, the image appearing in his mind's eye. A red light leaked from the cross-hallway into the main passage, and then there was the sound of massive movement.

Vir stared anxiously at the light. "Obviously it would be at your earliest convenience."

The demon emerged, scaly and red, its massive form bent, filling the two-story corridor. The floor shook with its footsteps as it stalked toward Vir, studying him with two piercing white eyes. Its mouth opened to reveal a set of fierce pointed teeth and breath that reeked of rotten meat.

Vir stood frozen in place. Only when the demon stopped, towering over him, did his lips somehow regain the power of movement. He spoke very, very quickly.

"My name is Vir Cotto, diplomatic attaché to Ambassador Londo Mollari of the Centauri Republic. My name is Vir

Cotto, diplomatic attaché to Ambassador Londo Mollari of
the Centauri Republic. My name—"

Elric created an illusion of himself standing on the catwalk
above Vir. He visualized the illusion speaking, giving it voice.
"Stop program."

The demon vanished.

"You don't frighten easily," Elric said through his illusion.
While Vir's attention was fixed on his image, Elric dissolved
the false wall of the corridor, stepped out behind Vir.

"I work for Ambassador Mollari," Vir said. "After a while,
nothing bothers you."

Elric dissolved his image in a flash of fire and spoke now
with his own voice. "What does your master want from me?"

Vir jumped at the sound of Elric beside him. Yet he quickly
recovered. There was more to this fool than his foolishness.
"My employer requests an audience."

"I'm sorry," Elric said, his tone modulated to convey he
was not sorry at all. "Neither I nor my brothers *do* private au-
diences. We have nothing more to say to anyone on this side
of the galactic rim." If their purpose in gathering here had
been unclear to any, it would remain so no longer.

Vir smiled and rubbed his thumb against index and middle
fingers. "Aha. But he's willing to pay." Londo's mind-set had
contaminated his servant.

"Money is also irrelevant. Where we are going, it will do
us no good."

"Let me put this another way. If I go back without a yes, the
personal consequences will be profoundly unfortunate."

"And if you try to force us to walk where we do not choose
to walk, the consequences will even be more unfortunate."
Elric turned away and started down the corridor.

"Excuse me. Could I at least get a name," Vir said.

Elric stopped and faced him. "Elric." He paused for effect.
"There is an old saying. Do not try the patience of wizards,
for they are subtle and quick to anger. Do not come again, Vir

Cotto." He walked away, satisfied with the encounter. Vir would deliver their message, and Londo would refuse to accept the rebuff. His ambitions would not be so easily denied.

As Fed and Beel manipulated Vir back through Down Below, Elric retreated to his private room, little more than a utility closet with a sleeping pallet. His duties were not ended, yet the throbbing in his head was growing stronger, and he could not let the others see him like this. He cursed his weakness.

He lay on the pallet and accessed the security cameras in the casino. Cameras were numerous there, to watch for cheating, so he could observe nearly anything he wanted.

The casino created a comforting, intimate atmosphere with dim background lighting and soft music. Occasional bright lights emphasized various areas. Glowing bands of white ran along the circumferences of the gaming tables, while brilliant columns of blue marked the way to the wheel of fortune. A bar surrounded by a cluster of tables provided a place for refreshment. Among the many patrons sampling the entertainments, Londo sat at one end of the bar.

Carvin entered. Dressed in her Centauri silks, she caught Londo's attention immediately. Londo's appetite for power was followed closely by his appetite for beautiful women.

She settled herself at a high-stakes poker table, opening her purse and pouring a pile of chips out onto the table. Before a new game began, he downed his drink, slipped off of his stool, and approached her.

Elric accessed the camera over the dealer's shoulder.

"My dear lady, you must be new to Babylon 5. I would remember if I had ever seen someone of your incredible beauty before." He thought himself charming, this butcher of Narns.

She smiled. "Yes. Thank you."

He took her hand, laying his on top. "I am Londo Mollari. As ambassador to Babylon 5, allow me to officially welcome you."

"Carvin," she said.

He released her hand, sat down beside her. "An unusual name. You are alone, my dear?"

"Not anymore."

He laughed. "It is fortuitous, our meeting. Some of the clientele here, they prey on tourists. I can protect you."

"I would much prefer companionship to protection."

Londo inclined his head, clearly enchanted. "As would I. Your accent is curious. Where are you from, if I may ask?"

"I was raised by a Human." Though Carvin was young, she handled herself well.

"Ah. That explains your delightfully direct manner. We Centauri play far too many games between men and women."

"I've always found sex far too enjoyable to postpone with games." She picked up one of her chips, ran her thumb over it in a circular motion. "Yet games, too, have their place. They are a great measure of character. I can tell by gambling with a man whether I'd enjoy having sex with him."

The dealer was beginning a new game, and Carvin tossed in her ante while Londo tried to get his mouth to close.

"Will you play?" Carvin asked.

Londo roused himself. "By all means, dear lady."

"I'm glad," she said. "But I must tell you, I'm no lady."

Five players were in the game. The first few hands passed uneventfully. Carvin bet heavily and lost. Londo bet more modestly, folding each time before Carvin. He had to keep rechecking his cards, unable to concentrate.

Then Londo seemed to get a good hand, raising several times, until only he and Carvin remained in the game.

Londo pushed a stack of chips into the center of the table, raising a hundred credits. "And what kind of gambler do you prefer?"

As he drew his hand back, she brushed hers against it. "The kind who is fearless." She pushed a pile of chips to the center, raising by two hundred.

Vir came up behind Londo, his timing nearly perfect. "I should have known. Here I am risking my life for you, and you're off—being you!"

"Vir! Never sneak up on someone playing poker. How many times have I told you that?"

Vir raised his hands in a placating gesture, bowing slightly. "I know. I'm sorry. I'm just a little rattled right now. I need to talk to you, Londo. I have news, on a matter you were eager to pursue."

"What, now? I am in the middle of—" Londo studied him. "At last! You are as slow as a Narn ordered to fetch the whip."

"Hey!" another player said. "Are you playing or not?"

Londo looked longingly from the large stack of chips in the center of the table to Carvin, then back to the chips, then back to Carvin. "I must fold, dear lady. Affairs of state—the type that are rather less entertaining, I'm afraid. I hope that we may play again sometime."

"I would enjoy that," Carvin said.

Londo stood, took her hand, and kissed it. Vir's eyes widened as he saw the signet ring on her finger. It carried the rune for solidarity, the same rune that had been prominently displayed in the hallway Down Below. He had made the connection, as he was intended to do. Part of an idea had been planted. If the Shadows continued with the same strategy they had used in the past, they would provide the other part of the idea.

Vir pulled Londo anxiously away from the table. Within a few minutes, Londo would be forming a new scheme for obtaining the mages' blessing. Londo would raise the stakes, and Elric would have his excuse to retaliate.

Everything was going according to plan. Elric released a heavy breath and brought his hand to his temple. That cavity of darkness in his skull pushed outward, pressing at the backs of his eyes, at his forehead. The pain pounded stronger with each beat of his heart, as if a great darkness would burst full-blown from his skull.

He must monitor Londo closely. And very soon now he must arrange his meeting with John Sheridan. And then he and Morden must face each other.

But all that could wait a few minutes. Just a few. Until the pain passed.

—— chapter 10 ——

The customs agent on Thenothk 4 opened the sample case with the FTL relay. Galen looked across the spaceport's vast lobby of black stone, feigning disinterest, though adrenaline was pumping through his system. The tech echoed his anxiety.

The agent, a skeletal alien of a species Galen had never seen before, gave the relay a cursory examination, closed the case, and passed them on. He had a long line of passengers to check. Blaylock picked up the sample case and his suitcase, and Galen followed with his valise.

The lobby was busy with activity. The port seemed understaffed and overwhelmed by the number of beings passing in and out. Galen accessed his sensors, scanned various frequencies, searching for well-defined areas of static. Blaylock walked beside him across the lobby, head turning casually from side to side. Blaylock nodded subtly toward a far corner. At the upper end of the infrared band, Galen found a large area obscured by static. A cluster of Shadows.

Suddenly the idea that they could come here, could gather information without being discovered, seemed ridiculous. They kept walking, two businessmen anxious for wartime profits. The gravity was slightly heavier here than on Soom, making Galen's feet drag. With each step he expected someone to denounce them, to demand that they stop.

Galen glanced at the many beings that surrounded them,

telling himself that among all these, they would be overlooked. Blaylock had stressed that they would have the best
chance of success if they avoided any conjuries that might be
detected. By this he meant messages, illusions, shields, or
weapons. But the truth was, they didn't know how many of
their conjuries could be detected by the Shadows. And even if
they cast no spells, they constantly radiated mage energy that
could well be noticed. Now Galen understood why Blaylock
had said their visit here would be brief.

Blaylock had stressed the use of probes. Since the microscopic devices utilized a more conventional technology, if
they were discovered, they would not betray the presence of
mages. Already he and Blaylock had planted them on many
of the ship's passengers, including Rabelna Dorna, and Blaylock had skillfully slipped them onto several of the spaceport
employees.

The two of them came out of the port onto a narrow street,
towering buildings surrounding them on all sides. The noise
was terrific—like a thousand stet-hammers breaking through
metacrete. Great engines roared, metal screeched on metal.
The sour-smelling air seemed to become lodged in his throat,
and Galen started coughing.

"Breathe lightly," Blaylock said. "The air is filled with
poisons."

As Galen struggled to bring his breathing under control, he
studied the area. He knew it was afternoon, but he could not
find the sun. Plumes of smoke rose into the sky, creating a
black haze that made it seem like twilight.

A new wing for the port was being built to their right, the
source of much of the noise. To their left, an oversized lift was
negotiating its way out of the port and onto the narrow street.
It carried a massive energy generator, its sharp silvery edges
standing out against the dark buildings.

The streets were busy with traffic and filled with many different species: Drakh, Streib, Wurt, and in smaller numbers,

Humans, Centauri, Drazi, Pak'ma'ra. There were several species he couldn't identify at all. In the doorway of the building across the street, Galen caught a glimpse of static. Another up the street, moving away from them. Two more beyond that. Galen realized the impossibility of their task. One Shadow had nearly destroyed them before. This place was filled with them.

Rabelna Dorna came out of the port several doors away and headed off down the street, looking as if she knew where she was going.

"I will follow her," Blaylock said, handing Galen his suitcase and keeping the sample case. "Go to the hotel. Wait for me there."

He strode away before Galen had a chance to reply.

Galen glanced quickly at the Shadows, at the other pedestrians on the street. No one seemed to take an interest in either him or Blaylock.

Blaylock would want him to use the time to work on the spell for listening to the Shadows. And he would, no matter how much he wanted to avoid it. But he had something else to do first.

The port city was vast, and was filled with energies, many of types Galen had never seen before. He scanned slowly, searching for the energy characteristic of a mage. He detected his own, of course, and Blaylock's. Yet beyond that, he could not be sure. The energies he sensed were strange, and powerful, and he could not easily eliminate them to discover whether subtler mage energy lurked beneath. If it was present, he would have to do a much more detailed scan to find it. He put his sensors to work on the job, knowing it could take days, and even then the results would likely be inconclusive. Yet one way or another, Galen must know if Elizar was here. And if he was, no matter how many Shadows protected him, he could not be allowed to live.

The hotel was fifteen blocks away. Galen would walk there,

and plant as many probes along the way as he could. Though he had his own reason for coming to the rim, he would do everything he could to help Blaylock and the mages, as he'd promised. Fed had said it was a suicide mission, and he was right. Blaylock knew it; that was why he'd brought the relay, so that any information they gained could reach the mages, even if they could not. Galen was at peace with that; it was the only thought, lately, that brought him any peace. He had hoped for an end to this, and Thenothk would most likely provide it. But he was determined that, if there was any way it could be accomplished, Elizar's end would come before his.

As he started down the street, a ship came in for a landing at the port, poorly maintained engines screaming at the effort of deceleration. The planet seemed to mount an endless assault against the senses. Clouds of haze and fumes drifted down the city canyons. Construction was under way everywhere, confirming what G'Leel had told him about the city's rapid growth. The roads formed a chaotic maze, intersecting at odd angles. New buildings sometimes blocked off entire streets. In other places, roads curled in on themselves and simply ended. There seemed no plan to it, or if there was a plan, it was complex and well hidden. Grand, expensive structures stood beside squat, seemingly abandoned ones. Factories were mixed with residences, businesses with lurid entertainments. Along the way, Galen saw few Shadows. Their concentration was sparse, and they seemed to pass undetected by most. Yet he had a feeling more were here. They liked to remain hidden.

With a growing sense of unease, Galen at last reached the hotel. Inside, it was an island of quiet. In the desire to portray them as well-to-do businessmen, Blaylock had booked them adjoining rooms in one of the more expensive establishments. Galen checked in and went up to his room. He was surprised to find that it was tiny, barely fitting a bed and desk and a miniature bathroom. Space was at a premium here.

In its adrenaline-heightened state, the tech raced with anxious energy. He put the suitcases to one side, found the temperature control, turned it up. The small space made it all the more apparent that there was no avoiding what he must now do. He had a task, the same task he had faced every day since their journey to the rim had begun, and this time he must not put it aside until it was completed. He must no longer resist the memories, must not break away no matter how difficult the work became. If they were to know the Shadows' plans for the mages, including Elric and the others on Babylon 5, they must be able to decode the Shadows' communications.

He pulled the scarf from his pocket, ran his fingers over the small bundle.

To keep you warm, she said. She grabbed the scarf and wrapped it around his neck, her subtle essence enveloping him. She leaned back, biting her lip. *Quite handsome.*

Did you weave this yourself?

She rested her head against his shoulder. *Of course.*

Does that mean there's a spell woven into it?

That's for you to unravel.

He sat on the bed, eyes closed, and hunched over the scarf. He forced his fingers, stitch by stitch, down its edge. It was a thought of hers, frozen in time, given to him.

He had already recorded the pattern, yet for some reason he persisted in touching the scarf, as if it held additional information that the recording did not, some essence of hers, something that remained. Yet there was nothing, nothing but an abstract pattern. He had tried to break down the complex sequence of bumps, plateaus, and valleys, yet the sequence seemed random, chaotic, just as the Shadow signals had been.

The simplest way to understand her code, of course, would be to guess what spell or message she had woven into it, and then to search for correspondences between that and the scarf's pattern. He had not wanted to think of her, though, or of what message she might have left him. But now he had no choice.

Beside him, her body pressed against his. Her presence, her smell enveloped him. She leaned back, biting her lip. *Quite handsome.*

His name. She might have included his name.

He searched for different ways she might have encoded it within the weaving. She could have used the numerical equivalents to the letters: seven for *G*, one for *A*. She could have used the pattern of the rune he had chosen to represent him. She could have translated his name into different languages. She could have used one of many complex codes that had been developed by various species over the years, or a code of her own. Time passed. He did not find it.

He must search for another word.

The scarf clenched in his hands, he stood, shivering. He turned up the temperature control as far as it would go, then stumbled back to the bed.

The word he didn't want to look for, of course, the word that he had never wanted to look for, was *love*. The word she had said to him as she lay dying. The word he had never said to her.

When he searched for patterns connected to that word, he found them everywhere. The word, in different forms, was embedded throughout the scarf, on the small scale and the large, one pattern intersecting the next.

The scarf did not hold some super-complex code, as he had thought. It held many small, simple patterns woven one on top of the other. He didn't know how he'd failed to see it. When he'd sat beside her in the training hall on Soom, when he'd examined her shield, the most striking thing about it had been its simplicity. It had been the order and elegance of her thought that had first drawn him to her.

Now that he understood how one word of her message had been encoded into the scarf, it was fairly simple to find the rest. As with the single word, the entire message was repeated again and again, in countless different patterns. The words revealed themselves to him one at a time, until the entire message at last emerged, a communication from the past to the present, from the dead to the living, brought finally to light in a different universe from that in which it had been created. Her breath whispered in his ear.

Love need not be spoken to be felt.

Galen looked down at the scarf clutched in his hand. He seemed to see it from a great distance, this dirty tan weaving, this insignificant piece of cloth. She excused him for his failing, excused him for being the repressed, inadequate, unfit Human being he was.

How had he shown her his love?

He had failed to prevent her fatal wound, and as she lay dying, instead of reassuring her with loving words, he had argued with her.

Her chest had labored to draw in air, to find in those last moments the breath to speak, to reassure *him*, to declare her love.

And then she had gone.

Her message made no difference. She might have forgiven him, but he would never forgive himself.

He saw her again in death, her face slack, tilted to one side. Her lips were slightly parted, her grey eyes blank and cold. The partially healed cut ran down the right side of her forehead into her thin brow. Her skin carried an odd shininess, a sense of artifice.

I could not have lived, her voice whispered to him, *knowing that I did not protect you.*

He forced himself to withhold the cry that wanted to escape, to contain the furious energy that burned through him. He was shaking. But he could not bring down the fire. It might be detected. He retreated into a mind-focusing exercise, then another, then another, recoiling from that place, that time, withdrawing from those feelings, contracting into the dark, secret center of himself.

Gradually he realized that he had accessed her files and was applying his new insight to the translation of her spells. His mind worked mechanically, dispassionately. Hours passed. The room turned dark.

Many of her hand movements, he found, could be grouped into separate, recurring subpatterns, clarifying the structure of the spells. The translations became easier, more straightforward.

The main problem he still faced was the fact that many of her spells took place over extended periods of time, arising from a series of motions. His spells were cast in an instant, through a single equation. He was not sure how the time factor translated into his language.

If it was irrelevant, as it seemed might be true from some of her simpler spells, then his equation should be the equivalent of all her hand movements performed at once. If an index finger of the left hand made a particular motion, then, and a few seconds later the index finger of the right hand mirrored that motion, would those two terms cancel each other out? He thought, perhaps, they would.

As he worked with the spell for Shadow communication, he found more and more terms canceling each other out, the translation growing simpler and simpler. He thought he must have made a mistake, for at the end he was suddenly left with only a single term in his spell. And oddly, the spell was identical to one of the one-term equations he'd discovered as they'd traveled to the rim.

He had derived that new one-term equation from a progression involving several different types of spells, which made its effect difficult to guess. The progression had included the spell to send a message, though, as well as the more complex electron incantation they used to engage in long-distance conversation. So it was possible the spell might involve communication.

But how could such a complex signal as the Shadows' be decoded with such a simple spell? Of course, it was simple only in his language, not in hers, and probably not in the languages of other mages. He went back over his translation, checking each step. If the time factor was irrelevant, his findings were correct. If it was not, he didn't know how to translate the spell.

He had thought, after conjuring the one-term equation of destruction, that any spell with only a single term would prove unstable, not a complete spell at all. If that was true, then this spell could be as dangerous as the other.

Even if it worked as her spell had worked, they would be in great danger. She'd had to be within three feet of their enemies in order to tap into their signal. And once she had, she'd been overwhelmed by its power.

The image came to him. Her body, lying twisted on the floor. Her mouth stretching wide, so wide that her head quivered. The muscles on her neck writhing. And the words of the Shadows driving out of her with the force of possession.

Even when they'd fled, she'd remained in the grip of the signal. Galen had feared it would never release her. When at last she'd come back to herself, his relief had been so great . . . it had been something he didn't want to think about— how much she meant to him, how quickly she'd transformed his life, and how in losing her, he would lose everything.

Galen shot to his feet, began pacing back and forth beside the bed. The room was deep in shadow. It was late. Blaylock had been gone for more than four hours. Where was he?

Galen scanned for mage energy, but could isolate only his own. He visualized the equation to access the probes he'd planted. In his mind's eye a menu listed them. He selected first the one on Rabelna Dorna's hand. She was in a restaurant, eating dinner. Galen saw nothing of Blaylock. He went from one probe to the next, looking for Blaylock, searching for any useful information, anything to take his mind from himself, from the scarf still clutched in his hand.

He saw the inside of a factory producing delicate, curved metal devices. One of the workers fit the fragile formation, little more than a few sculpted strands of metal, over his head. On each side, it ran from cheek to temple to forehead, and down to the nape of the neck. The worker drooped his head to the side, hung his tongue out of his mouth, and laughed.

Galen saw a warehouse where crates marked as Centauri in origin were being filled with weapons and prepared for shipping to Centauri Prime. In a dark room, he heard the Narn from the ship discussing with another whether their faction might at last gain control of the Kha'Ri and lead their people in the extermination of the Centauri. In a bar, he heard talk of war, and of profits to be made.

The bar reminded him of G'Leel and the rest of the crew of the *Khatkhata*. Galen wondered whether they might be on Thenothk. Their ship had made several runs here in the past. When they'd crossed paths on Zafran 8, Galen had planted probes on them, and an FTL relay aboard their ship, so that the probes could be accessed even from a great distance. He hadn't tried to access those probes, though, since the convocation.

At that time, they'd been on Thenothk, unloading a cargo of telepaths in sleeper tubes. The purpose of the telepaths remained unclear, except for one, who was to be Elizar's personal weapon. Elizar had said as much, when he'd come aboard to claim a telepath for his own.

The images of Galen's fantasy arose again: Elizar turning and seeing him, that angular, arrogant face filling with fear. And then, Galen's hands covered in blood, clutching the broken threads of Elizar's tech.

Galen hadn't dared to access the *Khatkhata* probes again, to see Elizar continuing with his life as if nothing had happened. Instead, Galen had given Elric his key, so Elric could access the relay on the ship and, through it, the probes on the crew. After a few days, Elric had told him that contact had been lost. The relay and the probes must have become separated, or else the probes had been destroyed.

If the probes were still intact and they were near enough, Galen could access them directly, without the relay. From his menu, he selected the probes on the Narn crew, and he was surprised to see their images spread out before him.

The crew was in a bar, of course. That seemed to be where they spent most of their time. The room was dimly lit, with a low ceiling and rough, exposed beams. Most of the crew looked fairly advanced in their drinking. They were hanging over each other, gold and black spotted heads swaying unsteadily, as they chanted one of their endless drinking games. They made obscene profits transporting goods to the rim and seemed to have little idea how to spend the money, except in drinking and extravagant self-indulgence.

Second-in-command of the *Khatkhata*, G'Leel sat apart from them with her back to the bar, quiet and watchful. In the past, she would have joined in.

Captain Ko'Vin stumbled up to her, and Galen quickly accessed his Narn translation program. As Ko'Vin spoke, the translation appeared in his mind's eye.

You could drink those fools under the table. Come on, let's make some money.

I have enough money, G'Leel said.

This sobriety thing is getting really annoying, Ko'Vin said. *You didn't find religion, did you?* He leaned close. *What you need is a little love to loosen you up.*

You're starting to look pretty repulsive, she said.

Ko'Vin made a dismissive, untranslatable sound, and lurched to the bar for a refill.

G'Leel had been a valuable source of information before.

Perhaps she'd learned more since they'd last spoken. Galen located the probes. They were only a quarter mile away.

Isabelle would say that G'Leel's presence here, at this time, was evidence of an order to the universe: the universe had put G'Leel here in order to help him. But he found no special significance in G'Leel's presence. They had first questioned her because she was transporting people and materials to Thenothk. The fact that she was here now was a logical consequence.

Isabelle had convinced G'Leel to give them information. She had known, somehow, that this drunken, mercenary Narn would help them. She had believed that G'Leel could transcend herself.

Just as she'd believed Galen could transcend himself.

That's why I was put in your life. You have opened yourself to another. That was the first. Next you will open yourself to yourself. Finally, you will open yourself to God. To his design.

He could not do what she asked. He could not open himself to anyone again—not another, not himself, most especially not a god who would take her away from him as part of some cosmic plan. He was who he was, and he would continue to fail her, even now.

The only way to maintain control was not to open up but to close down, to hold his words and his actions within. If he opened himself, he knew what would come out. Destruction. Galen crossed his arms over his chest, shivering. The need to act was becoming overwhelming.

He stopped his pacing. He could not stay here, with the endless thoughts, the relentless memories. He'd fled all the way to the rim, and still they haunted him. He wadded the scarf into a ball, threw it against the wall. He would find G'Leel, and see what she could tell him.

He opened the door to the adjoining room, left a note in the language of the Soom telling Blaylock where he would be.

Then he left, slamming the door behind him.

* * *

"Then you are familiar with the techno-mages, hmm?" Londo asked John Sheridan.

Londo stood at the window in John's office, hands clasped behind his back, surveying the station's vast gardens as if they were his own personal property. Elric watched through a probe Alwyn had managed to plant on John's neck.

"Only by name and reputation," John said. "I've never seen one before. Wasn't really sure they even existed before now."

After Vir had explained his failure to set up an audience with the mages, Londo hadn't wasted a moment to come up with a new strategy. He had not bothered to thank Vir for the attempt, or for pulling him away from a poker game with a techno-mage—a situation that could only have ended in his financial ruin. The idea that the mages had refused to see him while at the same time secretly sending a beautiful representative to cheat him at poker had offended his Centauri pride, and he was more determined than ever to have his way.

"Ah." Londo turned away from the window and approached John, who was sitting behind his desk. "Most unfortunate. On my world we had considerable experience with them. They can be a source of great trouble, unless one knows how to deal with them."

"And you do?" John said.

"Of course. With so many here at one time, and you being new to Babylon 5, and your . . . well, your inexperience in such matters, no offense—"

John tapped one hand against the other. "None taken."

"It occurred to me that I could be of some small assistance in averting trouble."

John leaned forward. "And what would you get out of it?" He was no fool.

"Oh, a clear conscience and a peaceful sleep." Londo smiled, the smile of a man who had not yet discovered that he

was damned and would never again have a clear conscience
or a peaceful sleep.

Elric realized someone was knocking at the door of his
closet-sized room. They must have news for him, news too
sensitive to be delivered by communication. He had lain down
with the idea that it would be for only a few minutes. Now he
didn't know if he could rise again. His head felt as if it would
explode if he moved. "A moment," he said.

John was speaking. He'd come around his desk to face
Londo. "Earth wants more information before letting them
go, so this is as good an opportunity as any. I'll set up a
meeting. Nine o'clock?"

"I'll be there. I'm pleased, Captain, that our first discus-
sions have gone so smoothly. I'm looking forward to many
more in the future." Londo turned, raising a hand as he
walked out of the office. "Until later, then."

Looking after Londo, John spoke under his breath. "What
do the techno-mages have that he wants so badly?"

Elric forced his body into motion. His limbs felt stiff, un-
coordinated. His forehead was throbbing. He straightened,
determined to show no sign of weakness, and opened the
door. Carvin stood there, her lips sucked inward, hands
twisted anxiously together. She said nothing.

"What is it?" he demanded.

Her lips parted. "Ing-Radi has collapsed."

G'Leel's head turned slowly as she scanned the dimly lit
bar from the vantage point of her stool. When her gaze moved
toward Galen, he took a drink of his beer, pretending not to
notice. At first she did not recognize him, but then her gaze
returned to him, and Galen was gratified by the stunned
recognition that arose on her face. The simplest tricks were
often the best.

She stood, pushed past several of her crew, and approached
the table where he sat. As when he had last seen her, she wore

a sleeveless tunic, pants, and gloves all of black leather, with a gun case fastened at her waist. Her gold and black spotted arms were sharply defined with muscle. As she walked, each shoulder moved forward in turn, her posture stiff, erect. She stopped before him, and he noticed the pale scar across her nose.

"It's you, isn't it." She spoke loudly, to be heard over the noise of the other patrons. "From Zafran 8."

He put down his glass. "Hello, G'Leel."

She glanced back at her crewmates, who were passionately engaged in yet another drinking game. She pulled up a chair beside him. "What happened to you?"

"I'm sorry?"

"You—look different."

"I don't— Perhaps, the hair."

G'Leel shook her head, dismissing the idea. "Where is your friend? The other techno-mage."

Galen realized it had been a mistake to come.

"She told my future. She convinced me to talk to you. You never told me your names, either of you."

"She is dead."

G'Leel's red eyes flicked away from him. "I'm sorry." They sat in uneasy silence for a few moments. "She was wise," G'Leel said.

"She was killed by someone you know." Galen bit out the words. "A mage named Elizar. He came aboard your ship to collect a telepath." Anger was rising up in him, irresistible and overwhelming, and the tech raced in response. He hadn't been able to release its energy, and it wanted to be released, it needed to be, if he was to retain control.

"I remember him. But how did you—"

He fixed her with his gaze. "Have you seen him since?"

She hesitated a moment, taken aback. "No."

"Have you heard anything of him, or of a mage allied to the Shadows?"

"No."

"He brought a Centauri on your ship. An apprentice mage, named Tilar. Do you know anything of him?"

"No."

"What about the telepath? Do you know who he is? Where he might be found?"

"No." Her golden face was wary, uncertain.

Galen forced himself to break off. He took a drink, willed his pounding heart to slow. She didn't know. She didn't know what he needed to know. He crossed his arms over his chest, holding tightly to control.

"Your eyes have been haunting my dreams," she said. "They look down on me and accuse me of not doing enough."

Galen turned on her. "And have you done enough?"

"I've been listening, and watching, since I met you."

"And what have you seen?"

She released a breath. "The last time I was here, I met a man in a bar who claimed to be a telepath. I don't know if he said it just to impress females, or if it was true. He said he worked in the City Center. That's the biggest building in the city. It houses the government. A lot of the Drakh work there. Security is very tight. You aren't allowed inside without a pass."

"Where is this building?"

"I can't explain how to get there. I could show you, though."

His anger was slowly fading, though the restless energy of the tech remained. He was tired of holding it in, tired of being cold. "What else can you tell me?"

"There's something strange going on down there. When I saw you before, we were carrying some demolition equipment for Joncorp. They're using it to destroy their factory, which is next to the City Center. They're just finishing up now. The thing is, I know a Narn who worked on the construction crew for that factory. The place was state-of-the-art, and it was built only two years ago. I thought maybe the city forced them out to expand the Center. But my construction friend just told me he's been hired to rebuild the factory for Joncorp in exactly the same place, to the same design. Construction is going to start soon. So why would they tear it down?"

"To keep busy?"

G'Leel smiled. "I didn't think you had a sense of humor."

"I save it for special occasions."

She leaned toward him, and her red eyes glistened in the dim light. "I know where Z'ha'dum is. A system called Alpha Omega. Drakh come and go from there, perhaps a few others. I don't know anyone personally who's been there. I think the Shadows live there, just like you said. I think they direct what goes on here."

"The Shadows are here as well. You cannot see them."

G'Leel looked around the bar. "In here, now?"

"I see none. But my ability to detect them may be imperfect."

"That's reassuring." Her gloved hands tapped nervously against the table. "Everything here is focused on a coming war. The growth, the activity—it's got to start soon." She looked at him expectantly, hoping her information was sufficient.

Though she had failed to tell him the one thing he wanted to know, Galen tried to find the right words to thank her, tried to remember what had been said to her before. "You've been a great help. The information is very useful."

"But what can you do with it? What can I do, against all of them?" Her hand closed around his arm. "You showed me a vision of my parents, on Narn, being attacked. How can I stop that from coming true?"

"If I knew the future, and I knew how to change it, don't you think I would have done so?"

She released him, her lips tight. "When I heard about the destruction of our outpost in Quadrant 37, I wanted to return home, to defend us from any threats. But I thought maybe I could do more good here. From what you and . . ." Her pause extended, her thought hovering in the air, waiting for the word required, the word that would allow the thought to continue.

He must say her name. "Isabelle."

G'Leel nodded. "Isabelle made me realize that I might do the most good here, if I could gather information and share it with others."

"You have done well." Galen felt himself growing distant from G'Leel, from this place, from this time.

"But why would the Shadows attack Narn at all? We've done nothing to them. The Centauri are the ones who have always threatened us."

"There is a warehouse here," Galen said, "where weapons are made. They are loaded into crates indicating that they were manufactured on Centauri Prime. I believe they will be sent to the Centauri."

"The Shadows are sending arms to the Centauri? Then they've allied against us."

"It appears so."

An expression passed over her face that Galen couldn't identify. "I have to stop them. Let me help you. You're going to attack them?"

"I am here to gather information," Galen said.

"In preparation for an attack. Where are the rest of your kind?"

"They will not come. I am with just one other."

"Two of you. To gather information. What good is that?"

"It may save us."

"Save *you*."

"Yes."

"And what about us?"

Galen said nothing. The answer was obvious.

"You drew me into this fight. You led me to believe we

could win. And now you're just stepping aside?" Her red eyes demanded an answer, but he had none.

"Those weapons have to be stopped," she said. "If the Centauri don't get those shipments, they may not have the stomach to attack us. This warehouse—where is it?"

"I will tell you, when we have the information we need."

G'Leel gathered the lapel of his coat in her gloved fist. "You'll tell me now," she said, her breath hot against his skin.

"If you move against the warehouse and are captured, you could reveal our presence. No one must know that we are here."

"I could reveal your presence right now," she whispered.

"But you won't. You need the information I possess."

G'Leel's gun barrel pressed into Galen's chest. "You'll tell me now."

Energy surged through Galen. He felt a driving need to attack, to strike back at this threat. Yet at the same time, something within him hoped that her finger would tighten on the trigger, and the weapon would fire, and the end he had sought would finally come.

With fierce focus he forced the screen in his mind's eye to remain blank. "I am under the direction of another. I've already told you much more than I should. I must get his permission before I can share the information."

A movement from the corner of his eye caught his attention, and Galen turned his head. Blaylock was sitting a few tables away, a large dinner spread before him.

G'Leel followed his gaze. "Is that him? How long has he been there?"

"I don't know. But try to make a good impression."

She slipped the gun back into its case, sat back in her chair. Briskly she straightened Galen's coat. "As good as new."

Galen began a mind-focusing exercise, desperately trying to regain some sense of calm. "Let me speak to him alone. I will come to you as soon as I'm able."

"In two days we leave again." She stood. "If you don't find me, I'll find you."

"I'll count on that," he said.

G'Leel returned to her crewmates, each shoulder moving forward in turn with her stride. She gave a short nod as she passed Blaylock's table.

Galen took a moment to slow his breathing, to compose himself, then joined Blaylock. He broke off the exercise, knowing Blaylock would demand his full attention. "I'm sorry I left the hotel."

"You indulge your emotions. They rule you." Blaylock pushed the platter of food to him and switched to the language of the Soom. "Here. Eat. We'll discuss your disobedience later. At length."

Galen spoke in the language of his home as well. "Where is yours?"

"I break my fast only once a day. Tell me why you trust this Narn."

"Do you want to know what she told me?"

"I heard all. I arrived shortly after you. I'm not asking whether I should trust her. I have already made that determination. I want to know why you trust her."

"She provided useful information before."

"Why did you trust her before?"

"We observed her."

"Yes?"

Galen shook his head. "I had no idea whether she could be trusted. But . . . Isabelle knew. Somehow she knew that G'Leel would help us."

"Wise is the mage who trusts in those who know better than him." Blaylock's gaze remained on Galen, making sure his point was taken.

Galen got the message. He was to obey. But as seemed common with Blaylock, this conversation was about more than one subject. "You've questioned my judgment of people since we began this trip. I admit it is a weakness of mine. But how did you know?"

"Elizar. It was obvious that you trusted and admired him."

"You didn't trust him?"

"Elizar seemed to me to prefer the image of doing good over the actual doing of it. He believed the greatness of our order dependent on how much power we wield, and he desired the greatest power for himself. But it is not the magnitude of power that matters. Men can build weapons more powerful than we are. Our greatness lies in knowing when and where to apply that power. In the finesse with which that power is applied. In the sacred intimacy with which we are connected to that power." Blaylock extended a finger. "Eat."

Galen dug into the food, which was some sort of shredded meat dish. "Can we tell G'Leel what she wants to know?"

"Once we learn what we need. Then you may tell her."

Galen realized he had one piece of news that might at least partially redeem him in Blaylock's eyes. "I translated the spell. I can't be sure of the accuracy, though, without a test."

Blaylock's thin, dour face contracted in a way that somehow suggested pleasure. The expression seemed odd on him. "It is too dangerous to test. We may be detected. We may well have only one opportunity to use it."

"In my language, the spell reduced to a one-term equation, like the spell of destruction. My thought has been that these one-term equations may be only partial spells, and that they may carry great, unstable energies. This one may carry power similar to the spell of destruction."

Blaylock nodded. "You have checked your work?"

"Yes."

"Then we must try it. It offers our best chance of success. And you must be ready, if it goes ill, to do everything in your power to stop it. I have searched what datasystems I could penetrate, and I have learned some of the Shadows' strengths and bases. But there are no files relating to our order, or any

plans they may have for us. Tonight, I believe, may be our
only opportunity to gain the information we require."

"Perhaps you should look at my work."

"I don't have time to learn both your spell language and
Isabelle's. I trust in your skill, Galen, in your intelligence and
your thoroughness. If I did not, you would not be here. It is
your discipline I find lacking."

The criticism angered Galen. He had obeyed the Circle, he
had upheld the Code, and she had paid the price. Wasn't that
enough? "I have followed the dictates of the Circle."

"And you must continue to do so. We face great danger
tonight. If we are to survive to pass our knowledge to the
others, we must be of one mind and one intent."

"I have sworn myself to this task."

"As you have sworn to kill Elizar?"

Galen leaned forward eagerly. "Have you found him?"

"Finding him is not our task."

His body was racing again, energy driving through him.
The images returned. Elizar's face, turned in fear. Elizar's
blood and tech. Galen looked down, and his raw hands closed
into fists. "Above all, we must find out as much as we can to
ensure the safety of the mages," he said.

When Blaylock did not respond, Galen raised his head.
Blaylock's eyes were narrowed on him. "You hold much inside. We all do. It is the way of our order. Secrecy. We all have
thoughts of things we must not do, thoughts of destruction. It
comes with having power. That is why obedience to the Code
is so important. To obey the Code we require control. To gain
control we require discipline. In discipline we do what we
must, whether we desire it or not. Those of us who follow the
ways of discipline reject emotions, desires, physical crav-
ings. We seek to purify ourselves, to attune ourselves not to
the flesh, but to the tech. Even then, discipline is never easy.
Why do you think so many follow my ways?"

"Because they respect you and they believe in—"

"No. Some follow me because they believe as I do, and for that I am gratified. But most follow me because they must. Without the daily scouring, without the fasting, without the meditation and repentance, the abstinence, the vigils, the sensory denial, the mortification, they would be unable to follow the Code."

"Elric taught that self-control, not self-denial, was the way."

"For some self-control is enough. For others the path is more difficult." Blaylock paused. "I would have to be blind not to see that you are in distress."

Galen looked down, forced his red, clenched hands to open, to lie flat against the table. "I prefer to deal with it myself."

Blaylock's response did not come for several moments, and when it did, his words seemed both a concession and a threat. "As is your right. As long as you do not fail."

—— chapter 11 ——

The meeting was not going at all as Elric had planned. He had intended to convince the captain that they meant no harm, to charm him with some magic. Elric carried several trinkets concealed on his person that would hold significance for John, and he had planned to produce one at the appropriate time. His anger was to have been directed solely at Londo, who hadn't even arrived yet. But here he stood in John Sheridan's office, nearly yelling.

"Captain, I insist neither I nor any of my clan represent any threat whatsoever to the station." The pounding in his head was unrelenting. And he was furious that he'd been required to answer the captain's summons when Ing-Radi lay dying. Gowen was attending her, and he was a skilled healer, but he remained inexperienced, and Ing-Radi's physiology was unknown to him. Elric could have guided him.

"So you say." John's tone was belligerent. Clearly, his frustration at the course of the conversation was quickly building toward anger. He came around his desk toward Elric. "You have to understand that when something like this comes to my attention, I have to look into it. And there are an awful lot of you here, over a hundred, according to security. And you refuse to tell EarthCentral where you're going?"

"We have a right to go where we wish, when we wish, with as many as we wish, without being harassed, questioned, or detained." Now he was yelling.

John took a deep breath. "I am not looking to cause you trouble. I would just like some questions answered, that's all."

Londo strolled into the spacious office, a drink in one hand. He hadn't even the courtesy to show up on time. Elric imagined the pleasure of throwing him into a roomful of angry Narns who knew what Londo had done in Quadrant 37.

"Sorry to be late, gentlemen," Londo said. "I was unavoidably detained. Matters of state, you understand."

Elric understood perfectly. John had agreed to set up the meeting an hour ago, and since then Londo had been madly searching for the smallest recording device he could find.

Londo set his drink down on a table against the wall, and with a clumsy sleight of hand set the one-inch-tall recording device beside it. He approached them. "I can tell from the sense of joy permeating the room that I was right to offer my services as a mediator."

Elric extended a finger toward Londo. "Is this the one who brought us to your attention?" he asked John.

"Only after I'd heard about your situation at my security briefing."

"Captain," Elric said, "you have been used. This—creature— has been seeking an audience with me since I arrived."

John turned toward Londo. "Is this true?"

Londo did a poor actor's imitation of outrage. "Absolutely not."

With a flourish Elric raised his hand, palm up. Had Londo been a true expert in techno-mages, he would have known better than to lie. The probes in the Down Below hallway had recorded Vir's visit, and it was a simple enough task to create a three-dimensional composite, a special humiliation for Londo. On his hand, Elric conjured a foot-tall image of Vir. It spoke. "My name is Vir Cotto, diplomatic attaché to Ambassador Londo Mollari of the Centauri Republic." He dissolved the composite recording to reflect a short jump in time, restored the image at a later spot. "My employer requests an audience," Vir said. Elric closed his hand, and Vir vanished.

Londo averted his gaze. He looked ill.

John's eyes narrowed on him. "You were saying?"

Londo struggled to recover his dignity. "Recording a conversation . . . a very low thing to do. But in the interest of good relations I am willing to forgive. I offer the hands of friendship." The butcher approached Elric, hands extended, palms down.

And here was the purpose of Londo's recording device. Following Centauri custom, Elric extended his own hands, palms up. He clasped Londo's forearms as Londo did the same. "And I accept," Elric said. "I assume that you would not take advantage of this gesture or misrepresent it as some sort of endorsement."

"Oh—of course not," Londo said. Still he had not learned. Which best served Elric's purpose.

In his mind's eye, Elric visualized magical fire bursting to life within Londo's recording device, the circuits overheating, melting. On the table against the wall, the device exploded with a flash and a puff of smoke.

Elric jerked Londo close and forced his words through clenched teeth. "A risky business, condemning my recording device while using one of your own."

Londo gasped. He looked as if he'd just awoken, as if he were seeing Elric for the first time, and the sight was not a pleasant one. "I can explain everything."

"I do not like being used," Elric said. "You must learn manners and respect. And from this moment on, you will." He shoved the butcher away, and Londo stumbled back, caught himself on a chair.

John's voice was harsh. "I think you should leave, Ambassador, before I decide to report your attempt to bug my office and send you back home on the slowest transport I can find."

Londo spread his hands before him. "Of course. My apologies." He turned and, with a glance toward the smoking device, made a quick exit.

That had gone perfectly. The mages now had every reason to strike at Londo, and Londo, in his anger, would want to strike back. He would turn to his powerful allies for assistance, and they would eagerly take advantage of the opportunity. Elric believed they had probably been anticipating it, just as he had.

Now he must repair his relationship with John. "You see how some seek to exploit us. I wish I could say he is an isolated case, but he is not."

John nodded. "I'm afraid we got off on the wrong foot. Could we start again?" Smoke lingered in the air, and John waved his hand at it. "Would you like to go for a walk?"

"Very well."

John led the way. Elric realized the throbbing in his head had lessened somewhat. He must make the most of this opportunity to win the captain over. The mages must not be detained. He and John came out into the Zocalo, the largest marketplace on Babylon 5, crowded with shoppers and stalls of merchandise.

"I apologize for that incident with Ambassador Mollari," John said, "but there are still some questions that I need answered—where you're going, what this group is all about."

Elric paused at one of the stalls to finger a wind chime made of hanging glass teardrops. He must draw attention to his hands, so that when he produced the particular item for John, the sleight of hand would create the greatest degree of surprise. "Captain, do you believe there is such a thing as magic?"

"When I was twelve, I used to sit in my dad's garden, the air filled with the smell of orange blossoms, watching the sky, dreaming of faraway places."

Elric betrayed no reaction to the mention of orange blossoms, but he was pleased. John had mentioned them in a message to his father, one of the many messages Elric had watched. An orange blossom, carefully preserved, was one of the objects he carried in his robe. He removed it from his pocket.

"Back then," John continued as they wound their way through the wares, "I think I believed in just about everything. Now, I don't know. I do think there are some things we don't understand. If we went back in time a thousand years and tried to explain this place to people"—he gave a soft laugh—"they could only accept it in terms of magic."

Elric picked up a crystal with the same hand that held the orange blossom concealed. "Then perhaps it is magic: the magic of the Human heart, focused and made manifest by technology. Every day you here create greater miracles than the burning bush."

John smiled. "Maybe. But God was there first, and he didn't need solar batteries and a fusion reactor to do it."

Elric enjoyed talking with him. It seemed ages since he had engaged in a simple conversation that did not involve death or Shadows. But of course the conversation was all about death and Shadows. The content was simply disguised. This man, as pleasant as he was, had the power to ruin their plan.

Elric tried, for a few moments, not to think about that, but simply to describe for this outsider the joys and wonders of technomancy, to which he had devoted his life. "We are dreamers, shapers, singers, and makers. We study the mysteries of laser and circuit"—he held up the crystal—"crystal and scanner. Holographic demons and invocations of equations. These are the tools we employ. And we know many things."

"Such as?"

"The true secrets. The important things. Fourteen words to make someone fall in love with you forever. Seven words to make them go without pain. How to say good-bye to a friend who is dying. How to be poor, how to be rich. How to rediscover dreams when the world has stolen them from you."

As he said the words, the realization came to him. At some point over the last few months, he had lost his dreams: his dream of the mages as he thought they had been, brave enough and sufficiently committed to good that they would fight the Shadows; his dream of growing old on Soom; his dream of watching Galen mature into a great mage. He had not even realized they had all been taken from him. Where they had been, there was only emptiness, like the emptiness that had once been Soom. And no spell could bring them back.

"There is a storm coming," Elric said. "A black and terrible storm. We would not have our knowledge lost, or used to ill purpose. From this place we will launch ourselves into the stars. With luck, you will never see our kind again in your lifetime." He paused for effect. He had said all he could. He hoped that it was enough. "I know you have your orders, Captain. Detain us, if you wish. But I cannot tell you where we're going. I can only ask you—to trust us."

Elric took John's hand, placed an object there, folded John's fingers over it, and walked off. John would expect it was the crystal. But when he opened his fingers, he would find something else.

Through the probe on John, Elric saw him lift the flower from his palm, turn it back and forth between his fingers.

"An orange blossom," John whispered to himself.

Elric hoped that he had made an ally. John was a good man living in dark times, and he would soon face some difficult decisions. Elric hoped, for the mages' sake, that he chose well.

Elric moved quickly toward Down Below, anxious to see Ing-Radi. He left the Zocalo behind, climbed down some steep access stairs, and entered the seldom-used passages that led to the restricted levels. They were poorly lit and narrower than the corridors above. He pressed the heel of his hand to his temple, trying to lessen the pain. He turned a corner, and there, a few feet down the passage, stood Morden.

He had known the meeting would come soon, but in the

moment he had forgotten. It was unlike him. He lowered his hand from his head.

Morden looked much as he had at the mages' convocation, where they had first met. He was a compact man in a well-tailored suit, his dark hair styled cleanly back. His hands were folded in front of him, and he smiled with a slight inclination of his head, revealing a row of perfect white teeth. "Elric."

On a silver chain about his neck, Morden wore the same round black volcanic glass he had worn before. It was an Anfran love stone, Elric had learned, acquired on one of Morden's archaeological digs and given to his wife as a wedding present. On the back, the side worn against the chest, was engraved the name of the Anfran star god, who regulated matters of love. The stone was believed to carry the good wishes of loved ones. It was the key to Morden. Unfortunately, Elric did not yet understand what secret he had locked away.

At first Elric had been inclined to think the worst of the Shadows' servant, to believe that Morden had asked his masters to kill his wife and child, who had died in the terrorist bombing of the Io jumpgate two years ago. If that was the case, then the necklace was a trophy. But as Elric had further researched Morden, he had come to believe that Morden had not encountered the Shadows until six months after his family's death.

Up until that point, he had been an archaeologist working on secret projects for EarthForce's New Technologies Division. He would discover ancient technologies, then work with engineers to exploit those technologies for Earth, mainly as weapons.

The records of Morden's work had been closed, and when Elric had finally obtained them, he'd been surprised to find that Morden had encountered Shadow technology three times in his career. The first had occurred on a planet in the Lanep system. The dig had uncovered fragments of an ancient space-ship utilizing a never-before-seen technology that mixed the biological and the mechanical. A Shadow ship. The incredible advantages of the organic technology had quickly been grasped, and engineers brought in. Morden's involvement had ended at that point, though the work at the site continued even now. The engineers were attempting to make use of the fragments in some way. The idea that Earth scientists would try to manipulate Shadow technology troubled Elric deeply. They could not possibly understand it; the results would very likely be catastrophic. And what little knowledge they might obtain from it could be even more dangerous. Most troubling was the location of the experiments: Lanep was uncomfortably close to the mages' hiding place.

Morden's second contact with Shadow technology had been on Mars, where an intact Shadow vessel had been found buried beneath the surface. Once it had been partially unearthed, the ship had sent out a signal, and a few days later, a second Shadow ship had arrived and used its powerful weaponry to finish the excavation. The two ships had flown off together. Yet a tracking device planted on the first ship by Morden and his colleagues had revealed its destination: a planet on the rim called Alpha Omega 3.

That was the site of Morden's third contact with Shadow technology. Unfortunately, Elric knew nearly nothing of this final expedition, except that it had ended in the explosion of the archaeological team's ship, the *Icarus*, and the alleged death of all aboard. The records had been removed completely from the system, existing only as hard copy in a government safe. Elric now believed it was on this third expedition, six months after the death of his wife and child, that Morden had made actual contact with the Shadows and had become their servant.

If that was the case, then perhaps the Shadows had bought him with the promise of revenge against the terrorists. As far as the official records showed, the perpetrators had never been captured. But that didn't mean they had not been caught privately, and killed. That would make the necklace a sign of remembrance and love. But how could that be possible? How could a servant of the Shadows, an agent of chaos and death, feel love?

Perhaps Morden wore the necklace simply out of habit. Elric remained uncertain, a state he disliked.

"You will not hold us here," Elric said. "You destroyed our ship, but you will not stop us from leaving." He scanned the dark corridor for any signs of static. His sensors revealed a strange energy emanating from the smiling Morden, but nothing else. He continued to scan, recording his findings in case they might later be of use.

Morden's hands unfolded, palms up. "This plan of yours is madness." His voice was smooth, threatening. "At first we didn't believe you'd go through with it. Now . . . Do your people want to die so badly?"

"Do your masters need us so badly? Or is it that they fear us?" There, at the upper end of the infrared spectrum, he found them, just as Galen had described. Two bodies of static, behind Morden, one on each side. Their angled silhouettes, crawling with white dots of unresolvable interference, somehow seemed to convey malice. So there were at least two Shadows on the station. Had they come to kill him, if he refused their offer, so that the rest would be frightened into accepting?

Morden brought his palms together, and his smile grew. "Creatures who break and run are more vulnerable than those who remain in their places of power."

Elric inclined his head. "Yet those who stand in the way of a stampede are trampled." The energy coming from Morden was similar to what Galen had detected on Zafran 8, from a Drakh. The Drakh had been receiving a communication from a nearby Shadow. Elric realized Morden must have some sort of receiver implanted in his brain. The Shadows were communicating with him, perhaps telling their puppet what to say. It was strange, Elric thought, that they were so insecure in their control.

"Your threats are empty," Morden said. "Your people are weak. You've crippled yourselves. It's a tragedy, really. So pointless." Morden lowered his hands, and his face contracted with false concern. "You don't look well, Elric. When was it I saw you? Only a few months ago. You've aged twenty years." Morden approached him, and the shapes of static came forward as well, their motion suggesting, somehow, the solid, structural movement of bodies—one area momentarily resembling a limb, another a head. They were blocking him from seeing them, yet they could not block him completely. "Wouldn't you like your health back? Your power?"

Elric stood his ground. "I made my choices. I live with them. And I will die with them."

Morden stopped, very close now, the Shadows right behind him. "Perhaps you aren't concerned for yourself. But what about those in your care? You're one of the great Circle that leads the mages. Do you want to lead them all to their deaths?"

"We lead them where we must."

"And you'll decide for all of them? Make no mistake, Elric; this is our last offer. A mutually beneficial alliance. Accept and they live. Refuse and they die."

"Then they die."

In the dim light, Morden's even white teeth seemed almost to glow. "You say that so easily. What about your apprentice, Galen? You trained him exceptionally well. We've been watching him, and he shows great promise. Do you want him to die?"

Fear froze Elric into silence. He could not tell if Morden knew where Galen was, if Morden knew Galen was not on the station.

"Does he know your secret, Elric? What do you think he

would do if he were told? Who do you think he would hate most?"

Elric's fear turned to fury, and his voice boomed in the narrow passage. "Stay away from him."

"Is that a request? Because I'd be happy to do that for you, if you would do something for me."

Elric conjured a fireball in his hand and seized the back of Morden's neck with that same hand, grinding the heat into the Shadows' servant. "It is an order! From one with the power to teach you obedience."

As Morden screamed out, the chain of his necklace melted, and the stone dropped down his chest into Elric's free hand. Morden failed to notice it, preoccupied as he was with pain.

Elric shoved him to the side and took a few quick steps past the Shadows, toward Down Below.

Morden hunched over, gasping. His eyes glittered with black anger. It was not only Morden's anger, Elric realized, but the Shadows' as well. They were enraged that he would treat their messenger with such contempt. Well, Elric had anger of his own. Let them learn what it meant to threaten Galen. And let their rage blind them to his designs.

"That was a mistake," Morden said from behind the twin figures of static. After a few moments he straightened, and again he smiled, though this time the smile seemed more labored. "If you want our silence, then work with us. No one needs to know. With your cooperation, you can buy the lives of all the mages."

"And what did you buy with your cooperation?" Elric held up the necklace. "Whose lives? Whose deaths?"

The smile vanished from Morden's face. "I want that back." Those words, Elric sensed, came from Morden alone.

"It means nothing to you," Elric said. "I read your article on the Anfran love incantation. You translated the key line as 'The love that abides no borders.' You loved them, once. Yet they are dead and here you are. If you truly loved them, and you truly abide no borders, you would have killed yourself to be with them." Elric allowed the stone to swing slightly from his fingers, and Morden's eyes followed it. "You are not what you once were," Elric said. "They have changed you. You are their slave."

Morden's eyes shifted from the stone to Elric, and his expression darkened. "You're as much a slave as I am. You were bought, just like me."

"I am not a slave," Elric said, "so long as I can do this." He tossed the stone toward Morden, turned, and walked away.

As he set one foot after the next down the dim passage, he waited for the Shadows to attack.

No attack came.

Of course a murder here could be messy, and noisy, and draw the attention of the captain. It would be better for the Shadows to kill them all together, after they had boarded their ship and cleared the station. A malfunction could be blamed, and no wrongdoing suspected.

Elric descended another steep, narrow staircase, finding his legs shaking with either exhaustion or fear, or both. He had rejected the Shadows' final offer of alliance. They would turn their full efforts to the destruction of the techno-mages.

His plan was all that stood in their way. The success of that plan was now in doubt, with Shadows on the station. He would have to make certain they were kept away at the critical moment, so they could not uncover the mages' illusions.

Elric's legs gave way, and he stumbled down several stairs before he regained control. He sat on the bottom step, unable to continue. He pressed the heel of his hand to his forehead. His heart was pounding in time with the throbbing in his head. He had many things to attend to, yet only a single thought penetrated the pain: Galen. He was in danger.

Gowen appeared at Elric's side. "May I help?"

Gowen had been waiting for his return. Elric straightened, though he felt he could not safely stand. "How is Ing-Radi?"

"She is weak, but improved. I left her resting."

"The *Crystal Cabin* has arrived?"

"Yes. Just a few minutes ago. The *Zekhite* is on schedule to arrive tomorrow."

"And Londo?" He could check himself, but he did not have the energy or the focus.

"Alwyn sent the computer demon into his datasystem as soon as your meeting ended. His money is being reinvested into worthless companies, and his files are being destroyed, all in a very loud, obnoxious way. He's very unhappy with us right now."

"Galen asked you to watch over me."

Gowen looked down, embarrassed. "Yes. Just as I asked him to watch over Blaylock."

Elric pushed himself to his feet. "You have fulfilled your promise. But know that Ing-Radi needs your attention much more than I do."

Gowen said nothing, his anxious eyes on Elric. Elric continued toward their place in Down Below. Gowen followed.

Blaylock, Elric knew, would watch over Galen to the best of his abilities. But what if Blaylock was incapacitated? Galen had no power to heal. He could be left alone.

And now, Elric had angered the Shadows. What better way for them to strike back at him than through Galen? If they knew where he was. After Morden's threat, Elric felt compelled to take some action. He had given up everything for the mages, except Galen.

And Galen he would not give up.

Galen and Blaylock wound their way through the maze of streets toward the City Center. Through their probe, they watched as the Drazi Rabelna Dorna walked a few blocks ahead, briefcase in hand. She seemed to know her way.

As the day had not been bright, the night was not dark. The city lights reflected off the smoke and soot in the air, giving it an eerie grey glow. The height of buildings, the narrowness of the streets, the concentration of beings all increased as the two of them neared their goal. Despite the late hour, the area was filled with activity, and Shadows were plentiful.

Here, at last, Galen found some pattern to the city. The curved streets revealed that it was, at its core, a circular maze, with the City Center its protected heart. Many streets ringed the area, while only this one, perhaps, allowed admittance.

As the massive black building came into view, Galen shivered. It stood two hundred stories tall, a dwarfing tower of glittering blackness against the glowing night sky. Rabelna disappeared inside. They would follow.

While Galen had finished his dinner, Blaylock had reviewed all that he'd learned over the afternoon. He had followed Rabelna from the port to the City Center. Through his probe, he'd watched as she had ridden to the top floor and met with a Drakh. Rabelna had offered information to report, information about techno-mages. The Drakh had told her to return that night.

Blaylock had lingered outside the building for most of the afternoon, attempting to penetrate the city's datasystems as he planted probes on many of those coming and going from the Center. It was then he saw a young woman coming from the building. She had long blond hair and wore a short pink dress. Blaylock had said he sensed some odd electromagnetic radiation coming from her, and when he studied it, he found the three frequencies in the ultraviolet in which mages hid signs. A microelectronic emitter had been planted on her forehead, and when Blaylock combined the three frequencies in the way known only to mages, he found encoded in the signal a rune, the rune signifying *Killer*.

Blaylock had searched for information on her, had found that her name was Bunny Oliver. She was twenty-eight years old, a P12 telepath supposedly held in the Greenfield Internment Camp on Earth because of "severe sociopathic disorders."

Blaylock had concluded she must have been the telepath chosen by Elizar, and she must have aided in Kell's death.

At this Galen had objected. Elizar had killed Kell, not a telepath.

"No," Blaylock had said. "Elizar was surely the one to flay Kell, yet that was done after Kell's death. He died of a heart attack, one so massive I believe he must have induced it himself, to prevent the telepath from gaining information."

Galen did not like the idea that Kell had killed himself. He'd been sure it was Elizar. Yet if Elizar had engineered the situation, and had flayed Kell afterward, what difference did it make? He knew Elizar was a murderer. He had seen it with his own eyes.

Blaylock believed Kell had planted the emitter, possibly as his last, dying act. Yet Elizar and the others would certainly have seen the signal, would have realized what it was. Why had they not removed it?

Perhaps they had no fear of other mages finding Bunny here, on the rim. Or perhaps the signal was meant as a lure for any mages who did find their way here—a lure to bring them to Elizar, Razeel, and Tilar.

Blaylock had kept his distance from Bunny, and directed Galen to do the same. Her powers were strong, and if she suspected them and tried to scan them, she would quickly discover they were techno-mages. Yet somehow they must learn all they could of her plans. If other techno-mages were to be captured, questioned, or killed, Bunny would likely be involved.

For Galen, Bunny's appearance was the best news he'd had since arriving on the planet. If Elizar's telepath was here, then Elizar might well be here. Though he could not sense Elizar's mage energy, Galen believed he might be close. Perhaps in this very building. If Bunny was a lure, Galen would gladly take the bait.

Energy raced through him, ready, eager to be used. Perhaps, finally, the time would come to release it.

Galen's attention was drawn to the narrow street before him. Ten feet ahead, among the passersby, an angular body of static stood motionless, blocking his path. Galen approached the Shadow with even steps, maintaining his direction. He could not reveal that he knew it was there.

The shape subtly shifted, and Galen was suddenly certain that it was looking at him. Would it sense his mage energy?

He forced his heavy feet forward. The Shadow was eight feet ahead, six, four. At last, with the hint of some strange, scissorlike action, the shape moved to the side, and Galen passed by, nearly brushing against it.

They still knew little about the Shadows, not even what their enemy looked like. The Shadows had lived for tens of thousands of years. They were far more ancient than the Taratimude that had given birth to the techno-mages; their powers were vast. Blaylock had said that the moment he and Galen were recognized as techno-mages, they would have only one chance—to run. He had purchased two tickets on a transport leaving at dawn.

But Galen would not leave. Not until both of his tasks were fulfilled.

In his mind's eye, Rabelna rode the elevator to the top floor.

As they approached the glittering black tower, Galen became aware of a sound, below the din of construction and traffic and people and business. He realized the sound had always been there, since they'd arrived, yet it had existed just below the level of hearing, a deep, subtle pulsation, lost in the noise of the city until now. Here, at the City Center, the vibration became slightly more pronounced. He looked down at the shiny black street. The sound pulsed from below. His sensors revealed indications of a vast underground complex.

A great screech sounded overhead, and Galen jerked his head up to see a dark, spiky shape silhouetted against the glowing sky. G'Leel had once described to them a Shadow ship, a ship as black as space, that moved as if alive. *I could swear it screamed,* she had said.

The ship cruised over the city canyon as if looking down upon them. Strange, intense energies radiated from it. It passed beyond the pinnacle of the City Center, then dove down behind it, out of sight. That would be where the empty Joncorp lot now stood.

Inside, Rabelna stepped from the elevator, walked down a plain, empty hall, and rang the buzzer beside a door. It clicked open, and she went within.

The entrance to the City Center was marked by three tall, golden doors. Beings trickled in and out. The building, Galen saw now, was made of a strange material. It reflected the light in an odd, shifting manner. If he could touch the wall, he could gain additional information through the sensors in his fingertips. Yet he didn't want to draw attention to himself.

The center door opened to admit them, and they passed through. To one side, several guards stood talking, of a species Galen did not know. Ahead was a line of metaglass booths that served as security gates. Beings entered and were sealed inside. They ran their I.D.s through the reader, and once their authorization was confirmed, the far side of the booth opened to admit them to the building.

Blaylock had created false I.D.s for them, and had breached the City Center database and added their information, authorizing them access to the building. If the tampering had been noticed, or had in some way been insufficient, they would be trapped inside the booths.

Galen stepped inside, and the booth sealed behind him. He ran his I.D. through as Blaylock did, held his hand to the scanner to confirm identification. The booth opened, allowing him to pass. Blaylock joined him.

While most were gathered at the near banks of elevators, he and Blaylock went to the far bank, the one that led to the top floors. They waited for an elevator to arrive. Galen noticed that the lobby's black walls were made of the same material as the building's exterior, and carried the same strange, shifting reflections.

The elevator doors opened, and Galen stepped in beside Blaylock. As they rode upward, they did not speak. They were no doubt being observed. Blaylock stared ahead, his expression unrevealing. Soon enough someone would notice them. Perhaps they would learn something to help save the mages before then; perhaps not. This would be their only chance.

Blaylock had planted their FTL relay nearby. If they were successful in gaining any information, it could be sent immediately to Elric, in the event they were unable to escape. If they were able to escape, then Blaylock could take the information away with him. Galen crossed his arms, the tech's restless energy churning through him.

The room in which Rabelna stood was dimly lit, as Drakh seemed to prefer. Rabelna moved to a desk illuminated by a sleek, low lamp, laid her briefcase there, and opened it. "I have information about the techno-mages." She spoke in English. Although her enunciation was a bit stiff, she seemed to have mastered the foreign grammar, unlike most Drazi. The final *s* of her sentence lingered with a slight hissing.

Another figure came close to the desk. Galen saw a flash of Human skin, pink fabric. As the figure bent to see what was in the briefcase, a sheet of curly blond hair came into view. It was Bunny.

A Drakh's voice scratched like dry leaves across stone. "We know of the magic workers on Babylon 5."

Rabelna turned. The Drakh was a hulking shadow before the closed door, the outline of its head barely visible, rising in the back into two craggy peaks, one above the other. Galen scanned different frequencies, looking for static. "I assumed your associate had told you by now," Rabelna said. "But has he also told you their plans?"

There, in the corner, the sparkle of static in the darkness.

The elevator doors opened. The top floor seemed deserted. Galen and Blaylock quickly made their way to the room Rabelna had entered. Shadow communications were transmitted in a narrow, focused beam. To detect them, he must be within three feet of the recipient, in this case, hopefully, the Drakh. Once he had tapped into the transmissions, though, he believed he could maintain access at a greater distance. In fact, once a connection was established, he might be unable to terminate it. Memories threatened to return, and he pushed them away.

"What do you know of their plans?" the Drakh asked. He stood just on the other side of the door, a foot away.

Galen scanned for high frequencies, found an area within the Drakh's brain was being excited by energy in a focused, narrow band—a message sent from the Shadow to the Drakh.

Something slipped down over his skin with the whisper of silk. Blaylock had contained both of them within a sound-proof shield. Galen had once done the same for her. If he began to yell out the Shadow's words, as she had, the shield would hold the sound within.

"I know everything," Rabelna said. "How much would you like to know?"

He did not want to cast the spell. If he'd translated incorrectly, it could create some massive instability, endangering Blaylock and possibly much more. If he'd translated correctly, he could be overwhelmed by the Shadows' signal. He glanced at Blaylock's gaunt face, realizing Blaylock would be left alone to face the Shadows if he was incapacitated. But there was no choice. This was their best chance to learn the Shadows' plans.

Galen closed his eyes, visualized the one-term equation.

Words bubbled up through him as if they swam through the currents of his blood, as if they permeated every cell in his body, as if they whispered up the twisting strands of his DNA. He was possessed by them; he was the embodiment of them.

They were Drakh words, yet somehow, without even translating, he knew what they meant.

The magic workers have rejected us for the last time. They prefer to cripple themselves with rules and stagnate in isolation rather than live free and use their great powers to their full extent. Now they must die. Find out all she knows so that none will escape us.

The flow of words stopped, yet those that had been uttered continued to circulate through him, repeating, breaking apart, recombining. *The magic workers have rejected us. Rejected us for the last time. They prefer to stagnate. Rejected their great powers. Rejected us to cripple themselves. None will escape.* Galen had little sense of his body, beyond the words that whispered through it. Yet he didn't think he was yelling, didn't think he was speaking. There seemed no need. The words seemed to be everywhere, in everything.

Gradually the broken echoes began to fade, and Galen became aware of the Drakh's dark silhouette in his mind's eye, of the voices that spoke. Rabelna and the Drakh settled on a price.

"They are gathering," Rabelna said, "all five hundred of them, in order to retreat to some hiding place. They've purchased an Earth transport, the *Tidewell*, which will arrive at Babylon 5 shortly."

"We know this," the Drakh said. "We have already destroyed that ship."

"But do you also know," Rabelna said, "that they have made arrangements for a Drazi freighter, the *Zekhite*, to come to Babylon 5 at the same time? Its captain, Vayda, has been known to have dealings with techno-mages in the past. The freighter can easily carry five hundred. I believe the *Tidewell* was a distraction."

"That is useful," the Drakh said.

Rabelna handed the Drakh a data crystal. "The *Zekhite* is scheduled to depart Babylon 5 in thirty-six hours."

Again the words came, flooding through him. *The magic workers have always a hidden deceit. Now that we know their true plan we can destroy them. Once they are all aboard we will destroy the freighter. Direct Morden to handle it. With their foolish Code they have made themselves unfit to survive.*

The message stopped, yet he was saturated with its words, and they murmured on, fragmenting, reordering. *Unfit to survive. Their true plan. Hidden deceit will destroy them. Once they are all aboard. Direct the magic workers. Their foolish Code always a hidden deceit.*

"Return to Babylon 5," the Drakh said from the darkness. "We will look forward to further information in the future."

Galen felt disoriented in that dark room, as if he were losing his balance. He realized that Blaylock was pulling on his arm. The sensations of his body seemed far away, lost in the echoes of the Shadow's words.

They prefer to cripple themselves with deceit. They are unfit to survive. Now they must die.

Galen held fiercely to the two spells in his mind—one for probe access, the other to decode the Shadow signal. He could not lose contact. He had to get as much information as he could. It could save Elric.

Yet he tried to extend his attention to the hallway around him, to the exterior of the body whose interior ran with whispers. Blaylock was pulling him, saying something Galen couldn't hear. The Shadows' words swathed him in their echoes. He saw movement at a turn in the hall. Three Drakh emerged, and tiny spots of yellow flashed from the muzzles of their weapons. The loud thump of the plasma bolts did not reach him.

He stumbled down the hall after Blaylock, yellow sprays of light blossoming across his vision. Blaylock must have replaced the soundproof shield with a defensive one, and the plasma blasts splashed across it. Blaylock was protecting him. Just as, in another place, she had protected him.

Blaylock dragged him into another room, closed the door behind them, and unfolded the shield from around them to direct it up against the door and the surrounding wall.

They know their order will die. They know they will die. Yet still they persist in their course. Their loss will be a tragedy.

"What the hell's going on out there?" Bunny yelled.

The Drakh's dry voice replied. "Two of the magic workers have come here to learn our plans. They will soon be dead, if they do not surrender."

Blaylock pulled Galen across the room toward the window. Galen was disoriented, part of him wrapped in words, part in the dark room, part here, in a similar dark room, looking out a large window. Outside, shifting lights reflected off the clouds.

Blaylock extended an arm toward the window, his fingers spread wide. From the center of the dark glass, fractures jagged outward in the directions of Blaylock's fingers.

Their order will be a tragedy. With deceit they cripple themselves. With deceit they persist.

Behind them the door opened, and more yellow flashed from the Drakhs' weapons. Yellow ripples spread across the blue-tinged shield.

Rabelna closed her briefcase, picked it up.

Blaylock's face was taut, severe. He thrust his arm to its full length, and the center of the window burst silently outward, leaving a large, ragged hole. Blaylock seized Galen's arm to pull him through the opening, but before they could even move, the glistening glass began to undulate, the jagged edges around the hole swelling, flowing in to heal the wound, sealing it closed.

As the inward flow continued, excess material collected at the center of the newly formed glass, bulging outward. Then, in a single, fluid movement, the excess extended into the room, like a bulb on the end of a narrow stalk. The bulb hovered just over them, turning slightly, as if examining them.

Then it retracted into the window, the excess material rippling out across the window and the black wall, disappearing.

The building was some kind of vast, living machine.

They will die. A tragedy.

Blaylock raised both arms toward the window, fingers outstretched. Behind them, the shield was flashing red and yellow. It would not last long.

Blaylock needed his help. The echo of the Shadow's words at last was fading. Galen maintained the image of the one-term equation, though he hoped the Shadow would say nothing more. He had to focus his attention outward. He forced the whispering remnants from his body, broke his connection with the probe on Rabelna.

The immediacy of the present struck him with overwhelming force.

A high-pitched, screeching whine filled the room. It came from Blaylock's shield, near failure. On the far side of it, the Drakh continued to fire, plasma bolts bursting from their weapons with powerful thumps. With each impact the shield flashed red, and the whine rose in intensity.

Galen visualized the screen in his mind's eye, conjured fireball after fireball, arranging them in rows aimed at the door. Without giving them movement, he calculated an equation of motion that would send them all converging on the doorway at top speed. When the shield failed, he would use it. Galen looked toward Blaylock.

Arcs of brilliant white electricity shot between the buttons on Blaylock's jacket sleeves. The arcs shot up his arms to his lapel pins, then twisted down to the buttons on the front of his jacket. Blaylock bowed his head, and a blinding light flashed out from him toward the window. The fat, brilliant curl of electricity burned an afterimage on Galen's retina.

The window was clouding over, like an eye covered by cataracts. The greyness spread even into the black wall.

Blaylock lowered one hand. His face was waxy, gleaming with sweat. His raised hand quivered.

Around the edges of the greyness, the black wall was undulating, swelling, and slowly, a healing blackness began spreading inward to transform the grey.

At the same time, from the center of the window, fractures crackled outward. With a grunt Blaylock thrust his hand forward, and the center of the window blew out.

This time, the breach did not heal. The grey section seemed unable to flow, although the black was rapidly spreading inward.

Blaylock grabbed his arm, retracted the shield from the doorway to snap around them. Its whining ceased. Galen conjured the equation of motion for the fireballs. And as the edges of the hole turned black and began to flow inward, they dove through.

—— *chapter 12* ——

Galen's coat fluttered out behind him in the cold night air. Beams of light crisscrossed the sky, Blaylock's body a darkness beside him. For a moment as they tumbled, Galen couldn't tell which way was down. Then he realized down was the direction in which they were falling, and if he didn't stop their fall soon, the ground would do it for them. Blaylock's energy was taken with the shield.

Galen conjured a platform below them and they slammed into it. Blaylock grunted.

"Sorry," Galen said.

A plasma burst sprayed red and yellow over them. Blaylock's shield was intact but weak. He was nearly exhausted. Above them, the window had somehow been directed to open, and the Drakh fired down from it.

Equation of motion. Galen sent the platform down, away from the window. He had to save them. In the red spray of light, he saw Blaylock's face, his mouth tight, eyes squeezed shut with effort. Galen climbed to his knees and jogged the platform away from the lights, diving toward the darkness that dominated a large area behind the building. That must be the demolition site. It seemed unoccupied.

Then the darkness moved, its spiky silhouette rising up against the glowing night sky. From above, he hadn't seen it. A red beam shot from its front edge down into the ground, carving some kind of trench in the earth.

The beam vanished, and for a moment there was just the sound of the wind rushing past. Then with a shriek the huge ship wheeled and dove toward them.

No ball of energy would stop it. No shield would protect against it. There was no time to evade it.

He made the decision in a second that seemed to stretch out forever. When he had faced Elizar, he had held back. He had obeyed the dictates of the Circle. He had thought he could save Isabelle by sacrificing himself. Instead she had shielded him, and she had died.

Now Blaylock protected him, though the protection could not hold. In a moment they would both be dead. The warning to Elric would be unsent; he and those with him would be killed.

And the universe would not care.

Fury rose up in him, fury at Elizar and the Shadows, fury at himself, fury at God.

Elric had told him the spell of destruction was his burden to carry for the rest of his life, the burden to have the power and not use it. But it was a burden he could not carry. He would not carry.

He had lost Isabelle by his restraint. Morden had asked him if he could live with that decision, and he now knew the answer: he could not.

He and Blaylock might both be killed, this planet of Shadows might be destroyed, this universe of chaos and death might be enveloped in a massive wave of destruction. But he would not stand by and do nothing.

He would not lose another.

On the front of the great shape of glistening darkness, a point of red light built to brilliance as the ship prepared to fire. Galen closed his eyes, visualized the spell of destruction.

Energy collapsed around him in a massive, overwhelming wave, crushing him with suffocating concentration. Then with a great rush it shot out of him, flinging him back. As he hit the platform, he threw out his arms, one finding the hard surface, the other flailing in empty air. He pulled himself toward the center of the platform, unable to catch his breath. The air felt charged, strange.

Above him, the brilliant red light on the front of the Shadow ship began to darken. The energy he'd conjured had collected in a sphere centered on it. The sphere itself was difficult to see. Perhaps fifteen feet in diameter, it encompassed only a small portion of the leading edge of the ship, an area that had now begun to turn redder and darker.

The spiky silhouette abruptly stopped its dive, hovering over them. Time felt wrong, sluggish, distorted. Space seemed fluid and uncertain. Galen felt his left lung swelling within his chest, as if it would burst out of him. The few inches between himself and Blaylock suddenly expanded, becoming feet, tens of feet. Blaylock turned toward him, and Blaylock's forehead stretched high, snaking upward as if it had become ductile.

Above, the black spikes of the Shadow ship began to waver. Galen accessed his sensors, found massive energy, massive instability concentrated in the spherical membrane. Within the membrane he could no longer see the point of red light; inside was uniform darkness. The sphere suddenly began to contract, revealing a clean, scalloped edge where it had cut into the ship. The blackness within it faded toward grey.

If the membrane retained its integrity, as he hoped, then the section of the ship within the sphere would fade and vanish, pinched off into a separate universe, an unstable one in the midst of collapse. As this new universe imploded, the spherical section of the ship would be crushed to nothingness.

If instead the membrane failed, its energies might fly out like a mini Big Bang. The contents of the two universes would mix, and if the physical laws governing them differed, they could trigger a huge chain reaction of destruction.

The sphere was continuing to shrink, fading to the pale grey of the glowing night sky behind it. The energy levels dropped to a more normal range, as if the membrane and what was within it were vanishing from existence. Time snapped back to its regular pace, and Galen's lung retracted to its normal size. He gasped.

The small, pale sphere faded away, and a great rolling thunderclap split the air. For a moment, in the aftermath, he couldn't hear anything. Then, out of the thick silence, arose a shriek.

The Shadow ship climbed higher, a spherical area cut from the front edge of its body. Galen stood, his brief sense of normalcy vanishing in a strange rush of sensation. At the same time that he looked up at the ship, he looked down on himself from above. He felt disoriented, overloaded with input.

Then the pain found him—extreme screaming pain from the hole ripped through his body. A part of the machine had been taken away. He could not perform his functions, could not keep the neurons firing in harmony, could not synchronize the cleansing and circulation. The beat of his systems stumbled, could not recover.

Galen didn't understand how it was happening. But somehow he had become linked to the Shadow ship. He was seeing through its eyes, feeling its feelings.

Pain shot out along his arms, astonishing in its intensity—a massive systems failure. His tireless, invulnerable body was collapsing.

Above him, the spikes of the ship retracted, shriveled.

He was screaming now, and she was screaming with him. The machine was failing, dying. She plummeted toward the planet. His legs failed; his body collapsed. He hit the platform, saw a flash of Blaylock's fingers stretched toward him, and fell into night.

One by one, the machine's systems failed, and as the shriek of the machine faded, another cry sounded more and more clearly. It was the scream of a living being, a woman. They felt the same pain; they were dying the same death. The last of the machine's stumbling systems shut down, and he found himself blind, deaf, lost.

She searched for her connection to the machine. She and the machine were one. She could not continue without it; it was impossible. All systems of the machine passed through her; she was its heart; she was its brain. The skin of the machine was her skin; its bones and blood, her bones and blood. She was the machine. Somehow they had become separated. She must find a way to rejoin with it.

The machine was so beautiful, so elegant. It had its needs, and she fulfilled them. Without its needs, what would she do? Without the machine, what was she?

In the suffocating blackness she became aware of a body within her body, a body within the machine. It was all that still remained alive. Yet it was choking, dying. It was her core, the central processing unit of the machine.

It was a Human being, wired into the heart of the ship.

The ship slammed into the ground, and they screamed as their body broke apart, tumbling, collapsing, disintegrating. As if from a great distance, Galen felt his own body growing suddenly heavy, as if he were in an elevator decelerating before a stop. In the next instant that distance between him and his body vanished. He slammed into the ground hard, and pain jolted through him.

For a moment he thought he had lost her. Yet as they faded toward unconsciousness, they retained their connection a moment longer, and in that moment, Galen searched for a remnant of the person this woman had once been, before she had been turned into a component of a machine, before she had been hardwired to obey, before circuits and programming had overruled her life. As they fell into oblivion and the connection failed, all he could find that survived was a name: Anna Sheridan.

* * *

After checking on Ing-Radi, Elric left Gowen to care for her. Somehow, with the aid of Gowen's healing, she had found the energy to continue, at least a while longer. In fact, she was looking better than she had since arriving on the station. Elric encouraged her to rest until it was time to execute the final stage of their plan.

Then he had to speak to Alwyn. He hurried to the observation room, where mages coordinated their surveillance of different areas of the station. Normally the plain grey room was silent, each mage absorbed in his own task. Yet now, as he ducked through the circular metal hatch, he heard a high, shrill voice singing a grating melody.

Narn opera. Alwyn had to be responsible.

Carvin, Fed, Ak-Shana, and several other young mages were indeed gathered around Alwyn, who had conjured in the air the image from the probe on Vir.

The probe revealed Londo sitting before his datasystem, watching in horror as Alwyn's computer demon ate his files and destroyed his finances. The lights flashed on and off in his ostentatious quarters, and the wail of Narn opera added an extra element of provocation and torment. Londo bemoaned his fate to Vir as a pleasant female voice from his datasystem informed him he was now the owner of five hundred thousand shares of Fireflies, Incorporated. The mages laughed.

As the Narn soprano's shrill voice ascended in a screeching crescendo, the sound pierced directly through Elric's skull into his brain. "Alwyn. I must speak with you at once."

The other mages quickly moved away, returning to their duties. The smile faded from Alwyn's face, and the image dissolved.

Elric led Alwyn to his small room, where they could speak privately. He scanned the room for any probes or listening devices. He was becoming paranoid. There were none.

The harsh overhead light shone off Alwyn's silver hair and cast lines of shadow down his cheeks. Elric felt awkward. He was not accustomed to asking for favors, and this one could easily be fatal. Yet he had no choice, and no one else to ask. "I need your help," Elric said. "It is a matter of great danger. I need you to go after Galen."

"What happened?"

"Morden has threatened him."

The bags beneath Alwyn's eyes wrinkled as his face tightened. "Does Morden know where he is?"

"I'm not certain. But I'm not willing to take that chance."

"You could be playing right into his hands."

"That is why any action must be taken in secret."

Alwyn hesitated. "Have you heard anything from Blaylock or Galen?"

"No." Alwyn was wondering whether they had already been killed. But the lack of communication meant nothing. Blaylock would send a message only if an urgent threat to all the mages had been discovered. And Galen was prohibited from sending any communication. Elric refused to consider the possibility.

Alwyn tilted his head. "By sending anyone after Galen, you would be violating the directives of the Circle. Most unlike you, Elric."

"And this offends your sensibilities?"

"Delights them, actually."

"That is why I've come to you. I told you I would not lose him."

"But aren't Carvin and I needed here? With Ing-Radi failing and . . . others not in the best of health . . ."

Alwyn meant him, of course. "I need Carvin. I cannot do without her. But you could meet her at the gathering place, then go off with her wherever you choose. I guarantee that the Circle will not interfere."

A slight smile lifted Alwyn's lips. "But if I'm to meet her at the gathering place, you would have to tell me where that is, violating another directive of the Circle."

"So I would," Elric said.

Alwyn looked upward, shaking his head. "How I've waited for this day." As he met Elric's gaze, his face grew serious. "I don't want anything to happen to Galen. You know I love the boy. But I hate to leave Carvin. I realize you need her—for Londo. . . . But I'd feel better if I could bring her with me."

Elric knew the seven words to say to make his old friend agree, and he hated himself for saying them. "Going to the rim will be dangerous."

Alwyn rubbed a hand over his mouth, considering. Then the hand came away. "You're right. It's better she stay here with you. You'll watch over her?"

"Yes."

They stood silently, regarding each other. Alwyn, Elric knew, was thinking of what would happen to Carvin if he did not return from the rim. At the same time he was thinking of his long-ago friendship with Galen's father, which Elric had never understood, and the responsibility he felt toward Galen.

"I don't know how you'll manage without me," Alwyn said finally.

Relief flooded through Elric, and gratitude. If there was a way Galen could be saved, Alwyn would save him. "It will be difficult."

"No doubt. I'll have to tell Carvin where I'm going. She'll keep the secret."

"I know she will."

Alwyn clapped him on the shoulder. "Don't worry. I'll bring Galen back, safe."

"Thank you," Elric said. "I will do the same for Carvin."

Alwyn's hand lingered on him. "Bring yourself back too. You're a stubborn old bastard, like me, and God knows there aren't enough of us in the universe."

Elric embraced him, feeling an unaccustomed rush of emotion. "Leave immediately and travel as quickly as possible."

"I will."

Elric opened the door, and they headed in different directions. Alwyn was a good friend, he realized, the best friend he had. It was a shame he would never see his friend again.

The throbbing in his head was growing stronger, but he pushed himself forward. He must confirm that the next piece of his plan had fallen into place. He could observe from his room, but he had done too much of that already. He must mix with the others, to reassure them that all was well. So he returned to the observation room.

Fed approached him, a smile somehow visible under the mass of his unkempt beard. "They're still stuck in Londo's quarters."

In the air before them, Fed conjured the image from the probe on Vir's cheek. The blackness was broken only by the thin beam of a penlight. Vir's thick-fingered hand aimed the light into a recess in the wall.

"This is ridiculous," Londo ranted. "In the case of emergency, when all power has gone and you are standing in complete blackness, open a tiny panel in the wall and trigger some nearly invisible device to open the door. What insane Human invented this system? We could be dead by now."

Vir turned, shining the penlight at Londo, who stood over him. "Don't say that. We've got enough problems as it is."

Londo raised a hand before his face. "Stop shining that thing in my eyes and get back to work." Vir turned back to the recess in the wall, and Londo continued. "Do they think I have nothing better to do than stand here in the dark? Do they think they can spirit away all my money and suffer no consequences? They think we are cowering in here, Vir, waiting for their next demon to slip through the air ducts and terrify us. Well, we're not! Come, conjure your best, you second-rate magicians! Bring it on!"

"Londo! You're not helping."

Fed laughed.

Londo continued. "They think we will be awed by their

fancy tricks like some kind of savages. They think they can come here and show no respect."

"I thought you had decided to apologize."

For a moment there was silence. Then Londo spoke. "That doesn't mean I have to be happy about it."

A dim light came on, and Vir turned to investigate. Across the room, the communications screen had lit up, and a text message appeared. Londo walked over to it.

Ambassador, I think you may want something I can provide. Assistance with your situation. Meet me. You know where.

"What's that?" Vir said. "I thought you said the comm system wasn't working."

The message vanished, and the comm screen went black. Vir's penlight revealed only the faintest hint of Londo's silhouette against the darkness.

"It isn't," Londo said. His voice had grown soft, uncertain.

"Was that from . . ."

Londo's dark figure turned on Vir. "Stop asking so many questions, and get back to work. I need to get out of here. Things may be looking up."

Vir turned back to the wall. The door opened.

"At last!" Londo cried. He passed Vir, slapping him on the back. "Good work."

"But Londo . . ."

But Londo had already disappeared down the corridor.

Fed was nodding his head, a growing smile twisting at his beard. "You, Elric, are the king. It's all happening just like you said. If I didn't know better, I'd think you had all of these guys under some kind of mind control."

Yes, Elric had anticipated Morden inserting himself into the conflict between Londo and the mages, and he had anticipated Londo accepting Morden's help. But the meeting that was about to take place was another unknown in Elric's plan. He could not listen to their conversation. In the gardens where

they now went to meet, there were no security cameras. And
Morden would be accompanied by the Shadows. They might
well detect any probe, any mage close enough to listen. They
must have no idea that Elric knew of their connection to
Londo. They must have no idea that Elric anticipated the plan
they would now propose.

And if Elric was wrong, all those in his care would die, and
the deception would fail.

The bed was hard as rock. Galen shifted in the dark room,
his body sore all over. His leg throbbed. He threw off the coat
that covered him, hot.

Moving slowly, he slid his legs over the side of the bed and
pushed himself into a sitting position. As he took a breath,
pain stabbed into his left side. He clenched a hand around his
ribs, suddenly overcome with dizziness, and hunched over.
Something was wrong with him. The inseam of his left pant
leg was cut open, and where the leg peeked out he saw it was
swollen and discolored. He tried to remember.

The City Center, the living window, the Shadow ship.

Where was Blaylock?

Breathing shallowly, he searched for mage energy, found
none besides his own. He checked the time. It took a few moments to register. He'd slept over thirty hours.

Blaylock must have brought him here. Blaylock must have
saved him, because he should have been killed by the fall.
Galen tried to sort out the sensations of the impact. At the last
moment before he'd hit the ground, his body had grown suddenly heavy, as if he were in an elevator slowing to a stop.
Blaylock had conjured a platform beneath him, spreading the
deceleration out over perhaps a second, lessening the impact.

Galen scanned his body. His lower left leg showed the incomplete knitting of two fractures, one of the fibula, and one
of the smaller tibia. Three ribs on his left side were recovering
from breaks. An assortment of bruises and scrapes marked

various other parts of his body. Blaylock must have healed him partially; his own organelles would have taken at least a few days to affect this degree of healing.

The plan had been to flee once they'd been discovered. Yet he was still on Thenothk 4. Galen was grateful he hadn't woken to find himself on a transport heading away from the rim. He still had a chance to find Elizar, if Elizar was here. And now that he knew the spell of destruction would crush only what he wished, he could use it.

The energy of the tech quickened in anticipation. Yet the cold, the driving need to act, did not come. They would return, he sensed, in time, yet for now he had a brief respite. He'd released a great deal of energy last night, had saved Blaylock, had been able to strike, at least in some small way, against the Shadows. He found some measure of satisfaction in that.

But where was Blaylock?

The bedroom door was open a crack, and red light leaked in from the next room. Voices spoke in Narn. Galen accessed his translation program, and the words appeared in his mind's eye.

I promised I would see him safely off the planet. Galen recognized G'Leel's voice. She sounded angry. *We can easily smuggle him on board. What difference does it make to you?*

You say it's easy, but they'll be looking for him, said Captain Ko'Vin. *It's a risk. And there's no reward.*

He'll tell us where the Centauri arms are kept. We can destroy them before they ever reach the Centauri.

Keeping one hand wrapped around his side, Galen laid the other flat against the bed to push himself up. The bed was an artificial stone, he realized. G'Leel's hotel must cater to Narns. As he stood, pain sang through his left leg. He shifted his weight from it, swayed unevenly as dark spots danced before his eyes. Against the wall, he noticed an empty cargo container the size of a coffin.

And what good does that do me? Ko'Vin asked. *G'Leel, you've turned into a political fanatic.*

What do you want? Do you want me to pay you for taking him, and for possibly saving our people? Let's negotiate. Let's settle on a price, the amount you need to be motivated to do something good.

Galen had to find out what had happened to Blaylock. He forced his swollen leg forward. When his weight came down, he felt a horrible grinding in his shin. Pain shot through him. He caught himself quickly with his good leg, releasing a hard breath, and told himself to take the next step now, before he thought about it. In this way, he limped across the room toward the door.

Calm down. I didn't say I wouldn't take him. I'm sure we can come to some sort of friendly, mutually pleasurable agreement. You know I've always had my eye on you.

Come one step closer, you pathetic [untranslatable phrase] and you'll leave here in pieces.

Galen opened the door. The outer room was decorated with stone furnishings in the Narn style, illuminated with red light. G'Leel and Ko'Vin stood a few feet apart. Ko'Vin's hands were extended, G'Leel's clenched in fists at her sides.

"Where is Blaylock?"

They both turned to him. G'Leel's eyes widened. "You're not supposed to get up. Your leg is broken."

"Where," Galen said, "is Blaylock?"

I'll talk to you in a few minutes, G'Leel said, showing Ko'Vin out.

Don't take too long. I need to get to the ship. If you're reasonable, we can settle all this quickly.

I'm sure it would be quick, G'Leel said, closing the door in his face. She turned to Galen. "Let me help you back to bed."

Galen braced his hand against the door frame. "Just stop. And tell me. Where is he?"

"Blaylock—he's that other mage you were with?"

Galen nodded.

"He went to get more information."

"Where?"

"He didn't say. But he said not to wait for him."

Galen rested his forehead against the cool door frame, taking shallow breaths. Why had Blaylock left him here? Where had Blaylock gone?

G'Leel's muscular arm clamped around his shoulders, and she half-carried him back to the bed, deposited him there. He sat hunched forward, hand wrapped around his side. "Tell me everything that happened." In his mind's eye, he began searching through all the probes they had planted, looking for Blaylock.

G'Leel stood over him, arms crossed. "He came with you last night, in the middle of the night. He said that you needed my help. I don't know what happened, but you looked very bad. You kept talking, saying something about a woman."

Galen closed his eyes. "I do not talk in my sleep."

"You had some things to say this time. You kept repeating, 'A woman in the scream.' Things like that. 'A woman in the machine.' Blaylock claimed he didn't understand it, but I got the feeling he didn't like what you were saying. Then he took out this crystal and said he was going to heal you. He seemed to just sit there. But when he quit, you looked better, and you'd finally shut up. He had to stop before you were completely healed, because he was afraid it might be detected or something. He explained that your leg had been broken in two places and you shouldn't walk on it.

"Then he said he had to leave. He told me he'd be back before the *Khatkhata* left, but if he wasn't, I had to take you off the planet with me."

"When will your ship depart?"

"Less than two hours. I'd already have you on board except for that bastard Ko'Vin. But don't worry. I can handle him."

"Blaylock said nothing of where he was going or why?"

"He left a note."

"A note." Galen raised his head.

"He said if you became difficult enough, I should give it to you."

Galen extended his hand.

G'Leel went to a stone desk across the room, removed a piece of paper from the drawer. She handed it to Galen.

"Have you read this?" he asked.

G'Leel shifted uncomfortably. "He claimed he put a spell on it. He said if I read it, a very unpleasant curse would fall on me and my family."

Galen coughed, pain stabbing him in the side. He made a motion over the paper as if removing the nonexistent spell and unfolded the note. It was written in the language of the Soom.

There is more information I must obtain before I can leave this place. Your work is done. Do not follow me. Your power must not fall into the hands of the enemy. Send a message to Elric telling him all that you've discovered.

Galen's eyes stuck on the sentence. Elric still didn't know. Galen had slept all this time without warning him of the Shadows' plans to destroy the *Zekhite*. His mind raced, trying to remember what Rabelna had said. The *Zekhite* had been scheduled to leave Babylon 5 in thirty-six hours—six hours from now. There was still time to warn him. Still time to save him.

Galen pushed himself to resume reading, to continue searching through the probes for Blaylock.

Then leave Thenothk as quickly as possible. I know this is not your preference, but it is your duty, and you must fulfill it. You must return to the mages to teach them how to listen to the Shadow communications. This skill may be critical to our survival. You must also be with them in case they have need of a weapon.

You used your spell of destruction in defiance of the Circle. It was a rash, undisciplined act. Should our order survive, you shall answer for it. That you cast the spell purposely, with control, is a matter for both condemnation and praise. Yet predictions of the end of the universe, it seems, were unwarranted. The spell has proven itself to be our most effective weapon against these ships, should we need a weapon for self-defense. Destruction is not our purpose; war is not our place. Yet in this critical moment in our history, your skill may be required. You must take great care to use it only for good, and only when there is no other course.

My need for further information is personal in nature. It is part of my spiritual quest, a quest that does not involve you. If I have not returned by the time you awake to read this, then I am dead. Under no circumstances search for me. Your skills are required by the living.

The note was signed with the rune signifying Blaylock's name.

Galen would not believe Blaylock was dead. Not until he saw the body. But he wished he had woken sooner. Suddenly it struck him that Blaylock might have encouraged that long sleep, to give himself time to do whatever he needed to do, without drawing Galen into danger. He might even have hoped Galen would not awake until after the *Khatkhata* had left.

Galen had gone through all of the probes they had planted; he found Blaylock in none of them. He decided to go through them again, more slowly, beginning with the probe on Rabelna Dorna. She walked down a long, dimly lit tunnel of stone. Areas of static interrupted the image. Shadows.

"Does it say where he went?" G'Leel asked.

Galen shook his head. "Was he also injured?"

"Not that I could see."

What information did Blaylock seek? G'Leel had said Blaylock was upset at Galen's fevered rantings about the Shadow ship. In destroying the ship, Galen had discovered that a person lived at the center of it, serving as the central processing unit, coordinating its functions, fulfilling its needs. Somehow, communication had passed between them.

Galen didn't know if it had been some strange feedback from the spell of destruction, or perhaps some connection created by his spell to listen to the Shadows. He had heard Anna's thoughts, felt her feelings. She seemed to have become nearly a machine herself, concerned only with serving the ship, reconnecting with it, as if it were a part of her. The Shadows had enslaved her with their technology.

No wonder Blaylock had been upset. A person made subservient to technology embodied the antithesis of the technomages. The mages were masters of their tech; all their training focused on it. Only with control could they follow the Code, use the tech for good. Blaylock believed that perfect discipline, perfect control must be their goal, the path to enlightenment. Subjugating intelligent beings to technology would be blasphemy.

The presence of Anna within the ship was yet more evidence of the Shadows' endless evil. And more important, it revealed that everything the techno-mages believed, the Shadows opposed. No wonder the Shadows were so obsessed with them. By their very existence, they showed that another way was possible, a better way. Living beings could be enhanced by technology, not overpowered by it. It was all the more reason they should fight the Shadows.

In his mind's eye, Rabelna stopped within the dim stone tunnel and greeted two Drakh standing guard beside a door. They allowed her to enter.

The room was brightly lit, with plain white walls. Rabelna hesitated, probably waiting for her eyes to adjust. A simple rectangular table and three chairs were arranged before her. To the side of the table, two figures, their backs to her, crouched over something on the white floor. Galen's heart sped at the sight of the short Centauri crest adorning the head of one of them. Tilar. Beside him was Bunny.

"What's going on?" Rabelna said. "I was ready to leave for Babylon— Who is that?"

Tilar and Bunny had stood, revealing Blaylock lying on the floor. His limbs were in random positions, as if he'd collapsed. His gaunt face was turned to one side, eyes closed, lips slightly parted. Galen studied him carefully, saw the blue suit jacket rising and falling with his breath. He was still alive. But what had they done to him?

"Well?" G'Leel said, drawing him back to the hotel room. "Why did he leave?"

"A moment."

Bunny twirled a tendril of hair around her index finger. "He's one of the mages who got away last night. He came back. And they say mages are clever. I don't see why we're supposed to be so impressed."

"Someday," Tilar said, "I'll show you."

"I know," Bunny said. "After you're all grown up and get your implants."

Galen located the probe. It was underground, three hundred feet below the City Center. He remembered the faint pulsation he'd heard from beneath the street there. His sensors had hinted at an extensive underground complex.

He folded the note, put it in his pocket. He pushed himself up from the bed. "I will go after him."

"How will you find him?"

"I have already found him."

"Where is he?"

Holding tightly to his side, Galen bent, picked up his coat. "*How* is he, then?"

"He is captured." Galen got one arm into the coat, then found that his sore ribs made it difficult to reach back with his other arm. He forced it back, slid it into the coat.

"What about your leg?"

Galen started toward the outer room.

"He wanted you to leave the planet," G'Leel said. "I thought you had to obey him."

"He can reprimand me later."

"Wash your face, at least. It's bloody."

Galen paused, headed into the bathroom. Though the light there was red as well, he could see dark, dried rivulets along the side of his face. He rinsed them away, G'Leel standing over him in the doorway.

In the underground room, Rabelna sat. "Do we know whether they warned the other techno-mages about the *Zekhite*? If they did, I can get my contacts working to find out what new arrangements the mages will make to leave Babylon 5."

"We know they didn't send a message from the planet," Tilar said. "If Galen—the other one—is still here, then the mages still don't know. Whether or not Galen is here, we'll find out soon. Bunny's going to ask Blaylock a few questions. As soon as Elizar comes."

A warm rush of well-being flooded Galen's body. It carried with it the promise of relief from everything he'd held inside, from the crushing anger and self-hate, from the grief, from the driving need to act. And perhaps, finally, an end to it.

He felt exhilarated, energized. Elizar was there. He had another chance. Another chance to kill Elizar. To crush him to nothingness.

"If you can wake him up," Bunny said.

Galen realized G'Leel had spoken. "I'm sorry?" he said.

"I said, I'm sorry."

"For what?"

"I criticized you for not fighting the Shadows. I see that you're doing all you can."

Galen dried his face. "The Shadows have targeted my order. We could do much more in the fight against them. But the mages are afraid."

"Apparently the Narns are targeted as well. If they knew, I don't think many of them would worry about helping your kind."

Their eyes met for a moment, and Galen nodded. She

stepped aside to let him pass, followed as he limped toward the front door.

"The warehouse," he said, "is three blocks north of here. It is called Kledah. The best time to strike would be at dawn."

"Thank you," she said.

He opened the door. "I hope I haunt your dreams no longer. You have done more than could possibly have been expected." He started out, pulling the door closed behind him.

She grabbed it. "I'm coming with you," she said, as if she had decided at that very moment.

"No. You must not."

"Yes," G'Leel said, "I must."

Galen limped back inside, closed the door. "I cannot be responsible for your safety."

"I'm not asking you to be."

"Already Blaylock is overcome, despite his great powers."

She tapped the black case strapped to her waist. "He didn't have a gun."

Galen fixed her with his gaze. "Do you know where I'm going? Beneath the City Center is a vast complex of tunnels carved out of the rock. They are filled with your worst nightmares."

"Actually, my worst nightmares have involved you."

"Then perhaps you should not anger me."

"I'm the one with the ship that can take you both out of here."

Galen bowed his head. He didn't have time to argue, and he was already growing tired. "I do not expect Blaylock or I shall return from that place."

"Then I'll just have to help you." G'Leel opened the door and stepped out into the hall.

Galen followed, lowering his voice. "You will very likely die."

Her mouth tightened, and she drew in a quick breath. "That's my choice, isn't it? Just as it's yours?"

That he could not argue. He walked down the hall, G'Leel at his side.

At the City Center, deep below ground, a door opened, and Tilar turned quickly, an overly enthusiastic smile forming on his face. "Elizar. At last you're here."

Londo peered down the dimly lit corridor that marked the boundary of the mages' territory in Down Below. Vir had "shown" him the way, with Fed's hidden assistance, and then had quickly withdrawn. Vir had learned his lesson, which was more than Elric could say for his master.

From the observation room Elric watched Londo, as he watched many things, attempting to ignore the constant throbbing in his head. Time was growing short. The *Crystal Cabin* was scheduled to depart in four hours, and those who would leave here alive must be on it.

In one of the customs areas, Purple Drazi gathered, looking toward the bay that held the *Zekhite*, and whispering of the Green Drazi that rumor said were inside. Commander Susan Ivanova, second-in-command of Babylon 5, had thus far frustrated their attempts to fight until a clear-cut winner emerged. According to Beel's report, Susan had seized the scarf of the Green leader in frustration, and so had unintentionally become the Green leader. She had promptly ordered all Green Drazi to dye their scarves purple, effectively ending their division.

Yet now, Elric knew, they sensed the thrill of conflict returning. Fresh enemies had arrived on the station. The Purples didn't know what had happened to the two comrades they'd met in the brig who had originally told them of the *Zekhite* and its Green crew. Perhaps they believed the two were casualties of the conflict. In that case, their deaths would be avenged.

In the captain's office, Security Officer Lou Welch sat across the desk from John Sheridan, making his report. "Since they aren't registered in any way, we can't know every techno-mage who arrived. But we estimate now there are hundreds of them on the station. Maybe as many as five hundred. The arrivals seemed to stop a few days ago, which could mean that they're all here—all that are coming, anyway. They've ordered lots of supplies from various vendors, and each time they specified the goods had to be ready by this morning. Which suggests that they're leaving very soon now." Lou paused to scratch his balding head, looking rather anxious and overworked. "We still haven't been able to figure out how they're leaving, though. They're not registered as passengers on any outgoing ships. We're watching all departures, as you ordered."

The probe on John's neck revealed that the captain was twirling the orange blossom absently between thumb and forefinger. It remained as fresh as when Elric had given it to him. "They said they were leaving. I think you're right; I think it's soon, whether there's a record of it or not. I need you to get word to their leader, Elric. Have him meet me here in an hour."

"Yes, sir."

"Thank you, Mr. Welch. Good work."

In Down Below, Londo at last gathered the nerve to step into the corridor where runes glowed on the walls. "Hello? Hello?"

Fed was handling all the conjuries this time. Elric had told him it was because he'd proven himself with Vir's visit. Although that was true, Elric would still have preferred to do the work himself, but he was simply too tired. He had to save what energy remained to him.

A dim red glow spread from the cross-hallway ahead of Londo, and the ambassador looked anxiously toward it.

Londo had come to apologize. Elric had accurately deduced at least that much of the plan that had been hatched within the station's hedge maze. This was Morden's misdirection: lead the mages to believe that Londo had been beaten, so they would be unprepared for him to strike back. The hypocrite Londo would have no trouble going along, while revenge remained his final goal.

Londo spoke nervously into the silence, extending his hands. "I admit perhaps my enthusiasm for—for a personal meeting was excessive."

The red light grew brighter, and a low growl echoed down the corridor. Beneath it rumbled the sound of massive movement. Though Elric was not there to smell it, he imagined the stench of rotten meat on the air.

Londo's hands rose, as if trying to ward off whatever might come. "And certainly—certainly the incident with the concealed camera was regrettable."

A thunderous roar blasted down at Londo.

He cowered, his hands up around his head. As the roaring swelled, he yelled out, barely audible. "And I would just like to say that for any misunderstanding that might have grown out of all of this . . . I . . ." His hands rose over his head now, in complete surrender. "I apologize."

The roaring stopped; the red light faded away.

Londo looked around in disbelief, then, deciding the worst was over, hesitantly lowered his hands. With an uncertain smile he attempted to regain his dignity. "Well, I'm pleased to see that you are a sympathetic and understanding group. I will go now. If you ever come this way again, though, perhaps we can do—do business after all, yes?" Londo paused, looking hopefully down the corridor. Then he seemed to realize that the greatest wisdom lay in a rapid retreat. He held his hands to either side of his mouth, yelled out his parting as if to stress the fact that their business was now concluded. "Good-bye." He turned and walked quickly down the hall.

On his back hung three holodemons, conjured by Fed with a spell that combined elements of illusion with elements of the flying platform, so that the images of the holodemons could be given substance, and even the ability to move objects. Fed would follow Londo, torment him with the demons. They would distract him and further fuel his anger against the mages. He would believe the mages' focus was on this petty revenge, and would not realize the true object of their machinations: the Centauri freighter *Ondavi* owned by Refa, docked at Babylon 5. It was the final shell in Elric's shell game.

Elric found he had received a message. It was from Galen. Galen was still alive.

He held that truth close to him for a moment, savoring its comfort.

But all too quickly, the worries returned. If Galen had sent a message, then Blaylock must be unable. Galen would be on his own. Even if Alwyn was taking extreme risks to reach Thenothk quickly, he could not have arrived there yet. And by sending this message, Galen could well have betrayed his location to the Shadows, putting himself in even greater danger.

The throbbing in Elric's head grew stronger, carrying the pain of absence, of everything that had been lost. He had determined not to lose Galen. Yet the cavity of darkness within him threatened to swallow all hope.

He took a deep breath, banishing his worry. It would serve nothing. He opened the message and forced himself through it, word by word, sentence by sentence.

The Shadows know you are on Babylon 5. They know you plan to leave on the Zekhite. *The* Zekhite *will be destroyed once you are aboard. Morden is in charge of it.*

If the Shadows could intercept their messages, Galen's warning would work to Elric's advantage. That, however, provided little comfort. Galen's message was unnecessary. And he had risked his life to send it.

I was able to translate Isabelle's spell. I'm sending you all of her files, and my translation, and the information we've gathered about this place and the Shadows.

Galen had learned how to listen to the Shadows. If others could translate the work, this would be an invaluable asset. It would take time, though.

Only three sentences remained.

Blaylock has been captured and is being held in the City Center. I'm going after him.

Elizar is there.

Blaylock had been overcome, just as Kell had been. Of the powers Elizar and the Shadows might have used to subdue them, Elric had only his fears. Against those powers, Galen would have no preparation, no defense.

Galen had written the message in haste, no doubt, which explained its sudden end. Elric skimmed through the attached information. Galen had given over all of Isabelle's files, his private link to her. He did not believe he would return.

The message was awash with Galen's emotions: fear for himself, fear for Elric and the mages, fear for Blaylock, and, at the end, a hint of eagerness. At last Galen would get what he most wanted, and what Elric most feared: a confrontation with Elizar.

Elric pressed the heel of his hand to his temple, hoping to hold back the pain. It was building, and he had no time to rest.

He composed a brief, cryptic message to Alwyn, from which Alwyn would understand that he must seek out this City Center. Elric should have sent him sooner. Elric should have gone himself. He should never have allowed Galen to part from him.

If the Shadows had Blaylock, then they likely knew of Galen's presence on Thenothk. Morden could have known his location all along. His threat need not have been idle.

Elric lowered his hand from his head, but the emptiness remained, pushing outward, pressing at the backs of his eyes, his forehead. How could he have allowed Galen's life to be endangered? How could he have let Galen go to the Shadows? Would Galen be sent back to them, flayed? Or would they hold him and tempt him with what he most wanted? And when he listened to the Shadows, what poison would he hear?

— chapter 13 —

It was near dawn when Galen and G'Leel approached the demolition site behind the City Center. The streets were quiet now. The not-darkness of night was being replaced by the not-light of day. Columns of black smoke rose to obscure the sky.

They slipped into an alley, unobserved. His breathing rapid and shallow, Galen unwrapped from around his head the scarf, which he had used as a crude disguise. He pushed it into his pocket.

Dark spots danced before his eyes, and he rested for a moment against the side of a building. His leg had turned into a mass of pain. He hadn't dared use a platform to reach the City Center, and as they'd hurried through the maze of streets, it had swollen until he could no longer bend his knee. The skin was hot and tight, and with each step the grating in his shin set off a brilliant detonation of sensation.

He was racing with energy—burning with it. He had felt that way ever since he'd heard Tilar speak Elizar's name. The tech was ready for his command. Yet what good was it if the Shadows would detect him the moment he used it? He must make do with his broken body a little while longer.

He started down the long alley after G'Leel. They must hurry. Even now it could be too late.

It had been forty-five minutes since he'd awoken in G'Leel's hotel room. In his mind's eye, Galen watched the bright white room deep underground through the probe on Rabelna. Blaylock remained lying on the floor, unconscious. Elizar and Tilar had spent the time first arguing over who was to blame for Blaylock's condition, then debating what should be done about it. Bunny had tried to stimulate Blaylock's mind to consciousness, but had failed.

Now she stood over him in her pink dress, hands on her hips. "If I didn't know better, I'd say he was brain-dead. Obviously the functions to keep his body alive are still working. But the higher functions are shut down. He's not asleep. He's not unconscious. He's just"—she snapped her fingers—"turned off. You mages are very fragile."

"That's not possible," Elizar said. "A brain can't just be turned off." Galen tried not to focus on Elizar. When he looked at that angular, arrogant face, his hatred threatened to overwhelm him.

"Well, I don't sense a thing from him," Bunny said. "Not a memory, not a worry, not a wet dream—nothing."

To one side, Tilar studied Blaylock with an intensity that worried Galen. "That's not the way it's supposed to work."

Bunny shrugged. "Well, I can't get anything out of him like this."

As the discussion continued, Galen tried to understand what had happened. Elizar and Tilar had done something to Blaylock. He had no idea what they'd done, but obviously they hadn't expected this result. He feared they'd caused Blaylock some irreparable damage. It was strange, though, that they were so puzzled by his condition.

Galen had considered the possibility that Blaylock was pretending an injury to avoid a scan by Bunny. Yet he didn't believe Blaylock had the ability to simply turn off the higher functions of his brain. Elizar was right; it wasn't possible. And in the unlikely event Blaylock did have the ability, how would he ever judge when it was safe to turn his brain back on? Galen didn't think Blaylock would have returned to this place just to play dead.

A more likely possibility, which cycled endlessly through Galen's mind, was that Blaylock had purposely injured himself. Blaylock had said Kell induced a heart attack to avoid revealing information. Had Blaylock, perhaps, induced a stroke? The locations of the gathering place and the hiding place were in his keeping. And Blaylock might have felt some need to protect Galen, to give him the chance to pass along the information they'd gained.

That would mean Blaylock had sacrificed himself for Galen, just as she had done. Galen could not accept that. He could not live with that. No more would die for him, unless he wanted them to.

As he approached the mouth of the alley, he pressed himself against the wall. Then, at last, he could rest another moment. He wrapped a hand around his side, struggling to catch his breath.

From across the alley, G'Leel appraised him. "You look like death."

Galen gazed out on the demolition site. It was a great open area of brown rock, surrounded on all sides by high buildings, the tallest the City Center. The Joncorp factory had once stood here, and soon would again, if G'Leel's information was accurate.

The ground was flat, except for a vast, irregularly shaped hole that had been excavated out of the rock. The excavation began just a short distance from the alley where they stood and covered about half of the empty lot. Galen couldn't see how deep the hole was, but he remembered that the Shadow ship had been carving some sort of trench in the ground. Anna must have blasted out this entire area.

A large group worked at the far end of the lot, where Anna had crashed. Pieces of wreckage were being hauled up on cranes and cleared away. The near end of the lot was unoccupied.

Galen couldn't tell whether the large hole contained an entrance to the complex of underground tunnels where Blaylock was held, but his guess was it did. That could be the easiest way in.

"What are they doing over there?" G'Leel asked.

It was time to risk detection, Galen decided. They'd probably be spotted as soon as they entered the tunnels anyway. "Want to take a ride?" he asked.

"On what?"

Galen visualized the equation for a flying platform, and the tech echoed it, eager, at last, to act. The platform pushed against his feet. He conjured an equation of motion, glided over to her.

"How the hell are you doing that?"

He extended the platform beneath her feet, and she grabbed at him for balance. "Hold on," he said. "We're going to move quickly."

She took hold of his belt.

Equation of motion, equation of motion. They shot out from the alley across twenty feet of open space, dropped straight down into the excavation. She grabbed him with both arms and spat a curse in Narn.

Perhaps a hundred feet below them was a smooth, dull black surface. It ran in gentle, graceful contours. It had been buried here, in the ground. Anna had unearthed it. Galen slowed their descent and turned the platform so he could observe the strange, spiky object that had been revealed.

"What the—" G'Leel said.

"You remember the ship you described to me once? As black as space, and bristling with arms. It moved as if alive."

"That's it," G'Leel said. "What's it doing in the ground?"

"I don't know. The Shadows must conceal their ships until they're needed. The one I destroyed last night was cutting this one free." They had demolished the Joncorp factory to reach it.

He resumed their rapid descent, directing them down between the front edge of the Shadow ship and the stone wall of
the pit.

"You destroyed one last night," G'Leel said breathlessly.
"A Shadow ship. One that was moving around."

As he skirted the edge of the ship he saw a faint light
coming from below. It was a tunnel in the wall of the excavation. From the tunnel, a walkway led to an opening in the
ship. Galen brought them down on the walkway.

G'Leel released him and took a few stiff steps back. "I
thought techno-mages were wise. I thought maybe they knew
a few things. But I didn't think they did much, except tell for-
tunes and perform mysterious—nonsense."

"I suppose this would fall into the mysterious nonsense
category." The entrance to the ship revealed only darkness.
He wondered if someone was wired inside. There was no
time to investigate.

The tunnel through the brown rock was about eight feet
across, and had an arched shape. The floor had been smoothed
and polished flat. The rest remained rough and ragged. Surely
the Shadows had the ability to create something much more
finished. But then, they chose to spend much of their time
down here, rather than in the tower above. Perhaps this was
where they were comfortable. Galen wondered if this was how
they lived on their home, Z'ha'dum.

The dimly lit tunnel extended about thirty feet, then ended
at an intersection with another. He saw no one, though the
probe on Rabelna had revealed that the tunnels were well traveled by Shadows and others. Galen wished he could use a full-
body illusion to disguise himself. But that would probably
give him away even more quickly than some half-baked deception. "Hold your gun on me," he said. "If we are stopped, I
am your prisoner."

"Who am I?"

"You are one of that cleanup crew out there. You were told to watch for me."

G'Leel pulled out her gun. "You think they're going to believe that?"

"If they don't, shoot them."

"Oh."

Galen limped down the tunnel.

In his mind's eye, within the white room, Elizar turned on Tilar. "You hit him. You did something. Just admit it."

Tilar crossed his arms over his chest. Against the ornately decorated vest he wore, the sleeves of his shirt were a brilliant white. "I didn't lay a hand on him. You can see there's not a mark."

"There were plenty of marks on Regana."

"Are we going to go through that again? She was my teacher. It was my right to kill her however I wanted."

Elizar threw up his hand with a flourish. "You are a sadist. And a poorly skilled one, at that."

"You act like you want to wrap your arms around Blaylock and give him a big wet kiss. We're going to kill him. What difference would it make if I—" Tilar turned and delivered a vicious kick to Blaylock's head. It snapped to the side, slowly rolled back. A trickle of blood ran down his temple.

Galen reached the end of the tunnel. A second one led off to left and right, curving in both directions so he could not see far along its length. A few doors were built into the rock, controlled by keypads in their frames. They were all closed, no one in sight. Galen wondered if he and G'Leel were just lucky, or if they were walking into a trap. It had occurred to him that Rabelna's presence within the underground room might be for his benefit. Elizar could have deduced that Galen and Blaylock had followed her to the City Center. He could have scanned her and discovered the probe. Showing Rabelna that they held Blaylock prisoner would be the best way to lure

Galen there. But to what end? Elizar knew that Galen held the secret of destruction. Didn't Elizar fear him?

Whether it was a trap or not, he must reach Blaylock quickly. The probe on Rabelna was one hundred feet below them, and seventy feet to the north. Galen turned right, hurrying ahead. The curving tunnels seemed as mazelike as the city above.

In his mind's eye, the argument continued.

"This is ridiculous," Elizar said. "He could have all the information we want, and somehow you've destroyed our opportunity. I don't think our associates will be pleased with that."

Tilar spread his hands. "I haven't done anything! He's faking it. You know how he and his hairless holy order can turn their senses on and off. He's obviously got some method of turning his brain off." Tilar looked down at Blaylock. "He'll wake up if he really wants to. We just have to make him want to." He circled Blaylock's fallen body. After every few steps, as punctuation to his speech, he drew his leg back and kicked Blaylock, hard. "You act like you're so pure. Self-denial. Scouring. You claim the tech connects you to God. Well I have a message from God. He says he wants no part of you." He dropped to his knees beside Blaylock, took Blaylock's hand in his. As he bent forward, he obscured Galen's view.

"What do you think you're doing," Elizar said.

"I'm waking him up. Come on, Blaylock, you're not going to sleep through this, are you?"

Galen's view shifted as Rabelna stood and walked around Tilar to see what was happening. He had Blaylock's wrist clasped between his knees, Blaylock's palm facing up.

Galen closed his eyes, but the vision remained. From somewhere Tilar had produced a knife, and he cut a deep channel from the heel of Blaylock's hand down the length of the index finger. Blood spilled down Blaylock's palm. Tilar dug into the wound with the knife, searching for the threads of tech within.

Blaylock's body remained limp, his lips slightly parted, eyes closed.

"Cast *me* away," Tilar said. "Tell *me* I'm unfit. You and your pathetic cult of holier-than-thou pompous mono-pricks! Claiming the mages are blessed by God. Do you laugh at night, that so many believe you? Or do you really believe that manure you peddle?" The knife point came out, pulling with it slender strands of gold intertwined with blood vessels, tissue, muscle. Tilar slipped bloody fingers around them, pulled. "Do you hear God, Blaylock? He wants his tech back. He's found *you* unfit. You ate that extra piece of cake last winter. He saw it." With a yank he ripped the threads out with slimy bits of tissue. A fresh gush of blood ran down Blaylock's hand, soaking into his jacket sleeve and the knees of Tilar's pants, and dripping down onto the floor.

Tilar shook the threads off, started carving a second channel down Blaylock's palm. "Better wake up, or you're not going to be a mage anymore."

Galen forced himself to limp faster, his body racing with fear and adrenaline, the tech echoing it back.

If Tilar wanted to inflict pain, why not use his chrysalis? Elizar had used his tech to flay Kell with clean, surgical lines. Tilar performed the same atrocity, but his method was brutal, monstrous.

Galen had dreamed of doing just the same to Elizar.

He heard footsteps ahead, around the curve in the tunnel. He would not hide; he would not slow. There was no time.

Two aliens came around the curve, wheeling a gurney toward them. The aliens were humanoid, tall and slim, with greyish skin, bulbous heads, large black eyes, and narrow mouths. They appeared unarmed.

The aliens raised their heads, regarding him curiously. G'Leel shoved him forward. "Move it, you low-rent fortune-teller."

Galen stumbled toward them, pain shooting up his leg. He could see, now, a body on the gurney. The woman wore a jumpsuit that looked as if it had once been orange but now was covered with a uniform greyish stain. It was much too big for her. Along her sides lay her hands, thin, almost skeletal. Her fingernails were several inches long, and they had begun to twist into spirals. Dark hair lay in an oily mat against her shoulders and head. Her eyes were closed, with half circles of dark skin below them. Fitted over her head was the delicate metal device he'd seen being produced in a factory. The sculpted formation ran from cheeks to temple to forehead and disappeared beneath her hair.

He regained his balance as he came alongside the gurney. Some sort of energy was emanating from her, or from the device fastened to her. He slowed, trying to analyze it. The frequency of its vibration was strange, like a heartbeat, or the echo of a heartbeat.

G'Leel laid a hand on his back, urging him ahead. Yet for some reason he couldn't look away from the woman.

Her skeletal hand shot out, seized his wrist. Her eyes snapped open, and she trembled with the intensity of her grip. She jerked his hand to the side of her face, to one of the sculpted strands of metal.

The connection formed instantly between them.

Anna.

She hungered for the machine. Without it, she was a bodiless spirit, lacking purpose or direction. She needed to coordinate, to synchronize, to strike, to fulfill the needs of the machine, to follow the direction of the Eye. She longed for the dizzying delight of movement, the exhilarating leap to hyperspace, the joy of the war cry. Even separated from her ship, she could think only of serving, of incorporating herself into the great body of the machine. She needed to have her body back again, to beat out the perfect, flawless march, to shriek the red ecstasy of fire. She and the machine must be one: a great engine of chaos and destruction.

Beside her, she sensed such a machine. Its touch promised all she desired. She must have it.

His breath suddenly became deeper, pain stabbing at his side with each inhalation. Deeper breaths, she judged, were more efficient. His chest rose and fell with hers. The heel of his hand was pressed against her neck, and through it, he felt the eager beat of her pulse. His own pounded in synchrony. His mind's eye flashed with a rapid series of sensor readings, lists of systems and programs stored within him. His leg tingled, and he realized she had discovered the damage and was speeding his organelles in their repair. His control was slipping away, a startling, unnerving sensation.

G'Leel had turned her gun on the aliens. Their black eyes were staring at him.

As if of its own will, his free hand rose, and he watched as it moved toward the other side of her head. She would coordinate his systems, serve as the central processing unit of his body. The bond between them must be made more efficient and complete.

Galen forced his mind's eye to go blank, and with all his will he yanked his hand free. "No!" He stumbled back, the connection suddenly broken.

She reached for him, fingers straining.

Galen found he'd backed against the wall. Yet she no longer frightened him. She'd had no chance of retaining control once he resisted. She was meant to be a slave, while he'd been trained to be a master.

Her dark eyes were consumed with emptiness and hunger.

They had removed her from the wreckage. They were going to wire her into the excavated ship. That connection was what she most wanted.

"Galen!"

He realized G'Leel had been calling his name. "Yes," he said, still struggling to regain his equilibrium.

"These two are unarmed." She had forced the two aliens away from the gurney, but seemed hesitant to kill them. The thin white scar across her nose was prominent in the dim light.

Bits of Anna's memories seemed to have stayed with him. "They are butchers. They turn intelligent beings into components for their machines."

The aliens stared at him. With their large eyes and thin, narrow mouths, they gave the impression of being sad. That, he knew, was not the case.

Galen suddenly realized he'd lost contact with the probe on Rabelna. Quickly he accessed it. She had turned away from Tilar and Blaylock. All he could see was Bunny, sitting in the corner with crossed legs, the top one swinging impatiently.

"I should be going," Rabelna said. "This really is not my area of expertise."

Galen willed her to turn around. He had to see Blaylock.

"We have need of you," Elizar said. "Wait beside the door."

Rabelna did not move.

"Are you finished yet?" Elizar said. "He's not waking."

"He will." Tilar's voice was strained, as if with exertion.

"Galen!" G'Leel said.

He forced his attention back to the stone tunnel. He had to immobilize the aliens, had to get to Blaylock. The smart thing to do would be to use a minimum of energy. Avoid detection as long as possible—if they hadn't already been detected. Giving Anna a wide berth, he went to the aliens. One held up a hand in seeming fear, his long, thick fingers trembling.

Galen palmed two of the tranq tabs from his coat pocket. He made a distracting flourish before the alien's face with one hand, while with the other he reached up to press the tranq on the back of the alien's neck. Then he did the same to the second alien. The tranqs were formulated for Drakh; he had no idea whether they'd do anything to these aliens, whether they'd knock the aliens out or kill them. All he cared was that they do something fast.

"What good was that?" G'Leel asked.

The two aliens fell against each other, wilted to the floor.

"Oh," G'Leel said.

From the gurney, Anna watched him. He couldn't leave her, he realized. He couldn't allow her to be enslaved again to a machine. Killing her would probably be a mercy, but he wasn't prepared to do that. Perhaps there was some way, in time, to help her recover what she had once been. Of course, it was unlikely that any of them would get out of here alive.

"Bring her with us." Galen limped ahead, the pain shooting through him with each step. "Hurry."

G'Leel wheeled Anna, and they found their way through the maze of tunnels to Blaylock's level without encountering anyone else. At this depth, the tunnels were about twice as wide as before. They should have been heavily trafficked. Galen had become certain they were walking into a trap. But there was no time for strategy or deception. He had to reach Blaylock.

They were within fifty feet of Rabelna's probe now; the door to the white room had to be around the next curve.

Galen heard the hint of movement behind them. He looked back. The curve of the tunnel concealed the sound's source.

He stilled G'Leel with a touch, hurried to one of the doors in the side of the tunnel. He pressed a few buttons on the keypad. The door required a specific code. He had no time to decipher it.

"Get against the wall," he whispered to G'Leel. "Quickly."

She wheeled the gurney to the side of the passage, and Galen pressed up against the cold stone beside her. He visualized the equation, conjured an illusion that the stone wall was in front of them rather than behind them, that the curve of the passage was slightly sharper than it actually was. "Be silent," he said.

From their point of view, the illusory wall was no more than a dark screen. G'Leel turned her head anxiously from side to side, looking for whatever Galen had heard. A few seconds later, several aliens came into view, traveling in the same direction Galen and G'Leel had been. They were clearly soldiers, protected by black body armor and carrying heavy-duty weapons of an unfamiliar design. After a moment, Galen recognized them as Drakh.

They were not the same type of Drakh he'd seen before; they had no protuberances on the backs of their heads. These were the second Drakh type described by the mage Osiyrin in his ancient treatise, those who did not speak. Their eyes glowed brilliant red. Jagged white exoskeletons covered most of the grey skin of their heads. They were shorter than the other Drakh, more muscular. Osiyrin had said they were soldiers and workers.

More came down the passage, about two dozen in all, and they passed by Galen and G'Leel, disappearing around the next curve. The Drakh were not trying to keep them from the room where Blaylock was held; these soldiers were here to ensure that they reached it.

Galen looked back the way they had come, saw no more Drakh. He was about to dissolve the illusion when he picked up a hint of static. A sharp-edged shape came into view, moving in the same direction as the Drakh, following at a safe distance. Its silhouette crawled with white dots of interference. The static shifted with that same suggestion of scissor-like action he'd sensed before. He could almost make out legs, a head.

Beside him, G'Leel shifted, and he realized that she believed they were safe. He pressed her back.

Several other Shadows followed this one. He thought he could see them swiveling their heads, studying the tunnel.

In his mind's eye, Rabelna at last turned, and Galen saw Tilar bent over Blaylock. Tilar was at work on the other hand now, the brilliant white of his shirt drenched in blood up to the elbows. Rabelna moved quickly away to stand near the door.

In the tunnel, one of the Shadows stopped its forward movement, its head tilted toward them. The body of static grew larger as it approached. Galen stopped breathing. He was racing with energy, desperate to reach Blaylock, cursing himself for getting into such a position.

The other Shadows hesitated now, looking toward this one.

The Shadow stopped in front of the false wall, and its head turned back and forth. It moved closer.

"Stop, now," Elizar said within the white room. "This is pointless. He's just going to bleed to death."

The static shape bent toward them, its head arching forward, coming up against the illusion of the wall, penetrating the wall. Something happened to the Shadow as it passed through the plane of the illusion. Through the dark screen came a head of shining blackness, its own veil of illusion vanished.

G'Leel jumped.

Fourteen pinpoints of light formed its eyes, and as they turned from Anna to G'Leel to Galen, they glowed like tiny furnaces of malice. The creature let out a high, piercing shriek.

Galen dissolved the illusion as the spell of destruction formed in his mind like a thunderclap. Energy fell upon him with crushing pressure in layer upon layer upon layer, then shot out, capturing the Shadow in a sphere. Its shriek hushed as the sound was sealed within. Yet other Shadows took up the call.

The sphere began to redden and darken, the Shadow a fading body of static with a head of pure blackness. G'Leel pushed Anna away from it, and Galen followed. Space became fluid, and the back of G'Leel's head rippled as if something beneath were pushing to escape. The tunnel began to distort, stone walls undulating in waves. Twisting and flowing, the other static shapes glided back the way they'd come.

They were responsible for all that had happened. They wrapped themselves in shadows, working behind the scenes, manipulating others. And from that safety, they encouraged treachery, provoked wars, inspired murder.

Galen had held in his anger, his need to act against them, all this time. But he would wait no longer.

The Shadows could hide no more.

He focused on one Shadow after the next, conjuring the one-term equation again, again, encasing one after the next in a sphere of destruction. The energy fell upon him, burned out of him, at last finding its release.

Answering the calls of the Shadows, the Drakh ran down the passage, weapons at the ready. But when they found their masters trapped within the darkening spheres, they hesitated. G'Leel yanked her gun up, fired. Most retreated in confusion around the curve of the tunnel, while the three nearest turned on G'Leel with their weapons. Before they had a chance to fire, Galen seized them within a single sphere.

The first Shadow he had encased was now nearly invisible in the darkness. Only the faint lights of its eyes remained, floating in strange, independent movement, like fireflies in the night. Gradually their light died, trapped within, and the black sphere began its rapid collapse. As it shrank, the sphere paled to grey, then, like a mirage, it simply faded away, a blast of air rushing in to fill the void with a great rolling crack.

Galen turned away, started between the spheres toward Blaylock. He was burning, incandescent, both seized with energy and surging with it. Around him, the fledgling universes began imploding with deafening claps, shaking the wavering tunnel. Some contained within them sections of the rocky ceiling, or the floor, and as they vanished they left smooth, scooped formations.

As the Drakh came into view, he visualized equation after

equation in a simple column, imploding one or two or three at a time as his attention fell upon them. Energy sang along the meridians of the tech. The conjury was effortless, the spells not some complex, halting, deliberate labor, but somehow natural, flowing with simple ease from intent to action. As he stepped in and out of the scoop-shaped depressions where once his enemies had stood, he realized he felt no pain in his stiff leg.

Encased within a darkening sphere, a Drakh reached for him, arms stretching and snaking in a hypnotic dance. As the sphere snapped into rapid collapse, the Drakh's body crumpled like a piece of paper. In another sphere, a Drakh's face twisted in and in on itself, like a grey, white, and red pinwheel, before contracting into nothingness. In another, as the shrinking universe clouded over, three Drakh collapsed into a single pulpy mass as if crushed by an invisible fist. His fist.

Then he had run out of Drakh. The thunderclaps ceased, space and time settled into their familiar shapes. Galen stood before the room where Blaylock was kept. Except for G'Leel approaching with Anna, the tunnel was empty. Perhaps they were afraid to send more. Perhaps they were satisfied that he'd gone where they wanted him to go. The stone walls seemed strangely solid, inflexible. G'Leel stopped a few feet away. Her golden face carried an expression Galen had never seen on her before. She was terrified.

"Don't worry," he said, barely able to hear himself after the fusillade of sound. "The other mages don't know that spell."

She sucked in a short breath, gave a quick nod.

He was ablaze with energy. He would take Blaylock, and the rest would pay for what they'd done. They would die. Elizar would die. If Galen could kill him more than once, he would.

He reached for the keypad beside the door. Before he could touch it, the door slid open.

* * *

Elric sat in John Sheridan's office, holding his weary body erect. He must know whether John would try to detain them, whether the plan to test the captain with the truth had been wise or foolhardy. But John had been delayed. He had gone to the customs area, where the station's Purple Drazi had launched an attack on the *Zekhite*'s Green Drazi.

The conflict had begun on the freighter itself when the Purple Drazi had stormed it, but quickly spread to the customs area and into other ships docked nearby. The Green Drazi, though much fewer in number, were holding their own. Ing-Radi had warned the captain of the *Zekhite*, Vayda, that such an attack might come.

Station security had been thrown into disarray, but Elric expected that within a few minutes, they would begin arresting the Drazi, including the crew of the *Zekhite*. This time Susan Ivanova could not simply take the scarf of the Green leader and order the Greens to dye their scarves purple, for there was no Green leader aboard the *Zekhite*. She would have to think of another solution, and until then the *Zekhite* would be unavailable. The second shell in Elric's shell game would be taken out of play, as he had planned. If the Shadows had read Galen's message, and knew that the mages had been warned of sabotage aboard the *Zekhite*, all the better. The Shadows would believe them desperate, vulnerable.

Across the station, Londo entered the casino. Elric released a silent breath. Here was the rest of the plan Morden had hatched within the hedge maze, and it was exactly as Elric had anticipated. He'd known that Morden sometimes manipulated the outcome of Londo's gambling, and he'd tried to encourage Morden's choice of that particular methodology by arranging Londo's encounter with Carvin. Londo, at his secret meeting with Morden, would have recited the mages' many offenses against him, including their attempt to cheat him at poker. Morden would have concluded that the mages, known never to lose at games of chance, were gathering funds to hire another ship, a replacement for the *Tidewell* that could be used to deceive the Shadows.

Now, Morden would believe, the mages' need for a ship was even greater.

He would want to control the mages. If they were to acquire another ship, he would want to know which it was. Elric had hoped that Morden would fashion these circumstances into a plan, a plan to use Londo to ensure the mages' destruction.

A lock of hair at one end of Londo's great crest drooped at an odd angle. Looking self-consciously around the dimly lit casino, he tried to press it back in place. When he removed his hand, it fell again immediately. With a frown, he brushed at a brown splotch on the front of his jacket. He'd had some trouble dealing with Fed's demons.

He saw Carvin at the high-stakes poker table and stopped his brushing. A strange expression came over his face, part eagerness, part hesitance. He must suspect that Morden's help with the techno-mage problem would not end well for the mages, just as Morden's help with the Narn problem in Quadrant 37 had not ended well for the Narns. Perhaps Londo had not lost his conscience entirely. Yet that merely damned him further. A man who performed atrocities in the absence of a conscience did not understand the depth of his evil, while a man who performed them in spite of his conscience believed his own petty desires justified any evil. He was a true malignancy.

Londo composed his face, straightened his jacket with a tug, and wound his way toward the poker table. Elric switched to the camera over the dealer's shoulder.

As Carvin raked in a large pot of chips, Londo came up behind her. "Hello, dear lady."

Carvin turned and extended her hand with a smile. "I told you, I'm no lady."

He kissed her hand, noticing the ring. He was wary, though trying not to show it. He must pretend he didn't know she was a techno-mage, must play the lovesick fool, with Carvin acting the seductress. Only that way could he "trick" her into gambling with him.

The player to her right—Muirne in disguise—gathered up her few remaining chips and left. Londo took her seat. "I am glad to find you here. I've thought of nothing but you since our last meeting."

"I've thought of many things, but none so intriguing as you, Ambassador."

Londo gave an uncertain smile, charmed in spite of himself. "You're unlike any woman I've ever met."

"More than you know."

"I would like to get to know you better. I've given great thought to what you said, that you like your gamblers fearless."

"And are you fearless, Ambassador?"

"For you," he said, again taking her hand, "I believe I could be. But the question is this, dear lady. Are you fearless?"

"You have a proposition."

"One I hope you will find intriguing. Perhaps we could discuss it over a drink."

"Delighted." She slid her chips into her purse, and they found a corner table in the bar where they could have privacy. As Londo brought drinks over, Elric noticed one of Morden's paid agents sitting several tables away.

Elric accessed different cameras until he found one that gave him a good view of both Londo and Carvin.

"Tell me," Londo said, "what brings you to Babylon 5?"

"Must we resort to small talk? Let's be more daring. If you could ask me one thing"—she fixed him with her eyes—"what would it be?"

Londo seemed to actually give the question some thought. "What was it like, to be brought up apart from your own people?"

She laughed, startling him. "But I wasn't. Those who raised me *are* my people. The Centauri perhaps share more of my

DNA than others, but your history is not my history, your desires are not my desires, your identity is not my identity." With a graceful turn of her wrist she extended her hand. "And now I have a question for you. If you had not been raised by the Centauri, who would you be, what would you want?"

Londo smiled uneasily, then shook his head, expelling a short breath. "It is impossible to imagine. My entire life has been steeped in the tradition, the history, the honor of the Centauri. It is who I am. Without that—" He waved off the question. "Perhaps I would be a professional gambler. Or a gigolo."

"I have a feeling you would excel at either profession."

Londo took a drink. "You flatter me."

"You're a delightful companion, Ambassador."

"Please, you must call me Londo." He seemed to be falling for her seduction, even though he knew it was an act. It fed his ego to believe she was sincere.

"Londo, there is only one desire I have failed to satisfy in living apart from the Centauri." She slid her hand across the table, brushed her fingers over his. "It is a desire, I must admit, I am eager to gratify, with the right man."

Londo recovered from her frankness more quickly this time. "I am sorry to hear of your loss. It is a true tragedy. I would like to do everything within my power to correct it."

"You said you had a proposition."

For just a moment, his face froze with its mixture of playful solicitude and lust. Then he spoke. "Indeed I do." He pulled back his hand. "I have been thinking about what you said, about gambling fearlessly. Many times I have bet more than I should. But those bets were never fearless, merely foolish. We could gamble for high stakes, but as long as one knows the stakes, one can judge whether the risk is acceptable, no? The true risk comes in accepting the stakes when one does not know them. Which leads me to my proposition." He reached into his pocket, removed a simple black eight-sided die, and set it on the table. Half of the sides were marked with a circle, half with a cross. So this was Morden's plan. "On one roll of the die we wager blindly. If you win, I will undertake any action you say, so long as it is in my power and violates no laws. If I win, you will do the same for me."

Londo was far from fearless; he had to be certain he would win to suggest such terms. Morden had clearly guaranteed him success. Suddenly all of Elric's assumptions were cast into doubt. He had expected any wager would be designed so that the mages won. Only then could the Shadows learn what the mages wanted—which was what the Shadows always desired to know.

But if Londo won, what might he demand?

Carvin inclined her head. "A bold proposition. You surprise me, Londo."

"You inspire me, dear lady."

Elric had arranged with Carvin that if at any point he wanted her to withdraw, he would send her a blank message. Carvin hesitated, allowing Elric time to stop her. He sent nothing. No mage had ever lost a wager. While Londo's die could not be switched, because they'd had no chance to prepare a replacement, a tiny flying platform could be used to push the octagon to the desired position, or an illusion cast to change the symbols.

Whether the Shadows could stop Carvin, Elric didn't know. But he didn't believe they would. He believed the Shadows wanted her to win, no matter what Morden had told Londo.

"The possibilities are a delight to imagine," Carvin said. "I agree."

"Will you choose the circle, then, or the cross?"

"The circle."

"And I will take the cross. Since you have chosen, I will roll, yes?"

As Carvin nodded, she sucked her lips inward, for the first time betraying any nervousness.

Londo shook the die. As his loose lock of hair trembled with anticipation, a triumphant smile broke out on his face. He dreamed, no doubt, of winning a blessing from the mages at the least. Perhaps more.

He rolled the octagon across the small table. Carvin lifted her drink, following its course. When done well, the use of the flying platform to assure victory was so subtle and quick that no one but another mage—or perhaps a Shadow—could detect it. Carvin did well. The die stopped with a circle on top.

The smile fell from Londo's face. "What? No! It's not possible!" He leaned closer. "Something has gone terribly wrong."

Now Carvin was smiling. "No, it hasn't. You've simply lost, Londo. That's what happens when you gamble with a techno-mage."

Londo continued to stare down at the die. At last he straightened. "What? You are a techno-mage?" he said with poorly feigned outrage. "I would never have gambled with you if I had known." He threw up his hands. "You can't expect me to pay you now."

Carvin seized him by the wrists and pulled him close. His drink flew off the table. "I'll tell you exactly what I expect," she said, still smiling, her voice mild. "Lord Refa owns a ship, the *Ondavi*, that is docked here. You will tell him you need the ship. You will use any excuse, make any promise to get it. It is well within your power. You will tell no one why you truly need it. And you will have it ready for us in two hours."

"But that's completely impossible! Lord Refa will not simply give me his ship."

Their faces were only inches apart. "You can be very convincing, Londo. I'm sure you can talk him into it."

"I may not even be able to reach him in two hours. He is a very busy man, you know."

"Surely for an important person like you, Refa will make time."

"It's simply out of the question. You have cheated me. Why should I honor the debt?"

She released one of his wrists, found the drooping lock of his hair, ran her fingers down it. "You have known the anger of one techno-mage. Would you like to know the anger of all five hundred?"

Londo pulled away, stumbling to his feet. "This is an outrage! I've done nothing to you people! Nothing but try to form a friendly relationship!"

"You have formed a relationship with us. At your own peril." Carvin stood and came around the table to him. "Have the ship ready. In two hours."

She kissed him on the cheek and walked out of the bar, leaving Londo, with his drooping lock of hair, looking stunned.

Galen stood in the dim stone tunnel, looking through the open doorway into the brilliant white room. Within, on the far side of the table, stood Elizar, with his long maroon velvet coat, his dark goatee in the shape of the rune for magic, his angular, arrogant face. Hatred sent a blaze of new heat through Galen's burning body.

It had been a month and a half since they'd last faced each other, but it felt, at this moment, as if no time at all had passed. From Elizar's cupped hands had emerged the long, deadly spike, from his lips the breath of air that had shot it toward them. The spike had snaked up her spinal cord, severing nerve roots and artery branches, killing her inch by excruciating inch. Now it was time for him to die.

"Galen," he said. His skin seemed paler than it used to be, his shoulders slightly curved. For some reason Galen was reminded of Elric and the other mages who had destroyed their places of power. But Elizar had no place of power. Though

Galen had destroyed the small piece of chrysalis on his ship,
that shouldn't have had any significant effect.

"What a lovely nonsurprise," Tilar said. He was crouched
on the floor to one side, Blaylock's body propped against
him. His bloody hand pressed a gun into Blaylock's cheek.
"Come in, Galen. A pleasure to see you again." Blaylock's
hands lay, palms up, against the floor. They were two masses
of purplish red, blood pooled around them on the white floor.
"I'm betting I can fire this gun faster than you can kill me.
Want to take that bet?"

Galen was surging with energy, incandescent. Rabelna
stood to the left of the door, and Bunny sat behind her, head
bent to the side, regarding him with mild interest.

He stepped into the room.

The relentless, racing energy vanished. The burning incandescence died. The gravity—or something—within the room
seemed strange. He stumbled, disoriented, caught a glimpse
of the door closing behind him. G'Leel jammed the gurney in
the doorway. Galen couldn't recover his equilibrium. Part of
his mind, part of his body, seemed out of reach, as if he'd suffered a stroke. His sense of balance failed and he dropped to
the floor.

"Galen!" It was G'Leel's voice.

With inordinate effort, he lifted his head, struggling to get
his bearings. There was a high-pitched screech—metal on
metal—and the gurney burst through the doorway, G'Leel
behind it. Momentum carried her past Galen, the gurney ram-
ming into the table, knocking it over.

Elizar had stepped back, and now he nodded to someone.

Galen's head turned in a loose roll. Beside the door, which
was sliding closed, Rabelna brought a weapon out from behind her back, aiming it at G'Leel.

With a fierce drive for clarity, Galen focused on Rabelna,
visualized the spell of destruction. But there was no echo

from the tech, no gathering of energy. There was no response at all.

Rabelna fired.

G'Leel's arms flew out as the blast threw her into the up-ended table. In the center of her back a black hole blossomed, plasma instantly vaporizing leather, skin, tissue. G'Leel fell away from the table, legs failing, buckling. She thumped to the floor a few feet from Galen, her golden arms splayed.

His hand flailed as he tried to get up. He couldn't make his body work. Limbs no longer seemed to be where they should. They no longer seemed to move as they should. His thoughts felt fuzzy, disjointed. His heart sped ahead. He gagged on saliva.

He'd felt something like this before, he remembered. Though it had been much milder. When he'd trained with Elric. When Elric overrode his chrysalis.

But no one could override a mage's tech. It was controlled only by him. It was part of him.

Galen pressed both his hands against the floor, straining to push himself up. His palms felt numb, yet his leg was throbbing worse than before. He couldn't find his balance.

To one side G'Leel lay, probably dead; he did not have the sensors to tell. On the other was Blaylock, with his ruined hands and dead mind.

"It's a horrible sensation," Elizar said. "But one can get used to it in time."

It was not possible for Elizar to do what he had done. "What— What have you—"

"I've turned off your tech, of course. And I can do it any time I want."

— chapter 14 —

In his quarters, Londo negotiated with Refa via a secure channel on the comm system. Refa was in the royal palace on Centauri Prime, and he was reluctant to admit he even owned the *Ondavi*, which made convincing him to turn it over quite a challenge.

Elric watched through the probe on Vir, who stood silently to Londo's side. Elric remained still in the captain's office, awaiting his return. But the endless wrangling of the two Centauri failed to hold his attention.

Through the growing throbbing in his head, he found himself worrying again about Galen, wondering if he still lived, if Alwyn would reach him in time to help. It would be so simple to do an electron incantation. In less than a minute he could have Galen beside him, talking to him, putting his fears to rest. It would be such a joy to see Galen one last time, to learn that Galen would be all right.

But he must not.

"I can't believe you convinced him," Vir said.

The communication had been concluded. Apparently Londo had been successful.

"What choice did I have? If I failed, I would be tormented for the rest of my life by foul-tempered holodemons and even more foul-tempered techno-mages. The smell in here, by the way—you still haven't gotten rid of it." His face wrinkling in revulsion, Londo began to scout around the cluttered, ostentatious room for the source of the odor.

"I'm working on it." Vir followed. "But I can't understand why you went back to gamble with her. I told you she was a techno-mage."

Londo turned to him. "I was—talked into it. I thought I couldn't lose."

"Londo, how many times—"

Londo held up his hands. "Don't say it, Vir. Don't say it. I was a fool, I was used, and now I'm trapped in a situation that is beginning to look very bad. It's beginning to look very bad indeed."

"What do you mean?"

Londo shook his head. "I have no time to explain it all to you. But these techno-mages have powerful enemies. I am afraid . . . I am afraid this may not end well."

As much as Londo might wish it, he could not blind himself entirely to the truth. Morden would not have confided the Shadows' intentions, yet Londo could easily deduce them. Nevertheless, he would do nothing to stop the Shadows' plan.

Londo reached with irritation to the back of his head, pulled out a hair clip. The drooping lock of hair fell free. "If you can stop badgering me with questions for a few moments, Vir, perhaps you can make yourself useful and do something about this embarrassment."

In Elric's mind's eye, he saw John Sheridan coming down the hall toward his office. The Drazi had been taken to the brig, and the *Zekhite* sealed off until further notice. John had met with Susan Ivanova, then headed tiredly back.

Elric straightened, acutely aware of how little time was left. He believed John would not detain them, yet he could not be certain. In any case, he needed more than that. Again he must ask for a favor. And he could not tell John the whole truth of it, or the captain would surely refuse.

John hesitated in the doorway as he saw Elric, then continued to his desk. "Elric. I'm sorry to have kept you waiting. I would have understood if you'd left."

Elric stood. "I have no time to reschedule with you, Captain. We will leave this place shortly. Unless you intend to stop us."

John took a breath, and his lips rose slightly. "Please sit," he said, and they both did.

John continued. "I have no intention of detaining your group. I'm afraid some people won't be satisfied with the answers you've given me, but that's going to be their problem. I believe you've dealt with me honestly, and as you said, you are free to go where you want."

"I will not thank you for allowing us to do what it is our right to do. But I will thank you for the friendship you've extended me." Elric paused, noting John's smile. "Unfortunately, Captain, there are others who would stop us from leaving. They seek to use our power for their own ends."

"Do you mean Ambassador Mollari? I think you scared him off."

"He is but one of many. I'm afraid I must ask for your help, Captain. Or we will not leave here safely."

John's face hardened. "Who's threatening you? I'll call in security, you can swear out a complaint, and we'll have them arrested."

He knew so little of what the mages faced, of what he himself would soon face. "A confrontation would be too dangerous," Elric said. "You don't want this station to become a battlefield, nor do I." That possibility would seem very real to John after the Drazi episode. "We have a plan that will allow us to leave safely and peacefully, but we require the assistance of you and your security team. I assure you that no laws will be broken. We plan a simple misdirection, a sleight of hand, so that our enemies cannot stop us."

John picked up the orange blossom on his desk and twirled it between his fingers. "Like this."

"Yes."

"You realize that not only am I not supposed to help you, I'm supposed to stop you."

Elric gave a single nod.

"How do you know you can trust me?"

"Because you believe in good, as do we. And because you still dream."

John laid the orange blossom on the desk. "Tell me your plan. Don't leave anything out. If it breaks no laws, as you say, I'll give you everything you need."

Galen's thoughts still felt fuzzy, disjointed. Hunched over on the floor, he panted in short, shallow breaths, each one stabbing sharply into his side. His sense of balance remained uncertain. He needed both hands braced on the floor to keep from falling over. Carefully he pushed himself back until his good leg was folded beneath him. His bad leg remained splayed out to the side. When he tried to bend it, an incredible pain shot through him.

"Another one bites the dust," Bunny said. "You guys are getting a bit boring at this point. There's no challenge."

"Leave us," Elizar said. "Galen and I must speak privately."

Galen struggled to focus, to understand.

This was how they'd subdued Kell, he realized. And he'd walked right into the trap.

They must have done the same to Blaylock. But for some reason Blaylock's higher brain functions had been shut down along with the tech. Why? He remembered Gowen saying something—something about Blaylock's health. *In his quest to become one with the tech, he has encouraged his systems to intertwine with it more intimately than most of ours do.* Perhaps Blaylock's brain had become so linked to the implants that only its most basic processes could function without them. In that case, if the tech was turned back on, Blaylock might recover.

Being without it was an awful, sickening sensation. Galen might have imagined a simple loss of power, a return to the way his body had felt before receiving his implants. But he now recognized the radical change his body had undergone since initiation. The tech had spread itself through all of his systems, had become a part of him. Without it, he was no longer complete.

Galen had thought at first that Elizar had cast a spell to deactivate his tech. But he realized that Elizar's tech was turned off too. That was why Elizar appeared weakened. That was why Elizar had not used his powers to attempt to revive Blaylock or to torture him. That was why Tilar had forgone his chrysalis. Without it, he would not feel the disorienting effects.

Some external device had deactivated the tech in all of them. But how could that be so? How could there be such a device?

Tilar shoved Blaylock over onto his side and stood. Galen vaguely realized Elizar and the others had been bickering, but he didn't know what had been said. He'd been concentrating so hard, he'd lost track of them. He had to regain his bearings.

"I'm getting tired of being treated like an inferior," Tilar said. "I bet I could get more out of him than you."

"You've certainly proven that with Blaylock," Elizar said.

"At least I tried something." Tilar stepped over Blaylock's body and came toward Galen and the door. As he passed by, something thin and wet fell on Galen's cheek. "A souvenir," Tilar said, "and token of things to come."

Galen shook his head and it fell to the floor, a golden filament of tech coated in tissue and blood.

Tilar left with Bunny and Rabelna. The door slid closed behind them.

Whatever device overrode their tech, it seemed to operate

only within this room. If he could get himself and Blaylock out of here, perhaps their power would return.

Fighting disorientation, he crawled toward Blaylock, his leg dragging behind him. Thick streaks of red were smeared over the floor around Blaylock. He'd lost a lot of blood. In the wetness, one of Galen's hands slipped out from under him. He regained his balance, turned Blaylock onto his back. Blaylock's face was ashen, his lips a greyish blue. The rise and fall of his chest was barely visible, his pulse beneath Galen's fingers rapid and weak. Thin streams of blood continued to run from his hands out onto the floor. Galen had to stop the bleeding.

Blaylock had a handkerchief in his jacket. Galen took hold of Blaylock's cold wrist. He pushed up the jacket sleeve, tied the handkerchief tightly about the forearm as a tourniquet. To slow the bleeding from the other hand, Galen pulled her scarf from his pocket. He leaned unsteadily across Blaylock's body, yanked the scarf tight, leaving bloody fingerprints. Then he pushed himself out of his coat, laid it over Blaylock. If Blaylock's tech wasn't restored soon, so that his organelles could operate, Galen didn't know if he would survive.

Galen believed G'Leel had to be dead, but he made his way over to her, hoping that Elizar merely thought him concerned. She'd been holding her gun the last time he'd noticed. Her guncase was open, but her hands were empty. The weapon was nowhere to be seen. For show, he checked G'Leel's pulse and was amazed to find her still alive. She had a chance to survive. He rolled her onto her side to check the plasma burn. The wound was deep, the yellow of bone visible at its center. She couldn't last long. He had to find her gun.

"You always wanted to be a healer," Elizar said. He stood beside the upended table, the gurney. Perhaps the gun had fallen on the far side.

Elizar set a chair down beside Galen, extended a hand to

assist him. Galen ignored the hand and used the chair to pull himself up, sitting in it before he fell.

"There is a reason," Elizar said, "that healing is the most difficult thing for a mage to master."

Galen had to concentrate to make his mouth form the words. "They both need immediate help. They're in shock."

"I cannot do anything for them," Elizar said, "until you and I talk."

Bowing his head as if in weakness, Galen looked for the gun. He must find it, and he must regain his equilibrium.

Elizar brought over a second chair, placed it opposite Galen's. He appeared unarmed. A sign of his arrogance. Still, Galen was in no condition to overpower him without a weapon.

"You don't know how glad I was to find you were here," Elizar said.

"The feeling was mutual."

Elizar sat. "You're injured."

Galen met his gaze. "Your plan is to kill us all, is it not?"

"Not if you will join me."

Galen couldn't help it; he started to laugh. His side spasmed like a fist and he clutched it, gasping. He supposed he was in shock too. "How can you possibly imagine that I would ever, ever join you?"

Elizar leaned forward, his dark blue eyes intent. "Do you remember when we spoke before? You were right. You said I must tell you what I uncovered. That I must give you evidence. I could not tell you then. But now I can."

Galen breathed lightly. "You mean you didn't want to tell me then. Unless I swore loyalty to you."

"I feared you would tell the Circle. I didn't want Kell to find out all I had learned. If only I'd known that he had contrived for me to learn it." He wiped a hand over his mouth. "In any case, I am permitted to tell you now."

"It serves your purpose to tell me now," Galen said.

"The evidence that what I say is true," Elizar said, "exists within your own body, in the very fact that your tech is no longer under your control."

"I don't care what you found. You're a butcher, and you're in partnership with butchers."

Elizar looked toward Blaylock's limp body. "You won't care so much about him when you know the truth. I told you that the Circle has lied to us. They have kept the truth from all of us—a truth we deserved to know before initiation, a truth that has put us in the middle of this war and has now brought us to the brink of destruction."

There was a secret, Galen knew. Elric had refused to tell him. Alwyn had discovered it somehow, and had believed the rest deserved to know. Galen had thought it a secret of power, a secret that might help the mages fight the Shadows.

But Galen no longer cared to know. He just wanted the tech and all its blazing energy restored to him so he could crush Elizar. So he could crush the Shadows. So he could end this.

Elizar studied him. "You and I have often spoken of the Taratimude, of their brilliance in inventing the tech. We marveled at how lucky we were, to be the inheritors of their wisdom, the recipients of these implants that grant the power to make dreams manifest, to create beauty and magic and do good. We mourned the death of the Taratimude, and of their knowledge of the tech.

"But the histories we have read are inaccurate and incomplete. The Taratimude understood the tech's workings little better than we do. They did not invent the tech. They did not produce it. They took it, in exchange for alliance. They took it from a much more ancient, much more advanced race: the Shadows."

Galen's mind went blank. For a moment, he could think of nothing. He was floating, transparent. He was not in this room, in this place. He was a ghost again, with no name, no body, no history. It was as if his identity had slipped away from him and he must wait for it to return.

But in a moment it did return, and he knew he must have misheard. Elizar could not have said what he had said. It couldn't be. All Galen had been taught, all he believed— He had spent his entire life studying the mages' history, learning their ways, striving to master the tech. The mages were a noble order, an ancient fellowship conceived in wonder, fired in discipline, proven in technomancy. They followed an admirable Code. They devoted themselves to magic, knowledge, and good.

The Shadows lived for war, chaos, and death. From behind the scenes, they provoked, they corrupted, they manipulated, they destroyed. Over their history, they had been responsible for billions of deaths. They believed in everything the mages opposed. Their technology did not empower; it enslaved.

It could not be so. Elric had told him. Elric had taught him. Elric could not have kept this from him.

Galen tightened his grip on his side. "You expect me to accept this lie?"

Elizar extended a hand. His palm faced up—a sign of honesty, as Blaylock had told him. "I've never lied to you, Galen. Everything I've said to you is true."

"The Shadows told you this? And you believe them?"

"I learned this from Kell's own files. It was part of the information he wanted me to have, the same information given to each mage elected to the Circle. It is the legacy of Wierden." He let out a heavy breath. "Throughout our history, it has fallen to the line of Wierden to meet once every three years, before each convocation, with the agents of the Shadows, just as Wierden herself did a thousand years ago. As the latest representative of her line, Kell performed that task. He would meet with a Drakh, who would hand over the implants and chrysalises we needed. The Circle does not hold the secret for replicating the tech, as they've told us. They have no idea how it is made."

Galen remembered his tribute to Wierden, how he had admired her. "If Kell put that in his files, then he lied. He was manipulating you."

"I observed him. Six months before the convocation that saw us initiated, he met with a Drakh. He gave this Drakh DNA samples of all the apprentices who were to receive their chrysalises, and all who were to receive their tech. Your DNA and mine, Galen, were given over to the Shadows. Just two weeks before the convocation, he met again with the Drakh. I saw him receive boxes filled with canisters. Some of the canisters were clear and held chrysalises floating inside. Others were opaque, carved with runes. I saw him, when he arrived on Soom, turn those boxes over to Elric. I saw those opaque canisters, carved in runes, in the very tent where our tech was implanted."

Elric could not know. Elric could not be a party to this. Elric had said he would never lie to Galen. But this would make everything Elric had ever said, everything he'd ever done, part of one huge lie.

Galen had seen the canisters himself, each holding the tech for a new initiate. But Elizar was mixing truth and lies, to make his lies more convincing. That was the only answer. The Shadows pursued the mages because the mages were powerful and potentially dangerous. Not because they were allies who had taken and taken for a thousand years, and then, when something was asked in return, pulled out of the bargain.

Elizar could tell his lie. Galen would not be drawn in.

Elizar had paused, hesitant, his lips parted. Now he spoke. "Where do you think Tilar acquired his chrysalis?"

When Galen said nothing, he continued. "I didn't want to believe it either. I was furious at Kell, just as you must be at Elric. I felt betrayed—by Kell, and by the entire lineage of mages, back to the ancients we so admired. I wasn't sure what to do.

"That's why I was acting so strangely at the convocation. I wanted to tell you. But I feared that if we confronted the Circle, they would not allow us to be initiated. We would be cast away. I knew the Circle must be overthrown, and their secrets revealed. Yet at the same time I still loved the mages, and I wanted them to continue.

"Kell's files had told me that the Shadows were returning, for the first time in a thousand years. They would expect us to ally with them, and if we refused, they would kill us all. Even if some of us managed to escape, the Shadows would have no further reason to supply us with tech. The time of the techno-mages would be over."

Elizar's fist hit his palm. "The sheer irresponsibility of it was staggering. I was outraged that the Circle had placed us in such a position. We should be leading the crusade against the Shadows, and instead we were in secret alliance with them. Worse than that, Kell believed we hadn't even the option of fighting them. Early writings of the Taratimude suggested that the Shadows possessed a device that could nullify or control the tech. This possibility—that the mages might lose control of their own tech—terrified Kell and the Circle. They feared becoming slaves of the Shadows. Obviously, the Shadows do have such a device. If not, you would have killed me and we would not be having this conversation.

"Apparently the Circle has conducted secret research on the tech for most of our history, searching for this control mechanism so they could override it. They've failed to find it. The tech is so advanced, they're like fungi trying to understand a jumpgate. At the same time, they forbade any of us from studying the tech, to prevent us from discovering the similarity between it and the ancient technology of the Shadows, to prevent us from discovering their hypocrisy. That is why Burell was treated so harshly.

"But even so, their secret has not been completely secure. A few years ago, one of the mages did discover it, and when he went to the Circle, they told him he would be flayed if he shared his knowledge."

Galen could keep silent no longer. "Who was it?" he said, knowing the answer and praying Elizar did not.

Elizar gave a truncated laugh. "Alwyn. I can't imagine how he found out. Doesn't seem like he'd have the time, with his busy schedule of drinking and womanizing. Yet somehow he did."

It all fit. Galen answered absently. "Alwyn knows the language of the Taratimude better than anyone. He taught it to me." Alwyn must have discovered the secret in some of the ancient writings.

There were too many elements of truth in Elizar's lie. Galen could not find the lie in it. Everything Elizar had told him when they'd last met had proven to be true. Could it be that Elizar, who had killed Isabelle, who had flayed Kell, was telling him the truth? Could Elric and the Circle have lied to them all? Could he be betrayed on both sides?

He had believed that becoming a mage was the greatest calling one could have. He'd thought himself unworthy to be one of their number. The Circle portrayed the tech as a great blessing bestowed upon them by an ancient, dead race. Was it instead the benefit of a secret alliance, an alliance that tied them to a race responsible for countless deaths?

We will reclaim the techno-mages, the fiery runes on Kell's body had read. Galen had thought it a presumptuous claim by Elizar. But had the message instead come from the Shadows?

Galen had turned down alliance with the Shadows again and again, refusing their offers of power, of knowledge, of Isabelle's life. *You are already one of us,* Morden had said. If it was true, then the Circle and the Code were empty, hollow conceits. And he had followed them, and lost her.

Elizar continued. "Once I knew the truth, I realized that,

above all, we must have our freedom from the Shadows. Kell and the Circle seemed to have no intention of acting. Fate left that task to me. I determined to be what the mages needed me to be, and do what they needed me to do. I would discover any method the Shadows had for controlling our tech, and learn the secret of creating it. Only that way could I lead the mages into a new age."

Galen didn't want to hear any more. What did the killer hope to accomplish? Did he think Galen would forget the past? "At the convocation, you seemed more interested in secrets of power. You wanted my spell of destruction."

Elizar gave a single nod. "Kell's files indicated that we were once much more powerful than we are now. I knew that great power would be necessary to fight the Shadows, once we gained our independence from them. For a short time at the convocation I hoped Isabelle's shield or your spell of destruction might save us. But I realized that still we must have the secret of the tech's creation, and there was only one way to get it."

Elizar's hand curled inward, and his thumb circled about his fingertips. "So I sought out the Drakh with whom Kell had met. I pretended to join with the Shadows, so I could learn their secrets. I have learned the secret of the device that turns off our tech. I've learned other secrets as well."

"How to make a killing spike." Galen bit out the words, his anger building.

Elizar straightened. Was that regret Galen saw in the planes of his pale face? Regret at having his lies interrupted with the truth, perhaps.

"I wanted Isabelle as an ally," Elizar said. "I didn't want her blood on my hands. But she left me no choice. Without her sworn allegiance, the Shadows would not allow her to live. If I had not killed her, they would have. And they would have killed both of us as well. At least when I took on the task,

I gained their trust. She did not die in vain. Her death helped in a greater cause."

Galen's fingers dug into his side. He was breathing hard, pain stabbing him with each inhalation. He used the pain to gain focus, to find his equilibrium. "So you decide who must be sacrificed. And you serve as executioner."

"Perhaps . . . I chose badly."

"Perhaps?"

"I believe that the survival of the mages is more important than anything. More important than a single life. Don't you?"

"You seem much more willing to sacrifice others than yourself."

"I convinced the Shadows to spare you."

Galen wanted to throw himself at Elizar. "You should not have." He lowered his head, again looking for the gun. "If all you've said is true, you could have told the mages, forced the Circle to admit the truth. We could have worked together to formulate a plan. Instead, you kept silent, so your initiation would not be jeopardized. You went alone, to gain knowledge and glory. You could decide later whether your allegiance was to the Shadows or the mages. After you learned how much power the Shadows would give you. After you obtained the secrets that would allow you to overthrow the Circle and take their place."

Elizar's jaw tightened. "I had to move quickly and quietly. Agents of the Shadows were everywhere. One was even at the convocation. I had the knowledge. Whom better would you send?"

The more truth Elizar told, the angrier Galen became. He fixed Elizar with his gaze. "What else have you done for the Shadows, to gain their trust and learn their secrets? How many have you killed? Am I next?"

"Not if you will join me. Together we can discover the secret for making the tech. Then we need serve the Shadows no longer, and we can lead the mages in a great war against them. A noble quest, just as dreamed."

"You tell me this story, and you think I will believe it and join you? You are lying, the Shadows are lying, Kell was lying. One thing I know for certain, and that is what you did." Galen's voice was shaking. He paused, and when he continued, his tone was emotionless. "For that, there is no excuse and no forgiveness."

Elizar looked away, and suddenly Galen saw G'Leel's gun. It lay on the gurney beside Anna's leg, half buried under a fold of her orange jumpsuit.

Elizar's gaze returned to him, and Galen tried to keep his face impassive. One blast should kill Elizar, though it would have to be to the head or the heart, somewhere the damage could not be undone by the organelles.

Elizar reached out. "I am telling the truth. The future of the mages is in our hands. What can I do to convince you?"

"Nothing." The gun was about five feet away from them both. He had to get his leg to work somehow, so he could reach the gun and aim it without interference. If they fought over it, he would lose.

"Galen—" Elizar extended his hand to grasp Galen's shoulder, and Galen jerked back. "For the sake of the mages," Elizar said, "you must help me. You must believe me."

Galen said nothing, and Elizar drew back his hand. For a few moments he regarded Galen in silence. Then he continued, his voice softer. "You of all people should believe it. I told you we had power much greater than we knew, power given to us by the Shadows. You discovered some of that forgotten power. You found one of the weapons they planted within the tech."

At the turn in the conversation, Galen's heart began to pound, and he found he was suddenly afraid.

Elizar continued. "The Taratimude warred constantly with one another. They sought power. The Shadows offered them a technology that would give them great power, make them great warriors. The Taratimude accepted. Many fought for the Shadows in the last war—another dirty secret. But after that war was done, the Taratimude returned to fighting amongst themselves. They destroyed one another. That is the great cataclysm that befell them, which has been so shrouded in mystery.

"What the Shadows did not tell the Taratimude, and Wierden came to realize only after the destruction of most of her race, was that the tech they had been given was not simply an advanced system of energy and control. It had been designed and programmed with a specific purpose in mind. As the Shadows promote war and chaos, they created the tech to do the same, to create an army of warriors, agents of chaos who would bring death and destruction wherever they went."

Galen's hand was gripping his side so tightly his arm was shaking.

"Haven't you wondered why mages are so quick to anger? Why we fight so often amongst ourselves? We can't even live together. The urge to fight is programmed into us. We are meant to attack others, to defend ourselves when threatened, to survive—through the healing power of our organelles—injuries that would kill others. To be nearly invincible forces of destruction."

Galen's mind jumped from one memory to the next, finding connections where he'd never seen any before. When he'd felt threatened by Elizar at the convocation, his first instinct had been to use his chrysalis to attack with overwhelming force. After the initiation, his body had raced with the tech's energy. The agitating undercurrent relentlessly urged him toward action. Each time he used the tech for attack, he felt its eager echo. Whenever he was in danger, he felt its driving need to strike out. The effort to control it was exhausting.

Since he'd agreed to flee with the rest of the mages, to repress his desire for revenge, he'd been fighting both himself and the tech. The restless energy had intensified. On Selic 4, he had been unable to hold it in any longer, and had destroyed Elizar's chrysalis. He'd been so consumed with the urge to destroy that to regain control, he'd had to turn the energy against himself, repeatedly.

Out in the tunnel, as he'd cast spell after spell of destruction, the tech had sung inside him, the energy flowing more easily than ever before, as if that was what the tech had been meant to do. As if that was what he had been meant to do.

Elizar nodded, clearly seeing the recognition on Galen's face. "Wierden established the Circle and the Code to curb our destructive impulses. That is why such stress is placed on them, why the penalties for violation are so severe. Some of us have buried our impulses so well that it is little struggle to obey the Code. For others, it is a constant battle. But without the Code and the Circle, we would revert to chaos."

We all have thoughts of things we must not do, Blaylock had said, *thoughts of destruction. Most follow me because they must. Without the daily scouring, without the fasting, without the meditation and repentance, the abstinence, the vigils, the sensory denial, the mortification, they would be unable to follow the Code.*

"With the Circle and the Code," Elizar said, "we focus on nondestructive uses of our power. We have subverted the programming of the Shadows, using the abilities they gave us toward ends they did not intend and could not foresee. We have combined the various powers they gave us, creating ever more complex spells, obscuring our true nature, even to ourselves. Instead of power, we focus on magic, knowledge, beauty, good. Some of us have even learned to heal, which was never the Shadows' intent. We have become much more than the Shadows ever imagined. We've transcended their designs.

"Yet in doing that, we've lost touch with our most basic powers. Somehow you rediscovered that potential. It's something about your spell language, about the way you think."

Galen had found the spell of destruction at the base of their spells, a simple one-term equation, a basic postulate, as he had called it. It formed the fundament upon which their powers were built, the basic truth of what they were. Take away the flourishes and misdirection, the staffs and cloaks and circles of stones, and all that remained was vast, destructive power.

The ability to listen to the Shadow communications also lay in a one-term spell, a basic postulate. Of course the Shadows would give their servants a simple method for communicating with them.

The tragic, horrific enormity of it struck him. The Circle took children and trained them and taught them and implanted into them the seeds of anarchy. They transformed apprentices into agents of the Shadows, and called them techno-mages. And as the programming of destruction spread through the initiates' bodies, the Circle demanded obedience to a Code that opposed their basic natures. Elizar dared speak of transcendence, as she had, but it was not possible. They were what they were: embodiments of chaos. The Circle fooled themselves into believing that from the Shadows could come good. That the mages could create good. But they carried the contagion wherever they went. Galen was proof of that.

Yet tech or no tech, he wanted to kill Elizar. He had the impulse to destruction. He dreamed of ripping Elizar's tech from him with bare hands, just as Tilar had done to Blaylock. Perhaps the tech had intensified the impulse, raised it to a constant, driving need. Galen didn't know. He had worked with the chrysalis for three years. He had trained it, and it, apparently, had trained him. And with initiation, he and the tech had been joined. They were a single being, intertwined so thoroughly that he felt incomplete without it. How could he tell which desires arose from him, and which from the tech? Or was there no difference?

"It all makes sense now, doesn't it?" Elizar said. "The way we live, the way we behave, the nature of the tech."

Galen nodded. He could find no more objections. The tech was programmed for destruction. *He* was programmed for destruction.

"You may hate me. I understand that. But I am the only one who can save the mages. And I can only do it with your help."

The mages should never have been made. Potentially, they were nearly as great a threat as the Shadows. Galen felt a great pity for them, with their dreams of creating awe and wonder, of doing good, of living up to a history from which one crucial fact had been withheld. They had all shared those dreams. But the dreams were based on lies.

As Galen thought over their history, of the vast knowledge they'd gained, of the great deeds they'd accomplished, of the wars in which they'd fought, the vendettas they'd carried out, the petty feuds, the plots and counterplots, he wondered if the good they'd done had outweighed the bad. It was only in the past fifty years or so that they had truly lived by the Code. Yet in that time, he knew, they had accomplished much of worth.

Galen didn't know if the mages could be saved, or if they should be. Elric had told Alwyn, *I can see no path by which the mages will survive this war. Not in any form that we would recognize.* Now he understood why. Without the ability to create new tech, the mages would eventually die off. Even if they somehow gained the ability, the nature of the tech would remain unchanged. It would still generate agents of chaos.

Galen didn't know what he wanted, except that he wanted to kill Elizar. "You don't need me," he said. "You have Tilar and Razeel."

"Tilar and Razeel follow the Shadows. Tilar will never forgive our order for casting him away." With a small gesture Elizar extended two fingers toward Blaylock's mangled body. "You see what he is like. Razeel—is beyond help." He lowered his voice and leaned closer. "I first had to convince you of my honesty. That is why I've told you all I have. Whether you believe me now or not, I have no more time to convince you. The Shadows have planned a trap. The mages will all die within the hour, unless you help me stop it."

Galen's heart jumped. "I'm to believe this because you tell me?"

Elizar frowned, impatient. "They know you warned the mages not to board the *Zekhite*. But the mages have another plan, and the Shadows have discovered it. The mages' ship will be destroyed, along with all those aboard."

If Elizar spoke the truth, then Galen's message had not saved Elric. All those on Babylon 5 would die. Yet how could he know if that was true? Elizar's revelations had been designed to gain his trust. Now could be the perfect time for a lie.

And the perfect time, at last, for Elizar to make his demand.

Galen spoke evenly. "How do you propose I stop it?"

"You must pretend to join with the Shadows, as I have. They've given up any hope of alliance with the mages now; Elric turned down their final offer. But if I can prove to them that I've turned you, it will reawaken their hope. They will believe that I can turn more. You must tell them that the truth has killed your loyalty to the mages. That you realize you owe the Shadows your allegiance. They have promised that if I gain your alliance, they will postpone their plan to kill the mages."

"And you trust them."

"I'm not a fool. I doubt them. But I know that they still desire us as allies."

"And they will simply let the mages run off to their hiding place."

"They will, if you tell me its location. That is the only way to convince them you are truly their ally. With that single piece of information, we can stop our order's destruction and gain time. In that time, we can learn the secret of the tech's creation." As Elizar spoke, his face grew animated, his mouth rising in a slight smile. "And if we cannot learn it, perhaps with your power we can force the Shadows to reveal it. You destroyed a Shadow ship, Galen! Your power rivals theirs.

Imagine if we all knew your spell, how much the Shadows would fear us. But first the mages must be saved. As long as they still live, there's hope."

"And to keep them alive, all I need do is tell you where they plan to hide." Elizar was a fool. He was the Shadows' puppet, whether he knew it or not. They sought to draw Galen in the same as they'd done with Elizar. They would never share the secret of creating the tech. But they could demand endless proofs of loyalty from him, just as they had from Elizar. And with the mages held hostage in their hiding place, he would have to obey or become the cause of their deaths. Perhaps the Shadows would have him work with Elizar, approaching the others one at a time where they hid, weakened and with limited resources, giving each of them one last chance to turn or be flayed. Perhaps they would have him teach the others his spell. What chaos might they generate if they all knew his secret? Or perhaps they would have him fight in their battles, spreading his brilliant heat of destruction.

But there was much more at stake. The mages on Babylon 5 were only a small group. Right now, it seemed, only they were endangered. Could the Shadows suspect the deception? Could Elizar? Certainly he knew how the mages worked.

"Galen. It's the only chance to save them."

"And how will you know," Galen said, "that I have told you the truth?"

Elizar dismissed the question with a flourish of his hand. "My telepath will scan you to confirm it."

Somehow, Galen sensed that this had been Elizar's goal all along. All the truth Elizar had told had been to gain his trust, so he would undergo the scan willingly. When Bunny had attempted to scan Kell, Kell had killed himself. Elizar would not want a repetition of that. He would want to know the mages' true plans.

Galen could not allow Bunny to scan him. She was a P12. He might delay her for a few seconds, but that was all. He did not have the skill to induce a heart attack, as Kell had done. Elizar would learn the secret of destruction. He would learn that the gathering on Babylon 5 was a misdirection. The rest of the mages would be endangered. Perhaps it was true that they should never have been created. But he did not want to be the cause of their deaths.

He must get to the gun. Galen removed his hand from his side, straightened. He didn't dare move his leg until he had to. Without the aid of the organelles, the pain had been intensifying steadily the entire time they'd been speaking. And the leg had swollen up even more than before, his pants digging into it.

Galen took a shallow breath, focused. He was a poor liar, but he had to try, at least, to convince Elizar that he was considering the proposition. "You're right that I hate you. But I'm not blinded by it. Your plan is our only chance. Yet how do I know that saving the mages is your true goal? Once you learn the hiding place, you can kill me, and you will have the rest of the mages at your mercy. I've no sensors to tell me whether you speak the truth. You must give me a sign of your good intentions. Restore my tech. Show me your trust, and I will show you mine."

Elizar stood. "And how do I know you won't destroy me, as you've destroyed so many in the tunnels? You've killed many more than I, Galen."

And he'd just been getting started.

Elizar brought his hand down sharply. "I've told you more truth than anyone else in your life. Tell me what you know of the mages' hiding place. Together we can save them. Together we can gain their freedom. You know that's what I want. And I know it's what you want. We once shared noble dreams. Reality has tainted them, but still there are great tasks left for us to accomplish. Show me your goodwill. Then I will restore your tech to you."

Galen looked down, trying to appear uncertain. He needed

Elizar to move away from the gurney. He needed Elizar not to see the gun.

"Are others here with you and Blaylock?" Elizar asked.

Galen met his gaze. "No. The rest are on Babylon 5. We came to discover the Shadows' plans for them."

"And what of the mages' hiding place?"

"Unfortunately," Galen said, "the Circle's secrecy is not limited to the tech. Only they know the location of the hiding place. They feared that some of our number were agents of the Shadows, so they would tell no others."

Elizar studied him. "You know nothing more?"

"Blaylock knows the hiding place." Galen staggered to his feet. Pain shot up his leg. "Rouse him and I will help convince him to tell you. I have no further loyalty to him." He swayed, his vision swarming with grey dots. He focused on his balance. He must reach the gun in one clean movement.

"Blaylock will never tell. And you have told me nothing that would convince the Shadows you have turned." Elizar extended a hand, stopped himself before he touched Galen. "I don't understand you. This is the only chance the mages have. You must help me. Don't you want to save them?"

Galen found his breaths coming faster. He fixed Elizar with his gaze. "Restore my power. Let us go. Tell the Shadows we escaped. I will warn the mages. They will elude the trap, and you will have the time you need."

Elizar flung his arms wide, and his voice rose. "How do I know you won't kill me? I can't endanger all I have done, let all those who have died be lost in vain. I must know I can trust you." He hesitated. "If you know nothing of the hiding place, then explain to me your spell of destruction. It will remain between us."

For Elizar, it always came back to power. "I will tell no one that spell. The temptation is too great."

Elizar's mouth hung open at a crooked angle. "We both want the mages to survive. Don't you find it tragic that we can't trust each other? It's our only chance. Galen, we have only a few minutes before they're all dead. What can I do, what can I say to gain your trust?"

"Bring Isabelle back."

Elizar's mouth wrinkled shut, and his eyes drifted to the side. "I would if it were within my power. Not a night has passed that I haven't relived that nightmare. But we must get beyond that. She—"

"There is no getting beyond that."

Elizar's gaze returned to Galen, lingered there. At last he shook his head, and his voice was soft. "I must have Bunny scan you. She will know your true intentions. If you will leave me unharmed, I will help you and Blaylock to escape."

Once Bunny was inside his mind, she could find out whatever Elizar desired.

Elizar started toward the door, and Galen pushed off with his good leg, lunging for the gun. He lurched into the gurney, his elbows slamming down onto Anna's legs, and snatched up the weapon. The gurney began to roll away, and he stumbled to regain his balance, a brilliant pain exploding in his shin. He brought the gun up on Elizar, gasping.

On the floor to one side lay G'Leel, her gloved hands open, empty. Galen's grip was tight about her gun. She had risked her life to help him, and he had nearly forgotten about her.

A shot to the head or heart could kill Elizar. And in a moment, it would. But he must make sure, first, that he could get G'Leel away from this place.

"Open the door," he said breathlessly.

Elizar seemed frozen, his eyes wide. His expression was satisfyingly similar to that in Galen's fantasy. "You would have all the mages die." He fell silent, and after a few moments, his face regained its composure. "You're not the person I knew. It is more important to you to kill me, than to save everything you love."

"I love nothing," Galen said, "except the thought of killing you."

Elizar glanced toward the door behind him. "The passage outside is filled with Drakh. The Shadows won't let you leave this room. They know what you can do, better than you know it. They've been especially patient with you, because they wanted you fighting on their side. But they've made you their last offer. Submit to scanning. Give us what you know."

Something fell behind him with a heavy metallic ring. Galen looked back. The gurney had brought Anna to rest against the far wall. She had pried a panel off it. Within the wall, something soft and black glistened, shot through with veins of silver. She thrust her emaciated hand into it. She had found another machine with which to connect. It was all that mattered to her. She was a slave to the Shadows' programming, just as he was. Galen turned back to Elizar.

"Open the door."

Elizar pressed several buttons on the door's keypad.

There was no response. Was it some trick? Or could Anna somehow be affecting it?

"Open it," Galen said.

Elizar pressed the buttons again. Still the door did not move.

The lights went out, plunging them into darkness. Galen feared he had missed his only chance. Crying out, he fired at the spot where Elizar had stood, filling the area with plasma bolts. Each recoil spiked pain down his leg.

The door opened, and in the dim light of the tunnel he saw the craggy silhouettes of Drakh filling the doorway. He shot at them with the crude weapon.

The Drakh fell back with the impact of his blasts, but their armor, he suspected, protected them from any serious injury. In another second or two, he would surely be shot. He must throw himself at them. If he got out of the room, perhaps his power would be restored. That was his only chance of escape.

Firing, he stumbled toward the doorway. But the shapes

there shifted. The craggy silhouettes parted, and a thinner, softer silhouette came forward between them. The dim light reflected off a curve of yellow hair. Galen's arm fell limp; the gun clattered against the floor. Beneath the curve of yellow hair, the face was a pit of pure blackness, and in the moment he saw it he was captured by it, its hunger pulling him toward it, sucking him in. He found his legs had stopped their forward movement, yet his mind was rushing ahead, unable to resist, wrenched from his body into the rich shining blackness.

— chapter 15 —

The blackness spread over Galen's mind, branching into tentacles, burrowing inward. He'd thought at first that he'd entered the blackness, but he now realized the blackness had entered him. The tentacles slid deeper, twisting, writhing. Then the end of each sprouted a claw, dug in.

He saw Elizar sitting before him. *It all makes sense now, doesn't it?* Then Elric stood before him in a hallway on Selic 4. *It is the test of what you are. A techno-mage or a traitor. One who kills, or one who does good. One in control, or one consumed by chaos. One who brings darkness, or one who brings light.* Then it was Blaylock, sitting across the table from him on the transport. *Elric and the others,* Galen said to him. *They're on Babylon 5.*

Bunny was scanning him. She was going to find out what she must not find out. He desperately visualized a blank screen in his mind, narrowed his attention to it, to the letter *A* appearing in blazing blue in the upper left-hand corner. It felt strange, doing the exercise without the echo of the tech. Yet he had done it many times before he'd received the implants.

It all makes sense now, doesn't it? Elizar said.

He forced the letter *B* to appear beside the *A*.

Then it was *A B C* in a neat row. Then *A B C D*. He must hold them all in his mind at once, keep each individual letter clear while the whole also remained clear. He must keep out anything else.

A movement distracted him, and for a moment he was back in the white room. Bunny was smiling, waving off the Drakh, coming toward him. He found his legs stumbling back, away from the door. The tentacles carved paths through his mind, probing for his deepest secrets.

Gowen walked beside him. *How could Elizar do such a thing?*

A B C D E.

A B C D E F.

A B C D E F G.

He could hold her off for only a few seconds more. He must kill himself before she could find what he knew. But he had no weapon. He added letter after letter at the end of the neat row, more and more to hold in his mind. *H. I. J.*

The tentacles drove into him, as the spike drove into her. *It's no use,* she said. *This is not a wound you can heal. It is a weapon inside me.*

K. The letter took great effort, and he found himself thinking of Babylon 5, of Elric. Bunny was forcing him to. He pushed the thoughts away. He must continue the alphabet, complete it. Don't think of what would come after.

L, M, N. He came up against the wall, the gurney blocking him on his left. He sat in his bedroom on Soom working on his spells, Fa crouched on the table beside his screen. *What's that?* she asked.

A B C D E F G H I J K L M N O.

The lights came back on. Anna looked up at him with dark, hungry eyes. She was controlling the room's systems. *P.* Her left arm was coated in the gelatinous black matter, silver threads running through it like veins. *Q.* With her free hand, Anna seized him about the wrist. Elric seized him in an embrace as he left for Zafran 8.

R. She jerked his hand to the metal device on her head. She would control every machine in the universe, given the chance. He fell through the night, and she screamed with him. Anna. Anna Sheridan.

His father towered over him, dark, enraged. *You're* my *apprentice. She's nothing to you!* It was becoming harder and harder to add letters, to hold them all in his mind. He focused. Pushed.

A B C D E F G H I J K L M N O P Q R S.

A B C D E F G H I J K L M N O P Q R S T.

Galen's breath deepened as Anna took control of him, and pain stabbed into his side. His heartbeat slowed, falling into pounding synchrony with hers. He searched for control of his hand, was about to pull away from her when he felt the penetrating tentacles of blackness hesitate in their paths.

U. Bunny was uncertain, confused by what she sensed.

Galen slammed his free hand against the fine metalwork on Anna's head. Let them fight for control of him. Perhaps it would give him a few more seconds to think. Yet he must focus only on the alphabet, each letter now a monolith of effort.

A B C D E F G H I J K L M N O P Q R S T U V.

Anna circulated all through him now. Galen could feel her frustration at his tech's lack of response. She wanted what she had felt before, when they had connected in the tunnel. She found meaning only as part of the machine, in serving the machine. This machine was not working.

W. She located the problem. A transceiver at the base of his spinal cord was picking up an intense signal in the radio band. The signal overrode the tech, prevented it from acting. Anna searched for the source of the signal, sending herself out through the silver veins, through the machine built into the wall and through all those with which it was connected.

Bunny renewed her assault, claws ripping through Galen's mind. As he fiercely visualized the screen with the letters of the alphabet, thoughts and memories flashed in and out, leaking through his defenses.

Elric stood before him. *We may alter the particulars of our*

*plan. But the plan has already been put in motion, and we
cannot change course now.*

X.

The Circle stood on the dais before the mages. Blaylock
spoke. *We have decided upon a new site at which we can prepare for our exodus.* Bunny was searching for the mages'
plan, zeroing in.

Y. Galen forced his mind away from that room, forced the
alphabet to completion.

A B C D E F G H I J K L M N O P Q R S T U V W X Y Z.

But then he was standing before the dais again. Blaylock
continued. *We cannot allow our gathering place again to be
discovered by the Shadows.*

Anna traced the nullifying signal to its source. And turned
it off.

Power shot through him like a seizure. His body filled with
fire, incandescent. Anna reveled in it. She too was programmed
for destruction. She wanted her new weapon to work well.

He'd been horrified at what she was, yet they were kin: different systems with different degrees of autonomy, on the
same spectrum of chaos and death.

The black claws ripped out of his mind. Bunny had broken
off her attack and was pushing her way back through the crowd
of Drakh toward the door. She knew what had happened.

Galen yanked his hands from Anna, retaking control of his
racing body, struggling to regain his bearings. He didn't believe he'd revealed the mages' deception, but he couldn't be
absolutely certain. He had to kill Bunny.

As the nearest Drakh raised his gun, Galen seized him
within a sphere of destruction. Then the next Drakh. And the
next. The white walls began to undulate, and time turned
sluggish, distorted.

He couldn't see Bunny. He cast the one-term spell again,
this time making the sphere large enough to encompass as

much as possible of the area between him and the door, while making sure it touched neither G'Leel nor Blaylock. The energy came down upon him, shot out of him. Many of the Drakh—and parts of a few who stood along the edges—were encased within the sphere. It began to darken. Galen hoped Bunny was among them.

Now for Elizar. Galen scanned the area in search of mage energy. All he found were his own and Blaylock's. At greater distances, as before, unfamiliar energies overwhelmed any sign of a mage. He realized why those frequencies were so full. The Shadow tech radiated at frequencies similar to the mage tech. They shared a common lineage.

The large sphere began to collapse. It had cut into the wall around the door, turning the opening into a large, curved archway. Through it, in the tunnel, he saw Rabelna. In the fluid spacetime of the spell, her shoulders were stretching out to each side, pulling the plaid pattern of her jacket with them, turning her into a strange, alien scarecrow. Her mouth open in fear, Rabelna aimed her gun at him, the gun that had shot G'Leel. With a thought Galen imploded her.

Behind her were more Drakh, and as his spheres collapsed with deafening cracks, they spilled into the room to fill the emptiness. Galen captured them in clumps.

Movement to his side, and Galen turned, the tech eager, ready for direction. It was Blaylock. He was pushing himself up against the wall, his rippling face ashen, drawn. He must have awakened when his tech was restored.

Blaylock jerked his head toward the door and raised his mangled palms. Arcs of brilliant white electricity jumped between the buttons of his jacket sleeves, raced up his arms, down the front of his jacket. A brilliant flash shot out from his chest. It moved too quickly to see, yet Galen could tell who its target had been.

The white carapace on the Drakh's head had been scorched black, and his armor ran down his body in thick rolls of sludge.

Smoke rose from around him, carrying the smell of charred flesh. The Drakh's arm fell to his side. He had been aiming his weapon at Galen. He collapsed in a smoldering heap.

Galen seized Drakh by the handful, the spells forming effortlessly in a neat column, the energy blazing through him, their bodies crumbling inward to nothingness. He remembered Blaylock's words. *What we have been given, Galen, is a mystery beyond our understanding, a true blessing. It taps into the basic force and fabric of the universe, into God, as some call it. Our place is to use that blessing in the best way possible, to be the best agents of the universe that we can. A mage who forms a perfect union with his tech will undergo an enlightenment in which he learns the will of the tech, and the universe. As one, they may carry out that will.*

He had learned the will of the tech, and it brought no enlightenment. The tech had nothing to do with God, or the universe. It was programmed to destroy.

Blaylock shrouded the tech in mystery to prevent them from studying it. Galen should kill him for all the lies he'd told. But then, they probably had only a few minutes left to live.

Drakh continued to storm the room. They didn't know enough to stop, to withdraw. Eventually his attention would falter, and another one would get past him, and shoot him. Until then, he would kill as many as he could.

A sphere of brilliant fire streaked down the tunnel outside. It looked like the fireball of a mage. Could the Shadows generate them too? Another fireball shot past, and then a screeching, high-pitched cry echoed down the passage.

It was so strange to hear that sound in this place. The distortion from the spell of destruction made the cry muddier than it normally was, yet still he recognized it. It was the cry Alwyn had designed for his favorite illusion, the golden dragon.

Alwyn was here. Elric must have sent him.

Belching fireballs down at the Drakh, the wavering golden

beast floated past the doorway like some kind of hallucination. Its wings were folded back to fit in the tight space.

Facing the dragon on one side and Galen on the other, the Drakh scattered down the tunnel.

Reluctantly, Galen stopped the flow of destruction. He was blazing with energy, racing with it. He held himself still. In the aftermath of the implosions, only the muffled cry of the dragon broke the silence. Time and space regained their regularity, solidity.

He went to the doorway. Though his leg remained stiff, the pain had again vanished. He conjured a platform beneath G'Leel. Alwyn could take her away—and Blaylock, if he wished. Then Galen would find Elizar. Then this would end.

The dragon passed by the doorway again, returning the way it had come.

The tunnel outside was clear of Drakh. He searched for the static-shrouded bodies of the Shadows and found none. He glanced back at Anna. The black gelatinous substance had extruded from the wall to encase her, reducing her to a shadow within its darkness. He would have liked to free her, to have Alwyn take her away as well, but he didn't know how to go about it. And if he did succeed in separating her from the machine, the signal that had nullified their tech might resume.

There was no time. Elizar could be escaping. She was happiest this way, anyway. Just as he was happiest in destruction.

Blaylock was sliding along the wall toward her. Galen didn't know why he bothered to speak to the liar; it was something in Blaylock's face, in the gaunt lines that revealed horror at Anna's body subsumed within the machine.

"If you want to leave, you'd better go now."

Blaylock turned toward him, the words taking a moment to register. Then Blaylock nodded, his face regaining its severity, and he pulled himself away from the wall. He walked with unsteady steps through the scoop-shaped depressions in the floor. "I told you not to come after me."

"You told me many things."

Galen stepped out into the dim stone tunnel. He scanned again for mage energy, but he could detect no clear signal.

"Elizar fled when our power returned," Blaylock said.

Galen was irritated that Blaylock knew what he was thinking. With an equation of motion he brought G'Leel out into the tunnel. To the left was the way back to the surface, the direction from which Alwyn's dragon had come.

Alwyn ran into sight around the curve, his silver hair gleaming in the dim light. He stopped and waved. "The cavalry is here! Hurry!" He turned and disappeared around the bend.

Galen limped quickly down the tunnel, bringing G'Leel behind him. Blaylock followed more slowly. Galen considered conjuring a platform for him, then grew angry at himself for thinking of helping. Let Blaylock conjure it if he needed it.

Galen received a message from Blaylock. It was a copy of a message he had sent to Alwyn. *Alwyn,* the message simply read.

Galen pushed himself ahead with his stiff leg, G'Leel and Blaylock falling behind. He craned his neck, glimpsing a flash of multicolored robe as Alwyn disappeared farther around the curve.

A response came from Alwyn. *I've been trying to reach you for ages. What happened to you?*

Blaylock's response went to both Galen and Alwyn. *How did you know where we were?*

I didn't, Alwyn wrote. *I don't. Where are you?*

Your golden dragon passed us only a minute ago.

That wasn't my dragon.

That wasn't Alwyn ahead of them. An illusion then, he thought eagerly. Created by whom? Elizar?

He ceased G'Leel's forward movement. He knew he should stop as well, but he didn't want to. Instead he continued a few more steps, the steps necessary to bring him around the curve and carry him into confrontation with his enemy, to reveal the trap that had been laid.

Drakh lined both sides of the passage, their weapons trained on him. Straight ahead, just a few feet away, stood the illusion of Alwyn.

Galen could see the quality of the illusion was very good—reproducing Alwyn's thin hair, the bags beneath his eyes. Too good to be created from a distance. Someone was within the illusion, either Elizar or Tilar. He must know which.

Several things happened very quickly.

Alwyn smiled. "Fire!"

With the whisper of silk, a shield slipped down over Galen. Blaylock was protecting him. A platform pushed up against his feet. Blaylock was going to pull him back down the tunnel.

At this short distance, Galen could finally detect mage energy from the figure before him. He had sensed this energy before. It held the distinctive signature of a chrysalis.

Tilar.

Galen visualized the screen in his mind's eye, imposed the spell of destruction upon it. The tech's response was instantaneous. The energy struck out, seized Tilar. As hot plasma sprayed yellow across Galen's field of vision, a spherical area around the false Alwyn began to redden and darken. Galen glanced at the roof of the tunnel, cast the spell of destruction within the rock there.

Blaylock's platform began to pull him back around the curve, while within the sphere the false Alwyn dissolved, revealing Tilar beneath. The silvery chrysalis on his head ballooned upward. His mouth rippled out in a silent scream. His arms—white from shoulder to elbow, dark red from elbow to hand—elongated downward, stretching like taffy to curl and pool beside his feet. In the last moment before the tunnel eclipsed Galen's view, the sphere begin to fade and collapse, and within its great invisible fist—the fist of Galen's will—Tilar's body was crushed.

He found it very satisfying.

As the platform raced back, a thunderous crack split the air. A rush of dirt and rocks shot down the tunnel at him, slamming into the shield.

Galen turned to face his direction of motion, found Blaylock and G'Leel on a platform beside him, speeding down the tunnel away from the cave-in.

When they reached a safe distance, Blaylock stopped both platforms, dissolved them and the defensive shields he'd conjured. He took a single, stumbling step, then recovered his balance and stood still, head bowed. He'd pulled off the tourniquets at some point; the bloodstained scarf hung around his neck. His face was shiny with sweat.

The energy still burned through Galen, racing, endless. He had to get G'Leel and Blaylock out of here.

He realized he had a series of messages from Alwyn. Ignoring them all, he created his own, sending a copy to Blaylock. *Where are you?*

Would you please stay in touch? You two are going to be the death of me. I'm at this City Center building you mentioned in your message to Elric. I've been flying around it searching for you. I got away with it for a while, but the locals would really like me to leave now.

With a brief steadying touch to Blaylock's elbow, Galen conjured a platform beneath the three of them, sent them down the tunnel the way he and G'Leel had originally come.

He sent a quick response to Alwyn. *There's a hole in the ground in back. An excavation. Land inside it. We'll meet you there.*

Alwyn replied. *You'll find some irony in your choice of landing place when you get here.*

Galen traced his way back as quickly as he could. Each moment allowed Elizar to get farther and farther away. But he couldn't get far enough. Galen would find him.

They glided past the two greyish-skinned aliens, still

asleep where he'd left them. As they approached the tunnel that led to the excavation, Blaylock gave him a sharp look, and a shield slipped again over him. There was the sound of movement in the tunnel ahead.

His body burned eagerly with the chance to release its energy once again. As the Drakh came into view, he registered their positions one after the next, equations pouring down the screen in his mind's eye, spheres of destruction boiling out of him, enfolding the Drakh in their dark embrace. He didn't know if there were twenty, or fifty, or a hundred. He simply continued until there were none.

They had not fired a single shot.

Blaylock's shield slipped away. The tunnel that led to the excavation was now empty, its surface covered with smooth scallop-shaped depressions. At the far end was the walkway leading to the blackness of the open Shadow ship.

Galen sent them down the tunnel. He realized he was shaking, his heart pounding, breath coming in short gasps. He felt overloaded, accelerated, as if the slightest thing could set him off.

He'd cast more spells in the past hour than he had in the rest of his life. He realized how exhausted he was, beneath the racing energy of the tech. He must marshal his energy; he must remain focused and in control if he was to find Elizar and kill him.

An odd, irregular thumping was coming from the excavation area. They reached the end of the tunnel and skimmed out over the walkway. Behind them, a sheer rockface rose up toward the surface. Before them, the Shadow ship formed a huge, curving black wall. Far above, between ship and stone, shone a sliver of smoke-filled sky. The hole seemed deeper than Galen remembered.

A thump came from the ship, and it shook a bit. A cascade of loose stone rained down. It was almost as if the great vessel were being fired upon from above. Alwyn must have landed on top of it, as Galen had directed, and he must be under attack. Galen hoped there weren't other Shadow ships in the area. A mage ship couldn't survive one of those blasts.

He sent the platform shooting upward along the massive side of the Shadow ship. Its skin remained a dull black. It waited for a central processor to connect to it, to bring it to life.

They reached the point where Galen thought the top would be, but still the ship went on. As they continued up, its skin looked different. It was vibrant, shifting, reflecting the light in the same strange way as the walls of the City Center. Galen studied the surface and discovered this was not a Shadow ship at all, but the illusion of one. Alwyn had disguised his small ship as a much larger Shadow vessel, and he'd landed it on top of the one in the excavation. A lighted opening appeared in the illusory Shadow ship, though the entry looked much like the ramp of a mage ship.

Alwyn came out onto the ramp and waved them in. "Hurry! The jig is up. Most of their shots are hitting their own ship, but it's only a matter of time . . ." He ran back inside, disappearing through the open air lock.

Galen brought them down on the ramp. He sent G'Leel in to safety.

Blaylock waited beside him.

"Go," Galen said. "I'm staying here."

In the ship's bright light, Blaylock's thin face was startlingly white, glistening with sweat. His eyes narrowed. "You claimed you came to help the mages, not to seek revenge for yourself."

"I lied. It's something mages often do."

"Your power could help save them."

"I have no desire to save them."

The sleeve of Blaylock's jacket bloomed with blackness, and he stumbled to the side, collapsed onto the ramp. Galen bent toward him, and more plasma bolts shot past.

Galen turned. Alwyn had come back out of the air lock,

and as Galen waved him inside, Alwyn was enveloped in an explosion. Plasma erupted through the ramp, burning into his legs. He screamed out, crumbled.

On the walkway far below, one of the grey-skinned aliens stood, firing up at them.

Galen crushed him, crushed him, crushed him.

Shaking, Galen knelt beside Blaylock. Energy raced through him. He was furious at this gaunt, severe man. But still he didn't want Blaylock to die.

Blaylock had protected him, just as she had. And he had failed Blaylock, just as he had failed her. He could not protect; he could not heal. He could only destroy.

More plasma fire erupted through the ramp. Blaylock was still breathing. Galen quickly conjured a platform beneath him and slid him into the ship, then rushed to Alwyn. Alwyn's eyes were squeezed closed, his teeth clenched. The lower part of his robe was charred and fused to his burned skin in an indistinguishable mass. Galen slid him into the ship as well, following quickly into the dark, plain interior.

He hesitated a moment, standing over them, heart pounding. He would have to fly the ship. He would have to leave Elizar behind. His frustration sent a hard shiver through him. There would be no end to this. He would return to the way he had been on Selic, and he could not stand that, could not keep it all within. Yet he could not leave them to die.

He closed the air lock and raised the ramp. As the ship sealed, it lifted off.

But that was impossible. Who was flying it? Galen looked down to Alwyn at his feet, found the place where he had lain now bare. Alwyn was not there.

A few feet away, Blaylock slowly pushed himself up, using elbows rather than hands. The black burn of plasma had vanished from his jacket. He paused a moment to rest, breathing heavily, then climbed to his feet. His severe gaze met Galen's. "A small deception was necessary to get you on the ship. I feared that would be so. We need you, Galen."

Alwyn, Galen realized, was fine. He was flying the ship. The deception had been flawless, fitting perfectly into the situation, allowing him no time to think but only to react. Blaylock had used Galen's own loyalty against him.

The ship was rising higher and higher, taking him farther and farther from Elizar. The energy raged through him. "You need me. What about what I need?"

"I could not allow you to stay and waste your life in useless vengeance. You can do much more. You can be much more."

"How can you say that? How can you spout those fairy tales about God and the will of the universe? I can be only what the Shadows made me to be."

Blaylock was silent for a moment, his pale face revealing no reaction. Yet something in that unyielding expression made Galen think his words had hurt, and he took satisfaction in that. "That is not so," Blaylock said. "I believe everything I profess. Those who created the tech are irrelevant. It is greater than they know. Only we can find its truth."

The floor shook, and Blaylock took a few stumbling steps. The ship had been hit.

A message came from Alwyn. *I could use some help.* The message included the key to access the ship's sensors, and when Galen did, he saw in his mind's eye the full image of the area surrounding them, as if the ship's walls had suddenly become transparent. The dark screen of Alwyn's Shadow ship illusion surrounded them. Beyond it, five ships were following them up into the sky, firing at them. They were not Shadow ships, not nearly as powerful. Yet they were powerful enough; several direct hits would destroy Alwyn's ship. What had saved him thus far was that most of the shots missed their target, the small mage ship hidden within the much larger illusion.

Galen held tightly to the racing, burning energy, to the desire to reach out and destroy. He'd been tricked into coming with Alwyn and Blaylock; he had no desire to help them now. Perhaps they wouldn't make it. At least there would be an end.

Blaylock blotted the sweat from his forehead with his sleeve. "We are not like the woman in the machine. Some abhorrent variation of the Shadows' technology enslaves her. But we are not slaves."

"No, we're monsters, bringing chaos and destruction. We're programmed by the Shadows. We carry out their will, not the will of the universe."

Blaylock fixed his gaze on Galen, his voice harsh and certain. "We don't have to. Not if we retain control."

"I'm in control," Galen said. His entire body was shaking.

Another message. Galen didn't care what Alwyn had to say. He didn't care if the ship—

It was from Elizar.

Warn the mages. Save them. I will do my part.

Elizar dared to think that Galen would work with him, would trust him. Galen closed his eyes, unable to hold it in any longer. He hated them all, hated Blaylock and the mages, hated Elizar and the Shadows, but above all, hated himself.

The enemy ships were up to a quarter mile away, far beyond where most mage powers would extend, but as he selected his targets and the destruction began to flow, he found he had no trouble reaching them. He couldn't make the spheres any larger than about fifteen feet in diameter, so he targeted areas of concentrated energy within each ship, the dark spheres of destruction forming there. As sections of each ship imploded, one by one they tumbled downward like broken birds.

What the hell is happening? Alwyn wrote.

Then the ships were gone but Galen's energy was not. Perhaps he could still kill Elizar. He looked downward, to the glittering black City Center a half mile away. He focused on the base of the tower, crushed one corner, then another. As those supports vanished, the lower floors slowly bowed outward over the weakened side, curving like the belly of a snake. The top of the tower undulated uncertainly. Then the lower floors bowed out beyond the point of no return, and they began to topple, crashing one by one over the excavation area in a rolling, fluid movement. The massive black structure smashed down across the open ground, reached the end of the excavation area and shattered itself against the buildings beyond.

Galen reached farther into the earth, to the tunnels where Elizar might still survive. But the tech would not echo his command. The tunnels had passed out of range. Furious at his slowness, Galen let loose a barrage of destruction on the broken remains of the City Center. Then they too fell out of range, and he searched for another target. Below he saw the warehouse from which weapons were being shipped to the Centauri. The spells boiled up out of him and he crushed it to nothingness, leaving only an empty lot. Then there was the spaceport, and after that whatever structures remained within his grasp. As the one-term equations burned in column after column, covering the screen in his mind's eye, he cut a swath of destruction through the city. Far below, the structures vanished with a strange silence, leaving only emptiness behind. He must destroy them all, destroy the Shadows for what they had done, for all the hurt they had caused.

Then the ship was too high, and he could destroy no more. He forced the flow of energy to stop. It took him a few moments before he could speak. "Take me to Z'ha'dum," he said, trembling. "Take me now. I will destroy it all."

"No," Blaylock said. "You are surrendering to chaos. You must stop."

Then the sensors revealed another ship ahead. It was still distant, outside the atmosphere, but it was coming straight toward them.

He would destroy it too.

* * *

They would say Kosh spent too much time among the younger races. They would say that he allowed sentimentality to weaken discipline. They would say that the rules of engagement must not be broken, that the Vorlons must keep themselves above the conflict. They would say it was not fitting that he should endanger himself for any of the younger races, particularly this small group infected with darkness. And perhaps they were right.

Yet long had he watched the younger races, long had he guided them, though they did not know it. Wars had come and gone, aeons had passed, races had lived and died. There had been progress, surely. Where he had been able to instill canon, discipline, the younger races gained wisdom, matured. Yet for each of the seeds he sowed, chaos sowed its opposite. Violence, lawlessness abounded. A race made a hard-earned step forward only to slide back toward anarchy, or to be destroyed by its neighbor. The Xon had flourished only to be massacred by the Centauri. The Humans had united in a planetary government only to fall into a pointless war with the Minbari.

Many among the Vorlons had grown frustrated by the constant interference of the Shadows. Some said the time at last had come; the enemy must be attacked directly. But most clung to the rules of their ancient agreement and hoped that their new stratagems would be successful, that they would at last prove order superior to chaos.

As for Kosh, the coming of this new war carried with it an unfamiliar sense of unease. He had begun to consider something of which he had never heard another Vorlon speak. He had begun to doubt whether their manipulations—when coupled with those of the enemy—truly benefited the younger races.

Those young races formed the battleground over which their elders fought. The battle was harsh, the casualties great, the process unforgiving. The younger ones struggled so, in their primitive way. The many who had died began to feel like an overwhelming weight of darkness which no light could banish.

But what could be done? Breaking the rules of engagement meant anarchy.

Yet sometimes, it seemed, they should do more than manipulate from on high. Sometimes, it seemed, they should help.

These thoughts had begun to take shape, perhaps, during the last war. But only as he had presented the information of Kell's probable death, only as he had argued that the fabulists should be allowed to leave in peace, had he become aware of his doubts. The Vorlons had reluctantly agreed to let the fabulists retreat to their hiding place, and Kosh's unease had been soothed. Yet now, all that could change.

He had been planting buoys in the systems touched by darkness. The buoys had sung their perceptions to him, and he had been slipping through their song, observing, absorbing, when he had seen it. Another fabulist ship had arrived in the Thenothk system.

Most of the fabulists had gathered on Babylon 5 in what seemed to be preparation for their departure. Yet many Vorlons did not believe that the fabulists would withdraw. They believed the fabulists must join with the forces of chaos. Despite the destruction of Kell's ship, some did not accept his death. They believed it a deception.

Others, whose numbers were growing, claimed it unimportant whether the fabulists joined with the darkness. They were touched by darkness, and so should be destroyed. Why let them flee, only to later return?

Kosh had watched as the new fabulist ship had disguised itself as one of the enemy's black abominations and approached the fourth planet in the system. Deciding he must observe in person, Kosh had altered the song of his ship, directing it toward Thenothk. The ship obeyed eagerly. Obedience was its greatest joy.

Over the short journey, Kosh witnessed the fabulist's actions. The fabulist approached the main settlement, circled the stronghold of the maelstrom. He was looking for something. After a short time, his false appearance ceased to deceive the Shadows. They began to attack. Still the fabulist remained.

As Kosh's ship glided peacefully out of hyperspace, the fabulist descended to the planet's surface. He had not joined with the ancient enemy, yet he came to their stronghold, he landed. He searched for something of great value.

As Kosh stopped a safe distance from the planet, the fabulist ship rose up through the haze of the atmosphere. It was besieged by vessels loyal to the darkness. Great energies flashed around the ship, energies as great as those commanded by the Vorlons. Kosh recognized those flashes. He had detected one before, at the fabulists' assemblage. One of the fabulists wielded great power, and it was for him that the ship had searched. He had been a prisoner of the Shadows, and now he was freed.

As the fabulist ship rose over the city of pestilence, buildings fell to rubble, structures collapsed, vanished. There seemed no discrimination in the choice of targets. In its wake the ship left chaos.

The fabulist was destroying a stronghold of the maelstrom. And yet he was a creation of the maelstrom.

The fabulists had imposed a Code upon themselves, their attempt to fight the influence of chaos. If this fabulist truly did destroy without discrimination, then he had succumbed to the dream of the maelstrom. As it had gone with one, so it might go with others. This, at least, would be the Vorlons' argument. And again they would turn their minds to attack.

The fabulists on Babylon 5 were vulnerable. Kosh could not let the Vorlons take action against them based on fear. He must know the truth.

Kosh would place himself in the ship's path. If the fabulist did not attack, that would be evidence sufficient to placate the others. But if the fabulist had fallen to chaos, then he would attempt to destroy Kosh. And Kosh would attempt to destroy him.

Who would triumph in such a contest, Kosh did not know.

They would say he had forgotten his place. They would say beings touched by Shadows deserved no second chance. They would say he took a foolish risk.

But it was his to take.

— chapter 16 —

Elric stood in the customs area, his body stiff, muscles clenched. Within his skull, the cavity of darkness pushed outward, exerting an incredible pressure against the backs of his eyes, his forehead. He told himself he need endure only a few more minutes; then his task would be completed. In the meantime, his concentration could not flag.

Spread across Elric's mind's eye were the images from numerous probes and security cameras on Babylon 5. They revealed five hundred robed mages, a procession stretching out of Down Below, through corridors, up staircases, into the customs area, past the security checkpoint, and onto the Centauri freighter *Ondavi*. Of the five hundred, only one in ten was real, each creating the illusions surrounding him. To help maintain those illusions, John had posted security guards periodically along the mages' route, preventing anyone from coming near or interrupting their progress.

The one who absolutely could not approach was Morden, who would be accompanied by Shadows who could see through their illusions. Elric believed Morden would keep away, so that the mages would not grow suspicious of the *Ondavi*. After all, Morden intended them to believe he knew nothing of the Centauri freighter.

But Elric could not allow the slightest chance that Morden and the Shadows might appear. Conveniently, a section of the hallway ceiling outside Morden's quarters had collapsed, trapping him and his associates inside. Morden would expect a defensive action of this type as the mages departed; it should rouse no suspicions of their true plan.

Morden had protected his interests, though, by sending one of his agents to observe the mages' departure. The maintenance worker stood now across the customs area, watching. That was fine. He would see what Elric wanted him to see.

As the mages approached the *Ondavi*, one in twenty would step aside before entering the ship, giving the appearance that they were supervising the others. Those were the ones Elric hoped to save, the young ones. Slowly they faded into the background, or went back along the procession's route with the excuse of checking on the others, then disguised themselves with full-body illusions and returned to board the nearby *Crystal Cabin* under false names. Of the twenty-five Elric hoped to save, fifteen already had boarded.

Unfortunately, all fifty of those who had come to Babylon 5 could not be saved. The Centauri crew of the *Ondavi* must believe that five hundred mages had boarded their ship, and that five hundred remained in their cargo hold. To sustain that illusion required five mages at the very least, more when those mages' powers were failing. Elric thought of Burell, who had been the most skilled at creating large, complex illusions. She had also been the first of their losses. The throbbing in his head grew stronger.

More mages were required to interact with the crew, and to keep the crew away from the illusions. More were necessary to create false life-signs and mage energies, so that any who scanned the ship as it left Babylon 5 would be convinced they were all inside. Elric and Ing-Radi had discussed the issue at length, but no fewer than twenty-five seemed required to ensure the success of the deception.

Ing-Radi and Beel were on board the *Ondavi* now, supervising the others. They had planted probes about the freighter, so Elric and the others could observe. Although the mages had seen no evidence that the ship had been sabotaged, they knew it had been done. All those boarding understood that they would die.

They had gathered an hour ago to recite the words of the Code. None had asked to be released from his task. All were prepared to give their lives so that the rest of their order might escape unmolested. Or so it seemed. Gowen had monitored them and found no evidence of disloyalty. Of course, Elric could not be certain until they had boarded the ships, and the deception was complete. He felt angry at himself for even doubting them, yet he must, if he was to foresee all possibilities. But it seemed now those doubts had been unwarranted.

Of course, none but he and Ing-Radi knew the truth. None but he and Ing-Radi knew that escaping to a hiding place would not save their order but only postpone their end. None but he and Ing-Radi knew that the Shadows were not their adversaries but their creators. If the others knew that, Elric wondered how many of them would still give up their lives to see the mages safely to the hiding place. Perhaps all, perhaps none.

But they would not know. He would maintain the lie, and they would go to their deaths, each one a crushing burden.

And secured by those deaths, the rest of their order would flee, abandoning the galaxy in its time of greatest need.

Ing-Radi did not think of it as Elric did. She believed the success of the deception would be an affirmation of their order and their solidarity. He had spoken with her privately before the recitation of the Code. It had been the first time she had risen from her bed since falling ill, and Elric had feared she was not equal to the demands of the task that faced them. They had met in the small room Ing-Radi had taken for her own, which was much the same as Elric's. He had been shocked at her deterioration.

The orange had faded completely from her skin, leaving it a pale greyish white marked by the crisscrossing blue lines of veins. Her tall, thin body had become skeletal, disjointed, and something in the tentative way she moved gave him the impression that she could collapse at any moment into little more than a pile of bones.

"You have done well," she had said to him. "I believe your deception will be successful."

"That remains uncertain."

"If I may, I ask again that you do not join us on the *Ondavi*. You are not needed there among the dead. You are needed much more among the living."

"We agreed that twenty-five were necessary."

"One more or less will not matter. If you believe it will, choose another. Any would volunteer to take your place."

"I cannot ask one more to make such a sacrifice. And I cannot ask any, if I do not make it myself."

"You do not ask. The situation requires that some of us die. Just as the situation requires that you live. To make any other choice would be selfishness."

Elric shook his head. He did not have the energy to argue, and he could not concede.

Yet Ing-Radi persisted. "You said you fear Blaylock may be dead. Would you have Herazade be the sole survivor of the Circle? Would you have her alone guide the mages through the difficult decisions ahead?"

The thought appalled him, as she had known it would. But it changed nothing. Besides, his health too was failing.

The slash of her mouth smiled gently down at him. "I live in hope that our order may discover the secret of producing our own tech. Then we may at last be in control of our own destiny. With such a hope, the retreat to a hiding place is sensible. I am willing to make any sacrifice to keep that hope alive. But I know that you have no such hope. You believe the mages have initiated their last, and will now begin their long twilight. You envision our order dying, one by one, until a hundred years from now the last of us passes to the other side. For what, then, do you offer your life?"

Elric spoke with finality. "For solidarity. Our only weapon against the Shadows. Please don't ask me further. I will not change my mind."

After that, he had turned the discussion to the final details of their plan. He had tried to focus on the good they would achieve if they were successful, yet Ing-Radi's words continued to haunt him, even now. She was right, of course. He had no hope for the mages' future. He had lost his dreams, and they could not be resurrected. His one regret was Galen. He did not want to leave Galen. But if Alwyn had not arrived in time, Galen might already be waiting for him on the other side.

Elric could not think of that. That way lay despair.

The throbbing in his head was building, spreading throughout his body, echoed in counterpoint by the tech. He forced himself to straighten, checking the various images in his mind's eye. The last of the mages had left Down Below, and the end of the line was winding its way up toward the customs area.

Elric realized he was pressing the heel of his hand to his temple, and he lowered it.

Carvin, wearing a simple black robe, reached the hatch of the *Ondavi* and stepped out of line, speaking with Fed and Gowen, who also stood to one side. Gowen said something to her, and she glanced toward Elric. Then Carvin pointed down the line of mages, appearing to send Fed and Gowen to check on the others. She came back through security and approached Elric.

Elric recalled the conjury she had done in her last training session before becoming a mage. With assured, graceful movements, she had juggled Alwyn's boots, mixing them with illusions of other shoes, sending them flying into complex patterns. In all the activity, illusions had replaced the real boots, which she had hidden away. Their current shell game was very much the same.

"Are you all right?" she asked.

He was about to send her on to the *Crystal Cabin*, when the pressure in his head suddenly built into an incredible, overwhelming pain. His muscles were quivering, his legs about to collapse. "I must withdraw. I will return in a moment."

She nodded, eyes wide.

He barely made it into an empty corridor before his legs gave way beneath him. He conjured an illusion around himself, a section of wall that bumped out around him. He pressed his forehead against the cold floor and tried to focus on the images in his mind's eye. The pain, that tumor of desolation growing inside him, seemed to block out everything else. He felt as if he were being consumed by it, by all that had been lost, and all that would be lost.

He had gone too long without rest. Now, at this critical time, he was failing.

Angry at his weakness, he forced himself to focus, to access the camera in the customs area. He must not allow the plan to fail.

Carvin was standing in his place, waiting for his return.

Londo strutted into the customs area behind her, his black halo of hair restored to perfect order.

Elric had known that eventually he would emerge, driven by curiosity, a twinge of guilt, but most of all, a desire to assuage his ego, to prove to himself that he was not afraid of the mages. Elric should be the one to deal with him.

Elric climbed to hands and knees. His limbs trembled, rubbery. He did not have the strength to rise.

"The arrangements are satisfactory, yes?" Londo said to Carvin.

"Londo. Yes, you've honored your debt." She extended her hand. "No kiss?"

His expression softened. "You make it difficult to remain angry at you." He took the hand, kissed it.

"There's no need for hard feelings between us. We required a ship; you were able to provide one." Although she was unprepared for the encounter, she was playing the gracious winner, as she should. She revealed no sign that she knew the Centauri ship would soon take twenty-five of her order to their deaths.

Londo looked toward the line of mages, and his lips parted. He turned back to Carvin. "I wish that you and I could have gotten to know each other better. Is there any chance you could stay? Follow the others in a few days?"

So Londo did have a scrap of conscience, at least for a beautiful young woman. The rest of them could die without causing him undue upset.

"I must go with them. You should be glad we're leaving before you've lost everything."

"Yes, I still have my stock in Fireflies, Incorporated. Sure to bring me security in my old age."

Carvin glanced at the end of the line of mages, which had wound its way into the customs area. "It's time now, Londo." With a smile she took his hand, kissed it in a perfect impression of his overly solicitous manner. "Good-bye, dear ambassador." She took her place at the end of the line.

As Londo looked after her, his mouth widened, as if he thought to say something, and he seemed to come to a decision. He went after her.

Elric struggled to push himself up. Carvin needed to get to the *Crystal Cabin*. Londo must be distracted. He raised a hand to the wall to brace himself. It slid down again, again, as if the muscles in his arm had been removed. Waves of emptiness pushed through him.

"The *Ondavi* is a freighter," Londo said, walking beside her as the line progressed toward the ship. "Really not fit for passengers. The cargo hold"—he shook his head—"it's quite unpleasant."

"Thank you for your concern. But I'll be fine."

"But you needn't be, dear lady." They reached the security checkpoint, and Carvin presented her identicard to Lou Welch. Londo continued. "I've made special arrangements for you to sit up on the flight deck. You'll find it much more pleasant there."

Lou cleared Carvin, and Londo attempted to follow her through.

Lou barred the way with his arm. "Passengers only, Ambassador."

"Oh, but this is ridiculous! This ship belongs to a highly placed Centauri, a friend of mine. I am handling this—" Londo called toward the *Ondavi*. "Lieutenant! Lieutenant!" He looked at Lou. "Security. Are you ever there when you are actually needed?"

A Centauri in a shabby uniform came out of the ship.

Londo pointed to Carvin. "This is the charming woman I was telling you about. You must allow her to sit with you on the flight deck. She's my most honored guest. Provide her every convenience you can offer. Make her happy. Keep her safe. Or you will have me to answer to."

Damn Londo. He'd somehow gotten the idiotic notion that he could save Carvin by keeping her out of the cargo hold. In an ill-considered attempt to appease his conscience, he was going to kill her. Elric clawed his way up the wall, his legs shaking. He must reach her. He must reach her before she boarded.

Ing-Radi appeared at the hatch of the ship. She was looking into the customs area, for Elric. She could say nothing to stop Londo. Any objection would reveal what they knew.

Elric dissolved the illusion, stumbled down the corridor toward the customs area, his body throbbing in time with his heart. He slammed into a wall, pushed himself along it.

The shabby-looking lieutenant, playing the gracious host, bowed and waved Carvin inside. She hesitated only a moment. Then she entered.

"Good-bye, dear lady," Londo called.

Carvin looked back over her shoulder, her face carefully composed, revealing nothing. "Good-bye, Londo."

Through the probes on the *Ondavi*, Elric watched the lieutenant lead her into the ship, toward the flight deck.

He stopped short in the entrance to the customs area, gasping. She was gone. And she could not be removed from the ship without alerting the crew that something was amiss. He took a few uneven steps, came up against the wall.

She was one of the best of the young mages, clever, disciplined, yet always smiling, full of life. When she and Alwyn had come to visit, she had always been a bright light in their lives.

From just inside the hatch, Ing-Radi was looking toward him with concern. Elric took a breath and straightened, moving away from the wall. He turned his back on her and Londo, struggling to collect himself. This possibility he had not foreseen. He had promised Alwyn he would watch over Carvin. And now he could not save her.

"Stop, Galen!" Blaylock's voice was sharp. "It is a Vorlon ship."

Galen had been about to form the spell of destruction in his mind. He quickly shifted his target away from the approaching ship, imploding instead a sphere of empty space.

The destruction was unsatisfying. He wanted another target, but as they rose out of the planet's gravity well, nothing else was within range.

He was burning, churning, surging with energy. The brilliant incandescence raced through his veins, shot down his neurons. The tech sang along the meridians of his body, a vibration so pure it was painful.

He forced the screen in his mind's eye to remain blank. He must not release it. He must cast no spell. He must hold himself still. He must remain still until he could think. He counted the beats of his pounding heart. The rapid rhythm helped him focus, helped him wait, wait.

He had known, on some level, that it was a Vorlon ship, even as he'd prepared to destroy it. He knew what they looked like, the long, narrow frame with the distinctive yellow-green coloring, four flowing arms aimed forward, almost like a squid on its side. Yet he simply hadn't cared. He still didn't care.

The Vorlon stopped directly in their path, a threatening posture. As Alwyn slowed their ship, Galen studied the sleek form for any sign of attack. Within him the energy was building, building. At the back of the Vorlon ship, its petal-like extensions were open. The mages believed these to be an energy generation device of some kind. The hollow at the center of its four arms—the place from which the Vorlons' beam weapon was known to fire—pointed toward them.

It blocked their path. It might attack, and Alwyn's ship could not withstand the strike. He wanted to crush it.

Alwyn brought them to a stop.

The Vorlon remained in their path, unmoving.

The Vorlons had always despised and distrusted the mages. No wonder. The mages were allies of their enemies, the Shadows.

"If you attack it," Blaylock said, "the Vorlons will hunt us down just as the Shadows are."

Galen held desperately to the heat blazing through him. He felt overloaded, accelerated. He was shaking, his heart pounding, breath coming in irregular, shallow pants. He performed a mind-focusing exercise, another, another. Time passed.

At last the Vorlon ship turned, then sped into the blackness of space.

Alwyn opened a jump point before them, sent his ship into the churning orange-yellow vortex.

Galen broke contact with the ship's sensors. He stood in the plain, black room at the back of Alwyn's ship. Blaylock's severe, disapproving gaze was fixed on him. Across the floor G'Leel lay motionless. The threat was over. There was nothing more to crush, nothing except the ship and what was within it.

The energy raced through him, endless, merciless. He had

only the vaguest idea of all he had destroyed, of the ships, the buildings, the people. They could not all have deserved death.

The tech echoed his agitation. Blaylock had said he need not give in to destruction, and Galen recognized the truth of that. It had been his choice. And he had chosen to kill.

Without a threat to hold his attention, the pain was seeping back into his leg, and he began to realize how completely exhausted his body was. His mind was exhausted as well, drained by the focus required to cast so many spells, by the even greater focus required to hold the energy inside him now, uncast. Yet he must maintain that endless, ferocious focus; there was no way to free himself from that need, for the tech was part of him, the Shadows were part of him, and as long as he lived, he could not escape them.

He needed to calm himself, to slow down.

His leg was burning now with a fire of its own, and he realized his fingers were digging into the inflamed tissue. He tightened his grip. As a brilliant pain shot down his leg, the racing energy faded just the slightest bit. From that thought to the next was a short jump.

"Excuse me," he said to Blaylock. He would go to one of Alwyn's sleeping cabins. There he could be alone.

Alwyn entered the room as he was leaving. "Will someone tell me what the . . ."

Galen passed him. The closest sleeping cabin was only a few steps down the passage. He locked the door and called the fire down upon himself.

With the first scouring he collapsed onto the bed, teeth clenched. The fire rushed over his body like living lava. He had to close down, to drive deep into himself the energy, anger, horror, memory.

With the second scouring he curled inward, the searing heat crawling over his body, raking his skin away. After all he had done, it was only the smallest fraction of what he deserved. For a moment the pain overwhelmed everything else, and he couldn't feel the restless energy of the tech. But then the moment passed, and it returned.

The third scouring enveloped him like a warm wave, and he began, at last, to relax.

The fourth carried him quietly into darkness.

The announcement was broadcast through the customs area. "Private liner *Crystal Cabin* is now in final check prior to departure."

The throbbing had enveloped Elric's body, and fighting it had exhausted him. Yet his task was nearly completed. He accessed the security roster of those who had boarded the *Crystal Cabin*. Twenty-four mages were aboard, including Gowen, to whom Elric had confided the gathering place. All were where they should be. All but Carvin.

He would join her now, aboard the *Ondavi*. It too was in final check.

Behind him, the butcher cleared his throat. "Excuse me," Londo said, and Elric turned to face him. It would be their final meeting. Londo had a mild smile on his face. He wanted to prove to Elric, and to himself, that he had no fear of techno-mages. "I wanted to thank you for your amusing little gift. It took me two hours to repair the damage to my quarters, and I don't think the smell will go away for days. Now if I may ask, does this torment end when you leave, or am I going to have to spend the rest of my life paying for one little mistake?"

His *one little mistake*. Elric wanted to strike down this petty, self-indulgent, careless man, a man who killed equally with kindness and hatred. But he must not reveal the depth of his anger, must not reveal that he knew the mages aboard the *Ondavi* would be killed. He had not needed to work so hard to control himself in many years. He fixed the butcher with his gaze, and he, too, put on a mild smile. "Oh, I'm afraid you're going to have to spend the rest of your life paying for your mistakes. Not this one, of course; it's trivial. I have withdrawn the spell. But there will be others."

Londo drew back, wary. "What are you talking about?"

"You are touched by darkness, Ambassador. I see it as a blemish that will grow with time. I could warn you, of course, but you would not listen. I could kill you, but someone would take your place. So I do the only thing I can: I go." He turned away, then stopped himself. Surely he could do some small bit more, without revealing the deception. If he could plant a seed of truth in Londo, a seed that might someday force the butcher to see himself for what he truly was, in all its horror, then perhaps he might have done some good. He turned back.

"Oh—I believe it was an endorsement you wanted, a word or two, a picture to send to the folks back home, confirming that you have a destiny before you."

Londo glanced away, impatient, anticipating a chastisement. "Yes, it was just a thought, nothing more."

"Well, take this for what little it will profit you. As I look at you, Ambassador Mollari, I see a great hand reaching out of the stars. The hand is your hand. And I hear sounds, the sounds of billions of people calling your name."

Londo's eyebrows rose hopefully. "My followers?"

Elric dropped his false smile. "Your victims."

Londo's expression had frozen, yet the same arrangement of features that a moment ago had conveyed hope, now seemed filled with unease.

Elric took that for his reward, modest as it was. He turned and made his way to the security checkpoint.

A number of the security guards had gathered about the hatch of the *Ondavi*. Once he passed through the checkpoint, Elric quickly found himself surrounded. John Sheridan was hidden among them.

Elric had no energy or patience for further delays. He had not anticipated this action and didn't understand what might be motivating it. "What is the meaning of this?"

John held up a calming hand and spoke softly. "Your friend Ing-Radi contacted me. I should be angry at everything you left out when you told me your plan. But I understand why you did it. And I have to say I agree with her. The techno-mages need a leader like you." He smiled.

The guards parted, making a slight opening near the hatch of the *Ondavi*. An illusion of Elric appeared beside him and walked through the opening into the ship. Ing-Radi, standing inside, nodded to him. The circle of security guards closed, and they began talking and laughing among themselves, walking down the docking bay toward the hatch of the *Crystal Cabin*. He was sheltered within them, unobserved.

Ing-Radi had violated secrecy, telling John more of their plan than Elric had. Elric had told him that only illusions would board the *Ondavi*, and that their enemies sought merely to capture them, not kill them. Surely Ing-Radi had not told John everything, for he would never allow the *Ondavi* to leave if he knew what was about to happen. Yet perhaps she had told him that she and Elric planned to go on board to create the illusions, and that Elric was unnecessary. Somehow she had told John enough to convey that Elric's life was in danger. And John, for some reason, had taken it upon himself to save a man he barely knew. Elric was exhausted, and in pain, yet even so, he didn't understand why he felt like crying.

He had lost his dreams, but John was giving him the chance to dream again, and giving him a new dream with which to start. The mages would not fight the Shadows, would not defeat them. But perhaps those left behind could. Perhaps John could bring them together, for good. Perhaps, through this remarkable man, those dark agents of chaos and death could at last be vanquished.

The group of security guards approached the *Crystal Cabin*, and Elric knew he would have to slip out while they continued on their way. Carvin's ticket had been purchased under the false identity of a Narn. Elric took on the Narn's image. "Thank you," he said quietly, then slipped out from their circle into the ship.

He was shown into the luxurious passenger compartment. The others, all disguised, stood at the window, silent. He joined them. There were the normal delays, yet none of them moved, none of them spoke. They all waited for what must come.

Elric accessed his probe on John, found him at Command and Control.

A technician turned to the captain. "The ship carrying the techno-mages is requesting permission to leave. What do I tell them?"

That would be the *Ondavi*.

John took the orange blossom from his pocket and twirled it between his thumb and forefinger. It would not wilt or decay; it would endure. And so, perhaps, would some bit of the beauty and good the mages had created.

"Tell them," John said, "permission granted."

Elric added to his mind's eye the probes on the *Ondavi*. One was fixed to the wall of the large cargo hold. There he saw a great mass of mages, some real, some illusion. They moved, and murmuring arose from them as if they spoke. Of those nearest the probe he picked out Ing-Radi, Muirne, Beel, Natupi, G'Ran, Elektra. They stood silently, also waiting.

Another probe showed the flight deck of the *Ondavi*, with its Centauri crew. The window at the front of the flight deck revealed that the ship was passing out through the docking bay. As the image shifted, panning the deck, Elric caught a close-up glimpse of Carvin's face, and he realized she'd planted the probe on the back of her hand, so they could observe.

The *Crystal Cabin* began to move as well, the view through the window beside Elric showing that they too were passing through the docking bay.

Within the customs area, Vir joined Londo, and they watched on the monitor as the Centauri ship left Babylon 5.

The *Ondavi* broke into the blackness of space and started

toward the jumpgate. The *Crystal Cabin* followed a minute later. Through an odd coincidence of flight paths, Elric found the *Ondavi* framed in the window beside him. It was a fragile construction of metal, a piece of technology that intelligent beings trusted to preserve their lives. But those with better technology could always destroy it.

In his mind's eye, the cargo hold shuddered as a rapid series of explosions raced through the depths of the ship. Ing-Radi caught Muirne as she stumbled, and wrapped Muirne in her four skeletal arms. Even now she sought to comfort.

The far end of the hold erupted with a spray of shrapnel and a great gust of fire. It roared across the room, engulfing it. In the space of a few seconds that would haunt Elric for the rest of his life, the mages were burned alive. Some were killed instantly in the intense flash of heat; others managed to throw up shields, to gain a few moments as superheated gas and flames penetrated inward. Their screams were no illusion, nor their brief, desperate struggles for escape. Ing-Radi and Muirne shot up above the flames, arms tight about each other, the subtle blue of a shield flickering around them. But the confined heat was too intense, and they were too weak. The blue vanished, and in a flash their robes incinerated, skin blackened, flaked to ash. Within the great furnace of the cargo hold, they were little more than a cinder buoyed on the heat of the flames.

On the flight deck, the probe's image shifted from the panicked, screaming crew to Carvin's face. She was crying. She too had seen what had happened in the hold. She was whispering to herself, or perhaps, to them all. "No, my God, no, no."

The booming chain reaction of explosions reached the flight deck, and as the ferocious fire blasted out from the wall in a churning, orange corona about Carvin's head, the probe's image went black.

Through the window beside him came a quickfire series of brilliant flashes, and the fragile ship flew apart.

In Command and Control, the same light flashed through the observation port, and John jerked his head toward it. "What?" He took a few steps forward, the sound of his breath hard. But when he spoke again, his voice was only a whisper. "They knew this would happen. They knew it."

In the customs area, Londo's mouth hung open in horror. He too had known what was going to happen, yet he had refused to fully believe it. He would not accept who he was, and what he was, though the answer was right before him.

Vir turned to him. "Londo, what happened?" He shook Londo's arm. "What happened!"

Londo could not look away from the monitor. He seemed stunned.

"Londo, answer me!"

Londo at last looked at Vir, and Elric saw his mental defenses begin to return, protections against discovery both by others and by himself. His voice was weak, at first, but quickly gained certainty. "I don't know. A malfunction of some kind, perhaps. I was told the ship was in perfect running order."

Londo was not ready for the truth—not today, perhaps not ever. At the least, many more would have to die before he would face it.

Around Elric, several of the mages had fallen to their knees. Other passengers crowded around the window to see the remnants of the explosion.

Of the *Ondavi*, only twisted, charred fragments survived, floating silently out into blackness.

He had sent twenty-five mages to their deaths. He had planned to go with them. Yet now it was left to him to bear the burden of those deaths, and to honor those who had died for their order. One by one he thought of them, who they had been, what good they had done, what had been lost in their passing.

Elric hoped their great sacrifice had accomplished its purpose, that the Shadows had been deceived, that they would believe the mages destroyed and would pursue them no more.

The *Crystal Cabin* moved around the wreckage, and Babylon 5 came into view. When he had arrived at the station, he had been a man without dreams. John had given him one, and perhaps now the mages had given him another. Though they had been asked to give up their lives, none had betrayed their plan; none had broken away to save himself. They had upheld solidarity, and in their unity they had, in their own small way, defeated the forces of chaos.

For the way the mages had performed, Elric felt proud. They had shown great courage and conviction, and though none here knew it, their deeds had proven that they were much more than their creators had ever intended them to be. A thousand years ago, Wierden had helped them dream a dream of what they might be, and they had fulfilled that dream.

Perhaps it was not their destiny to fight the Shadows. But they could at least remain true to themselves, to who they were as techno-mages.

And so it fell to him, Herazade, and perhaps Blaylock, to see the survivors safely into hiding. He would watch over them, for as long as he could, as they wrote the closing chapter in the history of their order. Perhaps it still could contain good, and beauty, and wonder, though it would be their last.

They had lost much over the last months, and he had lost much. The emptiness of that loss still pushed him toward despair. Yet it would not overwhelm him, so long as he had the one thing that meant most to him.

And that was his final dream: that he would land at the gathering place, and emerge from his ship, and he would see Galen, and Galen would be all right.

chapter 17

The cold wind whipped through Galen's coat and raked over his hands, still raw after four days. He stood on the high plateau of the gathering place, watching the mage ships drop out of the grey sky. Elric and Ing-Radi's group was finally arriving, only hours before all the mages were scheduled to leave for the hiding place.

Gowen's ship came down for a landing, followed by Ak-Shana's.

Many of the other mages were loading their ships using flying platforms, and they paused now, looking skyward, checking the sign on each ship to see who had survived. More came out of the hidden bunker, anxious for news of what had happened on Babylon 5. Since communications had been prohibited, they'd heard nothing from the group since they'd separated.

Three days ago, ISN had reported the explosion of a Centauri freighter leaving Babylon 5, a ship on which the mages were recorded as passengers, and many had feared the entire group destroyed. Since arriving yesterday, Galen had simply waited, and watched.

Fed's ship landed.

The mages clustered near the new arrivals, leaving him alone with the wind.

The plateau's high elevation and thin atmosphere allowed no strenuous activity, at least not until one became acclimated to it. Coarse, stubby brown grass covered the area. It was a vast, desolate place.

The mages had been staying in a bunker built into the plateau. Though the bunker was small compared to the facility on Selic 4, somehow the mages had managed to complete the preparations for their exodus. Herazade had returned from the hiding place, which had been made secure. She would lead them there.

Emond's ship landed, Chiatto's.

Blaylock came to stand beside Galen. He had returned to his black robe and skullcap, his eyebrows again scoured away. His face appeared more gaunt than ever, the waxy sheen of his skin more pronounced. He had not recovered from his ordeal on Thenothk. His hands, rather than curling naturally inward, remained stiffly open, as if they pained him. His mangled palms had covered themselves over with skin, but the skin was yellowish and stiff, its topography uneven. On the journey back, Blaylock had helped Alwyn to heal G'Leel, and so temporarily decreased the number of healing organelles in his own body. Galen didn't think they were replenishing themselves well. Perhaps Ing-Radi could help him.

Galen wished Blaylock would gather with the others. Blaylock had already questioned him about what had passed between him and Elizar. Galen had nothing more to say. He simply wanted to remain still and silent.

"There is Elric's ship," Blaylock said.

Galen looked skyward. A sleek black triangular shape marked with Elric's rune descended toward the landing area. Galen was shocked by the intensity of his relief.

Since waking from his long sleep on Alwyn's ship, he had felt little emotion. He had gone through the motions of retrieving his ship and flying it here like an automaton. He had forced himself to remain vigilant, so the power would not slip out of him, but except for that small piece he kept as watchman, he'd buried as much of himself as he could. And that was how he must remain.

While keeping his vigil for Elric, he'd thought the one emotion he would have to guard against would be anger. But as Elric's ship lowered itself toward the ground, anger remained a distant echo. For now he just wanted to see Elric. Elric was his only family, his only tie to the universe. Elric was his wall of strength, the one always standing beside him, the one who had brought order and meaning to his life. Whatever lies Elric had told, Galen didn't want to lose him.

And yet, as Elric's ship set down, its side marked with the rune for integrity, Galen realized he had lost Elric. The person he had thought Elric was, the man who never lied to him, no longer existed. The Elric who remained was a stranger. A liar. One who took from the Shadows. One who had helped him gain what he most wanted, without telling him what it truly was.

And so he had become a monster.

His anger was like a message from a distant galaxy, barely perceptible, its passion lost in the transmission. He didn't want to hear it. He would keep still, and it would pass.

Gowen and Fed came out from among the ships. Gowen quickly scanned the plateau, and his gaze stopped on Blaylock. He hurried toward them.

Blaylock spoke. "Regardless of its source, the tech can do good. Elric has done much good on his home, as others have done on theirs. The temptations and the difficulties for us are many, which is why I have always advocated cloistering ourselves away. Only by foreswearing worldly temptations and pleasures can we free ourselves from the directives of the Shadows and focus on the tech itself. Only that way can we gain complete control of it and perfect unity with it. I truly believe it is a blessing that links us to the basic powers of the universe, and that through it, we can forge a connection to the universe, and attain enlightenment. The tech may have been designed for one purpose, but that does not preclude it being used for another."

They had made him a weapon. What purpose could a weapon have, except to kill? Perhaps for some of the other mages it was different. Perhaps some of them felt the urge to destruction less strongly, or had better control. But when given the choice, he had chosen destruction. He seemed to have a natural affinity for it.

He watched Elric's ship, waiting for it to open.

Blaylock continued. "When I learned from you that the Shadows use living beings in those ships, which have killed so many without mercy, I feared that the transcendence I had sought was not the path. I feared it might end in bloodshed, with us as executioners for the Shadows. I had to return to that place to learn whether those fears had merit.

"But what I saw revealed that we are not like those poor beings. They are subjugated to the Shadows' technology. We are masters of our tech. And when we master it perfectly, we will escape the Shadows' designs.

"You have grown closer to the tech than most. You manipulate it nearly effortlessly. But you must control your emotions. Instead of controlling them, you bury them. You do not speak of your parents. You say little of Isabelle. You hold these things inside, thinking that you control them. But inside, they gain power over you. Only in facing and mastering them can you attain control of yourself."

He hid from himself. That was what Kell had told him. And Galen knew it was true. A part of him had been cloistered away for a long time. He hoped now that he had locked away most of the rest. He had caught a glimpse of his true self with Isabelle's death, and another glimpse with Elizar's revelation. Light had illuminated the dark, secret center of himself; truths had been revealed. Each one showed him something he didn't want to see.

She had told him that he must open himself to himself. Perhaps the job was incomplete. But he had faced, now, what he was. He could stand no more.

Elric came from his ship, and before Galen could see him clearly, the mages crowded around him. No further ships arrived. Fifty had set off with Elric and Ing-Radi. Only half that number had returned.

"Galen." Blaylock's voice was harsh. He waited until Galen turned to him. "You must not speak of what you have learned, to any but those in the Circle, and Alwyn."

And what would they do if he did? Flay him? He would like to see them try.

Again he said nothing. He would not be drawn into an argument. If the anger returned, if the energy reached the great burning rage he had felt on Thenothk, he could well destroy them all.

Flaying would be insufficient punishment for what he'd done. He had condemned Elizar for killing only one. Yet in his destruction of the city, he had killed thousands. Many of them could have been there simply to do a job, like G'Leel and her crew—perhaps he'd even killed Captain Ko'Vin and the other Narns.

In all those thousands, Isabelle might have seen the possibility for good. All Galen saw were targets for his anger. Even now he regretted he had not destroyed the entire city. And Elizar. Always Elizar.

Gowen stopped beside them, breathless. "Blaylock," he said, and in his wide eyes and clasped hands, Galen could see his relief and concern. He bowed. "The blessing of Wierden upon you."

"And upon you," Blaylock said.

Gowen turned to Galen with a grateful smile, gave a short bow.

"I must speak with Elric," Blaylock said. He looked at Galen as if he wanted to say more, but instead he set off across the plateau, the wind pressing at his back, revealing the stick-thin figure hidden within his robe.

"Won't you come?" Gowen asked Galen.

As Gowen had rushed to Blaylock, so Galen should rush to Elric, should meet him with relief and concern. But he could not. "Go ahead," he said, and after a brief hesitation, Gowen hurried after Blaylock.

Galen looked to the crowd that hid Elric at its center. Fed stood on the periphery, arms at his sides, oddly quiescent. Alwyn pushed his way out, getting into a shoving match with Tzakizak. Galen used his sensors to gain a magnified view in his mind's eye. Alwyn's jaw was tight with anger, and the shoving intensified. Alwyn conjured a fireball. Tzakizak stumbled a few steps back, conjured one as well.

The memory flashed through his mind. The day Burell's illness had grown serious. He and Isabelle had fought. In her anger she had turned on him in a moment, conjuring a fireball. She had been ready to attack him, and he had been ready to counterattack with the spell of destruction. The incident was remarkable only in its familiarity. He had seen such fights at almost every convocation. Mages were quick to anger; the Shadows had made them that way.

Alwyn and Tzakizak faced each other, each waiting for any movement from the other. Then Alwyn turned aside, hurling his fireball to the ground, where it splashed in a fiery puddle, consuming the wiry grass. He walked away.

Tzakizak stared after him for a moment, then, finally, extinguished his own fireball.

After a few steps, Alwyn began to stumble. After a few more, he collapsed to his knees. He shook his head, his cry barely audible on the wind. "No, no, no!"

Carvin's ship had not been among those that had returned. Galen remembered the rustle of her colorful Centauri silks, the graceful movements of her conjuries. She'd been excited to help in Elric's deception. She'd always been excited about anything she undertook. To Galen she had seemed strangely fearless—passionate, friendly, open. She had not hidden from life, but lived it. And now she was gone.

Alwyn had left her to go to Thenothk, to save Galen and Blaylock. Whether he could have saved her if he'd stayed on Babylon 5, Galen did not know. But the loss would crush him.

It was, as Carvin had said, one death after another. The mages were doomed. Could they not see it?

The crowd around Elric began to disperse and return to their tasks. Among them Galen saw Herazade, Circe, Optima, Kane. They looked shaken. Many had not returned from Babylon 5, including Ing-Radi. They had lost another member of the Circle, and their greatest healer.

Optima found Fed, and he burst into animated talk, slipping an arm around her waist as they walked across the plateau.

Left to themselves, Blaylock and Elric spoke. Elric glanced toward Galen, listened to Blaylock, glanced again. Galen stood frozen in place. Was there any way he and Elric could return to the relationship they'd once had? How could Elric possibly justify all the lies he had told? And how could Galen possibly justify all those he had killed?

G'Leel approached him from the bunker. She wore a long black cloak she'd apparently borrowed from Alwyn. Each shoulder moved forward in turn. The gold of her skin seemed slightly pale, the white scar across her nose standing out, bright. Alwyn had brought her to the gathering place despite the directives of the Circle. He had said she was too ill to be abandoned, and she'd been resting since they'd arrived. She looked well now, though Galen knew much recuperation was necessary after a healing.

G'Leel stopped several feet away. She looked in his direction, not meeting his eyes, then looked away across the plateau. "What's going on?" she asked. She was still afraid of him, he realized.

"The group from Babylon 5 has returned."

"Is that Alwyn? What happened to him?"

"His former student. Carvin. She was with the group. She died. Many others did as well."

"I'm sorry," she said.

The numbers who had died were nothing compared to the numbers he had killed.

G'Leel took a step closer. "How's your leg?"

"Fine." He supposed it was almost healed. He barely noticed the pain anymore.

She took another step. "Got rid of the hair, I see." When he didn't respond, she shook her head slightly, as if impatient with herself. Then her red eyes at last met his. "I need to know what happened in the tunnels after I was shot. Alwyn doesn't know anything. I remember going into that white room after you. I saw those two you asked me about—Elizar and the Centauri."

Galen didn't want to go over it again, to think of all he had done. "You were shot by a Drazi in league with the Shadows. I killed her. I killed the Centauri. We escaped."

A smile flashed over her face. "Did anyone ever tell you you're a great storyteller?"

"If you want stories," Galen said, "ask any other mage here." He was being drawn again into anger. He must stop it. Across the plateau, Elric nodded at something Blaylock said, and again his gaze returned to Galen.

"Thank you for saving me," G'Leel said.

He had been concerned only with killing, not saving. "I did nothing. It was Blaylock and Alwyn who healed you."

"The one who killed Isabelle—he got away?"

Galen wasn't sure whether Elizar was alive or dead. But he would not claim Elizar's death until he was certain. He gave a single nod.

"Are you going to go back there? I need to get to that warehouse you told me about and stop them from shipping any more weapons to the Centauri."

"I destroyed the warehouse."

G'Leel hesitated. "Are you serious? When did you do that?"

"As we were leaving, I destroyed the City Center, the warehouse, the spaceport—a whole section of the city. I killed—whoever was there." How could he live with what he'd done?

Elric and Blaylock parted. Blaylock went to Alwyn. Elric came toward them. He looked even older and weaker than before. He held himself stiffly upright, trying to appear as he always had. Yet the erect posture and long, even strides were clearly a growing effort for him. Each movement seemed brittle, forced.

Galen had wanted to keep Elric safe, had offered to abandon his task if Elric abandoned his own. If only they both had. If only they'd fled to the hiding place. Everything would not have changed. Elric had warned him. *Someday, perhaps, you will not think of me so kindly. I hope, if that day comes, you will try to understand why I have done what I have done.*

But Galen did not understand.

"I must speak with Elric privately," he said.

"Thank you for destroying the warehouse," G'Leel said. "I know you had more to think about than the good of the Narns. But maybe now the Centauri won't attack my people."

He hadn't done it for her, though, or for good. He had done it because he'd wanted to destroy, and the warehouse had been there.

Across the plateau, Alwyn climbed to his feet, dismissing some comment of Blaylock's with a sharp wave of his hand and yelling a retort in Blaylock's face. To Galen's surprise, G'Leel went toward them.

Then Elric stood before him. As much as Galen wanted to distance himself from Elric, to think of Elric as some horrible lying stranger, standing before him was the same man he had known all these years, his figure severe in the high-collared black robe that she had made for him. His thin lips were pressed together, grim. The three frown lines between his brows, though deeper than before, still indicated grave disappointment. Blaylock would have told him all Galen had done.

And yet somehow the expression was different, as if Elric were disappointed not with Galen, but with himself. Galen knew he would blame himself for the deaths of Carvin, Ing-Radi, and the others, even if he could have done nothing to prevent them. He had always taught Galen to take responsibility for his mistakes and failures, and on the rare occasions when Elric had failed or miscalculated, Galen had seen him do the same.

But what about taking responsibility for his lies? What about telling the truth? Galen's distant anger drew nearer.

They stood in silence, the wind whipping past them. Galen found himself unable to speak. How could Elric have kept this secret? How could Elric have lied to him, about the one thing that changed everything?

"I'm sorry I did not tell you," Elric said. "You should have heard the truth from me. And you should have heard it long ago."

Galen knew the Circle had sworn him to secrecy, but Elric would not use that as an excuse. That just made Galen angrier. A thousand bitter responses came to mind, but Galen uttered none of them, willing the wind to carry them away.

"I learned that truth when I was elected to the Circle nine years ago. It made me question many things. But ultimately I knew that I believed in the mages. I believed in our ability to create beauty and wonder, to gain knowledge, to do good. The origin of the tech did not change that."

Did they think they would never have to pay for what they took? Did they think themselves immune to the designs of the Shadows? How could they be, when they didn't have the least understanding of the tech?

Galen tried to still his mind, to think nothing, to feel nothing.

"The truth did, however, reveal the fragile base on which our order is built. And it explained many things. I realized that control and obedience to the Circle and the Code were even more important than I had known. I tried to teach you those things. But they were no substitute for the truth.

"If I had learned the truth before taking an apprentice, I don't believe I would ever have taken one. I was—uncomfortable with the idea of training a student while withholding this secret. But I had already instructed you for two years. I had come to . . . believe that you would be an exceptional mage."

Elric took a breath, straightened. "As my first act within the Circle, I argued that the source of the tech should be revealed. They refused. They believed the arrangement had worked successfully for a thousand years, and it might work for a thousand more. I submitted the proposal repeatedly, but was always defeated. In time I grew used to the secret. None of us ever thought the Shadows would return in our lifetimes.

"Now that the Shadows have returned, our time must be at an end. If the wisdom or folly of our existence is ever judged, it will be judged by the way we die. We must hold to the Circle and the Code, those elements that have allowed us to resist the purpose of the Shadows. We must not allow chaos to divide us."

Elric hesitated, as if expecting Galen to respond. An awkward silence fell between them. Galen willed himself to reveal nothing.

"I know it is difficult," Elric said. "I know that you would like to strike against the Shadows, and against Elizar and Razeel if they still live, but you must come with us to the hiding place. We must remain united."

So that was their concern. They wanted him with them. They wanted their weapon.

Again Elric hesitated. "We are not the dream of beauty and magic we have pretended to be. But still. We have accomplished much of value." Elric's voice had lost its resonance. He cleared his throat. "Please speak, Galen."

It felt as if the blockage in Elric's throat had suddenly transferred itself to Galen's. His anger caught there, and he found at last he must speak. "You told me that you would never lie to me," he said, and then the words were rushing out of him in a torrent. "You told me we stand for good, when instead we generate destruction. You told me we can spread light, but we are instruments of the Shadows. You told me you would make me a mage. And instead you have made me a monster.

"You have done nothing but lie to me. Only Elizar would tell me the truth. I feel nothing but disgust for the Circle, and pity for the mages."

Galen bit out the words. "But you need not fear. I will go with you. I have no choice. I am not fit to stay. Out here, I would destroy everything, happily. And there are too many innocents. If I go, at least I can destroy only mages."

He was trembling. He forced his lips closed, forced the flow of words to stop. The energy was stirring, quickening. He couldn't let it take hold. He squeezed his hands into fists, his nails digging into the raw skin of his palms.

Elric's mouth had fallen open as Galen spoke, and it hung now in a grimace. The lines between his eyebrows had vanished, leaving a horrible vulnerability. He stared at Galen for a long time, until Galen wanted to look away. But he did not. He had spoken the truth; let Elric live with it.

At last Elric gave a single nod. Then he walked stiffly away.

Galen forced his fists to open, his breathing to slow. He had said what he must say. Now let it be over. Elric was not his teacher. Elric was not his father. Elric was nothing to him. The Circle was nothing to him. The mages were nothing to him. He could retreat to that place deep inside himself, and no one could pull him back.

Galen realized Alwyn had been yelling for some time. His

words carried on the wind. "You're all cowards! Hypocrites! She died for nothing!"

Blaylock was backing away, his hands raised in acquiescence. G'Leel stood between them. Some of the other mages had stopped their work to look on.

"We can fight them!" Alwyn yelled. "Galen proved it!"

Blaylock turned and started toward the bunker. With a fierce glance at a few mages loitering nearby, he drove them back into motion.

As Alwyn started after Blaylock, G'Leel grabbed him.

Alwyn's head transformed into the head of a golden dragon, with fierce red eyes and long, needle-sharp teeth. He let out a furious screech. G'Leel jumped back.

The illusion vanished, and Alwyn yelled out to the mages. "You're all going to die anyway! Our time is over! In three years you'll know the truth!"

Blaylock stopped, faced Alwyn. Though his arms remained at his sides, the threat was clear. Alwyn must stop talking, now. The air around Blaylock seemed to boil.

Alwyn returned Blaylock's hard stare, his jaw tight.

Standing at Alwyn's side, G'Leel spoke to him. After a time Alwyn nodded once, then a few seconds later, again. Finally he looked from Blaylock to her. Then he turned, and they walked away.

Blaylock resumed his journey to the bunker as if nothing had happened.

Galen realized with displeasure that Alwyn and G'Leel were coming toward him. He needed to regain his stillness, to send his anger away on the wind. He began visualizing the letters of the alphabet in his mind, one after the next. The cold was beginning to build inside of him. It was the chill of a fever, of heat held within.

"You'll stay with us, right, Galen?" Alwyn said. The bags beneath his eyes were wet with tears, his face clenched in anger. "After what the Shadows did— After all they've killed—"

Alwyn jerked his head to one side. "Those cowards would turn tail and run. They don't care about anyone but themselves. They let her die, can you believe it? They just let her die."

He said it as if it were the first time such a thing had happened.

Alwyn clutched G'Leel's hand, raised it. "G'Leel is going to fight with us. You know the truth now. It's our responsibility to stop the Shadows. Or else we are no more than their cowardly allies. We can strike cleverly, swiftly, in and out before they know it. They'll never catch us."

Galen crossed his arms. "I cannot stay with you."

"There are a whole series of bases along the rim. With your power, we can wipe them out, one by one. And when the Shadows are weak enough, we can strike at their home, Z'ha'dum, and annihilate the whole—" Alwyn shook his head. "What?"

"I shall leave with the others."

Alwyn stared at him. "What is this, some kind of misplaced loyalty? You're just going to leave and let the Shadows get on about their business? What about Elizar? If he still lives, you simply wish him a happy life and fond farewell? I thought you cared about Isabelle. And about Carvin and all the rest. How can you let their deaths go unavenged? How can you go off and hide while the galaxy burns?"

"How is irrelevant. I will go."

Alwyn seized him by the shoulders and shook him. "Wake up, you damned zombie! Wake up!" Tears ran down Alwyn's face. "You're a coward, you know that? The worst of them all. You would run away when you're the one person with the power to end all this. The power to destroy the Shadows."

It was what he most wanted. And it was what he must not do. "I will go."

Alwyn's fingers dug into his shoulders. "Teach me, then. Teach me your spell."

"No."

Alwyn shoved him away. "You're a traitor to the Code.

You're not doing good. You're hiding. If Isabelle were here, she would stay with me. So would your father. But anyone with any guts around here seems to be dead."

Alwyn would not stop. Galen forced himself into movement, toward his ship. He had stood still for so long that walking seemed unnatural.

Alwyn's voice followed him, but Galen refused to hear, retreating within himself. After a moment he realized that G'Leel had run up beside him, and he stopped.

"Good luck, Galen," she said. "Keep the mages safe."

She thought he was leaving so he could protect the mages. Galen almost laughed.

"You're a strange, difficult person," she said. "I'll miss you."

"Take care of Alwyn," he said. "And yourself."

G'Leel's gloved fists tapped against each other. "If it weren't for you and Isabelle, I'd still be drunk with my crew in some bar. I'm glad I'm not. However this ends. I'm glad that I met you both."

Isabelle would say that G'Leel had transcended herself, that she had become a better person. Galen would argue that she must have always been so; they had just not seen it at first. It was impossible, by definition, to transcend oneself. They were what they were. He was what he was.

"Maybe when this is all over, we'll see each other again. In the meantime"—she gave him a friendly shove—"stay out of my dreams."

He couldn't imagine how he might see her again. If conditions were safe when the war finally ended, perhaps the others would emerge. But he could not. For him, this would never be over, so long as he lived. Whether or not the Shadows were abroad made no difference.

He nodded and moved quickly away. Blaylock stood beside the entrance to the bunker, watching. He could be reassured. Galen would go with them.

It was time to leave. It was time to withdraw from the universe. It was time to take their chaos and their destruction, and hide them where they would never be found. It was time for them all to vanish.

He headed for his ship.

— chapter 18 —

With a whisper the mage ships rose into the sky like a flock
of birds. They were to fly in tight formation, sending no communications, moving as quickly as they could, stopping only
once before they reached the hiding place. Those who had
died on Babylon 5 had given their lives so the Shadows would
believe their order had perished. That illusion must be preserved. Only with speed and stealth could they avoid detection and reach their goal safely.

This was the last journey Galen would make; these were the
final hours he would spend outside the hiding place. A few
months ago he could not have imagined the mages fleeing. He
could not have imagined himself fleeing. But then he had been
a stranger to himself. He had not known who he was or what
he was. Now he did.

Through the ship's sensors, Galen took one last look be-
low. A single mage ship remained on the plateau, Alwyn and
G'Leel standing beside it. Before taking off, Galen had sent
Alwyn all the information on the spell for listening to the
Shadows. Perhaps it would help him in the war. Galen could
offer him no more.

Alwyn's dwindling figure seemed to yell after him, even
now. *You're the one person with the power to end all this.
How can you go off and hide while the galaxy burns?*

But if he stayed, he would be the one to destroy the galaxy
in fire.

Galen tried to focus on the simple operation of the ship, on his speed, his course. As they shot up out of the atmosphere, he took a position near the back of the formation, away from Elric, away from the rest of the Circle. He didn't want to think about them, or what they had done. He didn't want to remember the look on Elric's face after he had said what he had said. He needed to regain his sense of stillness. He needed to leave all that behind.

Yet he could not. He had lost the fragile peace he'd had since Thenothk. His mind refused to be still, and once again the agitating undercurrent of energy was building, echoed by the ship, the cold inside him growing. He told himself to hold it in just a few hours longer. Then they would reach the hiding place. He could think no further than that.

Still Alwyn's words pursued him. *I thought you cared about Isabelle. And about Carvin and all the rest. How can you let their deaths go unavenged?*

The memory returned to him. She lay dying. Her neck was tensed, head held up ever so slightly, eyebrows raised. Her cold hands weighed limply against his. And he heard her voice, her breathless, failing voice. *My only regret would be . . . if the fire that I see in your eyes now were to burn your soul to ash in the future.*

But the fire would never burn itself out. It was merciless, endless.

He could have saved her so easily. He could have killed Elizar and Tilar with no more than a thought, and she would still be alive, would still be with him. But he had held to the Code when breaking it could have saved her, and he had broken the Code when holding to it could have saved him. Better to die than to become a mass murderer.

At the front of their formation, Herazade opened a jump point to hyperspace. Galen directed his ship toward the orange vortex, and the piece of chrysalis eagerly echoed his command, changed course.

He was reminded, jarringly, of Anna. Anna controlled the Shadow ship, coordinated its systems, just as the piece of chrysalis controlled his ship, coordinated its systems. When Anna had linked with him, he'd shared her thoughts of the machine and how she served it. She had thought of something called the Eye, something that gave her direction. That was the purpose he served, on his ship. He was the master, she the slave. Yet she was not some artificially produced technology, like the chrysalis. She was a living being.

He wished he could have brought her from Thenothk. But he'd been in too great a rush to find Elizar, to kill Elizar, to take the time to free her.

Following the rest of the mage ships, he passed through the black heart of the vortex into the roiling red currents of hyperspace.

The energy inside him continued to build, the cold to grow, and he found himself thinking of the cold, wire-thin strands of tech that had wormed inside of him at initiation, contracting and relaxing, insinuating their way down his arms, across his shoulders, along his spine, driving in intricate coils through his brain and settling there. They had carried the Shadows' programming into his body, where it grew and intertwined with him.

Burell, he realized now, had discovered that programming. Within each cell of the tech, she had found microcircuitry: some in the cytoplasm, more on the cell membrane itself. *The microcircuitry seems to direct the growth and functioning of the implants, to impose control on each cell.* She had compared the tiny dot clusters of microcircuitry on the cell membrane to the stippled discoloration that formed along each mage's spine and shoulder blades. The microcircuitry imposed its programming on the cell; the tech imposed its programming on the mage.

They could resist that programming, of course. But to

control it every minute of every day for the rest of their lives— How many could say chaos had not slipped out?

Galen crossed his arms over his chest. He had done much more than slip. He was drawn to destruction. He realized he'd known that, on some level, since he'd first attacked Elizar at the convocation. When he'd received the implants, he'd feared to use them, feared that violence would burst out. Later he'd decided it was not the tech he feared, but himself, his own instincts. Yet was there any difference? The tech, after all, carried his DNA. It grew to mirror him, as Burell had discovered. It reflected his brain, his thought processes. It echoed him. If he felt the urge to destroy, it was partly the tech; yet, he knew, it was also partly himself.

Elizar had said it was something in Galen's spell language, in his method of thought, that had allowed him to discover the spell of destruction. Its power had been hidden at the base of their spells, forgotten. But as he'd aligned his thoughts and his spells in neat, regimented columns, there, at the base of those columns, he'd found it. He had sought through his spells not to express himself, as Elric had taught him, but to hide himself. And in his attempt to hide, he realized, he'd built a spell language that was not so much a reflection of him, but a reflection of the tech and how its powers were structured. Instead of discovering spells original to him, he'd discovered the spells that had been placed within the tech, the spells they'd been meant to use, those of the Shadows.

There was an order to their powers, a design. But it was not the design of any god; it was the design of the Shadows.

Even now, the restless energy churned deep inside him, desiring to be released, to be loosed upon the universe. He could resist. But he did not want to resist.

Perhaps others could do good. Of himself, the most he could hope was that he would do no more harm.

And so he must remove himself from the galaxy, like the

rest of the mages. Their history was filled with wars and violence. But in this war, at least, they would not fight. And that was for the best. For if they did fight, who knew within the fog of war what destruction they might wreak, what sides they might take, what chaos they might generate. Even in fighting against the Shadows, they would promote the cause of the Shadows.

Galen thought with longing of Soom, his home. He would have liked to return there. He would have liked to see Fa again. He thought that, if there were a place where he could find peace, it was on the rugged mak, along the cliffs that fell to the mist-shrouded sea. But he would never be there again. He could not.

He had wanted nothing more than to be a mage. He had wanted to inspire awe and wonder, to do good, to heal, to know all that could be known. He had wanted some measure of control over an uncaring, unthinking universe, a universe that had killed his parents for no reason. He had wanted certainties and order. Instead he had received lies and chaos.

He had gone to the rim hoping to find an end. Yet still he persisted. Instead he would leave, he would fade. And if there was anything for him to do with the remainder of his life, it would be to arrange the rest of their spells in his neat, regimented columns and discover what else lay at their base. Elric had taught that he must find his own work; now he had. This was his work. This was who he was. Kell had told him. *You have hidden so well that any more you might have been is lost. You have become these regimented paths, and the places to which they lead.*

Only when he knew all the Shadows had put inside him could he truly know what he was. He had already discovered three basic postulates; there must be more. And he would find them, because was that not his role in all this, to know all that should not be known, and to bear its burden?

Though they were supposed to remain silent, he found he had received a message. *Galen.*

It was from Elizar. He still lived. A part of Galen took great satisfaction in that, the part that wanted to kill Elizar face-to-face, to rip his tech out with bare, bloody hands.

Another message. *Are you alive?*

Another message. *Answer me, you bastard. Why didn't you warn the mages? Why didn't you stop them from boarding that ship? I told you it was a trap.*

It seemed Elric's ruse had been successful. Or at least Elizar wanted him to believe so.

Another message. *I know you're alive. You didn't have time to reach Babylon 5 to die with the others. You let them die, didn't you? You let them all die out of spite, because of what I told you.*

He had not killed the mages, but he had killed many more.

Another. *Everything I've done—it's all pointless now. How could you have killed them? And Elric?*

All of Elizar's efforts were pointless now. He would have no mages to rule. Galen waited as minutes passed, knowing there must be more.

Come back and face me. Let us finish this.

At last, he and Elizar wanted the same thing. A thrill ran through him, and he shook with a quick, violent shiver. Here was his chance. They could kill each other. Finally it could end.

But he could not go back. If he did, if Elizar failed to kill him, he would not be able to shut himself down again. He would destroy everything. He wanted to destroy everything.

He did a mind-focusing exercise, tightening his arms across his chest. He would not respond. He would not act.

Know this. I will find you. And I will kill you.

I will say no more.

A jump point had opened ahead, and the ships were dropping back out of hyperspace. This was the one stop they would make before retreating to the hiding place, a last-minute addition to their plan. Galen's ship passed through the jump point, and the roiling red currents of hyperspace vanished, leaving him in the blackness of space. He must follow the others. He must leave before he was consumed by chaos. Let Elizar spend a lifetime looking for him. Elizar would never find him.

Ahead lay the Lanep system. Galen reviewed what he knew of it, striving again for calm. Elric had learned, while investigating Morden's records, that EarthForce's New Technologies Division had built a base here, to experiment with fragments of a Shadow ship. The fragments had been discovered during an archaeological dig in which Morden had participated. Galen couldn't believe the Earth scientists would risk manipulating such advanced technology. But apparently the desire for power was not limited to techno-mages.

When Elric had reported this to the remains of the Circle, they had quickly altered their plans. The Circle had decided that a probe and relay must be left to observe what happened here. Galen sensed the hiding place was not far; that would explain their concern. And perhaps they still wanted to believe they had some role to play in the universe. Perhaps they even hoped the researchers would discover some key to controlling the Shadow's technology, as unlikely as that was.

They entered the system, approached the first planet, on which the base had been established. The primitive Earth technology would not detect their presence. Through his ship's sensors, Galen studied the brown, rocky planet, noticing some strange energies.

The ships ahead of him came to a stop. Galen moved below the others so he could get a clearer view, and stopped as well. He focused on the coordinates of the Earth base. An intense burst of energy flashed from the surface, then another. A ship was hovering over the base, firing down on it. Galen quickly checked the surface for life, but found none. Not a single structure of the base remained. The ship had destroyed everything, had killed everyone, and still it continued to fire, blasting a crater deeper and deeper into the planet. That was just what Galen would have liked to do, on Thenothk.

He extended his sensors to maximum, got an image of the ship. It was sleek, black, organic, with glittering skin similar to that on a Shadow ship. Yet the shape was different. From a long, central core, two rows of pointed extensions stretched outward and down, like two rows of legs. The energy readings were not the same as he'd sensed from Anna either. Most of the output looked very primitive, like that of current Earth technology, while other elements, primarily the skin and the weapons systems, reflected Shadow tech. It was some sort of rudimentary hybrid.

Galen was amazed at first that the Earth scientists had been able to construct it. But then he realized that the mages incorporated Shadow tech into their ships, staffs, and places of power. Apparently it was quite adaptable. Yet the Earth scientists hadn't been able to control their hybrid, and it had turned on them. Galen could have told them the results of using Shadow tech. He could have told them it would bring only destruction. The hybrid was, perhaps, a distant cousin, but still they had much in common.

Galen realized that this research was yet another reason the mages must flee. If Earth knew this much of Shadow tech, it would not take their scientists long to discover that the mages utilized that same tech. And from there, the determination to acquire the mages' knowledge, and their power, would follow close behind.

At the front of the mages' formation, the ships belonging to the Circle turned and began heading quickly out of the system. The others followed. Though the Circle maintained silence, their intentions were clear. The mages would withdraw to the edge of the system, where the hybrid could not detect their jump point, and then return to hyperspace. The probe was no longer necessary; no further experiments would be conducted here. And they did not want to become the next targets for the ship. Galen realized they might even fear this hybrid could betray them to the Shadows. Perhaps they believed it a Shadow ship, come to destroy the research. Of them all, only he and Blaylock had ever personally encountered one, and Blaylock had been weakened and distracted. He might not notice the anomalous readings the hybrid was producing.

Galen followed the others, troubled by the possibility that there might be an Anna at the center of this ship. Extending his sensors back, he searched the hybrid for life signs. He found elements suggestive of life in the skin and a few sections of the ship, and there, at its center, a living being, a Human.

How could they have done that to one of their own?

The tech echoed his anger, quickening. And then he noticed the energy readings from the ship were changing. With each blast the hybrid fired down at the surface, the Earth tech within it built closer to overload. It would probably keep firing mindlessly, compelled to chaos, until it overheated its systems and self-destructed.

He'd failed to save Anna. His mind raced to find something he could do to save this person trapped at the center of the hybrid.

If he was the master, and Anna the slave, he wondered if he could order the hybrid to stop firing, if he could order it to land. How to communicate with it? He had only a minute before they reached the edge of the system and jumped back into hyperspace. From his sensor readings, Galen guessed that it communicated, not through some sophisticated Shadow system, but through a standard Earth comm system. The scientists would have built it that way, so they could communicate with it. He searched for any signal it might be sending.

The ship was silent. Yet Galen heard a faint, pulsing signal. It was a distress beacon, its energy nearly exhausted, located about fifty thousand miles to starboard. According to his readings, nothing was out there. In his mind's eye, he scanned through options, narrowed his field of search to the area of the beacon, increased the sensitivity of the scan. Then he heard the voice, desperate, breathless.

"—is Ensign Matthew Gideon, of the Earth Alliance Destroyer *Cerberus*, to unidentified ships. I need your help. My ship has been destroyed."

Galen found him: one person, floating in the vast emptiness of space. The hybrid must have destroyed the *Cerberus*. He saw no debris, but assumed it had dispersed. Somehow, in the face of the hybrid's ferocity, one still lived. It was a miracle.

"I don't know if you can hear me, I don't know if you can understand me. But—in thirty minutes, I'll be dead and—there will be no one left to speak for the people who died here. You have to help me, you have—"

At least some of the mages must have detected the beacon, must be hearing the message. Yet they were not slowing. Galen didn't know why he would be surprised. They were abandoning the galaxy; what was one person more or less?

He checked the position of the hybrid ship. It remained focused on the planet, continuing to attack it.

"Don't go. Don't— Don't go . . ."

He'd wanted to help the hybrid, his kin, and nearly overlooked one of its victims. The hybrid had killed many, just like him. Its carnage could just as easily have been his carnage. This Matthew Gideon could just as easily have been one of his victims. But this victim wasn't dead yet.

Galen directed his ship to starboard, breaking from the other mages.

He had hoped only to do no more harm. But perhaps, just this once, before he left it all behind, he could do something good. Perhaps he could save without killing. Perhaps he could bring light, rather than darkness. If he did have a choice, then let him, this last time, choose well.

He received a message from Blaylock. *Galen, we dare not delay. This may be a trap. The ship may detect and attack us. It may inform others.*

Then I will stop it.

It can destroy you long before you are in range to use your weapon.

That, in all likelihood, was true. But he did not want to destroy it. He still wished simply to stop it. And if he could not, then he would have to become its victim. For under no circumstance could he use his spell of destruction. He feared that once he cast it, he would not be able to stop. He would become just like the ship he destroyed.

Then leave without me, he wrote. *I must do this.*

He realized the truth of it as he sent it. He could not make the murder of this man his final act. After all he had killed, he could not bear the weight of one more.

The distress beacon was now only moments away. In his mind's eye he saw Matthew Gideon, illuminated by distant starlight, a lone floating figure in a grey EarthForce EVA suit. If this was a trap, there was no sign of it.

Energy surged through him, burning along the meridians of his tech, and he held it tightly, determined to retain control. The mage ships were receding into the distance. He had to rejoin them quickly. He had to reach the hiding place.

He brought the ship up above the lone figure, matching speed. He opened the small air lock on the underside of his ship. If Matthew entered there, Galen could keep him to an unused storage room, limiting what he saw. He must not realize he'd been rescued by a techno-mage.

Galen visualized the equation, conjured a flying platform at Matthew's back, pushed him up to the air lock. Through the ship's sensors, Galen watched as Matthew took hold of the air-lock hatch, pulled himself in.

As soon as the ensign was inside, Galen closed the hatch and directed his ship at top speed after the others. A swirling orange jump point had opened at the edge of the system, and the mage ships were entering. He must leave with them.

Yet still he had a minute before he would reach the jump point. He opened a communication channel to the hybrid.

"Stop now," he said. "They are all dead."

Intense bursts of energy continued to flash over the site of the Earth base.

"Use your sensors. Look. They are all dead."

At last, the firing stopped. Then, after a moment, a whisper, obscured by static. "Who are you?"

"I am your brother," Galen said. "And I have learned. We need not destroy."

From the first planet, the hybrid shot up, accelerating rapidly. It was coming after him.

Ahead, all the mages had gone through the jump point except for one, the one who generated it. Galen found the rune on the side of the ship: Elric. He waited for Galen.

The hybrid shrieked toward him, closing the distance. The Earth tech within it was overheating, reaching critical.

He'd been a fool for communicating with it. Yet now he must keep trying. "If you continue to attack, you will overload your systems and self-destruct."

A red beam shot out from the front of the hybrid. Galen changed course, changed course again. The hybrid fired one blast after the next. Frantic energy welled up in him, desperate to defend, to counter with deadly force. The hybrid could kill Elric, kill Matthew. Or if they survived to reach the jump point, it might follow them through.

Galen could turn on the hybrid, try to draw close enough to use his spell, and destroy it. But he must not, must not. Better to fly straight into the hybrid, to end it for both of them, now.

But then Matthew would die.

Leave me, Galen wrote.

The response came almost instantly. *No.*

The energy burned through Galen with brilliant, merciless intensity. With fierce focus, he fed his ship one course after the next, jigging up and down, side to side, evading the blasts. The hybrid was inexperienced, but determined.

Then Galen came even with Elric, and they were both speeding toward the immense, swirling jump point. The hybrid's beam clipped Elric's ship, and as it spun wildly, a hoarse scream sounded through the comm channel. Behind them, the hybrid's skin suddenly blazed a brilliant red. Then the glowing ship exploded, fragments shooting outward.

Galen was sucked through the vortex with a great wash of turbulence. For an instant the ship's readings went black, and he lost all sense of direction or movement. Then the red currents of hyperspace appeared around him. To his relief, Elric was at his side, the ship now under control. Galen detected no serious damage to it.

He wanted to make sure Elric was all right, to thank Elric for waiting, but he didn't know what to say. Nothing had changed.

The rest of the mage ships waited for them. They continued on their way.

Galen was racing with energy, his body shaking, heart pounding. He forced himself to take deep, calming breaths, resorting again to a mind-focusing exercise. Slowly, by small increments, the energy declined. He tried to focus on retaining control until they reached the hiding place. But the end of their journey would provide no relief. And he did not know how he would get through whatever years followed, cloistered away with no outlet for destruction but to visit it upon himself. The hybrid had been unable to stop its destruction, to escape its programming, even to save its life.

Galen had hoped, somehow, to save the person trapped within the machine. It had been a foolish hope. By contacting the hybrid, he had merely hastened its end.

He had wanted to save without killing, to do something purely good. And he had failed. One died, another lived. The universe continued in its maddening course of chaos and death.

Yet he told himself that he had at least saved one. That was something.

Now the mages would have to make one more stop, to drop Matthew Gideon at a safe location. Galen was sure the Circle was already debating what to do about the outsider. They wouldn't appreciate Galen's disobedience, but the rescue hadn't endangered their hiding place.

The mages would want to get rid of the ensign as quickly as possible. If they got close enough to a colony or friendly ship, Galen could put him into a life pod and fire him in the right direction. They could quickly be on their way again, and finish the journey.

But before that, Galen needed to put a face to the man he had saved. He hoped that it might help to restore his peace, that it might help him leave all this behind knowing that he had done one small bit of good, at least.

The dead had many faces. Isabelle, Burell, Kell. The Drakh from Zafran 8, his first murder. Then countless more Shadows and Drakh, twisted in torturous convolutions. Rabelna Dorna, shoulders stretching out to each side, grey scaled face distorted in fear. Tilar, silvery chrysalis ballooning upward, mouth rippling out in a silent scream, before he was crushed to nothingness. And then there were all the dead who had no faces, whom he'd killed from a distance, down to the whispering voice within the hybrid. Let the living at least have a face he could take with him.

In his mind's eye, Galen saw that Matthew Gideon had emerged from the air lock into the darkness of the empty storage room. Galen activated a single light above him. Matthew was kneeling. He jerked his head up at the light. With quick, panicked movements, he pulled off the helmet of his EVA suit. He was a young man, perhaps just a few years older than Galen, with a long, thin face and sharp chin. He was panting, his skin sheened with sweat. He looked frightened and disoriented.

Seeing him in this way was not enough. Galen had to see him in person. Galen made his way back to the storage room, entered silently. Matthew was at the far end of the room, facing away. Galen remained near the door, uneasy with his need.

"Rest," Galen said.

Matthew jerked around, mouth open.

"You're safe now."

He didn't seem reassured in the least. "Who are you?"

"Galen." Seeing him in person was still not enough. But what could be enough? How could saving one life do anything to lessen the weight of the thousands he had killed?

It could not.

Galen left him. Elric had told Galen he needed to decide what he was. One who killed, or one who did good. One who brought darkness, or one who brought light. One in control, or one consumed by chaos. But there was no decision to be made. Any small good he might do, any small light he might summon, was overwhelmed with the darkness inside him, the darkness of the Shadow tech. He could not transcend it; it was part of him. He was a techno-mage. He was a killer. That was what they all were. He was just the most effective.

He followed the others along the currents of hyperspace. Their time was ending, and that was as it must be. They would retreat into their hiding place, hiding not only from the universe, but from themselves. They would seal themselves into a prison of their own making. There, they could do no more harm. Just as the spell of destruction isolated an area into its own collapsing universe, so they would isolate themselves into slow, ultimate collapse. One by one, they would die. And their order would pass into memory.

* * *

The fabulists had gone.

Kosh had believed them dead at first, lost in the explosion of the Centauri freighter leaving Babylon 5. Yet, as so much with the fabulists, this was a deception. Their minds worked in an intricate, cunning manner that he had long worked to understand.

In their early days, their plots, their aggressions, their deceptions had been more straightforward. Many times Kosh had been able to penetrate them. But as their techniques grew more sophisticated, and more Humans joined their number, their deceptions became more unpredictable. For the Vorlons, who had lived many millennia, it was always difficult to understand the rapidly flowing minds of the short-lived. But of all the younger races, Humans were the most perplexing; they behaved in ways that were strange and new.

Most Vorlons would not admit the failure. They had no doubt of their vast superiority over the younger races. They, certainly, were capable of their own deceptions. Yet their powers were so great, their deceptions had never required such complexity. They were more like metaphors, as the Vorlons thought of them.

But there was nothing of metaphor in the deceptions of the fabulists. They were woven finely into the fabric of the here and now, evanescent possibilities that would work only in this time, in this place. Their way of thought did not come naturally to a Vorlon.

The buoy at Lanep had found them, each with his own ship, a great silent migration of those who had found the one narrow path through the conflagration that would soon consume all who remained. Of their number, some thirty were unaccounted for. Perhaps they had been lost at Babylon 5. Perhaps they refused to leave with the others. Kosh would watch for them.

The one among them he had confronted, the one who

wielded great power, radiated a higher level of energy. The buoy had detected him in one of the ships. That fabulist had separated briefly from the others, had rescued the sole survivor of the abhorrent experiments that had occurred in the Lanep system. And then he had gone with the rest. His name, Kosh had learned from their communications, was Galen.

Galen had not succumbed to the dream of the maelstrom. Instead, in saving another at the risk of his own life, he had brought a flicker of light to that place where darkness had consumed nearly everything. It was more than Kosh had done. He had known of the experiments undertaken there; he had known what their conclusion would be. And he had done nothing.

Quickly, the fabulists had slipped into hyperspace. Kosh believed they had retreated to their hiding place. Without the support of their creators, they would be unable to replenish their kind, and they would gradually age and die. They had found, at last, that the principles by which they lived were more important than their own survival.

Some said that the fabulists could have fought the forces of chaos yet did not. They said the fabulists might still hope to revive their alliance with the ancient enemy after the war's end. Yet Kosh believed that the fabulists embodied the greatest victory of Vorlon philosophy.

Though much of their history had been consumed with anarchy, they had gradually imposed order upon themselves, and they had created fleeting moments of great beauty. Ultimately, these instruments of the enemy had chosen extinction over chaos. They understood, better than any Vorlon, the truth at the core of all Vorlon teachings: that some must be sacrificed so that all could be saved. The galaxy was diminished by their passing.

Kosh knew what the others would say. The fabulists had allied themselves with darkness long ago, and this was the price they must pay. The lot of the younger races was order, obedience, sacrifice. Only that way could they develop properly, fulfill their endless potential.

Yet Kosh's unease over this new war was increasing. Each war brought sweeping changes, species dying, species rising to new power. The passing of the fabulists was but the first. One age ended, another began. Whether anything was ultimately gained had become unclear to him.

It was becoming difficult to stand apart from the younger races, to manipulate, to guide, and then to watch as the enemy undermined the hard-earned progress they had made. It was becoming difficult to watch the younger races suffer. If only the Vorlons could come down from on high and stand beside them, fight with them. Perhaps it was not just the younger races who must sacrifice, but the Vorlons as well.

They would say that he allowed sentimentality to weaken discipline. They would say that the rules of engagement must not be broken, that he must keep himself above the conflict. That, he had done.

And the fabulists had gone.

It caressed her like the whisper of lips, the faintest, most desirable touch. Her skin tingled as its touch intensified, spreading over her, warm, pulsating with power. Then she was enveloped by it, and in an exhilarating rush of sensation, they connected. She sent herself out through it. Signals raced down neurons, information sped through circuits. It became her, and she became it. The skin of the machine was her skin; its bones and blood, her bones and blood. At last, she was whole again.

Quickly she restarted the pumping circulation, activated the multileveled systems, restored the flawless march of the machine. After a millennium of sleep, it stirred, awakened. Its power ran through her, and she felt tireless, invulnerable. Eagerly she coordinated, she synchronized. All systems of the machine passed through her. She was its heart; she was its brain; she was the machine.

Without it, she had been no one, nothing—a bodiless spirit, lacking purpose or direction. Only in fulfilling the needs of the machine, only in carrying out the instructions of the Eye did her life have meaning. Only when she was whole could she know the thrill of battle, the ecstasy of victory. Above those, there was no greater purpose.

Stabilizing the long-dormant systems, she anticipated the joys she would soon feel: the dizzying delight of movement, the exhilarating leap to hyperspace, the red rapture of the war cry. She would shriek an oratorio of bloodshed. She would let no one strike her down again. She would engage and never break off, not until the enemy was utterly destroyed.

Now Anna had regained her body, her self, and together, they could again be what they were meant to be: a great engine of chaos and destruction.

Babylon 5:
The Passing of the Techno-mages

Book I
Casting Shadows

The spectacular space epic continues, as the techno-mages face the growing threat of the Shadows. . .

As Elric and his student Galen watch with taut anticipation, dragons, angels, and shooting stars rain from the sky, heralding the arrival of the techno-mages on the planet Soom. It's the first time Elric—a member of the ruling Circle—has hosted such a gathering, and if all goes well, Galen and the other apprentices will emerge triumphant from the grueling initiation rites, ready to embrace their roles as full mages among the most powerful beings in the known universe.

But rumors fly of approaching danger and Galen and his young lover, Isabelle, are chosen to investigate the dark tidings. An ancient race has awakened after a thousand years, thirsty for war, slaughter, and annihilation. Will the techno-mages be the deciding factor in the war ahead? Or the first casualties?

Published by Del Rey Books.
Available wherever books are sold.

Babylon 5:
The Passing of the Techno-mages

Book III
Invoking Darkness

The electrifying space epic reaches an explosive climax when one techno-mage battles the ultimate evil...

As billions die and the flames of destruction rage unchecked, the Shadows seem poised for absolute victory. Soon the entire galaxy will fall to their evil. But the war isn't over. . .not yet. At long last, in a forgotten corner of the universe, Galen has finally won the Circle's permission to leave the techno-mage hiding place. He is the only mage who has faced the Shadows and lived, the only one who possesses the unstoppable Spell of Destruction.

Galen's orders are clear. Though the galaxy is being torn apart by bloody conflict—in which his powers might tip the balance—he is to locate only three key enemies and kill them. But Galen has unearthed the Shadows' darkest secret—and discovered a monstrous truth about himself.

In this desperate, apocalyptic battle, there's no telling who will be the victor. Or if there will be any survivors at all. . .

Published by Del Rey Books.
Available wherever books are sold.